You are *the* Reason

Sands of Time

J.M. TRASK

NEWMAN SPRINGS PUBLISHING
320 Broad Street
Red Bank, NJ 07701

First originally published by Newman Springs Publishing 2019

ISBN 978-1-64096-994-0 (Paperback)
ISBN 978-1-64096-995-7 (Digital)

Printed in the United States of America

Dedication

To Audrey and Gavin, my daily inspiration, I love you.

To my mom, thank you for your unwavering support and love.

To Shane, thank you for your unending belief in me.

To Daryl, my handsome muse, may we always dance
among the trees and walk between raindrops.

And I'd choose you
In a hundred different lifetimes,
In a hundred different worlds,
In any version of reality,
I'd find you and
I'd choose you.

—Kiersten White, *Chaos of the Stars*

Preface

THIS WRITTEN WORK WAS TRULY a labor of love. It was several years in the making, and at moments, I wasn't sure it would ever be complete, much less published. The idea behind this book began with a dream and grew from there—an idea that wouldn't let me go until I expressed its creation.

All those I encountered along the way, all of life's circumstances, have acted as guideposts and inspiration.

There are too many people to offer my affectionate gratitude to list. During this process, I have seen and experienced that family is not that only born of blood, but soul family does exist and is often more akin to you than that you were born into. For them, I am eternally grateful.

My goal in writing this book is for the reader to feel, feel anything—anger, sadness, happiness, passion, desire, anything. In my previous phase of life in the corporate world, I would see so many people walking around numb, not feeling anything. My wish is that this creative work sparks emotion within and sets the reader upon their own journey of discovery. We each have our own hero's journey to embark on, and this was a part of mine. I hope this creative work activates the hero within and allows you to blaze the way for your best life. Happy trails!

Prologue

THOUSANDS OF SOULS STOOD BEFORE Prime Creator, floating amidst the perfect darkness, light emanating from each being of light. Prime Creator spoke in a language that did not use ears to be heard.

"The call went out, and your souls are the ones that are willing to take on the toughest assignment." The energy of the message radiated through each of our beings. "Humanity, as you all know, is in disarray. It was meant to be pure and balanced as my perfect creation, but it has been infiltrated by impurities and darkness, those that wish to hybridize with the human race and allow their impure genetic code infiltration and dark attachments through fear to keep humanity from rising to the light." Prime Creator paused. Each of us knew how much pain it caused Him to watch His beloved creation being controlled by the dark and fallen, controlled by a mutation of His creation.

"My children have been trapped for far too long. It is time to rid the world of this once and for all. Enough chances have been given."

The plan was both simple and complex, and very experimental. Earth's energy grid was failing. This energy grid was what supported corrupted human life and allowed Prime Creator's pure energy to be anchored into reality. The problem was, the infiltration was so abundant the grid could no longer hold the energy of the light that it was supposed to since we originally set the grid up at Atlantis. When Atlantis fell to the dark, we were forced to hide the crystals that generated and maintained the earth's energy grid in places they would never think to look.

A group of souls was sectioned off; they were called "light workers." They were meant to reincarnate on earth and hold the high energetic charge of the light to power and raise earth's new, pure energy grid. Another group of souls, the healers, was sectioned off and taken. They were to start practices to start removing large amounts of dark attachments causing false beliefs, physical ailments, and psychological torment. All would use their angelic body to fight the dark in dream space. There were a seemingly handful of souls that remained after the others departed. We looked at one another; we all recognized the plan and the reason for the break in groups.

"My twins," Prime Creator lovingly said, "my greatest warriors, my architects of light, for you all I give the impossible assignment. I give you the assignment of bringing love, real love, as I meant it to be, back to the Earth plane."

Each pair looked at one another, confident we could succeed in the face of almost certain failure. That was the hazard of being Prime Creator's children: we always had hope and believed in love. We were the anomalies, even in the spiritual realm. Each pair was one soul split into two parts: a male counterpart and female counterpart. One was guardian of the heart, and one was guardian of the mind. Although in each physical reincarnation back to earth, we could choose a different gender for our human body, we had our preference. We also did not necessarily find each other in each reincarnation due to the assignment or lesson we needed to learn or teach. Some of life's greatest lessons are learned through pain. As such, the twin pair was unable to hurt each other the way others could wound. This is where another group, the *karmic partners*, came in. This group was easily manipulated by the dark, so it was a hazard doing business with them. The karmic partner was there to help us learn and grow then move on to our next lesson.

I looked at my male counterpart; he looked back at me, the love between us so powerful and transformative it was unspeakable, the agony of the initial split of our soul never forgotten. We were Prime Creator's secret weapon. There weren't many of us, but there didn't need to be. The energy caused by the pull of the two halves of the souls coming together was massive and had huge impact. We were the original souls created by Prime Creator. We liked to say we were "older than dust." We were eons old—masters, if you will. We had to be, with that much energetic power, master being in balance. A twin being angry and out of balance had huge consequences.

"When your souls split at the beginning of time, my children, I promised when the work was done, you could be one again. This is that time. As this assignment is completed, your soul will be fused again, and you will be allowed to put down your sword."

Most of the twins departed, energetically understanding their assignment. Prime Creator held back two pairs, myself and my divine counterpart included, along with my twin sister and her divine counterpart. We were the originals. We had been with Prime Creator the longest; we carried the strongest light signature that could ever be.

"My assignment for you is to walk among the soulless into the pits of hell and destroy the dark from the inside. This will be most unpleasant, my beloveds."

It was our other sister who had fallen into darkness. She was created in the same love that we had been, but she had become power hungry and had fallen. Prime Creator had given many chances for her to change and come back to the light. We all hoped she would, but she refused, preferring instead to create legions of demons to support her ego and fear-based reign. Her name instilled fear in so many—*Satan*, our fallen sister. The challenge in defeating her was that she was instilled with the same knowledge as we were from Prime Creator, and in spite of her fallen nature, we loved her as Prime Creator did, desiring only that she return to the light. Since being cut off from Prime Creator, she had no access to the divine plan. All she could do was mimic and keep an ear to the ground as to what our plans were. This was why it was so essential to be covert.

There are fundamental truths and laws that are followed by the light and dark. As a light being, first, we do no harm. It is not to say that we can't help or participate in tough life lessons, but the intention must not be with malice. Second, the dark always serves the light. The dark may be permitted to do harm, but it will always serve the light's greater good. Third, the dark must always make itself known in the presence of the light. This is not to say someone you meet on the street is going to say, "Hey, I'm dark." It operates more subtly, as the dark does. It may be laced into a sentence, or they show you that their eyes are black. It is up to the soul to recognize this.

I looked into the face of my other half, our soul signature imprinted in gold on each other's face. We found ourselves standing on the edge of a cliff, all alone. I touched his face tenderly, as he did mine. We knew what lay ahead—the misery, pain, despair, anxiety, and wanting—all human emotions, so far from this place of perfect love where we currently stood. Yet the promise of being one again and never having to be separate again was worth it. It was worth walking through hell for. He and I looked at each other, knowing how horrendous this assignment was. We had returned to the earth plane to assist for eons, sometimes both of us, sometimes only one of us, the other remaining in spirit form to guide from the other side. We stood a long while, holding each other; it would be time to go soon. This understanding weighed on me and made these moments all the more sweeter. We both knew that when we returned to the earth plane, we would not remember each other, nor all of the healing gifts that Prime Creator gave to us. We would be acting in accordance with divine plan through using our intuition but would not have conscious knowledge of the plan or our mission on earth.

The task was great: to shift the consciousness of millions of people on earth, in a time where being open-minded was not accepted. My beloved and I would traverse the hell of the human condition, living among the fallen and soulless, blending in the best we could, all the while building the light grid to support higher vibrational living—that of the frequency of love. He would be imprinted with an intrinsic drive to find me. I would be in somewhat of a sleep state, to be energetically awakened once we met. Once we met in physical form, this would awaken me to the desire to come together with each other, activating the energetic grid we had built. Our coming together, in addition to the other light workers and twins, would help to raise the grid—bringing "heaven to earth," so to speak. It was essential to blend in and be inconspicuous. A proven challenge for old souls like us, our inherent empathic, psychic, and healing gifts were difficult to mask.

The time for reincarnation was drawing nearer, and I found myself standing with my twin sister and her male counterpart. We looked at each other, enjoying these last few moments of being completely saturated in unconditional love. In a moment, they were gone.

The soul works appropriately when both the heart and mind are clear and working in lockstep with each other. The heart knows no fear, so it leads where to go in life. The mind puts the plan together as to how to get there. It is a simple system, yet so many humans get it mixed up, allowing the mind to lead with fear and the heart to be ignored or caged.

It was time. Prime Creator nodded. My beloved and I were gone.

Chapter 1

"ANNALISE!" I HEARD MY MOTHER calling for me from our family's cottage. She must need me to take care of Jacque, my three-year-old brother, I surmised. I sat up and raced from my resting place in the field of lavender in front of our stone cottage. I slowed my pace as I neared the cottage and walked into the house, slightly out of breath. Ma smiled, spying the lavender I had tucked behind my ear.

"Here, take him. He's being cross, and Madame LeBouc will be here for some herbal tinctures I made for her sick daughter. I can't have Jacque messing about," Ma said.

"Yes, Ma," I said, taking a squalling Jacque into my arms. He immediately began to giggle and show off his dimples. I was four-teen years older than Jacque. He had been a surprise to my parents and the "anniversary gift that kept giving," according to my mother. I grabbed one of the warm rolls that had just come from the fire. Ma winked at me as I handed Jacque the bread. I closed the heavy wooden arched door of our cottage and walked down a well-worn-out path to the barn where my father spent most of his days.

As I looked in the barn, dark with the exception of the light shining through the open doors and slats of wood that made up the walls, filled with farming tools constantly needing mending, I saw Pa holding nails in his teeth talking to my sister's fiancé, Petyr. Petyr had been around since I could remember. He always seemed to linger around our house like a lost cat. He was completely taken with my sister, or my father, or my family in general; one couldn't be sure. Petyr's brother was the local leader of the church, which we never attended. It made me curious as to why such a well-read man would chase after my sister. Not that we weren't smart, but we were very different than he was.

"There's my baby girl," Pa said, maintaining the nails clenched in between his teeth. I was the youngest of my four sisters. I had been his baby for many years before Jacque came along. Pa was an imposing figure of a man. He was average height, but he was stocky. His hands were broad and thick, same as his shoulders and arms. He was balding a bit, but the hair he had was unruly light sandy brown with wisps of gray woven in. He had green eyes, the same as mine. His teeth were perfectly straight, and he had a booming voice. Everyone loved to listen to Pa telling stories.

"Hello, Pa. Hello, Petyr," I said. Pa smiled broadly, and Petyr nodded.

"What brings you out here? Going to help me shoe the horses?" Pa teased.

"Ma has Madame LeBouc from the village coming over and didn't want this little wild man running around."

"My son, wild?" Pa looked at me innocently.

"Yes, just like your daughters," I said, kissing Pa's copper-colored cheek.

He laughed out loud. "I don't know what I did to deserve to be surrounded by all of these women."

"You must have been a saint in your last life," Petyr interjected. I smiled.

"Must have been," Pa muttered. "Where are you off to?"

"I was thinking of taking Jacque to Bronwynn's so I could help her clean up before John gets back."

"Your mother will miss you."

"Pa…"

"I know, I know, you like to help your sisters. I'm just saying, there's a certain man that's been a-courtin' ya, and you'll likely be leaving the nest soon. You and your ma are closer than the rest, Lise. She'll take you leaving the hardest."

"I know, Pa."

"Why don't you go pick some wildflowers for your ma for the table for supper tonight? Bronwynn's got plenty of help from that ornery mother-in-law of hers," Pa said, gently touching the lavender

I had placed behind my ear. I had completely forgotten that it was there. I blushed, feeling childish.

"Okay," I said, kissing his cheek again. "See you, Petyr!" I said, planting a kiss on his cheek as well. Jacque waved at them over my shoulder as we departed.

"Where ya off to?" I heard my sister Raquelle yell from the side of the house. Raquelle and I were typically inseparable. We were called Irish twins; we were born within a year of each other.

"Picking some flowers for Ma. She wanted Jacque out of the house."

"Oh yeah, I heard the mean Madame LeBouc was coming over."

"Raquelle!" I chided, and we both giggled. Jacque giggled at us.

"I heard Henri spent quite a bit of time with Pa in the barn the other day."

"Yeah…"

"You don't sound very excited," Raquelle said.

"I'm not. I know I should be appreciative that he is showing interest…"

"But you don't want that thing coming at you in the dark?" Raquelle said, and we both broke into laughter. After we composed ourselves, Raquelle looked at me with more seriousness.

"Lise, you know what Pa and Ma are going to ask. Do you love him?"

"Of course I don't love him. I think he is a gross, woman-hating man that wants a slave and is intrigued by the way we live."

"I can't disagree," she said, pulling me into a side hug.

"I know physical appearance isn't everything."

"But it is something," Raquelle countered.

"I know," I said softly.

"He's gross, Annalise. He's got a potbelly so big that he can't see his feet, a bulbous red nose on that hideous face of his, he always looks unclean and unkempt, not to mention he's at least thirty years older than you and always uses strong perfumes to cover his stench. And for all the money he has, he always has grease stains from his last meal on his shirt. There, I said it for you!" Raquelle said, smiling.

"I love you, Ellie," I said, laughing so hard my stomach hurt.

"You deserve better than that," Raquelle said, squeezing me.

"I know, but he's got money."

"So? You're too beautiful of a person to be wasted on his money."

We made our way down the dusty country road, alternating the side of the wagon-wheel ruts we would walk in. We made it to my favorite wildflower field. It seemed to have every color of flower imaginable. I nuzzled Jacque's cheek before I set him down to waddle toward the field.

Then he plopped down and began to roll around, giggling. Raquelle sat down, and I laid my head on her lap amongst the flowers. She plucked a few white daisies and braided them into my long blonde hair. We had completely lost track of time, and both of us looked toward the late-afternoon sun. Jacque had fallen asleep on my lap. We both knew this wasn't a good place to be after dark and should probably be heading home. Raquelle slid out from underneath my resting head, and I awkwardly stood up, trying not to wake Jacque. Once standing, I carefully let Jacque's head rest on my shoulder. Raquelle gently dusted all of us off.

"Let's go the shortcut," she quietly urged.

"Okay, I guess," I said with hesitation.

We wandered through the darkening woods to a grass clearing. We could hear the sound of wood clanging loudly against one another. We confidently walked out of the woods into the clearing, passing about ten feet from a group of knights from the Lord's guard practicing different fighting stances with tall wooden poles. Some of the men had their shirts off. We politely did not look in their direction and kept moving. I could see lines of women sitting along the edge of the woods, waiting to catch the eye of one of the knights. My sister stopped when the man who was trying to court her, the blacksmith's son, Tomas Gagnon, came striding up from his seat by the opposite side of the woods.

"What are you doing here?" Tomas asked, seeming nervous.

"We were taking a shortcut through the woods to get home," Raquelle chirped.

"Well, you better get going—" he started.

"Hey, Tomas! Toss them a coin, and I'm sure they'll tolerate that pecker of yours!" one of the men from the field hollered.

Tomas blushed, looking at us apologetically.

"Toss them two, and I'm sure you could have both of those witches!" another one hollered.

All of the men started laughing at us. I saw movement out of the corner of my eye. I turned my head to watch a very muscular man casually walk over to the man hollering insults at us and hit him in the face with his pole, busting his lip and knocking him to the ground. I recognized that it was Liam Boutreau, captain of the Lord's guard. I had the occasion of running into Liam a few times already; none were in my best moments. They were all silent as the man spit blood into the grass. Liam came striding up beside Tomas a few moments later.

Liam had brown hair that curled a bit around his ears. His eyes were brown, and he had a perfect smile. His skin was tanned from the sun. He was shirtless. I could see his well-defined chest with scars etched across it from his battles. I gave him a slight smile.

"I didn't expect to be as fortunate to have such beauty come across my path today," Liam said, looking at me.

"You remember Annalise and Raquelle," Tomas offered.

"How could I forget such beautiful faces," he said, taking my hand and kissing it. Our eyes met, and we both smiled at each other.

Then I looked away blushing, hoping he didn't notice. "Nice to see you again, Liam," I said.

"It was. We really should be going," Raquelle said, pulling my hand.

"Can I call on you tomorrow, Raquelle McShaman?" Tomas called out.

"Maybe!" Raquelle said, giggling as we made it to the other side of the clearing and disappeared into the woods. I turned my head one last time to see Liam watching me, slightly leaning his face against his tall wooden pole, smiling.

"Liam seems quite taken with you."

"Oh, Raquelle, he uses women for sport. I'm sure he just wanted to get underneath my skirts." We giggled.

"Still, captain of the Lord's guard. Not too shabby, Annalise."

"Raquelle!" I chided.

"What?" she asked as I gave her a look. "All I am saying is that you could have a really nice life with someone like Liam," Raquelle said, bumping her hip against mine. I smiled in spite of myself, shaking my head.

We could smell the roasted vegetable stew as we drew closer to the house. A twinge of guilt ran through me; I wasn't home to help Ma with dinner. I walked into our cozy cottage with a sleeping Jacque on my shoulder.

"Well, look at the two of you. We were wondering if the wildlings were ever going to come home," Faith, my second oldest sister, said, smiling.

Ma glanced over her shoulder and nodded for me to put Jacque in his handmade bed in the corner. I laid him down in his bed; his cheeks were rosy from sleep. I covered him up with the blanket Raquelle had made him. Then I walked over to Ma and gave her a kiss on the cheek. She kissed my temple.

"You look a bit flushed, Annalise. Is everything all right?"

"Yes, Ma," I said, putting my apron on to take over stirring the stew.

"Ellie, will you please go get your father? I think he's still in the barn with Petyr," Ma said to Raquelle.

Raquelle exited and soon returned with the two men. We all sat at the long wooden table with two long benches on each side and a chair for Ma and Pa at each end. We all smiled at one another as we held hands and gave thanks.

"To whom do we owe thanks for these beautiful wildflowers on our table?" Pa asked.

"Raquelle, Annalise, and Jacque," Ma said.

"Did anything happen across your path while you were out there?" Pa asked. He and Ma both had excellent "knowing" abilities; it was always pointless to lie.

"We ran into Tomas," Raquelle offered.

"Oh yeah? He didn't want to join us for dinner?" Pa asked, winking at Raquelle.

"He asked if he could come calling."

"What did you say?"

"Maybe."

"Raquelle, you shouldn't tease," Faith said softly.

"And why not? Tomas can't just do as he pleases," Raquelle shot back.

"How do you ever expect to have a proper husband with that type of attitude, Raquelle?" Petyr asked.

"How could she get a proper husband without it?" I challenged.

A smile spread across Petyr's face, and then he cleared his throat. "Arcturis, I don't know how you do it," Petyr said, shaking his head.

"Oh, dear me, my girls are wildlings. They take after their mother, no sense in trying to control it," Pa said, and Ma took mock offense. We all started to giggle. Truth be told, both of our parents were free spirits. After dinner, I helped Ma wash the dishes in the washtub and then put them away on the shelf along the wall.

Ma put her hand on my forehead. "Are you sure you're okay, Lise?"

"Yes, Ma, just a lot of fresh air. I think I just need to lie down."

"Your sisters will help me with the rest. Why don't you go off to bed?" she offered.

I nodded. I walked into the small room I shared with my sisters. It contained four single beds with a wooden chest at the end of each that contained our clothes and extra linens. Pa had made all of our furniture with his own two hands. I slipped off my dress and slipped on my nightgown. I climbed under my soft covers and rolled onto my side facing the window. I lay in the darkness, and all I could see was Liam's face. I wanted to see him again. I closed my eyes and soon drifted off into a peaceful sleep.

Chapter 2

I awoke to a dark room and to tugging on my hair.

"Sis-sy," I heard Jacque's small voice say. I looked around the room. It was dark, but I could make out the silhouette of Raquelle and Faith in their beds. I could hear Pa's snoring echoing in the still house. I rolled over to see Jacque.

"What's the matter?" I whispered.

"Sis-sy, I wet," he said, holding out the handmade doll I had stitched together for him with our old clothes. I reached over and felt his cloth diaper; he was soaked. I got up and maneuvered through my room in the darkness. He toddled behind me out to the main room.

I found the squares of cloth in a basket in the corner. I changed his cloth diaper, tossing the old cloth by the door, as we were not permitted outside alone when it was dark. Now that he was clean, I swooped him in my arms and kissed his face. He hugged me tightly around my neck, still clinging to his doll. I smiled to myself.

I brought him back to my small bed and laid him in the bed with me; then I pulled the covers up over the both of us. I soon heard his little breaths slow, and sleep overcome his body.

As my eyes flicked open, I could see it was sunrise and heard Ma in her garden humming. I smiled as I recognized the tune as one she would sing to me as a little girl. I looked around the room to see Jacque, Faith, and Raquelle still sleeping.

I climbed out of bed so as to not wake Jacque and quietly got dressed. I grabbed a biscuit from last night's dinner that Ma had been warming by the fire and walked into the garden barefoot. I saw her squatting, tending to her herbs.

"Good morning, my lovely," she said softly.

"Good morning, Ma," I said as I tore off a piece of bread and shoved the rest into my pocket.

"I love this time of day. All things are new again," she said, inhaling the sweet morning air. In this moment, all the world seemed right.

"Me too," I said, smiling, beginning to help her pull weeds. After a moment, she gave me a sideways glance.

"You know, it's okay for you to seek new paths, Annalise," she said, working the soil with her small hand tool Pa had made for her.

"Yes, ma'am," I said, looking at her, considering her words for a moment. "How do you mean?"

"Do you see that dandelion right there?"

"Yes, ma'am."

"To most people around here, it is a weed, something to be pulled and discarded."

"But you use them," I offered.

"You're right, because I see its value and see it for the precious medicine that it gives," she said, smiling. I knew Ma had a vision of Liam last night. That was just the way Ma worked.

I smiled back at her. "True."

"Are you going to let him court you?" she asked.

"Yes, I mean, I would like for him to. He hasn't asked…I don't think…," I said, fumbling with my fingers and feeling my cheeks blush.

"I've seen the way he looks at you, my darling."

"It's the way Pa looks at you," I added quietly.

"Aye, like you're the most precious thing in the world to him," she said, almost drifting into her thoughts. She shook her head. "I think you both are well suited for each other," Ma said, winking at me.

Ma and I continued to work in silence. My mind flooded with thoughts of Liam. Faith exited the house with her basket, heading to the various places where the hens left their eggs. I heard the echo of the washboard and Raquelle scrubbing clothes. It reminded me that we would need to make soap and candles soon; I would need to gather a lot more wildflowers and lavender from the field. Most people didn't subscribe to washing, but we did, and Ma was specific about her recipe for both candles and soap. Soon I heard Jacque toddling outside in the yard.

"Sis-sy! Sis-sy! G-mornin'!" Jacque yelled as he giggled and ran to me.

Faith looked at him and shook her head. "That boy loves you too much," Faith said.

"There is no such thing," I retorted.

"Bronwynn still wants to feed him to the wolves, I think," Raquelle offered as she walked over to us.

"Not a chance," I said, kissing Jacque's chubby cheeks as he giggled. Ma looked up at me and smiled.

After my chores were finished, I brought Jacque with me to the field of lavender that day. Raquelle was helping Faith with the finishing touches on her wedding gown. It wasn't really as much a gown as a simple dress that had some fancier stitching.

I lay there in the field telling Jacque stories of Greek gods, which he always seemed to enjoy.

"Well, there was Perseus—" I started and then stopped as I heard a horse's footsteps pounding the earth. I shot up to sitting upright and scanned the road. My eyes caught on a figure riding toward us. My heart stopped; it was Liam. He immediately saw me and smiled, pulling back the reins and slowing his horse. I stood up; Jacque stood up too. I held his little hand, and we walked toward the road.

"You shouldn't be out here alone," Liam said, climbing down off his horse and walking to meet me.

"I'm not alone. I have Jacque."

"Is he your babe?"

"No, he's my brother."

"You're kidding!"

"No, I'm not kidding."

"Are your parents of age to still be having children?"

"Are you so foolish as to think just because one ages that the passion is sure to die between a couple?"

"Did you just call me foolish?"

"I called your thought foolish. Or am I to believe that you think me such a woman to devalue myself as to let a man have his way with me as he pleases?"

"I would never presume—"

"Because, Masseur Boutreau, that would be foolish as well," I remarked.

"I don't think I have ever been called foolish before." He smiled.

"Well, maybe it's the type of women you have been hanging around," I offered.

He snickered. "Perhaps," he said, gazing at me. After a long moment, he said, "You are so full of fire."

"Is there any other way to live but with passion?" I asked, watching his brown eyes set ablaze.

"You are so incredibly different than anyone I have ever met. You aren't like the other women."

"The ones that lift their skirts and spread their legs because you flash them a smile?" I asked.

"Yes, those ones," he said, extremely amused.

"You're right. I'm not them," I said, looking into his eyes.

"Why are you not afraid to be alone with me right now? You know what the people in town would say. I have quite the reputation, you know."

"They say those things about me and my sisters anyway. Besides, I am not afraid of you," I said softly. This seemed to register something in his eyes.

"So this passion you speak of…," he started.

"I'm not sure this is an appropriate conversation for two acquaintances."

"I don't want to be just acquaintances," Liam said with intensity.

I blushed. I could feel Jacque clinging to the back of my leg, hiding behind my skirt. "Regardless of what your friends in town say, I'm not a whore. So if you think—"

"May I call on you?" he cut me off.

I smiled in spite of myself. "I don't know."

"Please."

"I'm not sure."

"Don't make me beg," he offered.

I giggled. "Okay, yes," I offered with a smirk.

He smiled and grasped my hand, raising it to his lips. "Now that is settled, I would prefer you not stay out here alone. May I give you a ride back?"

"Jacque and I will be heading back soon. There's no need to worry. There's no one out here but us."

"Annalise, sometimes it's the danger you can't see. Please let me escort you and Jacque home," he offered.

I looked at him for a long moment. "Fine," I said.

As soon as the words left my mouth, he swooped me up on his horse. Jacque began to whimper. Liam handed him up to me. I sat Jacque in front of me, holding on to him tight. Next he handed me my basket of lavender, also eyeing the flower I had braided into my hair. He climbed up behind me with ease and grabbed the reins.

I could feel his body against the back of mine. The heat radiating off his body and his masculine scent were intoxicating. I felt so drawn to him.

"We ready?" he asked softly into my ear as he put his arms around my sides, holding the reins. As we got to the end of the path that led up my family's cottage, he climbed down and then helped Jacque and me down. Jacque took off running down the path with the lavender.

"Thank you," I said softly.

"You're welcome," he said, sweeping an unruly piece of hair from my face. I untucked a piece of lavender from my hair and tucked it behind his ear. His eyes were studying my every move.

"You should know I am being courted by Henri Venereilles," I offered.

"Is that right?" he asked with a smirk.

"Yes," I said softly.

"And?"

"And what?"

"Is that what you want?" he asked, his eyes penetrating mine.

"No, I want to be having passion babies with my husband when everyone thinks we should just be sitting in rocking chairs preparing our graves. I doubt that is Henri," I said with a smile.

As I turned to go, he grabbed my hand and kissed it once more. "Until next time, Annalise McShaman," he said.

I dramatically curtsied, and we both laughed.

I headed up the path to our cottage, unable to contain my smile. I could see Pa out in the garden with Ma. I picked up the clumps of lavender as I went that Jacque had spilled from the basket as he ran.

As I walked closer, both of my parents looked up at me and smiled.

"You look a little flushed, honeybee. Did you run home?" Pa asked, smiling.

"No," I said softly and smiled.

"Well?" Ma asked, still eying me.

"I picked a dandelion," I said to her, and she and I both started giggling.

Pa scratched his head. "A dandelion?" Pa asked, looking at the two of us. "With as long as I have lived with you ladies, I will never understand some things."

I walked over and gave him a hug. He swept me up in his arms, swinging me around like he would do when I was little. I let out a giggle. "Where would I be without my precious girls?" he said softly, setting me down but still squeezing me.

"There is a gentleman that may be calling on me, Pa."

"Oh yeah?" Pa seemed intrigued. Ma just smiled. "Another one? Who is this other fellow that wants to court my baby girl?"

"Liam Boutreau." I stopped.

Both of my parents looked at me thoughtfully, then started to chuckle.

"Liam, Tomas's friend?" Pa asked.

"Yes, sir."

"You should know that Henri asked me for your hand in marriage again," Pa said with all seriousness.

I plummeted into the ground from the high I was on. I immediately looked down, feeling my eyes begin to burn with tears. The thought of being trapped to a man like that disgusted me. My stomach began to hurt.

Pa tilted my chin up to look at him. "What's this?" he asked, wiping a tear that had escaped my eye.

Ma stood up, looking at me with concern. She walked over and hugged me.

"I know a partnership with him would be very favorable for us," I said softly, sniffling.

"You are more precious than gold to me, my baby girl," Pa said, squeezing me in for a hug.

"What did you say to him?" I asked, sniffing. I felt Ma smoothing my hair like she did when I was a little girl.

"I told him no, he could not marry you. I told him that an old fart like him needed to find someone his own age and that my daughter's beauty and passion wasn't going to be wasted on a man like him," Pa said, a smile breaking across his face. The three of us laughed as I wrapped my arms around his neck and clung to him.

"Thank you, Papi," I said, overjoyed.

He set me down, and I wrapped my arms around Ma. I knew she had played a huge part in this as well.

"So my baby has found a man she is interested in, hey?"

"Yes, Pa."

"Very well then. We'll see if he can earn my blessing," he said, kissing me on the cheek and Ma on the lips. He then proceeded to walk toward the barn.

"I'll finish up here. Why don't you go in and help Raquelle make some of the medicine packets?" Ma offered, holding the back of her hand to my cheek, looking at me with pride. "Then I want you to lie down and take a nap."

"Yes, ma'am," I said.

I pushed the wooden door open to see Raquelle sitting at the table with Jacque, grinning.

"You missed quite a show," she said as I sat down at the table.

"What happened?"

"Henri showed up with a bouquet of flowers for Ma and a gold locket plus some Fabergé egg thing for you."

"What!" I whispered.

"I know!"

"That egg would have set Pa and Ma up for life…," I said.

"Annalise, you know our parents don't care about that."

"I know."

"Anyway, Pa told him to take his stuff back to the serpent's hole he came from. Then he said, 'No daughter of mine is going anywhere near a shriveled-up pecker like yours,'" Raquelle said, mimicking Pa's voice.

Both of us set to giggling. When the packets were done, I did as Ma asked and made my way to my room, climbed into my bed, and slid under my covers. I slept. I woke up to Ma's hand on my face.

"Annalise, your gentleman caller is outside with Pa," she said softly.

My eyes flicked open, and I smiled. "Of course he is. We'll need to set an extra place for dinner," I said softly.

"Yes, we will," Ma said as she stood up.

I made my way to the large room and put on my apron. When dinner was ready, Ma asked me to go get Pa. As I walked to the barn, I noticed that not only was Liam in there but also Petyr and Tomas. They were all laughing as I pushed open the door. Pa waved for me to come over, and he draped his thick arm over my shoulder.

"Dinner is ready," I said, kissing Pa's cheek. Liam smiled at me.

"Then let's eat!" Pa said.

We made our way into the house. Tomas, Liam, and Faith sat on the bench opposite myself, Raquelle, and Petyr. Ma and Pa sat at the ends of the table, of course.

"Please hold hands," Pa started. Liam looked up at me from across the table and smiled as he held Ma's and Tomas's hand.

"Let us give thanks and gratitude for all we have been given," Pa said and nodded.

We all began to eat.

"So tell me, Liam, where are you from?" Ma asked.

"I live just up the road a ways, ma'am."

"With your parents?"

"With my mother."

"Any siblings?"

"No, ma'am."

"I understand you are captain of the Lord's knights?"

"Yes, ma'am. I can assure you I would always be able to provide for your daughter."

"Money is not the provision that concerns me, my dear," Ma said, smiling thoughtfully. He nodded; her comment clearly caught him off guard.

After dinner was done, each of us set off in pairs to walk in the moonlight. Liam walked close to me but did not touch me. I could see the profile of his hawklike features. My long blonde hair twisted and danced in the breeze.

"I didn't expect to see you this evening," I said.

"Didn't think I meant what I said?" he asked, giving me a sideways glance.

"No, I didn't."

"I would ask that you get to know me, Annalise, and not rely on my reputation," Liam said.

"And I would ask you to do the same."

"Agreed," he said. We both chuckled.

"You have a wonderful family."

"They are wonderful."

"I heard your dad wouldn't let Henri marry you."

"Yes."

"He is a very wealthy man."

"He does have lots of money. However, I am already a wealthy woman, but my riches aren't of this world," I offered.

He smiled at me. "I am glad your dad said no. Any certain reason why?"

"He didn't want me to waste my love on an old fart like him, nor my passion on a shriveled-up pecker like his," I whispered.

Liam started to laugh. "But a younger man like me…"

"Might be acceptable," I said, smiling.

"Acceptable?"

"Tolerable."

"Tolerable?"

"Adequate."

"Adequate? It keeps getting worse!" he said as I broke out into a laugh. "You fascinate me," he said after we both caught our breath.

"Oh yeah? Why is that?"

"You speak your mind, and you have all these beliefs that are different from everyone else."

"We were taught to love everyone and to speak your truth in kindness. The real secret is that everything you do should come from your heart."

Liam had lured me to a dark corner of the yard. I knew Ma would be calling for me soon.

"May I kiss you?"

"No."

"What?" he asked, surprised.

"I am not like your other girls, Liam. I am different."

"Of course, but—"

"I told you, I am not easy, nor am I a whore like everyone says that we are."

"Annalise, I didn't say that."

"Then what did you mean?"

"Your lips looked so beautiful as you were laughing. I wanted to kiss them."

"Oh," I said, blushing.

"I understand that you don't trust me."

"I don't."

"Then we will take it slow."

"Okay."

"Girls," I heard my mother say softly.

I smiled up at him. "It's time to go."

"Will you meet me tomorrow?"

"No promises. I am going to see where my day takes me."

"Good night, beautiful," he said, kissing my hand.

"Good night, kind sir," I said, and he chuckled.

As we walked toward the house, I felt Raquelle fall into step next to me, looping her arm in mine. I glanced over to see a red-faced Tomas. Apparently, their night had ended well.

"Good night, Tomas," I said as we headed toward the doorway.

Pa winked at us as he passed to shake Liam's, Petyr's, and Tomas's hands.

As we made our way into the main room, I could see Jacque was already asleep. Faith was already in bed. Raquelle and I slipped into our white nightgowns and climbed into our beds.

Chapter 3

THE NEXT MORNING, I WAS up at sunrise.

Ma looked at me thoughtfully. "Well, you're beaming this morning, my lovely," she said softly as I went to sit with her outside. As I took the seat next to her on the bench, I rested my head on her shoulder.

"Why don't you and your sister go have some fun today? Faith will help me with Jacque," Ma whispered to me.

"Are you sure, Ma?"

"Aye, Jacque needs to get used to you not being around," Ma said, tucking a stray piece of hair behind my ear. It made my heart squeeze at the thought that I would be leaving my family.

"I'll get the eggs and get the veggies from the garden before I go," I offered.

"Sure, my beauty, that would be wonderful," Ma said, pulling me in for a hug and kissing my temple.

Raquelle and I laughed as we ran through our neighbor's wheat field. We felt free, and we knew there was one place we wanted to go on a warm day like this. As we approached the road to cross into the forest, we saw Lord Farragut's carriage and guard coming in our direction. We stopped and knelt, as did a few other people along the roadside. The carriage stopped in front of us. We looked up. I could see Henri sitting next to Lord Farragut.

"You there, young maidens!" Lord Farragut said to us as his short, stubby body climbed out of the carriage, Henri followed and stood next to him. We looked at him and stood up.

"Yes, sir?" Raquelle said.

I saw a horse moving amongst the knights in the corner of my eye.

"I make it my business to know all of the beautiful young women in my province. Who are your parents?" he asked, his black eyes assessing us.

"Arcturis and Guinivere McShaman, sir," I said. I heard hoof steps of a horse walking toward us.

"Guinivere's youngest girls, very nice," Lord Farragut said. I found it odd he knew so much about my family. "Henri tells me you girls do healing magic like your mother?"

"No, sir, only some herbs and oils. Some may think it's magic when they feel better," Raquelle offered what we had been taught to say.

He laughed. "Well, I will know where to go when I am feeling poorly," Lord Farragut said, smiling and standing a bit too close. "You are both exquisite creatures, just as your mother is. The resemblance is striking," Lord Farragut said under his breath. I could smell the liquor on his breath and his heavy perfumes wafting in the hot air around us; it was making my head hurt. Lord Farragut reached up with his hands and simultaneously ran a finger along both of our chin lines. I could hear his corrupted thoughts of what he would like to do with us. They were similar to Henri's, who was shifting where he stood, glaring at me.

"Shouldn't we keep moving, my lord?" I heard Liam's voice slice the air. I looked up to see him in his full ceremonial dress on his horse, his sword anchored at his hip. I made no expression, afraid of what Lord Farragut would do. Liam did the same, not acknowledging me.

"Yes, Captain, quite right."

"I would ask that we keep on schedule, sir. Your safety is of my utmost concern,." Liam said with a tight jaw.

Lord Farragut laughed. "Quite right, quite right," he said, his look alternating glances at our breasts like we were a meal to devour.

"Sir, I think the captain is right. We need to get moving," Henri said, shifting his weight on his feet.

Lord Farragut licked his lips. Liam's horse stomped its hooves in place. Lord Farragut shook his head, gave us one last look, and turned around to enter his carriage, sitting down and molesting the goatee on his chin while looking at us with a smile.

"Annalise." Henri nodded at me. "Raquelle." He nodded and turned to get into the carriage, the support rods of the carriage squeaking under the pressure of the weight of the two men.

Liam then called out a command, and the entire caravan started moving forward. Liam winked at me as they rode by. I also caught a glimpse of the guard with the busted lip and bruised face from where Liam had struck him with the pole a few days prior. After the group was out of view, we continued our short journey toward the stream.

"That was close," Raquelle said.

"It was."

"We'll need to tell Ma."

"Pa's not going to like this."

"Well, he's got to hear it. It was weird he knew so much about us, specifically 'Guinivere,'" I offered as we slipped into the woods.

Raquelle and I found a wild blueberry bush and went to picking as many berries as we could find. As my sister reached to pluck a plump blueberry from the branch, I noticed the union mark on her wrist. I smiled.

"How did it go with Tomas?" I asked softly.

"It was magical."

"Was it what you thought?"

"It was amazing. It hurt like hell, Annalise. But there is no one else I would be with."

"Did you feel the energy?"

"Yes."

"What did Ma say?"

"Nothing much really. She just asked if I was okay."

"I like Tomas. He accepts you as you are, Ellie."

"I love him so much, Lise. I give him such a hard time, but I don't know what I would do without him," she offered.

I smiled and nodded. "I am pretty sure the feeling is mutual."

After we were satisfied that Ma would have enough berries, we made our way to the nearby stream. We found a secluded place on the bank of the stream where we disrobed and hung our clothes on a nearby bush. We glanced at them for a moment, and then we slowly made our way to the edge of the water.

Raquelle and I quietly slipped into the cool water of the stream, our naked bodies reacting with goosebumps everywhere. I kept eyeing my clothes on the shore. We both relaxed into the water, shoulder deep, briefly going under as to get our hair wet. When we popped out of the water, we looked at each other and giggled.

Raquelle and I were lost in conversation when we heard *kerplunk—kerplunk.*

Two small stones landed in the water close to us, splashing the both of us. We spun around to see Tomas leaning against a tree, grinning ear to ear.

"Well, what do we have here?" Tomas said.

"Get out of here, Tomas Gagnon!" Raquelle shouted.

Liam walked up from behind him, grinning just as big. "How do you ever expect to be able to support us if you are busy staring at naked women in a stream instead of learning your dad's blacksmith business?"

Instead of leaving, Tomas started to disrobe. "I already know his blacksmith business. Besides, my friendly neighborhood knight needed some assistance finding his way to a stream," he said, pulling off his boot.

"Tomas! Don't you dare! Annalise, cover your eyes, lest you be blinded!" Raquelle shrieked.

"What are you going to do about it? It seems your clothes are over there, Raquelle McShaman?" Tomas said.

I noticed Liam was beating him in the race to get naked. And in one final yank, Liam was fully naked and wading into the water.

"Liam!" Raquelle shouted. "Not you too!" She giggled.

I smiled at Liam as he came closer. For all of Raquelle's noise, we all knew that she and Tomas had already lain together—a lot. Tomas ran into the water, splashing everyone.

As Liam approached, I blushed. Liam's hands found my waist and pulled me to him. I wrapped my arms around his neck, and my legs around his waist. This felt so natural, and the whole world seemed to disappear around us. Although I could feel his desire between my legs, he made no move to force himself. Instead, he studied my face and my breasts, which would bob on top of the water every so often. He seemed to be studying every mark on my skin, taking in every detail. I did the same.

I ran my finger across a scar on his clavicle. "What's this from?"

"Tip of a lance," he said quietly.

As I closed my eyes, I could feel his battle-torn body. His battles had not been only physical ones; he needed a safe place to rest and heal.

I put my hand on his heart and opened my eyes. "How about this one?" I asked.

A slight smile tugged at his face. "Having to endure a life without you in it," he said softly.

I smiled, blushing. "You're incredibly charming," I said.

"I didn't say it to charm you. I said it because I meant it," he said.

I nodded silently, smoothing the hair back from his face.

"You are incredibly beautiful, Annalise," he said.

"Thank you," I said softly.

"I mean it," he said. "I've never seen a woman as breathtaking as you."

"I find you to be quite handsome," I said, and he snickered.

"I am not going to lie, Annalise. I didn't like Lord Farragut touching you today."

"I didn't either, but what was I supposed to do?"

"Actually, what scares me even more is what I could see myself doing to him if he had gone any further." He looked at me, penetrating my eyes.

"Liam," I chided.

"I wanted to cut his hand off. I'll not have another man touching you, Annalise. I couldn't bear it."

"Liam, it was just my cheek."

"Have you ever lain with a man?"

"No," I said, blushing, feeling slightly embarrassed but knowing his question was partly a concern for my safety. It was widely known

35

that there were many wealthy men that would pay dearly for a virgin. And my price went all the higher coming from a "magical family."

"You just need to realize men like him want exactly what you are," he said, sensing a bit of my unease.

"I know that, but…," I said, feeling flustered.

"But what?"

"What am I to do? I can't control that he is a pervert. I didn't know I was going to see him today."

"You can do as I ask and stay closer to home. You wander all over God's creation."

"And who do you think you are to have a right to ask that of me?"

"I am a man that is interested in keeping you safe because—"

"Because of what?"

"Because you are so precious to me," Liam said softly.

I smiled at him. This time, I wanted to kiss him. "You should probably know before you spend too much time courting me that I am barren. I could never provide you with children," I said, watching for his reaction. He seemed a bit amused.

"How do you know that?"

"Well, sometimes women just know."

"How do you know unless you try?" he said, giving me a smile. I giggled. "May I kiss you?"

"No."

"Why not, Annalise?"

"A kiss is incredibly intimate to me."

"And standing here naked with our nether parts bumping against each other isn't?"

"You tell me. You see women naked all the time, and I'm sure you do more than bump nether parts. Do you want to kiss all of them?"

"No," he said, thinking a moment. "But I want to kiss you," he said.

I blushed. I had begun to shiver. I looked around. Tomas and Raquelle were nowhere to be found; her clothes were gone. I knew they had found a quiet place to be together.

"We need to get out of here," I said. All of a sudden, I began to get an eerie feeling.

"Annalise…," Liam whined.

"Please, Liam," I said as my teeth began to chatter.

"Okay," he said, looking at me for a moment, sweeping my legs up and carrying me to shore as I clung to him.

I stood on the shore, and he gave me his shirt to dry off with. I slipped back into my clothes, as did he. I grabbed his hand. He looked up at me surprised and smiled.

"Come with me. We need to leave this place," I said softly.

He looked perplexed but followed. No sooner had we left than a stampede of religious crusaders came charging through the water on their horses in the exact spot where we had just been. Liam looked in disbelief. "Crusaders," he said under his breath. The riders hadn't seen us in the thick of the woods. I was still shaking. "Are you okay?" he asked, pulling me to him, rubbing my back, trying to warm up my body.

"I need to get into the sun," I said through my chattering teeth. He held my hand and led me through the woods. We found a clearing in the woods where the sun was shining through the trees surrounded by a thicket of bushes. It was perfect.

"Is this okay?" he asked.

"Yes. Will you lie here with me?" I asked softly.

"Yes, of course," he said, still studying me. He lay down, resting his shoulders against a tree. I lay down next to him, resting my head on his shoulder. He pulled me in closer to him. I wrapped my arms around his stomach and draped my leg over his. I closed my eyes and saw bloodshot blue eyes staring back at me. I flicked my eyes open.

"Are you okay?" Liam asked. "You were sleeping, and you jumped."

"Yes, I am fine," I said softly, running my hands slowly over his chest. We heard rustling in the woods. I sat up as Liam reached for his knife, and we both scrambled to our feet. Liam gently pushed me behind him. I could feel my mother's energy; she was looking for us.

"There you are!" Raquelle said, glowing ear to ear. "Ready to go?" she chirped.

"So soon?" Tomas whined.

"Ma's looking for us," I told her.

"How do you know?" Liam asked.

"There's a lot you have to learn about our family," Raquelle said.

"Can we walk you back?" Tomas asked.

"No, we need to go back alone," I said.

Liam gathered my hand and kissed it. "I don't like it," Liam said.

"We'll be fine," I offered.

He still wasn't pleased. "May I call on you again tonight?"

"Yes, I would like that," I said, blushing.

I looped my arm in Raquelle's as Tomas was getting in the last few kisses before our departure. When we were out of earshot, Raquelle looked at me.

"Well?"

"Well what?"

"How was it?"

"How was what?"

"Annalise, don't be dense with me. I told you about the first time I lay with Tomas—"

"I didn't lie with Liam, not like that anyway."

"What? Really?"

"Yeah."

"Really?"

"Yes!" I said, giggling.

She pulled me in for a hug. We held hands as we walked up the path to our stone cottage.

I could see that John and Bronwynn's wagon was here. Raquelle and I both looked at each other and smiled. We both took off running toward the house, mindful not to spill our berries.

We burst in the door looking around. We found our eldest sister and rushed her each with a hug. She giggled.

"There are the twins," she said, smoothing our wet hair. "And I see you have been swimming." She kissed our wet heads.

"We have missed you so," I said, squeezing her tighter.

"Me too," Bronwynn said softly.

Jacque tugged at my skirt "Si-ssy," he said, jumping up and down excitedly.

I released Bronwynn and swooped him up in a hug, kissing his chubby cheeks. He giggled. Faith walked in with some zucchini from the garden. She smiled at all of us.

"Now this is more like it," Faith said. Of all of us, Faith wanted the family together. She hadn't liked when Bronwynn had married John six months back and moved down the road. She was also hesitant to move too far away from Ma and Pa with Petyr.

"I understand a certain member of the Lord's knights is courting you," Bronwynn said with a grin. Raquelle elbowed me in the ribs.

"Yes," I said as Bronwynn motioned for me to sit down so she could comb my hair.

"He's quite taken with her," Raquelle said.

"Who is this knight?" asked Bronwynn

"Liam Boutreau."

"You can't be serious?" Bronwynn asked, clicking her tongue.

"What's wrong with that?" asked Raquelle protectively.

"He pays frequent visits to whorehouses and has slept with countless women all over the province. Is that really the type of man you want?" Bronwynn asked, turning my head to her.

"And what is wrong with that, Bronwynn? Maybe Annalise is different to him!" Raquelle challenged.

Faith was getting nervous; she was twisting her apron in her hand. I smiled and winked at her.

"Girls!" Ma said with hushed urgency.

"Bronwynn, why do you feel a man is judged solely by his past?" Ma asked.

"Annalise deserves better than a whoremonger who is going to just use her, Ma!"

"And what do you think John did before he found you to warm his nether parts? The measure of a man or woman is what's in here," Ma said, pressing her hand to my heart.

"Yes, ma'am," Bronwynn said.

Raquelle shook her head while she aggressively plucked feathers out of the poor dead chicken. Faith quietly set down the knife she was using to chop zucchini. Bronwynn took some lavender oil and smoothed it through my hair. We were silent except for Jacque, who quietly played in the corner with his doll.

As the room got stuffier with heat from cooking, I stepped outside to take a breath of the fresh air and admire the setting sun. I noticed Petyr's horse and even Tomas's, but I did not see Liam's. I would get hopeful at every sound, but he did not come. Liam did not show up for dinner, and I was disappointed, to say the least. Raquelle kept giving me a smile from across the table.

Tomas, who was sitting on my right, leaned in at one point and said, "He told me he was coming."

I nodded, feeling only slightly better. At the end of the dinner, the couples went outside, and I stayed to clean up with Ma. Pa took Jacque for a walk as well.

"One night's absence doesn't mean anything," Ma said quietly.

I nodded. "Yes, ma'am."

"Then why so sad, my lovely?"

"He said he was coming."

"Oh, I see. And you think his absence means everything he said isn't true?" Ma asked.

Sometimes I hated that she was right.

"Yes," I said softly.

"Everything unfolds the way it does for a reason," she said, and I nodded.

We worked to clean up quietly. Soon Raquelle and Faith came inside, followed by Pa. They both headed to our room. Pa sat at the table while Ma and I finished cleaning up.

"We ran into Lord Farragut today," I said quietly as I scored the stewpot.

"Oh?" Pa said. Ma paused and looked at me.

"He was very interested in you," I said, looking at Ma.

"I see," Ma said quietly.

"Why is he so interested in you?" I asked her.

"Some men seem to think they can buy women like a basket of eggs at the market," Ma said with disgust.

"Ya see, Lise, when we first arrived to the area and bought this land, Lord Farragut paid us a visit and took a liking to your ma immediately. Who could blame him?"

"Oh, pish posh!" Ma hissed.

"The only problem was me. I've always stood in the way of what he wanted. He even tried bringing her beautiful gifts of gold jewelry and precious stones—"

"I'll tell you where he can shove those precious stones!" Ma said quietly. I smiled.

"You can see how kindly your ma took to his gestures," Pa said, amused.

"A heart can't be bought, Annalise. It wants what it wants," Ma said with a penetrating look. I had never seen her so intense.

"Yes, ma'am," I said softly.

"Raquelle and then you came along shortly after that idiot tried courting your ma. He's always shown particular interest in you and Ellie because of it."

"Arcturis!" Ma hissed.

"What? It's true."

"So even you and Pa, with as much as you love each other, had people trying to interfere?"

"Always. People can't stand happy people who are in love. You just have to ignore them and stick to what you know," Ma said. "Now that's enough stories for one night. How about you get some rest?"

"Yes, ma'am," I said softly.

I then kissed her and Pa good-night and went to bed.

Chapter 4

IT FELT AS THOUGH I had only been sleeping for a few minutes when I was startled awake by a light tapping on the window. I jumped as a I saw a face there. It was Liam! He motioned for me to come outside. I quietly tiptoed, listening to my sisters' breathing and Pa's snoring. I tiptoed through the main room and lifted the heavy wood bar, slipping silently outside. He walked over to me and swept me up into a hug.

"Oh, Annalise," he whispered as he held me.

"Where were you?" I asked softly into his neck.

"Some last-minute business came up," he said, setting me down on my feet.

I looked at his face lit only by the moon. He had scratches on his face and a dark spot on his forehead.

"Come," I said, leading him over to a wooden box next to the house where Ma kept her healing supplies. I removed some oils and mixed them in my palm; then I gently caressed his face, his eyes studying me the entire time.

"Thank you," he said softly, lightly rubbing my arms.

"I didn't think you were coming back," I said softly.

"Why wouldn't I?"

"I don't know. You said you were coming, and then you didn't show up. It made me think—"

"I'm here now," he softly interrupted, and I smiled.

"Yes, you are," I said, continuing to touch his face.

"What's wrong?" he asked.

"My sister said that you are a whoremonger, and you asked me that question earlier in the stream. Is that why you are here?"

"Honestly?" he asked.

"Yes, of course," I said, preparing myself for his answer.

"No," he said and paused a moment then continued, "There was something different about you from the moment I laid eyes on you. Annalise, if you don't want me to kiss you, I won't kiss you... yet. If you don't want to lie with me, we won't. I just want to hear your voice, listen to your laugh, and see you smile," he said softly, caressing my face.

I blushed. "Okay," I said softly.

"I am going to make you my wife, Annalise, and you are far different than a woman in a whorehouse," he said, gently tucking a stray piece of hair behind my ear.

"Their occupation doesn't mean they don't have a heart, Liam. The next time you want to use them to warm your nether regions, think about that."

"I don't want them, for any reason. I am here, with you, Annalise," he said.

I smiled. "I should go back to my bed. I am sure Ma wouldn't be pleased."

"Tomorrow?"

"Tomorrow," I said softly, holding his face.

He swooped me up into a hug and swung me around. I buried my face in his shoulder to muffle my giggle. He set me back on my feet, and after another long glance, I quietly tiptoed to the house.

I slipped back into the house and closed the door, barring it once again. I stopped as I saw Ma sitting at the table with a cup of herbal tea. I could see a relaxed smile on her face from the reflection of the glowing embers in the fireplace. She gently patted the bench next to her, and I noticed there was another cup of tea that I hadn't noticed before.

I sat next to her, and she pulled me into a hug, kissing my forehead.

"Are you mad at me?" I whispered.

She smiled. "No, my precious baby."

"I didn't mean to wake you."

"It's no matter."

"He had scratches on his face, Mami."

43

"Did you heal him as I taught you?"

"Yes, ma'am."

"Good girl," she said, and I leaned my head onto her shoulder.

"How did you and Pa do it?"

"Do what?"

"Put up with all the people that wanted you to be apart?"

"Simple. I love your father."

"Were you ever tempted?"

"No, my lovely. When a heart finds its match, nothing or no one else in this world matters. I would live under a tree out of doors with your pa. All of this stuff doesn't matter—only him. It's as though once my heart found him, it sealed out everyone else. Does that make sense?"

"Yes, ma'am."

"Truth be told, your father lets me be free, as I do him. We have no need to control each other. We simply let each other be and do as we please."

"Some would take advantage of that to stray."

"True, but then they haven't found this type of love," she said, kissing my forehead.

It was true. I had seen men and women tiptoeing out of others' houses on our trips into town. I had also witnessed both of my parents be tempted away from each other. It had never worked. For a long time, I thought this to be a girlhood fantasy, but I was coming into the realization that I had taken for granted the love I had witnessed since birth between a husband and wife. I had never seen two people enjoy each other's company more than my parents. After all of this time, they still laughed and whispered together.

Ma and I sat with each other for the next hour until the sun came up, enjoying the silence and our tea together. We heard Pa begin to stir. He walked outside and returned, Ma making him his favorite porridge. He patted his thigh, and I sat down, draping my arms around his thick neck.

"You were wandering around outside a bit late weren't ye, pretty baby?"

"Yes, Pa," I said quietly.

"Liam?"

"Yes."

"Was he all right?"

"He had scratches and a bruise on his face."

"What did you see when you touched them?"

"Bloodshot blue eyes. They were angry. They were from an older person. I saw them in a dream earlier too."

"His mother," Pa said. He had the same gift of sight we all had.

"I think so."

"Some people don't come from loving homes, Lise."

"I know."

"It makes them no less valuable though. It makes them shine all the brighter."

"Yes, Pa, it does."

I stood up, and Ma served him his porridge. He smacked her on the rear end, and she giggled. I pretended not to notice but couldn't help but giggle. I went into my room and got dressed. I wanted to walk to clear my head.

"I am going for a walk."

"We're heading to Petyr and Faith's new place to help them fix it up. I know she's going to want you to go," Ma said.

"I'll be back shortly, I promise," I said, and Ma nodded.

I loved the light of the sunrise; everything was bathed in orange and red hues. All was quiet, and it allowed me to hear my voice. My thoughts fell to Liam. I realized I loved Liam, as crazy of a thought it was. It was inexplicable, but it was true. I had the attention of several gentleman callers over the years, but why did I love him, and so quickly? My peace was shattered by a horse and carriage coming down the road. I leapt off the dirt road into the grass.

I heard the carriage slow. My heart started thumping louder.

"Annalise!" It was Henri.

"Hello, Henri," I said, feeling uneasy.

"Your father declined my offer of marriage," he said, climbing off his horse.

"Yes, he did."

"That's a shame."

"Is it?"

"Well, of course, it is. I am a stubborn man, however. I don't give up that easy."

"I am being courted by someone else now, Henri. It's best you move on," I offered.

"Who is it? Who would dare do that?" he snapped. "Everyone in the area knows that I'm interested in you. Who would dare court you?" he hissed.

I remained silent.

"And Arcturis allowed it?"

"You can talk to my father about that," I offered.

"If you won't tell me, then I have other ways of finding out."

"Just move on, Henri. We aren't right for each other."

"Annalise, you don't mean that. Think of the life I could give you."

"I don't want that life!" I said, louder than I meant to.

"I should slap you for that. You should know your place!" he hissed, taking a step toward me, and raised his hand.

I turned and began walking away from him.

"Don't walk away from me, you slut!" he hissed.

Even though it wasn't proper or ladylike, I sprinted toward the house. When I made it to the dirt path to our cottage, I slowed to a swift pace.

I saw that Ma, Raquelle, Faith, and Pa were loading up the wagon; I was just in time. Jacque saw me and came running toward me. I scooped Jacque up in my arms and squeezed him.

"You ready to go?" Ma called out to me as I approached.

"Yes, ma'am."

"Ugh, I know that energy from anywhere," Faith said, looking at me as I stood next to her.

"Oh?" Pa said, overhearing. "And what energy is that you speak of?" he said, loading a crate into the back of the wagon.

"Henri," Faith said.

"Is that right, Annalise?"

"Yes, sir," I said softly, glancing at Pa. His face shifted to concern as he touched my face, damp and reddened from running. The understanding of my current state registered in his eyes.

"What did he say?" Pa inquired.

I could see Ma intently listening as she put the last sack of linens in the wagon.

"He was mad that I was being courted by someone else and that I wouldn't tell him who it was. He said he's going to keep trying," I said softly.

"Did you tell him to come and talk to me?" Pa asked.

"Yes," I said softly.

Pa pulled me into a hug. His strong arms always made me feel so safe.

"You did nothing wrong, lass. Some men get wrong ideas in their head, and they won't let them go," he said, trying to hide his irritation.

I nodded my understanding.

Raquelle, Faith, and I sat in the back of the wagon with Jacque sitting between Ma and Pa on the bench in front.

"Are you excited?" I asked as Faith braided small flowers into pieces of my hair.

"Sure," she said quietly. Her pale face and eyes were so delicate. She had gotten sick shortly after Ma and Pa arrived to France from Scotland. She was shorter and smaller than the rest of us. Her complexion was always more fair as well.

"You don't seem excited," Raquelle said.

"I'm going to miss my family," she said, kissing me on the forehead. We all hugged.

Faith had a three-year tumultuous courtship with Petyr. It felt more like she was forcing herself to do this than wanting to do this. Finally, after the seventh time of asking her to marry him, she agreed. Pa reluctantly agreed thereafter.

After a bit of bumping along the road, we arrived to her new house. It was an old stone cottage similar to the one we lived in, also similar to the one Bronwynn lived in just up the road. Petyr was in the front field, plowing. By the looks of it, he had been at it for a while.

We all got out of the cart. Pa went over to Petyr to help. I grabbed Jacque off the bench, and we all went inside. It was dusty, but we would make quick work of it. We had also brought all the bedlinens and curtains we had been sewing for the last month. Tomas had dropped off a huge metal kettle for their fireplace.

The day flew by as we had spent a good portion of the day dusting, scrubbing, and washing. The final chore was to get Petyr and Faith's bed ready. Petyr had attempted to try his hand at woodworking and to make their marriage bed instead of letting Pa make it. The result was an interesting piece that looked none too stable. Finally, Petyr relented and let Pa make one for them.

I heard Faith sniffling as we were putting ticking in her mattress.

"Are you allergic to the goose feathers? Should we use something else?" I asked.

She shook her head. "I'm scared, Annalise," she said in a small voice.

I dropped my end of the mattress. "Why are you scared?" I whispered.

"I don't know," she said, sitting on the floor.

I sat next to her and hugged her. "Is it Petyr? It's been three years. I'm sure he would wait longer…," I offered.

She started to giggle. "Yes…no…it's that everything is changing, and I'm not sure it's for the good."

"Oh, Faith," I said, resting my head on her shoulder. We sat for a moment. "Different doesn't mean bad though," I offered.

She shook her head. "What have I done, Annalise?" she said, looking me straight in the eyes, her eyes brimming with tears.

"It's never too late, Faith," I said, pulling her into a hug as she sobbed. My heart broke for her. She wasn't even married yet, and already she felt trapped. This wasn't how it was supposed to be, and it felt horrible. We sat there until all of her tears drained out of her. She sat back from me and held my face.

"Promise me that you won't do what I did. Promise me you'll marry for love, Annalise."

"I will," I said softly.

"Promise me!"

"I promise," I said, pulling her into another hug.

"If Liam is the one, hold on to him with two hands and never let go," she said softly.

I nodded, tears breaching my eyes. "I just don't understand… why can't you marry for love too?"

"It's too late for me."

"Faith! No, it's not!"

"I have to do this, Annalise. One day I hope you understand," she said, her words sounding ominous and eerie.

After a few more moments, we finished stuffing the mattress and sewing it up in silence. We placed the mattress on the handmade bed that Pa had made them as a wedding gift. I went to retrieve the handmade linens from one of the sacks in the wagon.

"Annalise?" Petyr said from behind me, and I jumped.

"Petyr, you startled me," I said.

"I'm sorry, I didn't mean to. Is everything all right? You seem flushed."

"I'm fine, just a lot of work today," I said, taking the linens out. I looked to see Ma in the doorway, watching. I smiled at her, and she smiled back.

"Don't work too hard," Petyr said softly. For a moment, I thought he was going to touch me. I nodded and held the linens to my chest and walked toward the front door.

As I approached the doorway, I realized Ma wasn't watching me; she was watching Petyr. I slid past Ma and went back to the bedroom where Faith was sitting on the edge of the bed, sniffling. I began to make the bed, and she stood, moving to the window to gaze out.

"Are you about ready to go?" Ma asked softly as she appeared in the doorway of the bedroom. I looked up at her and nodded. Both of our eyes moved to Faith.

"Yes," Faith said almost inaudibly.

"There are three of the most beautiful women in the world," Petyr said, coming up from behind Ma's small frame, and we all jumped.

"Come, Annalise," Ma said quietly. I nodded and made my way to Ma. She held my hand as though I was five years old again. I thought this strange. "Just like Maribelle," Ma muttered under her breath.

"What about Aunt Maribelle?"

"Oh? Nothing love," Ma said, not realizing she was mumbling.

We left Petyr and Faith in the house for a moment together while we climbed in the wagon. For most other couples, this would be a touching occasion. Faith came running out to the wagon, no expression on her face. Their union ceremony would be in three days. The sun was setting as we arrived home. We sat at the table eating some rolls and leftover stew. I heard a knock at the door. Pa looked at Ma and then answered it.

"Liam! My boy," Pa said, hugging him into the house. Everyone looked at me. I could see that his face had healed. He was holding a clump of wilted dandelions in his hand. Raquelle elbowed me.

"Please come in. We were just eating dinner," Pa said as Ma nodded and got Liam a plate of food.

"These are for you," Liam said to me from across the room. I nodded and stood, walking over to him to take them from him.

"They are lovely, thank you," I said as I turned to grab a cup, pouring some water from the pitcher. I placed them in the cup and set them on the hearth.

I returned to my seat across from Liam, who was enjoying the plate of food Ma set before him. He seemed famished.

"We finished Petyr and Faith's cabin today," I offered.

He looked up at me and smiled. "Is this the one just right up the road, the Gregors' old place?" he asked.

"Yes. I wanted to be close to Ma and Pa," Faith added.

"Understandable," he said, taking another bite of bread.

"We would love if you would come to their union ceremony in two days' time," Ma said. Pa looked at her and smiled. I knew why. There was a belief that the union energy was contagious.

Liam looked at me and smiled. "I will be there," he said softly, his eyes never leaving mine.

"You know you are going to have the toughest time of anyone courting her, don't you?" Raquelle asked.

"Oh yeah?" Liam asked amused.

"She's everyone's baby," Pa said, looking at me. "Gwen and I thought we were done with babies after Ellie. Annalise came eleven months after. Her sisters doted on her, and Gwen would hardly hand her over to me! She completed our family."

I blushed.

"Ya know, that arse you work for, Lord Farragut, has always shown special interest in her and Ellie," Pa said, watching Liam's reaction.

"I witnessed it the other day on the roadside."

"Oh yeah?" Pa said, looking at me.

"Truth be told, I wanted to cut off his hand when he touched her."

"He touched you?" Pa asked, glaring at me.

"He touched my chin."

"Annalise McShaman, you didn't say anything about touching," Pa said sternly.

"It was fine, Pa. Henri was there too. Liam helped move things along," Raquelle chimed in.

"Henri? Annalise!" Pa said, getting agitated with me.

"Yes?"

"Sir, if I may, the girls were walking along the roadside. The visit was unprovoked and unplanned. Lord Farragut left after a short conversation and touching each of them on the chin. Nothing more, nothing less," Liam stated matter-of-factly.

Pa nodded, lost in thought, considering this.

"Please excuse Arcturis. He has a long-standing issue with Lord Farragut," Ma said softly. Pa looked at her and winked. He couldn't help but smile.

Liam nodded, still looking at me. "You have a wonderful family," Liam said.

"Thank you, my boy. We always have room to add others into the flock," Pa said, winking at me. I blushed.

"How were drills today?" asked Raquelle, trying to save me.

"Excellent, always strenuous. Tomas says hello, by the way."

"Oh, how is he today?"

"Fine, he was doing some work on our swords for us."

"Oh...I see," Raquelle said.

We had all heard about the huge fight she and Tomas had the night before. I knew it hurt her that Tomas didn't come to dinner tonight.

After Liam hurriedly finished his dinner, Ma suggested just he and I go for a walk in the orchard. It was beginning to rain, although at the moment it was only a sprinkle. He interlaced his fingers with mine and walked toward the back of Pa's barn. He pulled me under the eve and into the shadow.

"May I kiss you?"

"Yes," I whispered.

He softly placed his lips on mine. His kiss was firm but delicate. He rested his forehead against mine. "I could get used to that," he said softly.

"Me too," I said softly, pulling him out of the shadows into the rain.

"How did you heal the scratches on my face?" he asked.

"It's hard to say."

"Annalise, no secrets."

"Ma's mixture of oils is really strong...," I hesitated.

"I've seen other people use oils before, and they don't work like that. What did you do?"

"It's the energy in my hands. It heals," I said quietly, bracing for his laughter.

"How?"

"The energy runs through me."

"Will you teach me?"

"Of course."

"Yeah?"

"Yeah, there are a few rules. The main one is that the energy must always be given and never taken," I said.

"I'm in," he said, nuzzling my face. "Thank you for healing me," he said as he pulled us against the house, kissing my lips again, this time with more need. I felt myself melting into him, and I began to get dizzy.

"I need to get going," he said softly, running his finger along my jawline.

"Will you really come to the union ceremony?" I asked softly.

"If you'll have me?" he said softly.

"Yes," I whispered.

He kissed me again, and I felt my knees about to buckle. "Good night, my love."

"Good night," I said as I watched him walk over and swing up onto his horse.

He waved as I went inside. I didn't think we had been outside that long, but everyone was in bed except Pa, who was sitting at the table, drinking a glass of his homemade apple brandy.

"He's a good man, love," Pa said quietly as he slowly spun his glass on the table.

"He is, Pa," I said, taking a seat on the bench next to him.

"I heard Bronwynn made ye a little skittish about his activities."

"I am not those women, Pa."

"You're right on all accounts," he said softly.

"Why do men do that?"

"They're looking for love, same as the women who allow it."

"Why don't they listen to this?" I said, patting my hand over my heart.

"Because they are taught or choose to ignore it and to do what everyone else thinks they should do."

"I don't want that," I said.

"Aye, I've always known that about you, Lise, my baby. I always knew that it would take quite a man to impress you. You're not easily convinced. None of you girls are."

"Are you disappointed about Henri?"

"No, babycakes, he wasn't right for you. I would live in a wooden shack if it meant I had your mother and my girls. Money is no matter to me. But your happiness is," he said softly as he kissed my temple.

I smiled as I braided a few strands of my hair.

"You know you are never a burden, Annalise," he said, knowing what I was thinking.

"I know, but I am getting older, and it would be less mouths to feed," I said softly, gazing at the wood grain of the table that had been rubbed smooth with use.

"My preference would be to have you all home with me and your ma for as long as possible. It's never easy watching you all go off. Ye take a piece of my heart with you when you go."

"I love you, Papi," I said, leaning my head on his shoulder.

"I love you too, my sweet baby."

We sat there a moment, and then I stood up, kissing him on the cheek. "Good night, Pa."

"Good night, lass."

Chapter 5

ALL THE PREPARATIONS WE HAD made over the last months for Faith and Petyr's union ceremony had paid off. We wrapped the wooden poles of the altar in leaves and flowers. Faith slipped on the gown that we made for her. We also made sure she had new nightgowns and food for the next few days packed in Petyr's wagon. Faith, who usually wore her hair in braids twisted to her head, wanted to wear her hair down today. She looked beautiful, like the Faith of our youth. She seemed happy but reserved as she sat in one of the chairs from our dining table. I braided a few pieces of baby's breath into her small braids that twisted from the sides of her head to the back. Raquelle finished the crown of flowers that she placed on her head. Bronwynn came over to her and grasped both of her hands to standing.

"Ready?" Bronwynn asked.

Faith nodded silently. Ma went to get Pa. In moment, he came bounding in the door with Jacque. It was just my family in this moment. This was when Faith was most content. She now seemed at peace.

"So a second one of the beautiful McShaman girls is ready to be in union, aye?"

"Yes, Papi," Faith said softly.

"We know that this has been hard for ye, Faith. My heart…" Pa got choked up; tears flooded his eyes.

Ma squeezed him and continued, "You're expanding our family and the love we can share with one another exponentially. You are so loved," Ma said.

Pa nodded and kissed Ma on the side of her head. Bronwynn, Raquelle, Jacque, and I exited into the morning light. I saw Liam standing amongst the circle of men: John, Tomas, and Petyr. He looked beautiful with the light reflecting off his features.

"Well?" Petyr asked nervously.

"Petyr, you've waited two years. What's another two minutes?" Bronwynn said, going to stand next to John.

"She's coming, Petyr. She just needed a moment with Ma and Pa," I offered. He nodded.

We took our places around the altar, positioning each one of the men in between us. Petyr and Faith would exchange their vows to each other under the altar while we held hands and created a circle around them. I had Tomas on one side of me and Liam on the other. Liam kept stealing sideways glances at me. I caught him once and started giggling softly. Ma and Pa exited the house arm in arm with Faith. They walked her to the edge of the circle. Each kissed her on the cheek, and she walked to Petyr under the altar. Ma and Pa took their place in the circle. We all joined hands. I began to feel sick. This felt all wrong.

Tears had already begun to fall down Faith's face; Petyr reached up to wipe them. Faith began, "You showed me a world I didn't know existed, and that love can thrive in the most unlikely of circumstances. I love you, Petyr Charowovski," Faith said, but her words felt empty and hollow.

Next it was Petyr's turn: "I never thought this day would come. I honor the light you bring to my life and look forward to walking into the next chapter with you. I love you, Faith McShaman."

Liam squeezed my hand.

Next, Petyr and Faith held their hands in the air, with their forearms facing each other. We could all see the healed marks where they had done the first part of the union ceremony. The memory of that day when Faith came home burned into my mind. They both grasped a piece of white ribbon between their hands as Faith wrapped their arms together. Then she said, "And so it is."

We all repeated, "And so it is." We all looked around and smiled. Petyr and Faith smiled. We released hands and rushed to hug them. Amidst the commotion, Liam grasped my hand in his and led me away.

I walked hand in hand with Liam to the apple orchard. Once we were out of sight from the others, he pulled me to him and kissed me.

"I want that for us, Annalise."

"Want what?" I said, smiling.

"The union ceremony."

"Do you?"

"Yes, Annalise. I want to be with you in every way."

I searched his eyes for a moment. "Did you notice the scars on their wrists?"

"Yes."

"There is a first part to the ceremony. I'm not sure we are ready for that yet."

"When?"

"When I know you truly see me and who I am to you."

"What do you mean?

"You'll know, and I'll know when it happens." I smiled, pulling him to me, kissing him.

"I want to marry you, Annalise. I want you to have my babies. I want to spend the rest of my life with you," Liam said.

"Aye, soon," I said, kissing him softly. "I have found myself falling in love with you in this short time we have known each other."

"You aren't the only one who's falling," he said, kissing me again. My heart fluttered.

"Annalise!" I heard Raquelle calling. We both stepped out of the shadows and walked back toward the house.

"There you are!" Raquelle said. "Ma needs help with dinner… and Jacque," she said, handing Jacque over to me.

Liam looked at me a long moment before walking to the barn where Pa was. I walked inside to help with the food preparations. As customary after a ceremony, we ate an early dinner.

Liam and I had trouble keeping our eyes off each other throughout dinner. If anyone noticed, they didn't say anything. After dinner, Liam and I walked outside. The sun was setting. Soon Petyr and Faith were climbing in their wagon and departing for their cottage. Not long after, Bronwynn and John left. Ma and Pa took Jacque inside, and Raquelle had disappeared with Tomas. I walked with Liam toward his horse.

"Meet me tomorrow?" Liam asked softly.

"Where?"

"Under the tree where we fell asleep."

"When?"

"Midafternoon. I'll be waiting."

"Okay," I whispered.

"Please be careful, Annalise."

I nodded, and he quickly pulled me into the barn. He pulled me to him and kissed me. This kiss was different. There was urgency, need, and passion laced with tenderness, love, and affection. After a few moments, we both came up for air and caught our breath. We smiled at each other.

"I've been wanting to do that all afternoon," he said.

"Me too," I said softly.

He kissed me again. "I have to get going," he said.

I nodded. "I wish you didn't," I said, pulling him into a hug.

He squeezed me and spun me around off the ground.

I giggled.

"Me too. One day, my love, I won't leave. It'll be just me and you," he said into my ear before he released me. We held hands as we walked back to his horse. He looked around before he snuck one last kiss.

"I love you, Annalise," he said softly.

"I love you too, Liam," I said, kissing him one more time before he swung up onto his horse with ease.

I walked into the main room where Raquelle, Ma, and Pa were sitting at the table. They all looked at me as I walked in the door. I hadn't realized how long Liam and I had been out there.

"Oh good! You're here!" Raquelle said, rushing up to me, grasping both of my hands. "Tomas asked me to marry him, and I said yes!" Raquelle blurted out.

I smiled and giggled, pulling her into a hug. "I am so excited for you!" I said, and we both giggled even louder.

"Oh, heaven help me," Pa said. "I don't think any other man has experienced more giggling in a lifetime than I."

"And it's your reward for being such a saintly soul, Arcturis," Ma said, chuckling as she got up from her seat and went to sit on Pa's lap. She hugged his neck and kissed him.

"I love you," she said softly, caressing his face.

"And I you," he replied, smiling broadly and kissing her. He looked at her like she was the only person in the world. They were so happy together, so in love, no matter what the circumstances. They had always been this way; it made it easy to know what to look for.

Raquelle and I left Ma and Pa to their moment and walked to our room. There were now two vacant beds. I knew we would be moving Jacque in here shortly. But for tonight, it was just Raquelle and me. After we changed into our nightgowns, I sat up on my bed. Raquelle came over and laid her head on my lap. I started to braid some of the small pieces of hair around her face.

"Everything is changing, Lise," Raquelle said.

"It is."

"I never thought there would come a day that I wouldn't see you every day."

"You won't live that far away, Ellie. We can still see each other, just a little less often," I offered.

"How about you come stay with Tomas and I after a little while?"

"No, thank you. I don't want to hear the noises coming out of that house," I said, and we both started to giggle. We sat there in silence as I continued to braid her hair.

"Liam wants me to meet him tomorrow," I said quietly.

"What time do we need to leave?" She gave me a conspiratorial smile.

I chuckled softly. "I need to meet him midafternoon by that tree where you found him and me."

"So we'll finish our chores early and head out after lunch," Raquelle whispered.

I nodded, smiling. She sat up and gave me a kiss on the cheek, then softly made her way to her bed, slipping under the covers of her bed. I lay down and smiled to myself in the darkness.

Chapter 6

As promised, we had finished our chores early and found ourselves walking along the dirt road toward the tree Liam and I had fallen asleep under. The day started out sunny, but thunderclouds were rolling in as the day progressed. Raquelle and I heard hooves of horses thundering down the road from behind us. We walked farther into the grass of the field to get out of the way, but the horses' pace slowed. We turned to see that the riders were some of the men from the Lord's guard. I recognized them from the field that day we were in the clearing. An uneasiness fell over me. I could feel it from Raquelle as well.

"Well, hello, ladies. Fine day for a walk," one of three men said, swinging down off his horse.

"Yes, it is," Raquelle said sweetly.

The man began to pace menacingly, circling us like we were prey. The other two men jumped off their horses and approached us as well. The look on their faces disgusted me. I could feel their anger and hate for us.

"So you are promised to Tomas, yeah?" the circling one asked Raquelle.

"Yes," she said softly.

Out of nowhere, he backhanded her. The hit was so hard she fell to the ground, holding her cheek in shock and disbelief, gasping for breath.

"Raquelle!" I shrieked as I dropped to my knees in front of her. I looked into her eyes, where tears had begun to pool. As I reached my hand up to touch her face, the predator seized me by the shoulders and pulled me away from her.

"Let me go!" I screamed as I wretched my body out of his grip and returned to Raquelle.

"Run, Annalise," Raquelle whispered through her tears.

"No! I'll not leave you," I said softly, tears stinging my eyes. He ripped me up by arms again.

"We have a feisty one here, boys," he said, laughing as I clawed at his hands. "You're Liam's whore. I should have known he would pick the wildest and sweetest fruit in the land. Why don't you do some sex magic for me that your family is so famous for, witch?" he said, flashing his disgusting teeth in what was supposed to be a smile. I spat in his face.

"That's how we're going to play, huh?"

"No! Don't you touch her!" screamed Raquelle, scrambling to her feet. Another one of the men lunged at her, grabbing her around the waist. She immediately began to elbow and claw at his arms. I saw a flash of lightning and heard the crack of thunder.

"You want to watch? Is that right?" her captor said into Raquelle's ear. She was fighting like I was to get out of her captor's grasp. I felt my captor clumsily fumbling with my skirts.

"No! Let me go!" I screamed, scratching and clawing at his hands. I shoved my elbow backward as hard as I could to hit something, anything. I heard my scream echo against the trees. His dirty, smelly hand held my mouth while he tried to find his way to my flesh between my legs. I bit his hand, and he threw me to the ground.

"I was playing nice, but you want it rough?" he growled as I tried to scramble to my feet. I found myself crawling backward as he slowly stalked me, untying his pants.

"Lise! No! Leave her alone!" Raquelle screamed, tears now streaming down her face as she kept fighting to get to me, struggling against her captor's grasp. I heard another clap of thunder from the incoming storm.

The heel of my boot caught on the back of my dress, and I fell backward. I scrambled to get up, but he was on top of me. "No! Please no!" I screamed, hitting him with my fists.

"No! Get off of her! Please don't!" I heard Raquelle scream, trying to fight off a sob. I could feel the thunder reverberate through the ground. The thunder became rhythmic; I realized it was hooves of a horse thundering against the ground. I tried to lean up, but he shoved me back down. I felt his dirty fingernail scratch my thigh as he tried to make his way under my skirts. I scratched his face.

"You whore! Quit squirming!" he said with clenched teeth.

"No! Get off of me!" I screamed, beginning to cry.

"Get off of her! Please don't!" Raquelle screamed.

I heard hooves on the path getting closer. I hoped it wasn't more of their friends.

"Ric!" I heard one of the men shout. "You may want to leave off this!"

My captor paused all motion and looked over his shoulder. "Shit," I heard him say under his breath, attempting to scramble to his feet.

"Help me! Please!" I screamed.

I strained to see around his shoulder to see Liam jumping off his horse even before the horse stopped. Liam sprinted over, shoving Ric, sending him stumbling backward. The man who was holding Raquelle let her go, and she came flying to me. We held on to each other. Dark clouds had begun to overtake the sky; fat drops of rain began to fall from the sky.

"Did you hurt her?" Liam yelled.

Ric stuttered, trying to find the words.

"Did he hurt you?" Liam asked me, the look on his face filled with rage. I shook my head no. "What were you doing, Ric?" Liam yelled.

"Oh, come on, Liam. We were just having some fun. You've never cared when we mess with your lady friends before."

"Fun?" Liam said, drawing his knife and holding it up to Ric's throat. The other two men took a step forward and thought better of it.

"Yes, why are you being so protective of some stupid sex witch whore, man?"

"She's not a whore. We're betrothed to be married," Liam snarled.

"What? You're marrying one of the sex witches?" Ric asked in disbelief.

Liam sliced him with his knife, not deep but enough to hurt. Ric growled as he grabbed his neck, bright-red blood seeping through his fingers. A boom of thunder shook the ground. Liam looked at the other two men.

"Come on, I'll take you both, but I think you know better than to challenge me, unless you want your entrails to fertilize this field," Liam growled. They both went back to climb on their horses. Liam's attention returned to Ric. He pulled his long dirty hair back, exposing his neck. Lightning flashed as rain started to pour down.

"You come near her or her family again, and you'll be missing this," he said, tugging on his hair and sliding the tip of his knife along the base of his neck. Ric nodded. "That goes for you too," Liam hollered, pointing his knife at the men on the horses. Liam released Ric and watched him climb on his horse. The men eyed him with disdain for a long moment and then rode away. Once Liam was satisfied they were gone, he returned to me. He knelt next to me. I lunged at him, throwing my arms around his neck.

"Did he hurt you?" he asked me softly.

"No," I said into his neck, unable to stop shaking. I began to sob uncontrollably. I felt Raquelle hug my back.

"It isn't safe for you out here right now. We need to get you both home," he said softly.

I released him and looked at him for a long moment. I noticed scratches on his neck. I turned and looked at Raquelle. She was rubbing her cheek.

"You okay?" I asked, sniffling.

"I'll be okay. I'm just glad he didn't—" She stopped, and we both acknowledged what was left unsaid.

Liam whistled, and his horse came trotting over. He lifted Raquelle on and then me. He climbed on behind me. I felt him reach for the reigns as I clung to my sister, laying my head on her back. The three of us were soaked by the time we arrived home.

"Raquelle! Annalise!" Ma yelled as she came running up to us. "My babies!" she shrieked as she clutched her abdomen. Liam hopped down and helped us off his horse.

"Come inside. You too, Liam," Ma said. I could see her face was pale.

"I don't want to impose."

"Nonsense. You're family," said Ma over the loud noise of the pouring rain beating against the ground. We stood in the doorway dripping.

Pa rushed over from where he had been pacing. "What happened?" Pa said, looking at us, eying Raquelle's cheek and my dirty dress. "Who did this?" Pa said, lightly touching Raquelle's cheek.

"Some of the knights from the guard," Raquelle said quietly.

"Your people!" Pa accused Liam.

"No, sir, not my people. I know them, but they are not my friends."

"Pa, stop," I said softly.

"Annalise, do you know what could have happened!" Pa said.

"He's right," Liam said.

"You are scared and worried for us. Liam had nothing to do with this. It was the usual issue we always have," I said.

"Liam stopped it, Pa," Raquelle said.

Pa considered this. "Let's go have a chat, Liam, my boy," Pa said, draping his arm around Liam's shoulder. They exited the cottage.

We slipped out of our wet clothes, and Ma examined the grass stains and mud spots. She ran her fingertips delicately over the fabric. Raquelle and I walked into our room and closed the door. We both slipped on a new dress and then hugged each other. We both started crying.

"I'm sorry," Raquelle whispered. "I couldn't stop them…"

"No, I'm sorry. I couldn't stop this," I said, sniffling.

Ma quietly opened the door and hugged both of us to her small frame. "My precious girls. I wish the world was a better place for ye," she said, kissing our heads. "Did he force himself on you?" she asked me.

"No, he was going to," I said.

"It shouldn't be like that for you for your first time," she said and then looked at me, lost in deep thought for a moment. "Let's go put something on that cheek," she said to Raquelle.

We walked out to the dining room to see Pa and Liam at the table. I sat next to Liam, still shaking, and laid my head on his shoulder. At first, he didn't know what to do since we were in front of my parents. He laid his head on mine. We all watched as Ma's sure hands put together some herbs and oils in her palm and then held her hand on Raquelle's cheek, rubbing the oil in. To his surprise, she then tended to Liam's scratches on his neck.

"Sissy! Sissy!" Jacque began to howl. He came running in from Ma and Pa's room crying. "Sis-sy, sis-sy!" he said through his tears as he ran over to me, lifting his chubby little arms up for me to pick him up. I smiled and set him on my lap. He turned and hugged me, sniffling.

"Thank you, ma'am," Liam said softly as Ma finished. She then took Jacque from me and sat in her chair.

"I should be going. Thank you for your hospitality," Liam said, rising to go. He shook Pa's hand and nodded at Raquelle and Ma. His eyes then fell on me, concern pouring out of them.

"I think the rain has stopped. Why don't you walk Liam outside, Annalise?"

"Yes, Ma," I said softly, following Liam outside, closing the door behind me. He grasped my hand and walked me over to his horse.

"Annalise, I was so scared when I saw...," he started.

I put my finger over his lips. "It happens all the time," I said. "Why?"

"The villagers think we are witches that practice sex magic, whatever that is, because of the way we live. They think they will be powerful if they can take it from us. They are also just as scared we would put a curse on them. I know that's an awful burden for you to—"

"I asked your dad for your hand in marriage, and he obliged," Liam said, cutting me off.

"He did!" I said excitedly, hugging his neck.

"Yes. Will you marry me, Annalise?" Liam asked.

"Yes!" I said.

Liam wrapped his arms around me and swung me around. We both laughed.

"Meet me by the tree tomorrow?" I asked.

"Annalise, I can't risk you getting hurt."

"I'll meet you in the lavender field, and we will ride together."

"Okay, but be careful. I can't have anything happening to you."

"I will," I said softly.

"I love you," he said.

"I love you too," I said.

He kissed me softly; then he swung up on his horse. He flashed me a smile as he rode away.

I went inside, and everyone was looking at me. "I said yes," I said, giggling. They all sprung up and rushed over to me in a group hug.

"Well, the boy has been asking me for ye hand since the first time he came over here."

"Did he?" I asked.

"Aye," Pa said, kissing my head. "Said you were the most beautiful woman he had ever seen."

"Pa," I chided.

"What? The man has good taste!" Pa said.

I blushed.

"I think I'm going to go to bed early, if that's okay, Ma?"

"Of course," she said, smiling.

Chapter 7

I FOUND MYSELF RUNNING TOWARD the lavender field from excitement. Raquelle had walked with me to meet Tomas in the clearing only a short distance away. I spied Liam waiting for me on his horse. When he saw me, he led his horse forward to meet me, leaning over slightly and pulling me up onto his horse with his strong arms. He wrapped his arms around me as he led his horse into the woods. I turned my head to kiss him. We arrived at the huge oak tree, where he tied his horse up. I led him to the edge of the stream. I found a soft, dry place on the bank of the stream that was secluded.

He watched as I withdrew a red ribbon. "Can I have your knife, please?" I asked. He removed it from its sheath. He held the knife out for me to take. I grasped the handle and then held out my other hand for his arm. I ran the knife blade across his wrist, creating a shallow cut. He winced slightly. Then I held my arm out and the knife for him to do the same. He nodded and lightly ran the blade over my wrist. Bright-red blood dripped down both of our arms. He wiped the blade on his pants and slid it back into its sheath.

I interlaced our fingers together and joined our bleeding wrists, the red drops of blood snaking down our arms. With my other hand, I took one end of the red ribbon and placed it between our hands. I then wrapped it around our arms, tucking the other end.

"Now and forever, for all of eternity," I said.

"Now and forever, for all of eternity," Liam repeated.

"And so it is," I said.

"And so it is," Liam said.

I kissed him, feeling the bubbling of love in my veins. I unwrapped the red ribbon from our arms. I took one step back away from him as I untied the back of my dress and let it slide to the ground. I let my bloomers fall to the ground. I stood completely naked in front of him, letting his eyes caress my body and the cool breeze lightly kiss my skin. I watched as he continued to study my body, his eyes catching on the scratch on my thigh from the previous day's events. He removed his shirt and then his pants. He stood fully naked in front of me, his eyes intent on searching every inch of my skin for its secrets. He stepped toward me and began to let his fingertips discover the feel of my skin. I began to lightly run my fingertips over his neck and down to his shoulders. Our fingertips softly ran over each other's skin, memorizing every inch. I closed my eyes, letting myself be wooed by the rhythm of the stream and Liam's touch. I felt his finger graze my most sensitive parts, making my breathing catch. My fingers found their way down to his obvious desire. I opened my eyes to look at him; so much love shone through his eyes. He led me over to where his clothes were, and he lay down on his back.

I straddled him, hesitating on lowering myself down onto him. I looked into his eyes, his hands softly caressing my thighs. I lowered myself slowly onto him. I whimpered from the pain. His look was intense as the resistance between our bodies broke. I let out a muffled moan as I took him fully into me. He let out a low moan and caught his breath. I didn't move, allowing us to be fully connected. I could feel the energy building at the base of my spine. His fingertips delicately ran over my hips. There were so many sensations—burning, pain, pleasure, and pressure. A few tears escaped my eyes. He reached his hands up to wipe my tears. He gently pulled me to his chest, our hearts beating as one. I kissed him.

In a singular move, he swiftly rolled us over so I was now lying on my back. He slowly and gently made love to me. Tears began to slowly escape my eyes again when I felt my body was going to burst from the building of all the sensations and emotions in these moments. I felt like I just couldn't take any more. I felt the energy that was resting at the base of my spine make its way all the way up my spine to the back of my neck. It felt as though the ecstatic energy released itself at the top of my head. I felt him release himself into me. He closed his eyes and moaned, whispering my name. He then looked at me and softly smiled, tears filling his eyes as well.

"Now and forever and for all eternity," he whispered.

I smiled. "Yes."

"My wife."

"Yes," I said softly, now fully grinning.

He leaned in a kissed me. "I love you, Annalise."

"I love you too," I said. We lay there together, kissing and nuzzling and touching.

"I have never felt something so intensely," Liam said softly, kissing my forehead.

I burrowed into his embrace. "I never thought this much happiness existed," I said softly into his chest.

"Oh, Annalise, this is just the beginning," he said, squeezing me harder, and I let out a giggle.

We had completely lost track of time until we heard Raquelle and Tomas tromping through the woods calling for us. We giggled quietly as we darted up. I spied the dried blood on his nether parts from me. My eyes lingered, and he smiled, his desire evident again. I looked into his eyes. We kissed again, both not wanting to part from each other. Our kiss was broken when we heard Raquelle and Tomas getting closer. We scrambled to get our clothes on. I grabbed the red ribbon, now stained with the blood from our wrists, and tucked it in his shirt. He smiled and kissed me, running his fingers through my long blonde hair.

We walked from our spot hand in hand toward Liam's grazing horse in the clearing. Liam lifted me up onto his horse. My breath hitched as I sat down, my body feeling very tender. He climbed up behind me. I leaned back and laid my head on his chest. We kissed again. I winced with each step his horse took; my lady parts felt more sore with each step. Once we were in the clearing, we saw Raquelle and Tomas riding on his horse; they came up beside us. Raquelle immediately noticed the cut on my wrist and some of the dried blood on my arm and smiled. I smiled back at her.

"I want to formally invite you both to our union ceremony in two weeks," Raquelle said, smiling.

"Two weeks?" I said. "That doesn't give us much time." I giggled.

"I know."

"Where will you live?" asked Liam.

"I bought a little cottage next to Petyr's on the way to town. The Rousches used to own it." Tomas said.

Liam nodded, seeming to know where it was. We rode alongside Tomas and Raquelle until we reached Ma and Pa's cottage. Both men helped each of us down and then headed to the barn to pay Pa a visit. We went inside to find Ma making dinner.

"There you both are. Did you have a nice day?" Her voice trailed off. I knew she could smell the blood on me. She turned and smiled, touching my face. "Was he gentle?" she asked quietly.

"Yes, Ma."

"Did you feel the energy?" she asked.

"Yes," I said softly.

"How do you feel?"

"I love him, Ma," I said softly, blushing.

She smiled, satisfied with my answers.

When dinner was ready, I went to the barn to kiss Pa on the cheek and bring the men in.

Pa's eyes caught on my wrist. "Go ahead, boys. We'll catch up to you in a minute," Pa said, pulling me into a hug. I noticed Liam only went as far as the doorway of the barn and stopped just outside.

"I noticed Liam has the matching mark to you. Are ye okay, baby girl?" Pa said softly, searching my face.

"Yes," I said, blushing.

"Because if ye aren't, I'll kill him where he stands," Pa said, sweeping my hair over my shoulder.

I giggled. "I love him, Pa," I said softly.

He smiled, but some sadness lingered in his eyes. The sadness of his baby girl growing up. "He's the one," Pa said.

"Yes, Pa," I said and hugged him again. I always felt so sure and so safe wrapped up in one of Pa's hugs. We both turned to exit the barn. Liam was still standing outside the doorway.

Liam interlaced his fingers with mine, smiling at me. The three of us walked into the house. Pa took his seat at the end of the table, and Liam and I sat down next to each other. I felt a need to be close to him; I didn't want to be apart from him. We ate and talked about Tomas and Raquelle's new home, determining what supplies we would need. We were going to go out and visit Bronwynn and Faith in the morning, so we wanted to make sure we packed some of their favorite breads and some items we had sewn for them. All throughout dinner, it seemed all I noticed was union scars. Ma's and Pa's were now barely a mark but still slightly visible on their wrists. In some way, it was comforting to know that they had performed the same ritual. Of course, Raquelle and Tomas, they both had a red scar on their wrists. Then I glanced at mine and Liam's, the scab and the remnants of dried blood on our arms. Liam caught me glancing and smiled. He shifted his calf under mine to reassure me. I scooted closer to him on the bench. If I shifted any closer to him, I would have been on top of him.

I missed the rest of the dinner conversation as I was lost in thought, thinking about everything that happened that had transpired that day. My life had changed forever.

After dinner, I walked with Liam to his horse. "I miss you already," he said, softly kissing me.

"Me too," I said softly, kissing him again. "I don't want you to go," I said shyly.

"Me either. I want to sweep you up on my horse and take you away with me," he whispered in my ear.

I giggled. "I love you," I whispered.

"I love you too," he said softly. He kissed me once more and swung up on his horse. He winked at me and then rode away, Tomas following close behind.

Raquelle hooked her arm in mine, and we turned to walk into the house.

Chapter 8

AT FIRST MORNING LIGHT, WE headed to Faith's house. It seemed like forever since we had seen her. Petyr was plowing the front field. Faith looked content but a bit uneasy, paler than normal, if that was possible. She excitedly told Petyr that she was going to Bronwynn's cottage with us. As per usual, Petyr agreed. On the way there, Faith's mind was in a different place. She hardly spoke as Raquelle rattled off her ceremony plans.

Ma drove the horses to Bronwynn's house, who happened to be outside feeding John's beloved goats. Bronwynn saw us, and she started running toward the wagon with a huge smile.

"Mami! Faith! Raquelle! Annalise!" Bronwynn hollered. I noted she intentionally left out Jacque. Bronwynn hadn't been that excited when Jacque came along. She wanted it to be just us girls. She also knew since he was the male heir, he stood to inherit all of what Pa and Ma owned. Prior to that, it would have been John that would have inherited our family's property.

As we all climbed out of the wagon, we each hugged her. She quickly glanced at my wrist and the red scab that was there. She smiled and nodded, draping her arm around my shoulders.

"Did you feel the energy?" she asked softly.

"Yes."

"Then you found your one," she said, kissing me on my temple.

We walked inside and went about cleaning and cooking.

"I heard that Liam cut Ric Raggon's neck defending your honor, Annalise," Bronwynn said quietly.

"What!" Faith gasped. "Not again. I thought this would have stopped now that Raquelle doesn't watch that horrid woman's children anymore," Faith added.

Raquelle took Madame Lemouex's four children into town one day and held the petals of a flower in her hand. She made them dance in the air above her hand without touching them. The kids were amazed, but the madame was appalled. We were spat at and had rocks thrown at us from that day forward. It had calmed some, but we were still known as witches.

"He was defending both of us," Raquelle added.

Ma was adding some oils to some jars at the table, just listening.

"Was it just Ric?" Bronwynn asked.

"No, there were three of them," Raquelle said quietly.

"What will you need help with for your union ceremony?" I asked Raquelle, hoping to change the subject.

"Well, let's see…," Raquelle started, but Bronwynn interrupted.

"No, wait a minute…what happened, Annalise?" Bronwynn asked.

"Ric was going to force himself on me, and he…he hit Raquelle," I said quietly.

"I don't know what would have happened if Liam had not of shown up," Raquelle added.

"I misjudged him, Annalise. I am sorry," Bronwynn said, touching my forearm.

"It's okay. It happens to us all the time." I gave her a slight smile.

"Well, I will definitely need help with my hair and dress and wedding nightgown," Raquelle added. We all started to giggle, even Ma. "I want a big feast where we all sit down and eat together!" Raquelle added.

"That will be lovely," Ma chimed in.

"When are you planning yours?" Faith asked me.

"I'm going to wait a bit," I said.

"Rumor has it, Liam will kill any man that comes near you, so I think you are safe." Bronwynn giggled. "Are you going to live in the manor house with his mother or in a cottage out this way?" Bronwynn asked.

Ma stopped what she was doing and looked at me.

"Definitely not with his mother," I said.

"Why not?" Faith asked.

"She's not right."

"How so?"

"She hurts him."

"How do you know?"

"He shows up to our house with scratches and scars."

"It doesn't mean she hurt him. He's a knight, Annalise. He gets scratches and bruises all the time," Faith offered.

"When I touch his wounds with oil, they are not from sparring or battle. I see angry bloodshot blue eyes. I feel her contempt for life," I added. They all stopped and looked at me.

"Annalise, Raquelle, go in Bronwynn's room now!" Ma commanded.

We dropped what we were doing and did as she said. We hid in the back room, listening. We heard a knock on the door. We heard a man ask for John. I recognized the man's voice. Closing my eyes, I could see that he was one of men that accosted us along the path. Bronwynn sent him away.

"Come out, girls," Ma said softly.

"He was one of them?" Bronwynn asked in disbelief.

"Yes," Raquelle said.

"That was Gustav, the preacher's son—you know, Petyr's nephew? It's getting bad, isn't it?" Bronwynn asked, sitting down.

"Aye," Ma said, patting her arm.

"I thought this would get better as we grew up and got married," Bronwynn said. "I don't understand why they hate us. We don't bother them. We only ever help them! I mean, Ma, how many of those ungrateful townspeople have you saved!" Bronwynn hissed in frustration.

"We are here to heal, my lovelies," Ma said calmly.

We all nodded. This was what she told us all our lives.

When we were done cleaning, dusting, sewing, and cooking, we each gave John and Bronwynn a hug and piled into the back of the cart. It was sunset by the time Ma stopped by Faith and Petyr's house. We dropped off Faith. She looked so sad and forlorn as the four of us rode away. She stood in the doorway of her house watching us leave, wrapping her arms around her waist. Raquelle sat on the driver's bench with Ma, and I climbed in the back of the wagon with Jacque. Jacque fell asleep on my lap as we rode home.

Pa was waiting for us with a grin on his face. "You ladies had some gentlemen callers, but all they found was me." He chuckled as he helped Ma down and began to unhitch the horse.

Raquelle took Jacque inside, and I gathered the remaining supplies from the cart and brought them to the lean-to shed on the side of the house. Then I went inside and changed into my nightgown. Raquelle was already in her bed.

"Ya know, the last time we left Ma and Pa alone, Jacque came along nine months later," Raquelle said, and we both laughed.

"I could only hope to be as in love as they are when I'm their age," I said.

"Amen to that," Raquelle said.

I climbed into my bed. As I did, I felt something. I grabbed it, thinking it was a bug. It was a dandelion; Liam had left it there.

Chapter 9

LIAM AND TOMAS SHOWED UP in the early afternoon to help Pa with some of his farm tools in the barn. I was in the garden helping Ma with her herbs. I waved at him as he looked in my direction with a huge smile, climbing down off his horse. I dropped my gardening tools and ran into his arms. He wrapped me up in a hug and spun me around, both of us giggling.

"I have missed you," I whispered into his neck.

"And I you," he whispered back. He set me on my feet, and we gazed at each other with stupidly happy smiles on our faces. Our moment was broken with Tomas whistling and motioning for Liam to join him in the barn. We both smiled at each other again, and I turned to return to the garden, unable to wipe that ridiculous smile off my face. Ma kept looking at me sideways and started to laugh.

"My goodness, Annalise!"

"What?" I asked innocently.

"I have never seen you beam so brightly," she said, still laughing.

"Oh," I said, blushing.

"It's beautiful, my darling," she said, chuckling. We continued to work in the garden together. After some time had passed. I made my way to work closer to Ma.

"Why did you say Faith is like Aunt Maribelle?" I asked.

Ma froze for a moment and then stood up, looking at me. She exhaled loudly, making her way to the wooden bench against the side of the house. She patted the seat next to her, and I went to sit next to her. She paused a moment and then began.

"Maribelle married a man similar to Petyr, one that was raised with a firm religious background. She and I were both raised the same, but she was more active in wanting to change people's minds

76

about social reform. She thought if she married into the mainstream, she could change their minds. Unfortunately, she became a tool for the dark. She had the same look that Faith does. Maribelle grew pale, but she was adamant all along that she was right. She even tried convincing me to leave your pa."

"Really?"

"Yes, it just goes to show, Annalise. Guard your heart, my lovely, for it is truly the wellspring of life. She was unreachable by the end, and she began converting people to her distorted view of the world. She took the beautiful values we were taught and twisted them to fit in. The dark can be subtle, never forget that," Ma said.

I nodded.

Ma patted my leg. "Help me with dinner?"

I nodded. "Yes, ma'am."

Again, Ma held my hand like I was a small child and led me into the house.

After dinner, Liam and I took off on our walk toward the apple orchard. He pulled me into the shadows next to the barn. I wrapped my arms around his neck and kissed him. I hopped up and wrapped my legs around his waist. He leaned me up against the barn, sliding my skirts up, pausing for a moment, looking for my consent. I nodded and smiled, seeking his lips once more. In moments, my skirts were hitched up by my waist, and I was having trouble containing my moan, full of pleasure and pain from the collision of our bodies. I clamped my lips shut and buried my face into his shoulder, each thrust sending the energy at the base of my spine shooting upward toward the back of my neck. I tilted my head back and looked at the moon. I gasped, feeling totally consumed by his energy. I heard a quiet moan within his chest as he clung to me and stilled, steadying both of us against the side of the barn. We kissed, completely engrossed in each other. We didn't stop until we heard footsteps. Liam set me down on my feet. We both straightened out our clothes. Liam turned around, standing in front of me, slowly removing his knife from its sheath. We stayed there in the darkness, silent as we saw a drunk man stumble past us. It was odd to see a drunkard this far from town. Not that it would have been unheard of for our neighbor to drink too much and wander through the orchard, but I did not recognize this man.

Liam called out to him and slowly took a step toward him, his hand gripping his knife firmly. "You there," Liam said, and the man twisted his face in his direction.

"Your mother won't be happy, Captain," the man said, seeming to recognize Liam.

"What are you doing trespassing on Arcturis McShaman's property?" Liam asked, taking a step closer to him.

The man looked around Liam to see me. I could see that his eyes were black; he looked more creature than man.

"Don't go any closer to him, Liam," Pa said, walking toward us from the house. "He's not drunk on alcohol. He's drunk on the dark," Pa added.

Tomas walked up from behind the house with Raquelle in tow. The man started to let out his sinister laugh, showing off his rotting black teeth.

"Arcturis, the most unholy of unholy," the man said.

"You speak blasphemy, you dark son of a bitch. Get off my land!" Pa said, taking a step closer, holding his hand out in front of him. The man was shoved backward six feet with no one touching him.

"Arrrgghh!" the man said, straining against the energy that Pa was sending. "I'm here as a messenger of prophecy. You can't run from us. We will claim you and your kind," the man said, his voice altering to a deep low tone. He looked at me with his black eyes. "Even a knight can't protect her, Arcturis!" he said as he started to laugh.

Ma walked up beside Pa; her face was angry. I had never seen her so angry. The drunk man fell to his knees, his dirty hands clutched at his ears as he screamed in pain. Dark blood began to trickle from his ears.

"There she is! Guinivere! I should have known this was you!" he screamed.

I took a step closer to Liam, holding on to him.

"That's right, come closer!" the man hissed, looking at me.

Liam stepped back, both of us walking backward, his arms holding me behind him. In that moment, the man's eyes began to bleed from their corners. The man looked at Ma. "You witch!" he hissed as he tumbled over in pain, trying to clutch his abdomen and ears, dark blood seeping from his shirt. He spat blood onto the grass in front of him.

"Leave and never return," Ma said sternly.

The man started laughing. "You bitch!" he said, and then he began choking on the blood pouring out of his mouth. He raised his arm in submission.

"I said leave and never return!" Ma said through clenched teeth.

"As you wish," he said, catching his breath. He glared at me; I held on to Liam tighter. Then the drunkard glared at Pa and Ma as he walked past.

Pa followed him, and when he was sure he was gone, he returned to us.

"I hate to sound dumb, but who or what the hell was that?" Tomas asked.

Ma and Pa looked at each other.

"That's a story for another night," Pa said. "I think it's time for the girls to come inside."

"Arcturis, with all due respect—" Tomas started.

"If you didn't believe that the dark walks the earth, I surely hope you believe now."

"Well, I gathered that. What do they want with you and Annalise and Guinivere?" Tomas asked. This was the question we all wanted to know.

Pa inhaled and exhaled deeply. "Like I said, that's a story for another night."

"Arcturis—" Liam started.

"Why would a bunch of Scots be living in France?" Pa interrupted. We were all silent.

"The darkness Ma saw before you came, it's here now," I said softly.

Liam squeezed me to him. "Should we stay? I can sleep out here," Liam asked.

"We'll be fine," Pa said. "Now we'll let you say your good-nights," Pa said as he put his arm around Ma's shoulders, and they turned to go into the house.

Liam spun around to look at me. "I can't leave you," he said, searching my eyes. "You heard him. He wants to get to you."

I touched his cheek with my hand and smiled. "I'll be fine."

"Please let me stay. I will sleep in the barn."

"You need to go sleep in your warm bed."

"I don't want to be anywhere you're not, Annalise," he said, resting his forehead against mine.

"Liam," I said, hugging him to me.

"Please don't make me leave you," Liam said softly. "I couldn't live with myself if something happened—"

"Soon we will tuck each other into bed," I offered.

"When?" Liam urged.

"I'll talk to Ma and Pa," I said, smiling.

"Soon, Annalise, no more waiting," he said softly.

"Okay," I said, kissing him. "Did you need to talk to your mother?" I asked.

"No," he said even before I finished. "I want her out of our lives. I never want her near you, Annalise," he said, kissing me with urgency.

"Liam." I giggled.

"I need to be with you," he whispered.

"Me too."

"Then let me stay," he urged.

"I think we need to get a good night's sleep."

"Tomorrow?"

"Tomorrow," I said.

He kissed me once more and led me by the hand to the front door. "Sleep well, beautiful," he said as he kissed me.

"I love you," I whispered with his face so close to mine.

"I love you too," he whispered back.

Just then, Pa opened the door and smiled. "Ah, there you are," he said.

"Good night, sir," Liam said, shaking Pa's hand.

"Good night, son."

Liam turned and swung up on his horse. He smiled at me and gave a little wave.

It was only a few minutes when I was in my room changing when I heard Raquelle come in the door, and Pa barred the door behind her. She came sweeping into the room.

"Well, that was some excitement," Raquelle whispered.

"Why did he want to get at me?" I asked.

"I'm not sure. People have always thought there was something special about the way you came into the world."

I nodded then tucked myself under the warm covers of my bed, closing my eyes and drifting off.

I awoke to a loud banging on the door—*THUD, THUD, THUD—THUD, THUD, THUD.* "Arcturis! Arcturis! Wake up!" a man's voice shouted.

I heard Pa moving rapidly out of his bed and toward the door. "Stay in your bed, girls," he said as he went to the door. "Who is it?" Pa barked.

"Benjamin! Please open up!" the man shouted through the door. I could see Pa look in our direction with the little light that the fire was giving off. Ma went to stand behind him. Benjamin was one of the farmers down the road. He was a friend of Pa's. Pa slowly opened the door, unsure of what awaited him.

"For the love of God, what happened!" I heard Pa gasp. I saw Ma cover her mouth and race to get her box of oils, herbs, and tinctures.

"I found them in a ditch on the way home from town. They were jumped as I heard it. Their horses were in the field nearby. I'll ride out to get them and bring them here. I don't want no trouble at my place," Benjamin said.

"Girls!" Ma called out.

We raced out to see Benjamin carrying in Tomas and then Liam. Both of their bodies were limp; their clothes were soaked in blood. Ma pointed for them to take them to the extra beds in our room. A tear squeezed out of my eye, which I quickly wiped away.

"Thank you, Ben," Pa said.

"I thought this was the safest place for them. Your wife is a miracle worker. I would have lost my youngest son to the black death for sure if it weren't for her," Ben said, holding his hat in his hand.

"You were right to bring them here," Pa said.

"Well, I'll bring their horses by later. Have a good night," Ben said.

Pa closed and barred the door behind him.

Liam wasn't responding. As soon as he was laid down on the bed, I put my head to his bloody chest. He had shallow heartbeat and was barely breathing. I removed his blood-soaked shirt to see stab wounds all over his perfect chest. His face was swollen, and his knuckles were bleeding. I could feel the fight he had put up. I could feel the energy from the anger of the men who did this. Ma brought in boiling water and rags. I cleaned his chest so I could see the wounds. He had so many stab wounds; all were seeping blood. I started to cry. Liam's words echoed in my ears; he had wanted to stay. Maybe this wouldn't have happened if he could have stayed in our barn. I let my tears fall onto his skin. I quietly sniffed. My eyes became blurry. I wiped them with the back of my hands, which were now covered in his warm blood.

"The dark would have found him anyway, Annalise," Ma said softly as she went to work, mixing oils and herbs, cleaning the wounds and then packing them with her mixtures. She poured some oil in my hands and then went to attend to Tomas.

I closed my eyes and could feel the energy running through my hands. I rubbed the mixture all over his face, chest, and stomach. After that, the only thing we could do was wait. I gently and lovingly cleaned his hands and knuckles, looking at his beautiful hands, the hands so strong and rough from work but gentle with his touch. Setting them next to him, I gently smoothed his hair. I dozed off sitting next to him. I woke to more banging on the door. I looked at the window. It must be early morning. Light wasn't coming through the slats in the shutters yet.

"Arcturis! Arcturis! We know you are in there!"

THUD, THUD, THUD, THUD, THUD, THUD!

"Arcturis!" an angry man's voice came through the door.

"What do ye want? You're waking my family!" Pa hollered.

I felt Liam's body flinch. I put my hand on him, and he relaxed.

"We know you're hiding them!"

"Hiding who?"

"Tomas and Liam!"

"What are you talking about?"

"We know you and your witch family!"

I now recognized the voice as one of the men from the village Pa used to barter with, Rainier Trappola.

"Get out of here before I kill you for trespassing on my land, Rainier!"

"We'll be back, Arcturis!"

I heard a clap of thunder in the distance. Liam's body flinched again, even though he wasn't awake. I rested my hand over his heart and laid my head next to his chest on the mattress. I heard the rain pour onto our thatch roof, and it lulled me to sleep.

I woke up, my body stiff from my contorted sleeping position. Liam still wasn't awake. He had a pulse, but his breath was still shallow. The swelling on his face had gone down, and his wounds had begun to heal as I expected. His color was returning to his skin.

I grabbed my dress and went into Ma and Pa's room to change. I noticed a sleeping Jacque in their bed, twisted up in the covers and smiled. I then collected Liam's bloodstained clothes, as I did, our red ribbon fell out. I picked it up and smiled, then went to tuck it under his pillow. I made my way into the main room where Ma and Pa were sitting at the table next to each other. I kissed Ma and Pa on the cheeks, and they both watched as I stoked the fire. I could tell neither one had slept since the arrival of our visitors. Then Pa got up and went outside, returning several times with buckets of water to boil the bloody clothes, in addition to Tomas's, which Raquelle had just emerged from our room with. Tomas had woken up a few hours before.

We went about reapplying oil to their bodies. I studied every mark on Liam's skin, eventually flipping his wrist over and staring at our mark. I felt a tinge of pain that he went through this because of me. He was so beautiful. I sat and held his hand; a few slow tears rolled down my cheeks.

We spent the rest of the day making tea packets and other various herbal concoctions that Tomas was choking down as Liam would when he woke up. Pa was outside chopping wood for the fire. We had been instructed to stay inside; he would handle the chores today. Everything was somber and silent except Jacque, who was now playing in the corner. I was sitting at the table doing some mending of Jacque's pants. Raquelle was mending one of Pa's shirts, and Ma was making some herbal mixtures. The silence was shattered.

"Arrrrrgh! Annalise! Annalise!" I heard Liam scream.

"Calm down. She's here," I heard Tomas say quietly.

"No, I need her. Where is she?" he asked, panicked. In a moment, he was standing fully naked in the doorway of the bedroom.

Ma began to giggle. "Lise!" Ma whispered.

I shook my head from staring at his beautifully scarred body. Raquelle giggled and averted her eyes.

"I'm right here," I said, jumping up and rushing to him. He groped the air in front of him, seemingly unable to see, though his eyes were open. I hugged him to me. His hands felt out the features of my face, and he inhaled the scent of my hair.

"Oh, Jesus, it's you. Where am I?" he asked.

"You're at my house. A neighbor found you with stab wounds and brought you here," I said as I led him back over to the bed.

"I can't see, Annalise," he said, panicked.

"It's okay," I soothed as I held my hands on either side of his head. A movie played in my mind as to what caused the trauma to his eyes. I then focused my energy on the damage.

"It tingles, love," he said softly, caressing my arms, his fingers feeling out the scar on my wrist.

"Yes, it should. It may pinch. I'm almost done."

"What are you two doing over there?" Tomas said from his bed. Raquelle raced in the door and hugged him. He groaned. I looked over to him; his one eye was blackened. I finished with Liam and held his hand.

"You may get sleepy," I said.

"So this is all it took to let me stay the night?" Liam teased.

"Not funny, Liam Boutreau!" I admonished.

"You'll not leave me?" he said, looking in my direction.

"I'll never leave you," I said, kissing him. His fingers were still rubbing the scar on my wrist. He closed his eyes and drifted off to sleep again.

"Tomas!" I heard Raquelle quietly admonish as he kept trying to kiss her. I smiled and went back in the other room to retrieve their clothes from the boiling water and hung them to dry. After a while, I poured some of the tea mixture in a cup for Tomas and brought it in. I handed it to Raquelle, and she began to slowly allow Tomas to sip from it. Liam woke up gasping. His eyes flew open, and he looked right at me.

"I can see you," he said, catching his breath. His hand reached up to my face, and a huge smile spread across his lips. I smiled, and after a moment, I departed and brought him back a cup of the warm liquid mixture. I sat next to him, holding his hand with one hand and holding the cup to his mouth for small sips with the other.

"I need you," Liam whispered.

I smiled. "I need you too," I whispered back.

"I mean it, Annalise. I never want us to be apart."

"I mean it too, Liam. I don't either."

"I found a cottage for us to live," he said, kissing my hand.

"Oh yeah? Tell me about it."

"It's much like this one. It has an apple orchard, grape vines, cherry trees. I can't wait to taste all the fruit creations you're going to make us." He smiled, caressing my face.

"It sounds perfect as long as you are there," I said.

He smiled. "I agree. You're my heart, love," he said, and I leaned down to kiss him.

"Did you tell her about the waterwheel by the stream?" Tomas added from across the room.

"A waterwheel!" Raquelle chirped. I smiled. A waterwheel meant we could grind grain for flour and barter with other farmers. It was another source of income and would be nice to have in the family as well. I smiled at him.

"Are you pleased? Could you be happy with me there?" Liam asked.

"It all sounds so lovely, but I just want you. We could live in a shed for all I care."

"I wouldn't ever let us live in a shed."

"I love you," I whispered.

"I love you too," he whispered back. I leaned in to kiss him again.

"How are the patients?" I heard Pa's booming voice from behind me. I blushed, realizing he probably caught me kissing Liam. I looked at him, and he winked at me.

"Our apologies, Arcturis," Liam started.

"We didn't mean to intrude or bring trouble to your home," Tomas added.

"Nonsense! We're family. We look after our own. You were brought to the right place."

"Thank you, sir," they both echoed.

"Now tell me, what got you in this condition?" Pa asked.

"Should we discuss this in front of the girls?" Tomas asked.

"I keep nothing from my girls. No secrets in this family."

They both hesitated.

"Is it because of your ties to my family? Your engagements to my girls perhaps?" Pa asked.

"Yes, sir," they both echoed.

"Okay then, be out with it! Tell us what happened," Pa said.

"We were leaving Tomas's blacksmith shop," Liam started. "There were quite a few men from the village that appeared as we were walking to our horses."

"Some were angered by Liam's engagement. It seems Annalise has quite a few admirers and enemies."

"Me?" I asked.

"Yes, some were Henri's friends or friends of Liam's family. Some of the legion was there. You'll recall their sentiments," Tomas added. Liam was studying my face.

"I'd wager you are leaving a few broken hearts behind as well, Tomas and Liam?"

"Yes, sir," Liam said. "I'm hoping they got this out of their system, and we can all just move on."

"I hope so too, my boy, but I'm not so sure," Pa said, rubbing his beard.

"I've bought a place down the way, sir."

"The place with the water mill?"

"Yes, sir."

"Very nice, my boy. I look forward to seeing it."

"Arcturis! I need more firewood, love," I heard Ma say.

Pa smiled and departed. I heard him making kissing noises and the two of them giggling together. We all started to snicker. I looked at Liam, smoothing his hair.

"I'm sorry this happened because of me."

"This is nothing. I would endure far more than a few pokes of a knife for you, my love." His words lured me in, and I kissed him.

"You aren't telling us something," I said, breaking the silence. "Where were you before the blacksmith shop?" I asked. Raquelle looked at me and smiled.

"Annalise...," Tomas chided.

"No, Tomas, where were you? Wherever you were caused the conflict," I said calmly.

Both men looked at each other in astonishment.

"The courthouse, petitioning for marriage," Liam said. I nodded, blushing.

"Petyr's brother, the preacher, was there," Tomas added.

My head was spinning; I began to feel nauseous. It seemed people who were close to us weren't who we thought. My mind drifted to a more innocent time when we were all little girls running through the fields, picking flowers, and giggling while we braided each other's hair. We were still able to go into town with Ma and Pa to pay a visit to the local shops. We were taught to love. This world of hate was confusing and made no sense to me or any of us.

A few hours later, Pa came in an announced that Benjamin had brought over Tomas's and Liam's horses.

Ma said she would allow them to leave after another night of rest. After we brought them dinner and made sure they were comfortable, Raquelle and I fell asleep in our clothes on top of our beds. We were more exhausted than we realized. I awoke in the morning with my quilt over me; I knew Ma had been in. Liam was sitting up, smiling at me. I sat up and rubbed my eyes, then walked over and knelt in front of him, examining his well-defined stomach. He caressed my hair.

"You look healed to me," I said, smiling up at him.

"You look beautiful when you sleep," he said softly.

"Liam," I chided, blushing. He lifted my face to his, and we kissed.

"I want to wake up next to you every morning," he whispered.

I smiled. "And I you," I said and heard a clap of thunder in the distance.

It was agreed that they would depart in a few hours after they drank a cup of Ma's special tea and a bit of food. I finished mending the holes in Liam's shirt. I delivered his washed, dried, and mended clothes to him. He smiled.

"You're welcome," I said as I set his clothes down.

He laughed, showing his perfect smile. "Thank you," he said. He searched the folds of his clothes, looking for something, panic starting to overcome his face. I reached behind his pillow and handed him the red ribbon. He smiled as relief flooded his body. He kissed me.

"I always keep this with me," he said.

"I'm glad."

"It was the best day of my life, Annalise. I want to always remember it," he said, looking at me with his beautiful brown eyes. I blushed and smiled.

I helped Liam to standing.

"Amazing," he said in astonishment, touching his stab wounds lightly. He pulled me to him and kissed me.

I giggled. "Liam," I chided.

"You amaze me," he said, looking into my eyes.

I smiled. I held Liam's hand as I walked Liam out to his awaiting horse. The late-day sun was glorious on my face after being cooped up in the house. The air smelled clean now that the thunderstorm had passed.

"Your mother hates me?" I asked softly

"Yes."

"Why? I didn't do anything but love you?" I asked quietly, feeling my eyes water.

"She hates everyone, mostly herself. You represent everything she's not and never can be."

"Why?"

"After my father died, she became bitter about life and obsessed with me and my life."

"Obsessed?"

"No woman is good enough to take me away from her. She's sick, Annalise."

"The scratches on your face..." My voice trailed off, now understanding the abuse he endured because of me. "I'm sorry," I said softly, looking at the ground.

"Look at me, Annalise." He tilted my chin to look at him. "I hate her, Annalise, and I love you. When we are married, I never want to see her again."

"Liam, she's your family."

"You are my family. That is all I need. Can you be that for me?"

"Yes," I said, hugging him.

"I'm going to come and get you tomorrow. We're going to ride to our new house together, okay?"

"Okay," I said into his neck. Then I kissed him, passionately, losing myself. When our lips parted, we both smiled. I watched as he winced, swinging up onto his horse. He gave a little wave and rode off, Tomas riding alongside him.

I went back into the house and promptly got the linens off the bed to boil white again. I opened the shutters in our room to let the light and cool breeze in. I sat on my bed, staring at my hands. Ma sat down next to me, and I curled up, laying my head on her lap.

"What's wrong, my love?"

"I don't like being in this place," I said.

"What place is that?"

"This in-between place."

"How so?"

"I just want to be with Liam, but we aren't married yet, and I love being here. I want to be a family, but his mother hates me. It just feels like I am not where I need to be yet," I said, trying to contain my frustration.

"That means you are in the middle of a transition, leaving something old behind, and the new hasn't come in to fill its place yet. The period in between is always the hardest," she said.

I nodded.

"Your pa was the worst courter. He wouldn't show up on time, forget when he would tell me he was coming, forget to bring flowers. I was always in a constant state of wondering if he was going to come through for me."

"He left his family for you and hasn't left you since," I said softly.

"Aye. My point being, when he was courting me, he was leaving his old ways, but he wasn't quite my husband yet. The in-between stage was awkward and frustrating. But the ending was beautiful," she said, kissing my temple.

I turned and smiled at her. "So you are saying, I'm in the messy middle part before the good stuff comes in?" I asked.

"Yes, my love," she said, smoothing my hair from my face.

I'm not sure how long we were like that before we both fell asleep.

I woke in the morning with Ma sleeping, leaning against my headboard and my head on her lap. It made me smile. When I moved, she woke up and smiled at me.

"Breakfast?" she whispered.

I smiled and nodded. We were surprised to see Pa up and the porridge made. He was sitting at the table spinning his glass of fermented apple juice.

"Did you sleep at all?" Ma asked him, making herself a cup of herbal tea.

"Maybe an hour or so," he said.

"And?"

"And what?"

"And what did that do for you?" she asked him.

"We can't outrun this, Gwen."

"You're right. But I don't know what to do about it."

"I didn't expect the girls getting married to stir up so many things. I thought it would settle things down."

"Hate is hate. It doesn't matter what we do. We are different," Pa said.

Chapter 10

As promised, Liam arrived early in the morning to take me to our cottage. We rode at a slow pace. I leaned back onto his chest; he kissed my temple.

"This is where our property begins," he said into my ear as we made our way down the wagon path. I saw apple trees as far as I could see on both sides. As we drew closer, there were fields that I could plant herbs and vegetables, lavender and wildflowers. I could see the rows of grapevines in one of the side fields. I gazed at the barn off to the left side, and to the right was a steady flowing stream. I could see the waterwheel peeking out behind the house. The cottage was stone and stucco with a thatch roof. Liam helped me down, and I hugged him, squealing with excitement.

"This is more beautiful than I could have imagined!" I said as he swung me around.

"You like it? You are pleased, my love?"

"I feel so happy, Liam," I said kissing him, his arms pulling me in closer.

"Let's see the house," he said as we both excitedly ran toward the front door.

He swooped me up in his arms and carried me in. I heard him bar the door behind us. Streaks of sunlight shone through the wood shutters. I saw a fireplace to the right and a nice open room. It was a bit roomier than other cottages; it had two good-size rooms and stairs up to a loft. Liam and I made our way up to the loft where I saw he had a blanket lying on the floor.

I looked at him and smiled.

"I want to make love to you in our new home, Annalise. Will you have me?"

"Yes," I said, slowly untying the back of my dress and letting it slide to the floor. He watched, letting his eyes linger on my breasts, and then his gaze dropped to my stomach and apex. He looked into my eyes, kissing me. My fingers tugged at his shirt as I lifted it over his head and let it fall to the ground. I untied his pants, and they also fell to the ground. Again, we let our fingertips dance and discover, drinking in the feel of each other's skin.

I lay down on the blanket, and he followed on top of me. He kissed me softly, then with more passion. He leaned his head up to gaze at me as he slid himself into me slowly. I whimpered as I held his face. I closed my eyes for a moment, feeling the energy at my back and slowly starting to pulse only partway up my spine. I brought his lips to mine and got lost in his being. There was no telling how long we were up there in the loft; we enjoyed each other for hours. As we lay there naked, we fell asleep to the rhythm of each other's heartbeat.

When we woke up, we opted for another round and then made our way down to the main room.

"Could you be happy here with me, my love?"

"Yes, you are home to me. Wherever you are is home," I said.

He kissed me again. "I've never loved anyone as I love you."

"Nor I."

"I'm moving in here to start fixing the place up," he said.

I smiled.

"After we are married, you will join me, sooner if your parents would allow," he said, kissing me.

I nodded. We walked hand in hand through the apple orchard, enjoying the sun on our faces as we picked some apples to bring back for Ma and Pa, then made our way back to his horse and departed for Ma and Pa's. Even riding on his horse with him was where I wanted to be. I meant it: wherever he was, I wanted to be there too.

When we arrived at Ma and Pa's, I brought the apples to Ma, and Liam departed to help Pa in the barn, but not before sneaking a kiss.

"Well?" Ma said as I stood next to her cutting vegetables.

"Well what?" I smiled.

"Did he do well?"

"Well on what?"

"Annalise Grace McShaman! Your new house!" she said, laughing.

"Oh! It's beautiful, Ma. He did well. I can't wait to start our life together!"

"He asked your pa if you could move in with him."

"What did Pa say?"

"Only if you have your union ceremony first," she said.

"Yes, ma'am." I nodded, understanding I would need to wait a few months. It would be a large expense for two of their daughters to have ceremonies close together.

"So we thought perhaps you and Raquelle could have your ceremony at the same time," Ma said softly.

"Really? Is Raquelle okay with that? I don't want to ruin her special day."

"She said it is more than okay!" Raquelle said, coming out of our room tying her apron and grinning ear to ear. "I would love to share that day with you," Raquelle said, hugging me.

"Double ceremony, it is," I said, squeezing her.

After dinner, I walked Liam to his horse, and he pulled me in for a kiss. I giggled at his urgency.

"I wish you could come home with me tonight. I want to feel you beside me all night and wake up to your beautiful face in the morning," he said, holding my face and caressing my cheeks softly with his thumbs.

I smiled. "We're having a double union ceremony with Tomas and Raquelle. It won't be too much longer," I said.

"I can't wait," he said, smiling.

"Me too," I whispered.

He kissed me. "I love you,"

"I love you too," I said, kissing him again.

He held my face a moment longer and then swung up onto his horse. Tomas came striding up beside him. Raquelle appeared beside me and looped her arm in mine. We gave them both one last wave, and then we entered the house together.

Ceremony preparations went into full swing. Liam would stop by some days to pick me up and bring me to our house where I would help fix it up or hang curtains that I had made. He would stop by every night after drills to eat dinner with us. As promised, he had moved into our house, completely cutting off contact with his mother. He seemed so happy now, so free. The two weeks had flown by with all of the preparations.

The big day had arrived. Bronwynn and John arrived early that morning. John went to help Pa, who had woken up early to roast a pig over a huge fire. Faith and Petyr arrived soon after that. I spied that Tomas arrived with Liam; it took everything I had not to run out and fling myself at him. Raquelle and I stood in our room and looked at each other after we had slipped on our white dresses. We smiled as tears brimmed our eyes.

"This is it, Annalise. This is our new beginning," Raquelle said.

"I'm so excited. I didn't know I could feel this happy," I said.

"Me either," she said, pulling me in for a hug.

Ma came in and sat on one of the beds, her nose red from emotion. "Are my girls ready?" she asked softly.

We both went to sit on each side of her on the bed. She sniffed. We both hugged her, and she began to cry. Then Raquelle and I followed in short order.

"Are you sad, Mami?" Raquelle asked.

"No, nothing like that, my lovelies. I can feel the joy, excitement, and love. It's overwhelming."

"What's this?" Pa asked, coming into our room, smiling. His eyes locked on Ma. He knelt before Ma, holding her hands. "The only advice I have fer ye girls is to follow your ma's example and love him fiercely," Pa said, looking into Ma's eyes, completely taken with her. I felt the jolt of energy he sent with his words. They smiled at each other; then Pa pulled all three of us into a hug with his strong arms. We heard Bronwynn and Faith talking as they entered the cottage.

"Anybody home?" Bronwynn called out and giggled. We smiled, and all stood up sniffling. Pa grasped Ma's hand and led her into the main room.

The day had flown by. Ma, Pa, Bronwynn, Faith, Raquelle, Jacque, and I stood in our home that we had shared so many memories in. We huddled close as Ma and Pa had tears streaming from their eyes.

"My babies, I was hoping for this day for ye but also dreading it fer myself," Pa said, chuckling and wiping his eyes. "Our youngest two girls, starting out on a new journey. Where has the time gone?" he asked Ma.

She sniffled and wiped her eyes. "You always have a place to come back to," Ma started.

"And we look forward to the love that will grow from these unions," Pa added.

"With all our girls here, we love you all so much. You are always our babies, never forget that."

With that, we all kissed and hugged. I straightened my simple white dress. I had braided part of my hair and left the rest down. Faith placed the crown of leaves and flowers on my head and then on Raquelle's. She kissed our cheeks and made her way out of the cottage with Jacque. It was just Raquelle and me with Ma and Pa.

"My wildlings," Pa said as he drew us into a hug with his big muscular arms. Ma hugged us from behind. We were totally cloaked in our parents' love.

"I love you," Pa said.

"I love you too, Papi," we both echoed.

"And I love you," Ma said.

"I love you too, Mami," we both echoed as we turned around and hugged her.

"Are we ready?" Pa asked, wiping his eyes.

"Yes, sir," we both echoed.

Pa led us out into the afternoon light, Raquelle standing on one side of him and me standing on his other. Ma looped her arm in mine as he led us from the cottage to the altar. Ma handed us each a bouquet of wildflowers with the white ribbon we would use for the ceremony tying the stems together. My eyes were fixed on Liam as his were on me; he looked striking in his nice clothes. He smiled at me, and I smiled back. Both Ma and Pa kissed our cheeks before we entered the circle. I went to stand across from Liam. His eyes began to water, as did mine. We smiled and let out a soft giggle, and we wiped our eyes.

He held my one hand that didn't have the bouquet and squeezed it. I hardly heard Tomas's and Raquelle's vows as I was so lost in Liam's eyes. This felt more right than anything I had done in my life. Tomas and Raquelle stood there with their arms bound together with the white ribbon while Liam and I started our vows. I handed my bouquet to Faith after I unwrapped the ribbon. I could hear everyone in the circle sniffling except Petyr. I took our hands and matched the scars on our wrists, then bound our arms together with the white ribbon.

"I never thought I would find you, but here you are before me, the one who was made for me. I now know what true love is and where I belong. I love you, Liam Boutreau."

"You are the air in my lungs and the heart that beats within my chest. You are my life. I love you, Annalise McShaman," he said, smiling through his tears as we raised our arms in unison with Tomas and Raquelle.

We were grinning at each other ear to ear as we kissed. Then everyone said, "And so it is!" We all cheered. Liam swooped me up, kissing me, and I giggled.

"You're mine, Annalise, and I'm yours," he said, nuzzling my neck.

"Yes," I said, kissing him again.

"This is the best day of my life," he said, his eyes tearing up again.

"Mine too," I said, resting my forehead on his.

"Now and forever and for all eternity."

"Now and forever and for all eternity," I said back to him. He kissed me once more before setting me down on my feet. From that moment, we were inseparable.

Pa had been roasting a pig for most of the day for the feast after the ceremony. It was delicious. We all sat outside and ate together. It was hard to get a bite in between Liam's kisses. I giggled. "I need my strength for later," I whispered to him. That made him growl and nip my ear and did not stop any of his kisses. Liam had actually purchased a wagon for us, as much as he detested them. Liam put my chest of clothes and some leftover food in baskets into the wagon before I gave my family a tear-filled goodbye.

I sat on the bench next to Liam, looping my arm in his as he guided the horses with the reins. He kept turning his head so I could kiss him. Tomas and Raquelle were leaving at the same time to go to their cottage. I turned back as we rode away to see Ma and Pa standing there with Jacque on Pa's shoulders. I smiled and leaned in for a kiss, which Liam gladly obliged.

I laid my head on his shoulder.

"This has been a long two weeks sleeping in an empty bed, my love."

"I'm glad to hear it was empty, I would hate to hear that it wasn't," I said, kissing him again.

"There is no one else for me, Annalise. If it's not you, it's no one," he said, looking at me intensely.

I nodded. We drove in silence the rest of the way, enjoying each other's presence. He maneuvered the horse down the driveway. Our cottage was lit only by the moonlight. When we arrived, I waited for Liam to unload the wagon and unhitch the horse. He led the horse into the barn and returned shortly to open the door for me and carried me in. I hung my crown of leaves over our fireplace as Liam brought in my chest of linens and clothes. I also helped bring in a couple of baskets of food. Once everything was stowed, we maneuvered through the dark cottage into our bedroom. The moon was shining through the bedroom window, giving just enough light. Liam immediately undressed, as did I. He held my hand as he led me into our bed. His lips found mine, and our bodies tangled with each other's.

"My wife," he whispered.

"My husband."

"I like the sound of that," Liam said.

"Me too," I whispered.

He kissed me with full fervor. We were lost to each other for the rest of the night and into the next day. We only put on clothes and emerged to get firewood from outside and start the fire. We also ate a few bites of food, but other than that, we were totally absorbed into each other. I had never been so taken with another human being before.

Chapter 11

Bronwynn and John

THE DAY THAT BRONWYNN MET John was like any other normal day. I was thirteen at the time; we were still welcomed in town. My sisters and I rode along with Ma on a visit to a very sick woman. Traditional medicine had not been able to help her, so her son called upon Ma as a last resort. As we were peeking in the little shop windows, we arrived at the bakery. We knew the baker, Simone, well. Ma had helped deliver their first baby. We walked inside.

"Well, hello, ladies!' Simone called from behind his counter. Bronwynn stopped dead in her tracks.

"Hello, masseur!" Raquelle called out.

"Winnie, what's wrong with you? Move your feet," I whispered, giggling. I peered around her to a young man standing at the counter awaiting some loaves of bread and a cherry pie to be tied up in a cloth with twine. I could tell he was a gentle soul. By the looks of it, he was a farmer. He had long brown hair tied back with a leather strip. He had soft brown eyes and a beard. He was just as mesmerized with Bronwynn.

"Hello, miss..." the gentleman said,

"McShaman, Bronwynn McShaman."

"Bronwynn," he repeated softly.

"And you are?" she asked.

"John Gremmer," he said.

"These are my sisters Faith, Raquelle, and Annalise," Bronwynn offered.

"How do you do?" He nodded; we all nodded back. "You're Arcturis's girls, aren't you?"

"Yes, sir, we are," Bronwynn said.

"What's your pleasure?"

"Pardon?"

"I mean, what are you buying today from the baker?"

"Nothing today, but the cherry pie is delectable."

"My mom loves them too. That's who this one is for," he said, blushing. Bronwynn nodded.

"Ma's waiting for us," Faith whispered. Bronwynn nodded.

"It was a pleasure to meet you, John." Bronwynn gave him a slight nod and turned to go.

"May I call on you?" John called after Bronwynn.

"You may," she said with a smile, exiting the shop and climbing up next to Ma on the bench in front of the wagon.

"Well, see anything good?" Ma asked, smiling.

"Winnie?" Raquelle asked as Faith and I snickered.

"Yes," she said quietly.

"I knew there was a reason you all were supposed to come to town with me," Ma said, winking at Bronwynn.

"We may have a guest for dinner," Bronwynn said to Ma.

"Wonderful!" she said.

As we rode through town, the villagers smiled and waved at us. Everyone knew our parents, and their daughters were known as much for their beauty as for their strange ways. As we passed the local orphanage on the way out of town, we were simultaneously silent, remembering our aunt Maribelle. Once we were well beyond the edge of town, we started up conversation again.

We arrived home to see Petyr's horse tied to the post outside the barn. Petyr had met Pa in town one day and came to help Dad quite often after that. He had taken a special interest in Faith, but she wasn't sold on him yet.

As promised, John arrived in the afternoon and met with Petyr and Pa in the barn for a bit before they all came in for dinner. We were used to having guests at dinner as we prided ourselves in welcoming those that were brought across our path. John seemed a bit nervous but relaxed some as dinner progressed.

"So, John, tell me, how is your father?" Pa asked.

"He's not doing well. He's ill," John responded.

Pa casually flicked his eyes to Ma, who shook her head slightly. This meant that there was nothing we could do for him, and we were not to intervene.

"I'm sorry to hear that, my boy," Pa said.

"Thank you, sir. Mother is trying to keep up as best she can."

"Does she need help?" Bronwynn asked.

"I'm sure she would love the company as much as the help, now that I'm the only one of her boys left. She misses the conversation, I think." He chuckled slightly.

"How about I pay her a visit tomorrow?" Bronwynn asked.

"That would be lovely," John said, completely taken with Bronwynn. We smiled at each other and looked away. I looked at Petyr and Faith. They looked at each other differently than John looked at Bronwynn and like Pa looked at Ma.

Bronwynn walked John out for a few moments that night and came back in the house flushed. We all smiled, knowing she had found the one. As we all lay in our beds looking up at the ceiling, Faith was the one who spoke.

"Petyr wants me to do the red ribbon ceremony," Faith said quietly.

"And?" Raquelle whispered.

"I don't want to," Faith said.

"Why not?" I asked.

"I'm not ready, and I'm just not sure," Faith said.

"Not sure about what?" Raquelle asked.

"Something is off."

"Did you tell Pa?"

"Yes."

"What did he say?"

"That he wasn't the one, or I wasn't ready."

"What did Ma say?" I asked.

"She said to follow my heart. The confusion comes when I don't."

"What does your heart say?" Bronwynn asked.

"No."

"Okay, so what's the problem?" Raquelle asked.

"It's just Petyr has put so much into this and has been trying so hard, and I know Pa likes him."

"Faith, it's your life. Besides, Pa's girls mean more to him than anything or anyone. You know that," Bronwynn said.

We all giggled and lay in the silence. We all drifted off to sleep.

As promised, in the morning, Pa took Bronwynn over to John's mother's house.

Ma was eight months pregnant, and I could tell she needed a break, so I took over for her making candles so she could rest her body.

"Oh, dear me, I am too old to be pregnant," Ma said.

"You know what causes that, don't you?" I asked. She started to laugh uncontrollably and swatted at my behind.

"Will you go get us some more lavender, Lise?" Faith asked.

"Sure thing."

I made my way to the front lavender field and got a bit distracted. I lay down and looked up at the sky, watching the shapes of the clouds. I may have even nodded off for a few minutes too.

I came to as I heard the creak of a wagon. I leaned up on my elbow to see that it was Petyr. He couldn't see me among the rows of greenery.

"Hello, Raquelle!"

"Hi, Petyr. Have you seen Annalise?" Raquelle asked.

"No. Would you like help looking for her?" Petyr asked.

"No, thanks. Pa isn't here. He's at Madame Gremmer's house."

"Oh, okay. Well, is Faith here?"

"She is. She is helping Ma make candles."

"Oh." He seemed lost and didn't know what to do.

"I'm here!" I said, waving at Raquelle.

Her face lit up. "I should have known," Raquelle said, running over to me to help me up.

"Can you get that basket for me?" I asked her.

"Ma's going to love this," she said, looking at all the blooms we had picked for Ma.

"Can I give you a ride to the house?" Petyr asked, smiling.

"That's okay. I'll walk," I said.

"Okay," he said, driving the wagon forward.

None of us were sure that Petyr specifically wanted to marry Faith; we all suspected he would settle for any of Pa's daughters. It seemed Petyr just wanted to be a part of the family; it didn't matter whom he married. He and Bronwynn had started off talking, but that fizzled out. He had moved on to Faith.

Faith was the one of us who struggled the most with following her heart; she wanted to please everyone. The irony was, everyone thought Faith would be the last to get married or never would because she enjoyed being with Ma and Pa so much.

It was only a matter of weeks until John asked Pa for Bronwynn's hand in marriage.

Chapter 12

Raquelle and Tomas

RAQUELLE, FAITH, AND I HAD walked into town to bring some of Ma's tinctures to the blacksmith's wife. When we walked into the shop, we noticed that the older gentleman that we were used to speaking with wasn't there. Instead there was a younger man with dark-sandy-blond hair, dipping a glowing orange sword into a barrel of water.

"How may I help you?" he asked, looking right at Raquelle.

"We have some tinctures for Madame Gagnon," Raquelle said, blushing. Faith and I looked at each other and smiled.

"Oh, I can take those for you. They are for my mother," the young man said.

"Thank you," Raquelle said as their hands touched, passing the precious medicine.

"I'm Tomas, Tomas Gagnon," he said, lost in looking at Raquelle.

"I'm Raquelle McShaman," she said as he kissed her hand. Raquelle blushed. They lingered staring at each other for a moment. I cleared my throat.

"Oh, these are my sisters Faith and Annalise," Raquelle said.

"A pleasure to make your acquaintance," he said, nodding at us. We nodded back.

"Tomas! How many of these are ready for the guard—" An older man with long brown hair tied back came to stand next to Tomas. It was his father, I presumed. He stared at us, the look on his face unreadable.

"Well, you have business. We should get going."

"May I call on you?"

"No."

"No?" Tomas asked, perplexed. We giggled.

"If you think handing over some tinctures is enough to call on me, Tomas Gagnon, you've got another thing coming," Raquelle said in true Raquelle fashion.

He started laughing, shaking his head.

Tomas must have ridden the path in front of our house at least three times a day for the next two weeks, hoping for a glimpse of Raquelle. She finally relented. One day, she and I walked to the lavender field by the road and began to clip chunks of flowers. Tomas, along with a few other men, came riding up the road. They stopped. I noticed that three of the men were part of the Lord's guard. The one riding beside Tomas was the most beautiful man I had ever seen; I was so taken with his presence. I caught myself, so I nodded and then ignored him.

"Well, if it isn't two of the McShaman girls," one of the men said.

"Well, it's good to see you're not blind," I retorted, continuing to clip flowers.

"That pretty little mouth of yours—" he started, and the knight next to Tomas all of a sudden slammed his fist into the man's chest, sending the man forward, gasping for air and furiously coughing. I tried to contain my giggle.

"Is that funny to you, sweetheart?" the other unknown man said.

I looked at him. "It is," I answered.

"Is it now? They say you're the sweetest one of all," he said.

I smiled, not sure how he meant it. The knight who had just slammed his fist into the chest of the other man stared at the other man, seeming to contemplate what to do next.

"Well, we should be heading back," Raquelle said.

"May I call on you?" Tomas said.

Raquelle acted irritated. "Yes!" she said, smiling.

Tomas's face lit up.

"How about you, honey? Can I call on you?" one of the unknown men hollered out to me.

"No," I said.

"What? Why not?"

"I don't like you," I said.

And everyone started to laugh. The knight next to Tomas looked pleased, and he winked at me. Raquelle and I started back up the path to our house.

As promised, Tomas called on Raquelle that night and every night for the next month.

One afternoon, I was hanging linens on the clothesline outside to dry when Raquelle came running up to me like a cat that ate the canary.

"Lise!" Raquelle hollered as she came running up to me. "I want to see Tomas tonight. Will you go with me?" she asked in a hushed whisper. This usually meant we were going to get into trouble.

"Where are we going?" I asked suspiciously.

"Into town," she said confidently.

"Are you sure that's a good idea?"

"Of course. Why not?"

"Well, do you think we can make it back by dark?" I asked.

"Please, Lise?" she begged.

"Okay, let's go," I said.

Raquelle and I arrived into town just before sundown. We stopped by the blacksmith shop, but Tomas was not there.

"The pub!" Raquelle said excitedly, leading me by the hand.

Raquelle and I arrived to the front of the local pub.

"Raquelle, I don't think we should be here. It doesn't feel right. The energy is dark and dirty," I said.

"Nonsense, Annalise, just for a few minutes. What's the harm? If we don't find him, we will head home, deal?" she said, holding my hand and walking into the pub.

The pub smelled like stale beer and sweaty, dirty men. All the men turned to look at us, and I immediately felt like retreating. I could tell that the only women that frequented this place were the ones who worked at the brothel next door. We were way out of our element. It could have been my imagination, but it appeared to me that these dirty men were licking their lips like we were prey. One man grabbed my arm and sat me on his lap, his rough beard scraping my neck as he tried to kiss me. I could smell the liquor emanating from his pores. He had clearly been drinking for a while, possibly his entire life. I struggled to free myself.

"No, sir!" I said, turning my head, trying to get away.

"Come on, I haven't seen one as pretty as you. How much?" he slurred.

Raquelle hadn't realized I wasn't behind her. She made it to Tomas's table where he was with some friends, including the handsome knight from the other day by the roadside. Tomas said something to Raquelle, and she spun around. Tomas and the knight walked in my direction, pushing their way through the crowded room.

"Whoa, whoa, whoa, she's with us, Cedric," Tomas said to the dirty bearded man making kissing noises, trying to reach my face.

"I saw her first!" he slurred.

"Annalise is mine, Cedric. I'll cut off your balls and shove them down your throat if you don't let her go," said the knight walking up from beside Tomas. I was in shock that he knew my name.

"All right, all right, Liam, you don't have to be such a spoilsport. There's no reason we can't share, aye?" Cedric said.

"I don't share," Liam said, grasping my hand and leading me out of the pub. Tomas followed with Raquelle.

Once we were down the street a bit, Liam let go of my hand, and Tomas turned to Raquelle.

"Are you crazy, Raquelle!" Tomas asked, exasperated.

"What? I wanted to see you," Raquelle said innocently. Tomas's look softened.

"I wanted to see you too, but you can't be out here with your sister at night. It's not safe," he said, pulling her into a hug, kissing her forehead.

"Why?"

"Because there are a bunch of men who think they can do what they please without any regard for what you may want. They'll think nothing of hurting you or Annalise," he said, looking at me.

I noticed a few of the men from the pub had begun to trickle outside of the pub and casually make their way down the street toward us. "We need to go," I said softly.

YOU ARE THE REASON

"We'll take you home," Tomas said, walking toward the post where several horses were tied up. Tomas and Raquelle walked hand in hand ten steps in front of us. I walked next to Liam.

"Are you okay?" Liam looked at me and asked.

"Yes," I said softly. "It's you, from that day by the roadside." I tried not to show how taken I was with him.

"I'm Liam Boutreau," he said, grasping my hand and kissing it.

"I'm Annalise McShaman, but it seems you already know that," I said softly. I stopped walking, and he stopped walking, looking at me perplexed. I wrapped my arms around Liam's neck and hugged him. He froze for a moment, unsure and not expecting it. "Thank you," I whispered.

He hugged me back. "You're welcome," he said.

I released him and blushed a bit, unsure why I had done that. Liam didn't miss a beat as we started walking again.

"You're the youngest of Arcturis's girls, yes?"

"That's correct."

"I'm honored to make your acquaintance and be in the presence of such beauty," he said, smiling.

"How did you know my name, honorable knight?"

"I make it my business to know all the beautiful maidens' names."

"I'm sure you do."

"Everyone knows your name, Annalise."

"What? Why?" I asked, shocked.

He laughed. "Apparently, you have high standards for your suitors."

"I do," I said softly.

"I like that," he said, smiling. I couldn't help but smile back.

We made it to where their horses were tied up. Tomas swung up on his horse, and Liam swung up on his. Tomas pulled Raquelle up, and Liam held his hand out for me to take. I smiled at him and placed my hand in his. He pulled me up to sitting in front of him. I could feel his body heat against my back. He readjusted to hold the reins, his arms on either side of me. He purposefully stayed back from Tomas and Raquelle.

"So why such high standards for a suitor?" Liam asked.

"I know what I want," I said.

"What is it that you want?

"A life of love from the one who is made for me," I said, feeling a bit naive.

"Doesn't everyone want that?"

"No, most people want easy and convenient. They want it so long as you fit into their life and don't make them uncomfortable."

"What's wrong with wanting that?"

"Nothing at all. Just don't call it love."

"So what is love to you?"

"Love is looking at your partner in the middle of a shitstorm and smiling because they are worth it."

"An angel with a dirty mouth. I like that too." Liam chuckled.

"Isn't that what you want too?"

"I've never thought much about it. Normal rules say that you find a woman you are well suited to and have children. Life is what it is."

"That's awful," I said.

Liam threw his head back and laughed at me. "Why is that awful?"

"That's so boring. Where is the passion? Where is the love? Where is the chasing of dreams?"

"Dreams, huh?"

"Yes, even if the dream is to own a barn, ten chickens, five pigs, two goats, one cow, and a tomato plant. Your partner should be side by side in supporting it."

"I like the way you think."

"Thank you."

"How did your sister convince you to come out tonight?" Liam asked.

"She's in love with Tomas. She wanted to see him. There really wasn't much convincing. She would have done the same for me."

"For the man that you're in love with?"

"Yes," I said quietly.

In a few moments, we were at the path to our cottage. Tomas was off his horse and trying to part lips with Raquelle. Both were doing a poor job of it.

"You're welcome," Liam said in my ear as he stopped his horse.

I smiled. "You didn't give me a chance to say thank you," I said, laughing.

He slipped off his horse and held me by the waist to swing me down. "Thank you for the wonderful conversation."

"You're welcome," I said, blushing.

He smiled as I turned to quickly walk down the path, leaving Raquelle to make out with Tomas. In a few moments, I heard Raquelle's footsteps.

"Annalise! Wait up!" I heard Raquelle say in a hushed whisper.

"Raquelle, this was not one of your best ideas," I whispered.

"Agreed, we won't do that again." She paused. "I think Liam is handsome, don't you?"

"Raquelle!"

"Well, do you?"

"He's very handsome, and full of himself."

"And very taken with you," Raquelle said, nudging my side.

"Now for getting back in the house," I said, wanting to change the subject. As we approached, we saw that the door was cracked; that meant Ma or Pa was up and knew we were gone. My heart sank.

We slowly pushed open the heavy wooden door to see both of them sitting at the table. They both smiled at us. This was going to be bad.

"I only have one question," Pa said as we sat down.

"Yes, sir?" Raquelle answered.

"Did ye learn ye lesson?" he asked, eyebrows raised.

"Yes, sir," we both echoed.

"Good, now off to bed with ye."

We both stood up and kissed him and Ma on the cheek then made our way to our beds. After we had changed into our nightgowns and slid under our quilts, we lay there for a moment in the silence.

"Well?" Faith said.

"Well what?" Raquelle asked.

"Did you find Tomas?"

"We sure did, and Annalise now has an official admirer," Raquelle teased.

"Who's that?" Faith probed.

"Liam," Raquelle said.

"Liam, as in captain of the Lord's guard Liam?"

"Yes, that's the one," Raquelle said.

"Sheesh, I should have come with you," Faith said, and we all giggled.

Chapter 13

Faith and Petyr

ALMOST AS SOON AS BRONWYNN and John announced their engagement, Petyr was begging for Faith's hand in marriage. Faith spent a good deal of time ignoring Petyr and pretending she didn't notice his requests. He would ask for her to walk with him down by the woods, and she would refuse, preferring to stay close to the house. Around this same time, two more suitors became interested in Faith. At one point, we were alternating dinner nights between the three. I remember a discussion over dinner one night that become fairly heated.

"Why will you not marry me?" Petyr asked Faith in front of all of us.

Faith blushed. "I'm not sure I want to."

"You're not sure you want to?" Petyr said, clearly feeling hurt. All of us avoided eye contact.

"Yes, I'm not ready," Faith said.

"When do you think you will be ready?" Petyr asked.

"I don't know," Faith said.

"Faith..."

"Petyr, I think that is enough," Pa said.

"Why won't you give me her hand in marriage?" Petyr asked Pa.

"She's not mine to control. She's mine to protect," Pa said.

Petyr nodded. "So I'm supposed to just wait? It's been over two years courting her, and I've been around your family much longer than that!"

"I would hope you would wait a lot longer if necessary," Pa retorted.

Petyr nodded, quietly stewing for a moment before excusing himself from the table and exiting the cottage. Soon we all heard the creak of his wagon leaving. No one went after him, and we ate in silence the rest of the dinner.

After dinner and the chores were done, I sat in our room with Faith combing her long light-blonde hair.

"Sorry about dinner," she said quietly.

"What do you want, Faith?"

"I don't know."

"Gustav seemed very nice," I offered.

"He's wonderful."

"Then what's the problem?"

"Petyr has been hanging around for so long. Pa relies on him."

"So what? Pa will make another friend."

"Petyr's already bought a house for us."

"So? He can live in it with someone else."

"Annalise, it's not that simple."

"Faith, yes, it is. You're making it too complicated."

"I know," she said.

"Maybe I should give Petyr a chance?"

"That's up to you," I said.

I had that conversation two months before they announced their engagement. After that, Faith changed. She started wearing her braids tightly pinned to her head. She would walk slightly behind Petyr and would only speak when she was spoken to. She became much more serious and hardly ever laughed or smiled. Looking back, it should have been clear to me what was happening: it was the beginning of the end.

It was a week before they announced their engagement when Raquelle was out with Pa in the barn, and Bronwynn was out with John when Faith came rushing into our room. I had just finished making our beds with fresh linens. I didn't have to look at her. I could smell the blood; I knew what had just happened. She lay on her bed and sobbed. I sat next to her and smoothed her hair.

"I didn't feel it, Annalise," she whispered through her tears.

"Maybe it just wasn't time yet," I offered.

"No, he's not right," she said, burying her face into her pillow.

"Why don't you tell Ma. She could do something."

"I'm bound to him now!" she whispered.

"It only works if it's love, Faith," I said softly.

"Please don't tell, Annalise!" she whispered.

"I won't tell if you promise you will."

"Okay, I will. I promise."

"Are you okay?" I asked, wiping the tears from her face.

"I hate this. I have messed up so many things. I can't go back."

"We can fix this, Faith."

"Stop, Annalise. You don't understand. It's too late for me," she said, almost lost.

I got up and walked outside and began walking down the path toward the orchard.

"Annalise?" Pa called after me. Ma was standing in her garden looking in my direction.

"Yes, Pa?"

"Where are you off to?"

"I need some fresh air."

"Is everything okay, my lovely?"

"No," I said as I kept walking. I saw him scratching his head out of the corner of my eye.

I made it to the apple trees and sat under one of them. My mind was troubled. I didn't like what Faith was going through. I didn't like that she had given up.

I sat against the tree trunk and closed my eyes, dreaming of days gone by when we were younger, when life was much simpler. My thoughts were disturbed by the sound of a boot cracking a fallen stick. My eyes flew open to see Grant Ferris.

"Well, if it isn't Annalise McShaman."

"Hello, Grant," I said as I recognized the local man from the village. He was only a couple years older than me. He had been interested in Faith, but she had turned him down. He had shown an interest in courting me not too long ago, but it had fizzled out. "What are you doing in my family's orchard?" I asked, getting to my feet.

J.M. TRASK

"Well, we"—he said as three more men emerged; I felt sick—"were looking for some shade and to have a snack."

"Well, enjoy. There are plenty of apples," I said, turning to go. Grant grabbed my wrist. "Please let go of me, Grant," I asked.

The other men snickered.

"Don't you know the struggle is what makes it fun?" he said, pulling me close to him.

I turned my head. "No, Grant!" I screamed, "Please let go of me!" I tried to jerk away from him, but he dug his fingers into my wrist tighter.

"Come on, Annalise…we just want to have some fun."

"Let go of me, Grant!" I screamed.

"What the—" Grant said and let me go.

I was astonished my request worked.

"W-we were just having fun, sir," Grant stuttered.

I spun around to see Liam in full Lord's guard gear, his sword resting at his hip. My heart leapt as I hadn't seen him since that day in the field when he hit the man in the face with the pole. I was mesmerized; I had never seen anyone so handsome. Liam flicked his eyes at me then hopped down, adjusted his sword, and slowly walked toward Grant, who took a few steps back. Liam grabbed Grant by the side of the neck and pulled him close to his face.

"Do you know the right amount of pressure to cut off someone's ear?" Liam asked Grant.

"No…no, I don't, sir," he stuttered.

"Funny, I do." Liam smiled, removing his knife from its sheath.

"W-why would I need to know that?" Grant stuttered.

"Well, you clearly weren't listening to what Annalise was saying, so you clearly have no use for yours," Liam said.

"Y-yes, sir…I mean n-no, sir," Grant stuttered. "I mean please don't cut off my ear, sir."

Liam paused, staring at him. "Say you're sorry to Annalise," Liam said.

"What? Sorry to a whore?" Grant spat out.

Liam tightened his grip on his neck and lifted him off the ground. "Whore? Cleary you didn't hear what I said," Liam hissed, tightening his grip further. Grant began coughing.

116

"Come on, man, just do it so we can get out of here," one of Grant's friends said.

"S-sorry, Annalise," Grant said, looking at me, his face turning purple.

Liam set him down on the ground. "Get out of here and don't come back!" Liam whispered.

"Y-yes, sir," Grant said, barely able to talk. Liam released his grip from his neck, and Grant sprinted away, rubbing his neck, his friends following. They looked back for a brief moment and then kept on going.

Liam then turned and looked at me. His look softened from only moments ago. I was standing at the neck of his horse. He smiled. "We need to quit meeting up like this, first in the pub and now in the apple orchard. You can't seem to stay out of trouble," he said, flashing his perfect smile.

"It seems a knight is handy to have around," I said, smiling back. I heard him chuckle.

"Well, you're welcome," Liam said, smiling.

"Thank you," I said, laughing. "Trouble seems to have a way of finding me," I offered.

"I would prefer it didn't," Liam said.

"I appreciated the Lord's guard's concern for my safety," I said as I turned to walk down the driveway.

He grasped my hand and pulled me back to him. "I'm not saying it as a knight. I am saying it as a man," he said seriously.

"Well then, thank you," I said.

"You're welcome," he retorted, smiling.

"To what do we owe the honor of a visit from the captain of the Lord's guard?" I asked.

"I came over hoping to get some dinner."

"Courting Raquelle?

"Raquelle invited me, but there is another McShaman that I am interested in."

"Well, Pa is already spoken for," I retorted.

Liam laughed. "As wonderful as your father is, I am not here for him."

"Ah, I see. Well, pray tell, who is it you are here to see?"

"You," he said, his look intense. "I haven't been able to get you off my mind."

"Well, I think the least we can do is provide you some food for your good deed today."

"Now I'm even more glad that I stopped by," he said, his eyes penetrating mine.

"We'll see about that," I said.

"What were you doing out here by yourself anyway? You could get yourself into trouble with some young group of men sneaking up on you."

"But now that I am in the company of a knight…"

"You're welcome."

"I already said thank you," I said, giggling.

"You're welcome," he said, lifting me onto his horse. He climbed up behind me and wrapped one arm around my waist, holding the reins in the other. He clicked his tongue, and we took off toward the house.

There was a stark difference in the energy of the house. Faith looked like a ghost. She wouldn't look at anyone. I heard Petyr's voice outside, and she didn't react. I volunteered to get the boys from the barn. As I entered, Tomas and John smiled at me. Liam winked, and Petyr eyed me warily. Pa wrapped his arm around my shoulder as we headed back into the house.

We all sat down at the table. Petyr sat next to Faith, but they didn't touch. Liam was on the other side of Faith, across from me. He stole glances at me as he ate his food. Faith excused herself after dinner, saying she didn't feel well and that she wanted to go to bed. We all watched as she went into our room and closed the door. I looked up at Ma, concerned. Ma nodded her understanding. After dinner, we left Pa and Ma inside, and we strolled out as a large group.

"Annalise, a word?" Petyr asked.

"What can't you ask in front of us?" Raquelle asked protectively.

"This is a private matter," Petyr said.

"What does Annalise have to do with your private matter?" Liam chimed in to my surprise.

"It didn't go the way it was supposed to. Your energies aren't right," I said.

Petyr looked like he had seen a ghost.

"That is what you wanted to know, isn't it?" I said.

"How did you know? How did you do that?" Petyr asked me, amazed.

"We all have gifts, Petyr."

"No, Annalise! I don't believe you! You're wrong!" Petyr said, running his fingers through his hair. "That stupid ribbon ceremony doesn't matter. I am her person!" he said, grabbing me by the shoulders and shaking me. "Do you hear me!"

I looked at Petyr's eyes. They turned black for a moment, then back to blue. "Your hands are burning me! What are you?" I asked.

Liam stepped forward, ready to choke him out. I felt Pa's energy. Petyr released his grip on me and was shoved back three feet by an invisible force.

"Petyr, it's time for you to go," Pa said calmly from behind us. We all looked in his direction. His tone was eerily calm.

"Yes, sir," Petyr said. As he walked by Liam, he chucked his shoulder into him; Liam shoved him in Pa's direction.

Pa gripped Petyr's shoulder hard; I saw him wince. "No man lays a finger on any of my daughters in anger, are we clear?" Pa growled.

"Yes, sir," Petyr said, still wincing.

"It's been an eventful day. We all need some rest," Pa said.

Petyr nodded, and Pa released his shoulder. Petyr continued along to the path toward his horse, combing his hair down. I hid behind Liam. He had draped an arm around me, holding me to him.

"Annalise, come here, my baby girl," Pa said softly, his anger gone. I went to him. "Show me your arms, please."

I raised my sleeves to reveal angry red handprints where Petyr's hands had grabbed me. "Sweet Jesus," Pa said under his breath.

"What is he, Pa?"

"I don't know," Pa said, raking his hand through his hair, turning around and walking into the house, lost in thought.

"Are you okay, Lise?" Raquelle asked.

"I'm fine," I said, smiling.

"How did your dad get him off you?" Tomas asked.

"Energy. Pa can move energy, so he gave him an energetic shove," I said. The men thought on this.

"What is he, Raquelle?" I asked.

"He's into wizard-and-witchcraft-type things, sacrificial druidry. That's all I'm getting right now," she said. Tomas looked at her in awe.

"Liam, take Annalise over there. He's coming back," Raquelle said.

Liam and I tucked into a shadowy corner of the barn and waited.

"I'm glad you are here," I whispered.

"Me too. I couldn't imagine anything happening to you," he said, blushing slightly. "What will heal your arms?" Liam asked.

"You," I said, looking at him. He looked perplexed. "Watch," I said, rolling up my sleeve where the red handprint was. I took the tip of his finger and touched a spot in the middle of the red. It turned my skin back to its normal shade.

"You are so beautiful," Liam whispered. I smiled. Our moment was interrupted as, sure enough, Petyr came riding back.

"Where is Annalise?"

"Just go home, Petyr. Rest and let this day settle," Raquelle said.

"I didn't mean to frighten her. I want to apologize," he said.

"Annalise is fine. Pa will be cross if he sees you here," Raquelle said.

"Where is she?" Petyr said.

I could feel his energy searching for me, and I clung to Liam. Liam wrapped his arms around me.

"Why can't I find her?" Petyr hissed.

Raquelle smiled. "There is so much you don't understand," she said.

"Where is Liam?" Petyr asked. "Is he with her?"

"That's none of your concern."

"Is that why I can't find her?"

"That's none of your concern either."

"Does Arcturis know what type of man he is?"

"Pa knows a lot about a lot of things."

"You know what happens when one of the McShaman girls gets deflowered by the wrong man!"

120

"Thanks to you and Faith, we all now know what happens!" Raquelle challenged.

"Tomas, you should really keep that one in check!" Petyr hissed.

"Calm down and just go home," Tomas said.

Petyr nodded, his eyes sweeping the yard for me. Then he rode away. When they were convinced he was gone, they motioned for Liam and me to come out. Liam went out first, holding my hand as he led me out. We strolled back to the horses.

Liam looked concerned. "What if he comes back?" he asked quietly.

I smiled and touched his face. "I'll be fine."

"This may sound strange since we just met, but I don't want to leave you," he said, searching my face.

"You'll see me tomorrow," I said, smiling.

"How do you know?"

"Because I do," I said.

He pulled me in for a hug and kissed the side of my head. "Please stay safe, Annalise," he said.

"I will." I smiled as I hooked my arm in Raquelle's, and we stood there and waved as they rode off.

We walked in the house to see Ma and Pa at the table, concern etched on their faces. I heard Faith vomiting in the bedroom.

"Let me see your arms, love," Ma said softly to me.

I rolled up my sleeves, and she eyed my red handprints. Her eyes caught on the white dot from Liam's fingertip. "Liam?" she asked, pointing to the white spot.

"Yes," I said.

"You showed him?"

"Yes, ma'am." I waited a moment.

"What's on your mind, Annalise?" Ma asked.

"Is Faith going to be all right?"

"Yes, but Petyr took some of her light and left his darkness in her. She is bound in dark magic, not light. The ceremony went awry, both parts," Ma said, clearly nauseated by that fact. Raquelle got up from the table and squeezed Pa.

"I don't like that he has taken such an interest in you, Annalise," Pa said.

"I'm sorry, Pa, I—"

"Nothing to be sorry about, my lovely. I'm just concerned."

"Well, I don't like the sound of that," said Raquelle.

"I don't either," I said.

"I don't want you wandering far from home. I want you to stay close to the house, do you hear?" Pa said.

"Yes, sir," I said.

After everyone had gone to bed, I sat up in my bed.

"He won't stop, Annalise," Faith said in the darkness.

"Who?"

"Petyr."

"Oh. What? Why?"

"If I marry him, he'll leave you all alone. Otherwise, he won't stop," she said, sniffing.

"No, Faith, don't do that. We can make this right," I whispered.

"I have to. I can't have him hurting you too."

"Faith, please, don't…," I said, starting to cry.

"He isn't that bad. He's just not my energetic match," she said. Her voice sounded hollow. "I messed up, Annalise," she said, crying.

I got up from my bed and found her in hers. I hugged her. "Faith, it's nothing that can't be fixed."

"I have to, Annalise."

Chapter 14

Guinivere and Arcturis

"SHE HAD THE MOST BEAUTIFUL eyes I had ever seen," Pa started, gazing at Ma, making her smile and blush. We all smiled as we had heard this story a million times, but we never got tired of it. "And her long reddish-brown hair was mesmerizing." His gaze still fixed on Ma. "I knew the moment I saw her I had found a home for my heart," he added, lost in love looking at his bride.

Ma smiled and winked at him.

"I immediately asked her father for her hand, and he said, 'Arcturis, she is already promised to another man. You must prove yourself to be worthy of my daughter's hand.' So from that day forward, when I would finish my work, I would go over to Gwennie's house and play music for her. And don't you think for a second that I wouldn't sneak her behind a bush for a sweet kiss in the moonlight whenever I could," he said, smiling huge. Ma laughed.

"After bringing gifts and eating dinner with her family almost every night, her father relented. But that was only half of it. The greater prize was that I had won the most beautiful woman's heart in all the land. And she was put here just for me," he said. Ma smiled like a schoolgirl. My parents looked at each other, so much love, passion, and joy flowing between them. "I find myself more in love with her now than I was that day. I never thought it possible, but it's true," Pa said, gazing upon Ma. She walked over to him and planted a kiss on his lips. We all giggled. She sat on his lap, looking at him, smoothing his hair from his face.

"Don't think for a moment, girls, that I had no part in this. When I saw your pa standing there, I knew there was no one else for me." She kissed him tenderly again. "I may have been promised to someone else, but I wanted no part in it. It was a business deal that was good for the family but terrible for me. Arc showed up right on time, and the other fella didn't have a chance. Arc even won over my father. I'm pretty sure it was all the half-dead daffodils you would pick from my neighbor's garden and leave on my doorstep." We all giggled.

"Shortly after we were married, we noticed a darkness spreading across our lands. The darkness was hate, contempt, close-mindedness, ignorance, jealousy, fear, self-righteousness—the darker side of humanity. Your father and I knew we had to get away. One day I was standing in our little cottage in the Scottish countryside and saw what was coming. Your pa sold everything, and we made a plan to leave everything we had ever known, including our clans. Your father, Winnie, my sister, Faith, and I got on a barge and came to France, hoping to escape the darkness. Raquelle came along soon after we arrived, as did Annalise. My wish for all of you is to find your perfect complement, the person that would sell every worldly thing you own and leave for a new life based on a premonition."

"How did you know Pa was your person?" Faith asked.

"He was the most beautiful creature I had ever laid eyes on. He still is," she said, kissing him.

"What do you mean?" Faith asked, struggling.

"When you are attracted to someone's soul and can see beyond physical beauty, appearances, and material things, that's when you know someone's true character. Soul-to-soul attraction just happens. You know when it's your person."

"I'm sure you had other male suitors, Ma," Bronwynn added.

"Of course, I did, but none like your father."

"How so?"

"He made my dreams grow and my heart fly out of my chest. The other men wanted to keep me in a box to pop out farmhands." We all giggled. "Your father wanted our children to be evidence of the love we share together, and a chance for that love to multiply and go out into the world."

"I had stiff competition. There were many young lads I had to compete with for your ma's affection."

"There was never any competition, Arc," Ma said softly, holding his face and looking into his eyes as if they were the only two in the room. We all smiled to one another.

Ma had grown up as part of a large family in Scotland. Her family passed on their healing gifts to all of their children. She had three brothers and four sisters, one of whom she was close to. Her sister Maribelle came to France with us. She had lived with us for the first five years we were here. Maribelle eventually met and fell in love with a man from the village who ran the local orphanage. He turned out to be a religious zealot that was more interested in converting Maribelle to his ways and taming her "wild spirit." She was trapped; there was nothing she could do since she was considered his property. Finally, one day she tried to run away. Her vengeful husband found her and killed her, leaving her for dead in the woods. Ma collapsed in the garden the same moment that Maribelle died. I was out there that day with her picking the sage for drying. I ran screaming into the barn to get Pa. He ran back out with me, scooping Ma up with his strong large arms, cradling her like a baby.

"She's gone. He killed her," Ma said as she hugged Pa tighter.

Pa and Ma were able to locate her body in the woods. They brought her corpse back here and buried her in a corner of the farm.

Pa had a large family as well. He had six brothers and two sisters. His family was a bit more traditional, but they still believed in mystical things. Pa was close to his family, and choosing Ma over them was a choice he never thought twice about. It was no secret his mother didn't want one of her precious boys going off with the wild likes of women like Ma. Pa listened to his heart and never looked back. Ma and Pa were feeling more and more pressure to conform to beliefs and ways that they felt were wrong. They could no longer stay in that energy. Then one night, Ma had a premonition of a huge dark shadow slowly making its way across Scotland. She saw it had begun to snuff out the light and burn so-called witches at the stake.

Anyone who did not believe what they did were considered witches. There was no telling how many innocent people were burned for not sharing their ignorant way of thinking. Ma and Pa escaped before it reached their clans. They had never heard from their family since, nor had they ever looked back.

Chapter 15

LIAM AND I TOOK TO married life. We fell into a bit of a routine. He only had to go to drills a few times a week now, so he would be home with me taking care of our farm. It was only two months until our bliss was shattered. Liam received orders that he had to go on a campaign for an undetermined amount of time. I cried as soon as he walked in the door; I had felt it coming.

"How did this happen?"

"My mother," he said quietly.

"What? Why?" I asked, not understanding.

"She owes taxes on her house. Since I am the male heir, I must serve to pay off her taxes," he said through his gritted his teeth.

"Liam," I started and then began to cry.

He pulled me to him. "I wish she would just die, Annalise."

"You don't mean that," I said softly, sniffling.

"I do, my love, with all my heart. I do. She is a curse to me. I wish to be rid of her for eternity."

"Can you talk to someone?"

"No," he said quietly.

"Can we borrow the money from someone?"

"Annalise!" Liam snapped. He had never gotten angry with me before. "Don't you see? They don't want money. They want me gone, away from you," he said.

"Why do they hate us?" I asked.

"Because we love each other, and they are miserable."

"What are you going to do?"

"I will serve my time, and then my debt is paid. I will have my walking papers at the end of this, if you'll still have me?"

"Of course." I hugged him harder and began to sob.

"Then I need you to trust and believe that I will come back, Annalise. Do you promise?"

"I promise," I said, kissing him.

We made love on our dining-room table, and when we were done, he carried me to our bed where we stayed the rest of the night.

Liam left in only a couple of days. We never left each other's side and were barely clothed for those two days. We sent word to Ma and Pa via Raquelle and Tomas. They offered for me to stay with them, and they said they would stop by to help me.

On his last night with me, Liam and I had stayed up all night together, making love, cuddling, talking, and dreaming—trying to escape the impending sadness of our separation. For the first time, I dreaded the daylight arriving.

When it finally did, he stood next to his horse, holding me.

"I don't want you to go. I don't know if my heart can stand it."

"I won't be gone for long,"

"Do you have to go?" I said, wiping the tears that were cascading down my face.

"Yes, I have to go, Annalise."

"I feel like I am never going to see you again," I said.

"I will always come back to you," he said, wiping the new tears that streaked down my face.

I hugged him, resting my head on his chest. "I love you," I said.

"I love you too, my love," he whispered.

I smiled. We kissed, each savoring these moments. Then he swung up on his horse and gave me a little wave. I returned to the cottage and sat at the table. I wept.

After I let the wave of sorrow pour out of me, I tried to keep my mind busy with chores for the rest of the morning. I fed the livestock. I checked the waterwheel as Liam had taught me to do. I walked through the orchard collecting apples for my fermenting pail. Waves of emotion would sweep over me; I would collapse from it and sob loudly. Finally, I decided to go work in my garden to quiet my mind.

I went and sat amongst my herbs, trying to stay busy with the weeds. All of a sudden, I felt a pulling in my heart, and I knew I needed to go to him. I immediately stood up and started running to where I knew the knights collected outside of town before they departed. I saw Liam on top of the hill, with the legion's flag waving behind him.

I ran to the top of the hill. I knew I wasn't supposed to be there for a myriad of reasons. He saw me and smiled. He pulled me up onto his horse, facing him. I wrapped my legs around his waist. I wrapped my arms around his neck and kissed him. A few of his men whistled. I heard a low groan come from within him.

"I miss you already," I said.

"Me too, baby," Liam said. "You shouldn't have come here. It's not safe."

"I know. I just had to come and see you before you left."

"Be a good girl for me. We'll work on that family we want when I get back," he said, kissing me.

I nodded. "Please come back to me," I said quietly, a tear escaping my eye.

"I'll always come back to you, my love," Liam said. "You're home."

I nodded.

"Will you wait for me?" Liam asked.

"Of course, I will. You're my heart."

"I love you."

"I love you too," I said. He helped me swing down onto the ground. My heart squeezed as I watched Liam leaving on his horse with the rest of his legion.

I heard the grumbling and guffaws of some of his men as they rode past me, but I didn't care. I stood there until Liam was out of sight.

I cried as I walked home. I was glad I was alone; I would have looked like a madwoman. I screamed from the pain I felt from him leaving growing further from me. I didn't want to be a moment without him. I visited our place in the woods. I sat where we had lain together, letting myself slip into the beautiful energy of those moments together.

After a while, I slowly made my way back to my house, the ache and sadness of his departure weighing down heavily upon me. I didn't realize I had made it to the edge of our property. I stood at the end of the worn grass path that led to our cottage. I proceeded slowly. With each step, more tears poured out of my eyes. I opened the heavy wooden door and closed it behind me. I went to our room and sat at the edge of our bed. I buried my face in my hands and sobbed. When I came to, I was curled up on our bed. I got up and fed the horse, our dairy cow, the chickens, our barn cats, and stray dogs that seemed to like to sleep outside our cottage door. Liam and I didn't mind; they kept other critters away. I had brought in the firewood during the last few moments of daylight hours as Liam had requested.

As I laid the firewood next to the hearth, I stared into the dwindling flame in the fireplace, getting lost in the dance of its burn. I barred the door and locked all the shutters. There were dozens of Liam's weapons hanging on our wall; I could lead my own army if I needed to. I chuckled to myself. My whole body ached. I slowly made my way to our bedroom. That night, I lay there alone in our bed, the quietness of the cottage drowning me and his missing presence thundering in my ears. The grief of separation came over me, the unknowing of when I would see him again. I sobbed and moaned in agony. I had never felt so much pain in all my life. The ache in my chest felt like my heart was being ripped out. I'm not sure when I finally fell asleep; it was more like passing out from being exhausted from crying. When I woke up, I lay there, not wanting to move but knowing I needed to get up and tend to my chores. I fell into my lonely little routine. As sad as I was, there was nowhere else I would rather be. After about two weeks of this, I decided I would pay Ma and Pa a visit. I saddled up our horse and started on my way over.

As I was riding to Ma and Pa's house, I got an eerie feeling. I decided to ride closer to the tree line so I could tuck myself out of view if needed. I turned and looked back to Liam's and my property, trying to shake the feeling. I stopped in our front field to pick some flowers for Ma.

"Annalise?" I heard someone say my name.

I shrieked as I spun around to see Petyr, wondering where he had been hiding as I hadn't seen him only moments before.

"What are you doing here?" I said, catching my breath.

"I guess I should be asking you the same thing," he said.

"I am picking flowers for my visit with Ma and Pa," I offered.

He nodded, seemingly unconcerned. I walked out from the tree line, and he followed me.

"So now your turn. What are you doing here?"

"Faith wanted rabbit for dinner," Petyr offered.

Now I knew he was lying to me. Faith didn't eat meat, and even if she did, there was no reason to come all the way out here to snare one; he had plenty at his house. I nodded, unsure of what was going on.

"Well, I'm going to get back to my journey," I offered as I made my way back to my horse. He nodded, a strange look on his face as he followed me. "Good luck finding the rabbit!" I said.

He didn't react but kept following me. Soon I saw a wagon appear and come down the lane toward us. The hair on the back of my neck stood up. I could see it was Henri as it drew closer. I went to pull myself up onto my horse, but Petyr grabbed me.

"Petyr, what are you doing?" I felt his hand burning into my flesh as I tried to get free. I screamed, "Let go of me! What are you doing?"

"This is for your own good, Annalise!" Petyr snarled.

"What are you talking about!" I shrieked.

"This is for the good of all of us!" Petyr growled back at me.

Soon Henri's wagon was upon us.

"Hello, Annalise," Henri said, jumping down from the wagon.

"What are you doing?" I screamed a Petyr, trying to break free.

"As promised," Petyr said.

Henri handed over a large pouch of coins. I had been betrayed; the dark had infiltrated our family completely. I had naively thought if he married Faith, it would satisfy his hunger.

"What have you done?" I screamed, looking at Petyr.

Henri immediately gagged me with a cloth and bound my hands and ankles. I tried screaming, but there was no one to hear it. He threw me in the back of the wagon. We bumped along the road for a long while; then we came to a stop. He yanked me up by my arms and jerked me out of the wagon.

We were at his manor house. It was a huge white stone building with manicured shrubs.

"Let's see about this magic, shall we?" he said, untying the binds on my ankles and leading me into the house. I squirmed to get away from him, which only caused him to tighten his grip. When we entered the house through the front door, I locked eyes for a moment with a servant girl. She nodded at me and then looked away, clearly ashamed of the dark secrets she had to hold. He threw me over his shoulder and brought me upstairs to his bedroom, throwing me on the bed. I scrambled to get up, but he shoved me back down. I felt him attempting to move my skirts out of the way; then I felt him force himself into me. I screamed. He slapped me repeatedly. I tasted blood.

"Shut up!" he hissed.

"No! Get off me!" I screamed, kicking my legs and clawing at his face. He pulled my hair back and then gripped my neck hard. I started to choke. Soon I blacked out. I came to on the floor in a dark cold cellar. My wrists and neck had a thick metal band around them connected to a chain that was bolted to the wall, like I was an animal. It was pitch-black. There were no windows, only light showing from the bottom of the door at the top of the stairs. The only way out was through the cellar doors. I squinted, trying to adjust my eyes and take in my surroundings. My chains dragged against the wall and floor as I tried to maneuver. I heard the cellar door open and turned my head as the light flooded the room. I heard the stairs creak as Henri made his way down the steps.

"I thought I heard you moving down here," he said, slowly making his way down the steps and eying me as though I was his prey.

"Why are you doing this?" I asked.

"I want your magic."

"What magic!" I asked, exasperated.

"The magic you use to heal people! The sex magic you use when you sleep with men?"

"Sex magic? I don't even know what that is!" I screamed.

"That's not what Petyr says. He says he gets bliss for longer than normal with your sister."

"That's it? That's love! Why are you all so ignorant!" I hissed.

He slapped me. "Your father never raised you right. You should hold your tongue with authority."

"You aren't my authority," I said, he slapped me again. "I'll show you authority," he said, untying his pants and forcing himself upon me again.

"Get off me!" I screamed, straining against my chains, trying to fight him off. "No! I don't want this! I don't want you!" I screamed, tears streaming down my face.

He slapped me again. I felt my lip split; I tasted blood.

"Why are you so wild?" he hissed.

"Get off me!" I screamed. He slammed my head against the concrete wall, and I blacked out again.

I woke up to my head throbbing and a sharp pain on my ankles. I looked down to see that it was a rat biting me. I kicked it and heard it squeak as it flew across the cellar. My ankle was bleeding. I tried to maneuver as to wipe it on the bottom of my skirt. The servant girl whom I had locked eyes with earlier came down the stairs; her steps were light and delicate. I sat up slowly, my head throbbing even worse.

"Hello, Ms. Boutreau. My name is Marci," she said sweetly. In spite of my circumstances, I loved hearing my name. I loved that I shared it with Liam.

"Please let me out of here," I said, tears beginning to stream down my face. "I just want to go back home," I said, breaking into a sob.

"Ssshhhh," she said softly. "I can't. I don't have the keys," she whispered.

"I have a farm and a husband. I need to get back to them. I won't tell anyone what happened, I promise," I said, breaking into a sob.

She knelt beside me, tears pooling in her eyes. She pulled me into a hug. "You're too beautiful of a soul to be here," she said softly, smoothing my hair. It reminded me of Ma, and my heart began to ache. Someone had to be looking for me. All of our animals would die if they weren't taken care of. Surely someone would have stopped by my house or seen my horse by the road.

"Why is he doing this?"

"He thinks he can take your magic," she whispered.

"I don't have any magic!" I whispered.

"If he knows you're awake, he'll come back. You have to be quiet miss," she whispered. "Here are some biscuits. Please eat for me."

"Thank you, I'll eat later," I whispered, sniffling. We both heard his heavy steps stomping on the floor upstairs. She quickly made her way up the stairs and softly closed the cellar door. It was a while before the rats were back. I tossed my biscuits to them. That seemed to keep them from wanting to feast on my ankles for the time being.

I lay down and began to sob. I missed Liam, and now I didn't know if I would ever see him again. I missed Ma and Pa. I missed my sisters. How had everything gone so awry in only a matter of days? I cried myself to a state of exhaustion and fell sleep.

I woke up to Henri on top of me. I started to fight him off, but instead I lay there limp. My body jolting from his thrusts, he slobbered on my cheek, although he may have thought it was a kiss.

"Think about it, Annalise. You could have had all of this had you just accepted my proposal."

At this, I looked at him. "You disgust me. I would rather live in the woods than be with you! You're more a creature than a man!" I hissed.

He slapped me so hard my nose began to bleed. "What is wrong with you? Why do you not control your tongue!" he hissed. I stared blankly at the wall, feeling myself shut down inside.

"There is no magic happening!" he said angrily and unable to release himself. He climbed off me and stormed up the steps. After a while, Marci came down with a wet cloth to clean up my nose. She couldn't have been more than seventeen. She was so loving and delicate.

"He forces himself with me too," she said softly. "He's so evil his pecker can't stay hard the whole time, so he never finishes," she whispered. I nodded lifelessly as she held a cup of water to my lips. I drank thankfully. She handed me two more biscuits. "Please eat," she said softly.

"I will later," I said softly.

She nodded and made her way up the stairs. My rat friends made their way out of the shadows. I tossed them the biscuits, and again they left me alone. I had to relieve myself in the corner of my prison. I went as far as the chains would allow.

In a few hours, Marci came back to clean it up and left me a pail this time. I felt embarrassed. She sat down next to me.

"He's passed out from drinking too much. We can talk freely," she said.

I nodded. "What is he going to do with me?" I asked her.

"I don't know. He hasn't done this before. He's been obsessed with you for a while. Ms. Claire helped to set this up."

"Ms. Claire?" I asked.

"Claire Boutreau," she said.

It felt like a knife stabbed me in my gut. Liam's mother had set this whole thing up. He had been right; she was as evil as he said. I began to cry. I missed Liam.

"Please don't cry, ma'am. We'll find you a way out of here, okay?" she said. "I'll find his keys while I'm cleaning," she whispered.

"You'll come with me?" I asked softly. "You deserve to be happy too, Marci," I said.

"I have nowhere to go. I have no family," she said.

"Now you do. You can live with me or live with my parents. They would love to have you," I said.

Her eyes swelled up with tears, and she hugged me. "Thank you," she whispered. "I'll look for the keys tomorrow."

"Thank you," I said. We dried our eyes, and soon she departed. I lay on my side, seeing Liam's face, and fell asleep.

I woke to Henri's heavy footsteps coming down the stairs.

"Get up!" he shouted.

"Why?" I sniped back.

"Because I said so!" He trudged his portly body over and yanked me up by my chains and slapped me. "You are so defiant!" he yelled in my face. "We are going to visit a fortune-teller."

"Why?"

"So she can tell me how to get the magic out of you!" he snarled.

135

"I keep telling you! I have no magic inside me, you stupid pig!" I screamed.

Henri hit me so hard I heard something crack. Then I felt pain radiating out from my cheek.

"Marci! Get her ready to travel!"

Marci came down and changed my clothes and combed my hair. My eye had begun to swell closed. Then she followed as Henri led me up the stairs. He tied my hands and ankles and gagged me with a cloth tied around my mouth. Then he put a sack over my head. He threw me in the back of the wagon and tossed a blanket over me. We bumped along for what felt like hours. I was yanked up, and the sack removed from my eyes. I looked around to see that it was dark, and we were in some sort of gypsy camp. I could feel the darkness that this group fed off of; I knew this wasn't going to be good for me. Henri led me over to a tent where he tied me to a cot. Thankfully, Henri slept on a cot across the tent from me. He snored loudly all night. I kept trying to remove my binds so I could make a run for it. I was depressed when morning light came, and there was a knocking on one of the tent poles.

Henri struggled to sit up with his portly belly. He shot a glance at me. "Come in," he snapped. A woman with dark energy came in; I immediately got a headache.

"Is this her?" she asked him, staring at me.

"Yes."

"You're powerful, yes?" she asked in her heavy accent.

"I don't know what power you speak of," I said flatly.

"You can move energy. Move me right now!" she said.

I looked at her like she was crazy. "What?" I asked in disbelief.

"Don't play stupid with me, girl!" she hissed.

"I don't know what you are talking about!"

"It's in there, Henri. Maybe you need to be more forceful!" she said, looking at me with an evil smile.

"Are you sure?" Henri asked.

"Yes! I can feel it!"

"I have tried everything. It doesn't work. I think this may have all been a joke," Henri offered.

"No! Try again!" she said.

Henri scratched his chin, seemingly unsure. After a few minutes, a wooden crate with holes was brought in. His manservant dropped me in there just as before and closed the lid. I then felt myself being lifted onto the back of the wagon and felt the bumpy ride home. I strained to look with my one healthy eye out the breathing holes to recognize something or someone. I felt myself then being lifted and carried back down to the cellar. When they pried the lid off, I gasped for air and sat up. The manservant lifted me out and reattached my chains. He carried the wooden box up the steps. Henri came down and sat at the bottom step, not speaking and just looking at me, contemplating. After a while, he spoke.

"This isn't what I wanted for us, Annalise," he said quietly.

I nodded. "I thought you were my friend, Henri," I said softly.

This made him soften even more.

"Everything has gotten so out of hand. I shouldn't have listened to other people," he said, lost in thought. "This isn't me."

"I know," I said.

He looked up at me. "After everything I have done to you, and you sitting here now, chained, how can you say that?" he asked in disbelief.

"I don't hate you, Henri," I said, and it was true.

He was shocked and stood up, making his way upstairs in his confusion.

Henri left to go out of town the next day. He was gone for two weeks. He had taken the keys to my chains with him. Marci found every tool she could to help get me out of my chains, but it was no use. I sank into a deep depression. I had quit eating altogether.

Chapter 16

UPON RETURNING FROM HIS TRIP, Henri walked down the stairs into the cellar. A sense of dread came over me in spite of him seeming like he was in a good mood. My stomach felt sick.

"So, my pet"—he laughed, seemingly amused—"tell me where this magic is. Everyone says I should be able to take it from you."

"Who is everyone?" I asked.

"The mystics, the fortune-tellers, the magicians, even the local witches' coven."

"They know nothing," I said.

"Oh yeah? You think you are so much better than them?"

"I am better than no one."

"Then why is it that they keep telling me you possess magic?" he hissed.

"They sense my energy."

"What energy is that?"

"I am a healer," I said.

He started to laugh. "So you are a witch priestess?"

"The magic they practice is weak."

"Why is that?"

"It comes from ego, control, and sometimes evil."

"And where does your energy come from?"

"Love, joy, and happiness—all of which are more powerful than that of the experts you seek."

"Why do I not have these powers? I have been intimate with you."

"What you have done is try to take it. It must be freely given out of love. You have not been intimate with me. You have been abhorrent," I said.

He slapped me. "You're lucky it's not worse for you," he snarled. "Don't you love me?"

"I love you like I love the turds that come out of a horse's rear end. I will love you for fertilizing the soil one day, just as they do."

He slapped me again. "Why will you not give me what I want!" he shouted in my face.

"You're not my person. I am not your person. Liam is my person. Claire is your person."

"What!" he said.

"She is of the same low vibrational match as you."

"She's disgusting and old," he said, slightly offended.

"Our person reflects back to us who we are," I said.

He slapped me again. My jaw was getting sore.

"That's it!" he said, turning me around, lifting my skirt, and forcing himself into me. I was now too weak to fight. My mind went black. I escaped to somewhere, anywhere but here. I only came to when I vomited. It kept Henri from releasing himself.

"You disgust me," he said, spitting at me and shoving me to the ground. Then he tucked himself in and made his way up the stairs.

I lay there on the dirty floor singing the lullaby Ma sang to me when I would wake up at night scared as a little girl. I closed my eyes, and I could feel my head on her lap, her hand smoothing my hair. As I lay there on my side, making the dirty hay spin and dance with my hand, thinking of how much Jacque would have loved to see that. My thoughts would drift to Liam, hoping he would rescue me from this hell. Or if not, that he would find happiness without me. He deserved that much. Thinking of Liam was dangerous. The initial thought of him was glorious, but then the pain from the realization of our separation was unbearable.

To my surprise, Henri had Marci bring me up from the cellar, stating that we were having a visitor. He commanded Marci to clean me up the best she could. I smiled as she tried to wipe the dirt off my face and give me clean underskirts. She gave me a wet cloth to wipe my lady parts. She also brought down a fancy silk dress for me to wear. She slipped it on. To her dismay, it showed my protruding ribcage.

"Here, miss," she said, handing me a biscuit. "I really wish you would eat."

"I'll eat later," I said, smiling. I was tired and had no energy. My body felt heavy. We both knew I would use the biscuit to try to keep the rats off me later.

She tried to smooth my dirty hair the best she could and rebraid it, but there was only so much she could do. She walked me upstairs and sat me in the sitting room.

"You look so pretty, miss," she said.

I gave her a weak smile. I didn't care about the fake beauty or this facade. I just wanted to go home. I sat there sitting amongst all his expensive and fancy trinkets, similar to what I was to him—a trinket, I mused. I saw the Fabergé egg that he offered Pa for me sitting on display on his huge mantle. I closed my eyes, drifting off, seeing Pa's face and hearing Pa's voice tell me I was more precious than gold. Tears stung my eyes. Marci quickly crossed the room and handed me a handkerchief. I wiped my eyes and nose.

"Oh God, there you are. I should have known by the smell," Henri said. I didn't look at him. Marci clamped her lips together. "Well, get up, you worthless whore!" he said as he backhanded me.

I fell back in the chair, dazed. I held my cheek. Marci got up to come to me but had to stop herself from coming over to me. I saw the tears in her eyes. I would have given anything in that moment to feel Ma's soft hand on my face and smell the scent of the oil on her skin. I took a deep breath and stood up. I caught a glimpse of myself in a mirror. I didn't recognize myself, with my hollowed-out eyes, protruding cheekbones, and sunken-in cheeks. I was so thin even my teeth seemed to protrude.

There was a knock on the door. I heard two men's voices; one was Petyr's. My heart leapt. In some part of my brain, I hoped he had changed his mind and come to take me home. Henri grasped me by the arm and brought me to the door. Petyr looked appalled at my appearance.

"Annalise…," Petyr said softly, tears filling his eyes.

I gave him a weak smile. "Please take me home," I asked with what remaining strength I had left.

Petyr looked away.

Henri laughed. "You stupid girl!" he said, laughing as he shoved me behind him. "There, you've seen her. She's alive!"

"Barely! That wasn't the deal! What have you done!" Petyr growled, shoving Henri.

"You got your money. Get out of here. She wasn't worth what I paid for her. You're as big of a liar as Claire was. She doesn't have any magic! And now she's just a bag of bones!" Henri snarled. He slammed the door and took me up to his bedroom and threw me on the bed.

"You smell terrible. You're lucky I'll even lie with you!" he said. His words didn't hurt because they held no value for me. I was lifeless as he lifted my skirts and forced himself yet again. I closed my eyes and turned my head. I let my mind drift to happier days of being with my family and picking lavender bunches with Jacque, braiding Raquelle's beautiful reddish-brown hair, hugging Pa, the first time I laid eyes on Liam. Tears slowly flowed from my eyes.

After he finished, he yanked me up hard. I felt and heard the pop as my shoulder dislocated. I made no noise, only winced slightly. The physical pain was so minor compared to the pain inside of me. He firmly gripped my elbow, leading me down the main stairs and to the top of the cellar stairs. He released my elbow and shoved me down the stairs with his foot against my lower back. I free-fell onto the cellar floor, facedown. I heard several cracks as I landed. I gasped and began to cough. I spat up blood, and my breathing became labored. He slammed the cellar door.

I was in complete darkness. Unsure of how long I had been lying there, I heard the cellar door softly open and close. Marci was at my side with a cool cloth, trying to clean me up and move me from the pool of blood I was lying in that had formed from my mouth. She moved me to lay my head on her lap, smoothing my blonde hair, now matted and stained red with blood. As she moved me, everything hurt, and I coughed up more blood. I could hear her quietly sobbing and sniffing. I couldn't speak, but with the last ounces of strength I had, I wanted to make her smile, this sweet soul that had tried to make my stay in hell less painful. I took the last amount of energy I had and made the dirty hay dance off the floor with my fingers.

She laughed through her tears. "Thank you," Marci whispered, trying not to cry. "I wish I could have gotten you out of this awful place," she added, breaking into a sob, rocking back and forth.

In my last moments of life, I felt no hate, even for Henri. I had never been taught to hate, only to love. I just wanted to be where the love was. I just wanted to be with my family. I just wanted to go home. I just wanted to be wherever Liam was especially. No revenge, no hate, no animosity—just allowing my soul to run straight for joy, for love.

Chapter 17

I FELT PEACE AFTER BEING released from that tortured body. I floated above watching as Marci mourned the limp, lifeless vessel I had inhabited. I watched as a day soon thereafter, Henri burned my body at the corner of his property where he burned his diseased livestock to get rid of any evidence of me being there. That same day my body was burned, Marci escaped from that hellhole to find Ma and Pa. She arrived at nightfall and meekly knocked on their door. Pa opened it; his face looked haggard from worry.

"Yes?" Pa said softly, the pain and grief etched in the lines of his face.

"Masseur McShaman?" Marci softly asked.

"Yes, that's me," Pa said suspiciously. "And who are you, my dear?"

"My name is Marci Ginglow, and I was a housemaid for Henri Venereilles. I know about Annalise," she said.

"Please come in. Is she with you? Do we need to go get her?" he said, his eyes brimming with tears.

"No, sir," Marci said, swallowing hard.

"Annalise, you said? Where is she!" Ma jumped up from her seat at the table.

"Yes, ma'am. I'm sorry to tell you, your daughter died three days ago. I was with her when she passed," Marci said softly.

"No! Not Annalise! My baby! Arc! No! Arc, tell me this isn't happening! Not Annalise! Not my baby! No!" my mother shrieked. She collapsed into Pa's arms. They held each other as they mourned my death.

"My baby girl," Pa kept saying over and over. They sat on the dirt floor of our family's cottage, holding each other, rocking back and forth. Marci sat on the bench at the table where we had shared so many meals, put her face in her hands, and cried. After a while, they both came up for air.

"How did it happen?" Ma said, blankly staring off as Pa held her to his broad chest.

Marci looked uncertain, and Pa nodded his head. I spied Jacque hiding in the doorway of the bedroom.

"She was shoved down the stairs, ma'am," Marci said quietly, sniffling.

"So it wasn't a quick death?" Ma asked.

"No, ma'am. I sat there with her head on my lap for a few hours. She made some hay dance for me," Marci offered.

Ma started sobbing again. "No, Arc, no! Not like this! Not for Annalise! We were supposed to go first! I want her back. I want to see her smile. I want to hear her laugh. I want to watch her grow old with Liam! Damn it, Arc! Bring her back to me!" she screamed before breaking into a sob again. The pots along the wall fell to ground, making Marci jump.

"Was he kind to her?" Pa asked.

"No, sir."

"Tell me everything," Pa said.

"After Claire got Liam away on assignment, Henri paid Petyr to capture Annalise. He kidnapped her a couple weeks after Liam left," Marci paused a moment. "She was on her way to your house."

"I knew it!" Ma said. "I knew she was on her way over here!"

"Henri wanted to take her magic," Marci said.

"Sweet Jesus, no," Pa said, understanding what that meant.

"He kept her chained in the cellar."

"He kept my beautiful angel chained like an animal with the vermin in the cellar?"

"Yes, sir."

"Dear, God. My baby," Pa said with tears streaming down his face.

"Where is her body? I want her body. I want my baby's body," Ma asked numbly, an unending stream of tears cascading down her face.

"He burned it a few days ago so that no one would find her," Marci said, crying.

At this, Ma broke down completely, unable to speak.

"Thank you. I know this wasn't easy for you, my dear. How did you know where to find us?" Pa asked.

"Annalise and I talked about escaping, but I told her I had nowhere to go. When I told Annalise that I had no family, she said that I could join hers. She loved you both and her sisters and baby Jacque and her husband very much. She would sing the lullaby you sang to her all of the time, ma'am," Marci said to Ma.

"I just want her back. I just want to hold her. How could they do this to my beautiful baby? Please say I am going to wake up from this. She can't be gone. Arc, I just want her back!" Ma said with a small voice, erupting into tears again. The wooden pegs where the aprons hung fell to the ground. Marci jumped again.

"Me too," said Pa. They clung to each other, crying and rocking back and forth.

"I should have gone to stay with her after Liam left," Ma said.

"Now don't go taking blame for this, Gwennie," Pa said.

"We should have protected her, Arc! We knew Petyr was never right! We knew Henri and Claire were horrid!" Ma said, weeping.

"We can't go into what-ifs, Gwen," Pa said softly.

"We just sat here! I let my baby die. I let those monsters kill my baby," I heard Ma say before she broke down.

I watched as Marci exited to get some fresh air. She leaned against the barn and began to quietly sob. Jacque toddled out of the house to find her and hugged her leg. When she heard the squeak of wagon wheels and the sound of horse hooves beating the ground as they came up the path toward the cottage, she grabbed Jacque and hid. She peered around the corner to see three wagons, two loaded with men and one loaded with logs. Six of the men entered the house; the other four went to digging a hole to stand one of the thick wood poles upright on its end.

Four of the men barged into the cottage and seized Pa, yanking him up; the other two grabbed Ma.

"What do you want?" Pa shouted.

145

"We're tired of your kind!"

"My kind? What kind is that? We haven't bothered anybody!" Pa yelled.

"You've been practicing witchcraft!"

"What nonsense! We would never!"

"People said they have seen you!"

"Seen me doing what exactly!" Pa yelled. The men looked at one another. "That's what I thought! This is nonsense! Now let me go and get out of my house and off my land!

"No magic stuff, you two," one of the men said.

"I just found out my daughter is dead. Can you please leave us alone?" Ma asked.

The men laughed.

"That was one down, three more to go. I heard she went quietly," he said.

"How would you know that?" Ma said through clenched teeth and lunged at him.

The man laughed. "She was feisty and evil just like her witchy mother. She had to go," the man said, restraining her. "She was really nice to look at, and according to Henri, she was a good time in the sheets, although Henri didn't think there was much magic to her when he got done with her." The man snickered.

Ma vomited all over her captors.

"I'd hate to see what's going to grow on ya now that ya got her vomit all over you!" Pa hissed.

The men looked at one another. One of Pa's captors punched him squarely in the jaw. Pa spat out blood from his busted lip.

As Pa and Ma were being held, I then watched as the angry mob arrived at John and Bronwynn's house. They hit John over the head with a club, not meaning to but killing him. I saw his soul leave his body. He came to watch with me as they dragged a pregnant Bronwynn crying and screaming from their cottage. She was bound and gagged and thrown in the back of a wagon. They slaughtered all of their livestock and set fire to their fields.

They brought Bronwynn back to Ma and Pa's house, where they tied her to a stake and set fire to her. She screamed as the flames consumed her. The angry, hate-filled crowd watched with pleasure on their faces, pleased with themselves and their self-righteous pursuit. I watched as Bronwynn was burned to ashes. Her soul came to join John, her male counterpart, and me.

I saw that the madmen had already bound Ma and Pa, holding each of them now at knifepoint. It took four men to hold Pa back. Both had tears of agony streaming down their face as they heard Bronwynn go silent.

Faith was next. Petyr and Faith were sleeping but were awoken to beating on the door. Petyr answered and tried to put up a fight at first.

"Get out of our way, Pete. This is what you wanted," one of the men said.

"No! Not like this!" Petyr screamed.

"You did this?" Faith asked, the betrayal registering on her face. "I shared myself with you, and this is what you did?" Faith screamed, tears streaming from her eyes. Petyr wouldn't look at her.

"Look at me, you coward!" she screamed.

He looked at her. "Yes, I did this! Your family had to be stopped!" he growled.

"Stopped from what? Stopped from loving, stopped from healing!"

"Stopped from witchcraft!"

"Witchcraft!"

"Yes, you and all of your witch sisters! And witch parents!"

"You can't be serious!" Faith screamed, jerking against the hold of her captors.

"You can go quietly like Annalise or loudly like Bronwynn," the captor said into her ear.

I watched as Faith's heart broke. "I did this. I allowed you access to my beautiful world. This is the price I will pay for not following my heart. You are a disgusting man, Petyr!" she screamed.

A group of men took Petyr away and locked him in a stone shed where he wouldn't be in the way. I watched as he tried to get out and dislocated his shoulder. They bound and gagged Faith. Her captor, in the back of the wagon, high on the excitement, forced himself on her. She lay their lifeless as her body jolted from his thrusts. As Bronwynn's ashes smoldered, they tied Faith up and set the huge logs ablaze beneath her. She screamed as the cloth fell off her mouth. "Mami! Papi!" she cried.

Petyr frantically tried to escape his temporary dungeon, but he could not. Her screams went silent, and her body went limp as the flames consumed her. Again, a disgusting look of pleasure registered on the crowd's faces. I watched as Faith's soul left her body and came to be with now Bronwynn, John, and me. We all watched as Ma clawed at her captors and Pa trying to fight off four men holding him back. The agony of knowing of their daughters' deaths and listening to their daughters scream in agony tore through both of them. Ma went limp and collapsed. Her captor tried to continue to hold her upright. Ma's pain was etched on her face as she blankly stared at Pa, tears streaming from her eyes, so overcome with pain she couldn't speak and could hardly breathe. Her mouth gaped open; only a haunting low moan came from it.

An angry mob arrived at Tomas and Raquelle's house. Tomas fought a few of them off, but he wasn't able to keep all of them away. They tied him up and took Raquelle. They bound and gagged her and took her to where Bronwynn's and now Faith's ashes now smoldered. Raquelle was pleading with them to let her go. They tied her up. Tomas escaped his binds and raced his horse as fast as the poor animal could go. We thought he was going to make it, but he was too late. He leapt off his horse while it was still running. As he sprinted toward the fire, the crowd grabbed him and held him back. He was there to look into her eyes one last time before her soul left her body. Raquelle came to join us. Tomas screamed and collapsed. He went mad with despair, shoving those around him, tears streaking down his face.

We watched as Ma vomited uncontrollably and continued to dry-heave. Her captor pulled her beautiful long auburn hair back, exposing her neck, and slit her throat. Blood poured out. She landed on her side, coughing and gasping. They left her there as they thought she was dead. But she wasn't. She then had to watch as they disemboweled Pa, running a scythe through his gut. He collapsed onto his side. They both lay on the ground looking at each other, unable to speak, their physical pain only lessened by the extreme emotional pain coursing through their bodies. The last thing they heard was Jacque screaming for me, wandering through the crowd of strangers, tears streaming down his chubby cheeks, clenching on to the now severely soiled doll I had once made him. He had no one. It was Marci who had been hiding in Pa's barn, who took him to the next town to a church. He unfortunately had been delivered into the religious group that was stirring all this mess. They would go on to raise him to be one of them.

We all watched as Ma's and Pa's souls left their body and came to join us. My soul smiled to see my soul sister again and her male counterpart.

We all watched as, a week later, Liam came home. With me dead, his mother made sure Liam's assignment was ended promptly, and he was released from his duty. He returned for me as he had promised. He rode immediately to our house and couldn't find me there. Our livestock were gone, everything was overgrown, there were holes in the thatch roof of our cottage. He was so confused. He then rode to Ma and Pa's house, looking for me there but only to push open the door and find the rotting corpses of Ma and Pa inside. He found the burning post and three partially burned skulls lying amongst the ashes. I watched as he vomited repeatedly and cried out. He left everything as it was and rode to John and Bronwynn's to find the aftermath of bloated, rotting livestock and burned fields. Next he rode to Faith and Petyr's. The house had been ransacked, the furniture overturned, broken pottery on the ground. No one had known that when Petyr finally escaped, he left France by foot, choosing instead to wander the countryside. Liam rode to Tomas and Raquelle's cottage, which sat amongst blackened fields. Tomas hadn't been back in their house since that night. Liam walked in to see Tomas's binds still lying on the floor in the main room. Tomas's parents had gone to retrieve what livestock survived. Liam could see there was no sign of life.

Liam rode with breakneck speed to Tomas's blacksmith shop in town and beat on the door. Tomas opened the door, drunk.

"Where is Annalise?" Liam demanded, grabbing Tomas by the shirt.

"They're all gone, brother," Tomas said, starting to cry.

"What do you mean gone?" Liam screamed, tears threatening his eyes.

"They took them and killed them," he said, sobbing.

"All of them?" Liam said in disbelief.

"Yes."

"Annalise?" Liam said with tears brimming his eyes.

"Yes."

"No, that's not possible."

"I'm sorry. It's true."

"She didn't do anything wrong. Why would they—" Liam said, trying to process everything.

"Henri kidnapped her right after you left. They say he raped her, chained her up in the cellar, and killed her. She's dead, Liam. My Raquelle is dead. I couldn't save her. I was there and saw her burn. They burned Bronwynn and Faith too. I went into Arcturis and Gwen's cottage. They were dead on the floor. They're all dead," Tomas slurred, wiping his eyes and taking another sip of his liquor.

Liam collapsed to his knees and started screaming, "No! No! No! Why! She can't be gone! Where is her body?" he screamed.

"He burned it," Tomas said, weeping.

"No! This can't be happening! I love her! She's my family! I'm home now! Everything can go back to normal! I can keep her safe now!" Liam said, breaking down.

"I'm sorry I couldn't save any of them," Tomas said softly, taking another sip from the bottle.

"Will you help me bury what's left?" Liam asked.

"No, I can't go back there."

We all watched as Liam went back, dug graves, carried my parents' remains in addition to my sisters' charred skulls, and buried them on the corner of the farm where my aunt Maribelle had been buried. He broke down and cried after he was done, sitting under the apple tree where he had saved me that day. He finished a bottle of liquor and broke it against the tree.

He walked slowly into the house, careful to step over the two huge black spots on the floor where each of my parents had been slain. He went into my bedroom and sat on my bed, putting his hand on the pillow where I had laid my head for so many nights. He lay down on my bed and began to cry.

After he was done, he got up and closed the door to my parents' cottage. He made his way to our cottage. He looked around for a moment. His emotions consumed him as he screamed in agony. He punched the walls. He knocked all of his prized weaponry off the walls. Then he collapsed on our bed. He held his face to my pillow. He lay there as though he was holding me. He spent a while there, shut in our cottage, mourning and grieving. I could feel that it wasn't helping; the agony was so deep.

We all watched as he closed the door to our cottage and rode his horse as fast as he could to the place in the woods by the stream where we had performed the red ribbon ceremony. He pulled the white and red ribbons out from his shirt and held them to his face. Grief washed over him. He collapsed to his knees and sobbed. I heard him talk to me.

"Annalise, please say this isn't happening. This can't be real. You're all I have. You're my family," he said between sobs. "You were supposed to be here when I got back! We were supposed to start a family! Don't make me live this life without you! I don't want to be here without you!" he said before his grief overcame him again. He stayed in that spot, alternating between screaming and crying, clenching the red ribbon in his hand. I could feel that his rage wouldn't subside.

Liam then got on his horse and rode to his mother's house. He kicked in the door. The one manservant they had took one look at Liam's face and walked the other way. His mother peeked out of her drawing room and walked toward him with open arms as though she was going to hug him.

"Liam! There you are, son! You're finally home!" she said with a smile.

As soon as he was close enough to her, he grabbed her by the neck and held her against the wall. "You did this," he growled.

"Liam! How dare you! What are you talking about?" she choked out.

"I should have killed you before when I had the chance," he said, drawing his sword.

"Liam, you're home now. Everything can go back to normal," she choked out.

"No. You took everything in this world that I loved away from me!"

"Don't you love me?"

"No, I hate you. You deserve to rot in the dark place from which you came from for eternity for the evil things you have done and light you have snuffed out from the world," he said, holding his sword to her neck.

"That little witch whore turned you against me!" she hissed.

"Who? Annalise? You're speaking of Annalise Boutreau, my wife?"

"You married her?" she asked in disbelief.

"Yes, it's the happiest I have ever been. And you took her away from me," he growled.

"She cursed you!"

"No, Mother, she loved me. And I love her and always will. She won. How does it feel?"

"Liam, I love you," she whined.

"No, you're sick. This isn't love. This is the last time you will see me. Forget you had a son as I will forget that I ever had a mother."

He slid his sword into her neck and removed it in one swift move.

"Liam—" She tried to scream but could only gurgle as she clung onto his arm. He threw her off him and walked out the door. He climbed onto his horse and took off, leaving this hate-filled little village. The memories were too much to bear.

I watched as, for the next month, he let his grief consume him, living by the drink. He wandered from town to town. He had no home, no place to go. He was lost.

Until one day, Liam was sitting at the local pub when a man who recognized him from his days on the Lord's guard noticed him.

"Well, if it isn't Captain Boutreau?" the man said.

Liam didn't acknowledge him.

"Did you hear me? I was talking to you!" the man said, becoming irate.

"It sounds like a horse's arse taking a shit to me. Kind of smells like it too," Liam said, staring at his empty cup.

The man took Liam by the shirt and threw him outside. Liam stumbled.

"Horse's arse, eh?" the man said, punching Liam in the face.

Liam didn't wince. "You punch more like a woman than a horse," Liam said, returning the blow to the man's face. The man's nose began to bleed.

"I heard your wife moaned like a whore when Henri got a hold of her," the man said.

Liam pulled his knife from his sheath and stabbed him in the gut with one smooth move. Liam didn't see the man's friends coming from behind him. They all stabbed him multiple times. They left him for dead in the street, but miraculously, Liam dragged himself to a dirty alleyway. He propped himself up against the side of the building. He pulled the red and white ribbons from his shirt and held them to his face. He closed his eyes as a few tears escaped. His head slumped over as I watched his soul come to be with me. I was overjoyed to see him. Now I was truly at peace—the other half of my soul had returned to me.

We all realized our plan was severely flawed; it had failed. We had underestimated how dense the energy was and how entrenched the dark was in the human psyche. We had learned a hard lesson, but through this lesson, we were able to regroup and figure out what we needed to do to make it work this next time. When it was our turn to return to the earthly plane, we all stood in deep understanding when we chose our next mission. This time, we would succeed. This time, the light would win.

Chapter 18

I GRUMBLED UNDER MY BREATH as I pulled at a stubborn weed that refused to release its grasp from the flower bed in front of my porch. It finally released its stronghold from the soil, and I lost my balance, falling backward and landing on my rear end. I looked to the left and to the right. I didn't see any of my neighbors out or within view. I stood up and looked down at myself, dusting off my now throbbing buttocks and the front of my mesh athletic shorts. I looked up. It was a beautiful Saturday morning. The sun was shining, and there wasn't a cloud in the bright blue sky. I always reserved Saturdays as my days to work out in my yard. The routine and structure I had built into my life helped me to maintain control; I could depend on that. I thrived in the order and predictability of my life. Working during the week and keeping up with Braeden, my eight-year-old son, left me very little time for anything else. This particular Saturday felt different for some reason. Although, for all intents and purposes, it was like any other ordinary Saturday.

Before I had started my latest endeavor of weeding my flower beds, I had just finished mowing my five-acre yard. My house was somewhat secluded and private, yet close enough to neighbors if I absolutely needed something. It was truly a haven for an introvert like me. It was going to be a warm one today, but the cool breeze coming from off the water reminded me that fall was just beginning to tip its hand here in coastal Virginia. I wiped my face with my dirty gardening glove and was pretty sure that I smeared dirt across my cheek, making me look like a pro football player. I removed my gloves and stood for a moment, tilting my head back to absorb the warm sun's rays on my face.

When I closed my eyes, I could see Sam's smiling face, his sandy-blond hair and blue eyes, perfectly straight teeth. Then the same sad movie began to play in my mind, as it did every time I would think of Sam, the happy memories of starting a life together and ending with my memory of his broken body in a hospital bed. Lost in the memory of holding the hand of a love that had already passed, the color of his skin fading as his vibrant life's essence faded with it. It is the same movie that played in my mind whenever my attention wandered. Then the what-ifs would soon follow: *What if I had taken Braeden to school that morning? What if I had stayed home that day? What if I have left a few minutes later? What if I had called him that morning? What if he worked from home that day? What if he was driving my car or a different car?* All of these questions cycle through my mind but always go unresolved as to what I could have done to change the series of events.

Sam was a good husband, and I had loved him. We had met in college. I was the nerdy bookworm, and he was the outgoing statesman. I could hear the filmstrip rhythmically slap the projector as the movie reel in my mind stopped. I felt my skin lightly tingling then I heard the crunch of gravel from my driveway behind me. I had been so lost in thought I hadn't been paying attention to my surroundings—why should I? I was in the middle of a tiny town no one could pronounce the name of!

"Laney," a male voice said from behind me.

Startled, I dropped my gardening gloves, my heart stopping and then began thrusting itself into my throat at the sound of the familiar voice. *It couldn't be,* I told myself. I had to be hearing things. I inhaled deeply and spun around quickly to see two men standing about three feet in front of me. I instantly recognized the face to whom the voice belonged. My heart leapt again at the recognition of his being. How long had it been since I had stared into those deep and mysterious hazel eyes? He was the last person I expected and yet the only person I wanted to see standing in front of me. Why was he here? Why now? I felt like my heart was racing so fast that I couldn't regulate my breath. His unknown companion was just as muscular and a few inches taller than my five-foot-nine height. His head was clean-shaven, and he was taking in our surrounding with his bright blue eyes. Both of them looked like they had just finished a run in their athletic shorts, T-shirts, and sneakers.

"Brad, I...I can't believe it's you!" I managed to stutter a little too enthusiastically. The sex-kitten voice in my head was rolling her eyes at me and wondering how long they had been standing there or at least were in eyeshot. I wanted to leap over and hug him, but I couldn't move.

"Hello, Ms...?" the shorter man said in an even tone before Brad could respond.

"Masterson...oh, where are my manners? Please, call me Laney, and you are?" I said, flashing him my best Southern-hospitality smile and extending my hand out to him.

"Jesse Allister. How do you do, ma'am?" he said.

My gaze fell back to Brad. I stood there grinning at him, feeling as though time was standing still. Jesse cleared his throat, and I realized that I needed to collect myself. I cleared my throat, hoping to clear the familiar but forgotten magnetic-like pull toward Brad as well. Brad extended his hand to me and clasped my hand in his. I immediately felt a tingle go up my spine that made the hair on the back of my next stand up. My cheeks felt like they were ablaze. I looked into his hazel eyes, and I felt unable to move. I studied his perfect mouth as he flashed me his best GQ smile and studied his lips as he spoke.

"I'm surprised you remember me, Laney," Brad teased.

I was lost in thought, diving even deeper into my memory pool. I blinked rapidly, trying to bring myself into the present moment.

"Of course I do...," my voice trailed off. Time seemed to be suspended as I looked into his eyes. "I can't believe it is really you... how long has it been?" I said, lost in my thoughts, not able to contain my smile.

"Ten years," Brad responded almost before I finished my question. He seemed just as lost in his own thoughts.

"How have you been? You look great! I see you still enjoy working out," I said with the excitement of a schoolgirl talking to her crush.

"I have been well, and I see you have done very well for yourself. This place seems to agree with you," Brad said, gazing at me like a sculptor looks upon their masterpiece.

"It does...," I said, my voice drifting off, completely taken with him and lost in his beautiful hazel eyes. I didn't want to talk anymore; I just wanted to be in his presence. I just wanted to look at his beautifully chiseled face. It had been that way between us all those years ago too. From what I could tell, he didn't seem to want to move either.

Jesse cleared his throat, bringing me back to reality. I blinked rapidly. "Could I offer you both some water?" I asked, not moving my eyes from Brad's. There was so much there, so much being said but remaining unspoken.

"We would love some," Brad said.

"Of course...I'll be right back," I said as I turned and briskly walked into the house.

Once inside and out of eyeshot, I leaned up against the wall and inhaled deeply, then slowly exhaled my breath. I continued toward the kitchen, only briefly stopping to look at myself in the hall mirror. "Ahhhhh, crap!" I whispered to myself. I saw that I did smudge dirt on my cheek and forehead. The unruly bun on top of my head that contained my long fine brown hair had somehow collected a few small leaves in it, and to top it all off, small grass clipping had stuck to my sweaty skin all over my legs, arms, and chest. I hurriedly tried to pick the yard debris out of my hair and dust some of the grass clippings off my skin. The dirt on my face was a little bit more stubborn. Then I quickly walked to the fridge and collected two bottles of water. As I walked outside, Brad's gaze was steady on me, scanning my body up and down. It made it hard to breathe. I felt like I was about to go sing on stage in front of a thousand people. Jesse's eyes were scanning the house and yard. I made it down the stairs without falling, thankfully. I handed a bottle of water over to each of the men.

"Thank you. You have a beautiful property here. The view is breathtaking," Brad said as I handed him a bottle of water.

I swallowed hard. His eyes were steady on mine. I noticed he wasn't looking at the land or house.

"Thank you. It is a lot of work, but I wouldn't have it any other way. When Sam and I purchased this house, he wanted to tear it down. But as you can see, I prevailed. I think the imperfections make it beautiful, ya know?" I said, suddenly blushing and trying to figure out why I told him that.

"I believe I do," he said with a slight smile tugging at the corners of his mouth.

"I have to be honest, I have no idea where you went when you left Mendelson. Do you live around here?" I blurted out, sounding more like a pick-up line than a question.

Brad was about to open his mouth to speak when a car came speeding up the driveway—gravel, dirt, and dust stirring up into a light-brown cloud behind it. Brad and Jesse turned in tandem to look at the pickup truck as it came to a stop ten feet in front of us. Braeden hopped out of the back passenger side door and ran over to me, excitement written all over his face.

"Mommy, I weighed in, and I can play football!" he squealed.

I laughed—as this had been the topic of discussion at our house for the last two weeks—as he ran over to me and into my arms.

"Braeden I would like you to meet some friends of mine, Brad and Jesse."

"Hi." Braeden gave a little wave. Then he looked at me, clearly disinterested in our guests. "Can I go play now?"

I smiled at his angelic face, his hazel eyes were from one parent who had brown eyes and one who had blue, but everything from his sandy-blond hair to the way he walked was the spitting image of Sam.

"Sure, but straighten up your room first," I called after my son, who had already darted off toward the front door.

Ugh, now for the unpleasant part: dealing with Mark McCauley. Mark strode up with his normal cocky swagger and chest puffed up. He awkwardly stepped in the middle of the small triangle that Brad, Jesse, and myself had formed. He could have stood beside me instead to make a square, but that wasn't Mark's style. It dawned on me that his primary goal was to wedge himself between Brad and myself.

Facing Brad at an incredibly awkward and close proximity, Mark said, "Hi, how do you do? Mark McCauley." He had extra emphasis on the *k* at the end of his first name. I tried to conceal my amusement by clamping my lips together and looking down at my hands.

"Hello, Mark. Braxton Green. This is Jesse Allister." Brad provided no extra explanation of his visit. I could see by Brad's face he was amused but was running out of patience for Mark's intrusion. I knew that Brad did not suffer fools.

Mark narrowed his eyes. "Wait, are you *the* Braxton Green? Didn't I see in the newspaper that you bought the 260-acre waterfront parcel next to Laney's here?" Mark said as though he had solved a *Jeopardy* question.

Mark's statement stunned me. Brad was going to be my neighbor. As that statement registered, I immediately found Brad's eyes again.

Brad's gaze was on me too. "I did."

Still between both of the men and me, Mark turned around to face me. He was making this awkward and himself look stupid all in one try. I took one step back to allow more personal space.

"Are you coming to Lucas's party tonight?" His eyes were looking at me hopefully. Unfortunately, there is no good way to burst a bubble.

"I'm sorry I can't. Jenna and Josh are coming over for a sleepover." I watched as his face melted. A pang of guilt twanged in my stomach; I felt embarrassed that this exchange was in front of Brad. I needed to change the subject. "Thanks for taking Braeden to weigh-in today. I'm glad he'll get to play. Did Lucas do okay?"

"Daddy! I want to go home!" Lucas, Mark's son, who had rolled down the car window, was hollering to his dad.

"I'm coming!" Mark yelled. "See you later, Laney." He leaned in and gave me a kiss on the cheek, then eyed the men one more time and then returned to his car. It felt like I was a tree that Mark had peed on to mark his territory. Brad's gaze was still on me. I could see his jaw was tight. I felt myself blush. It was apparent that Brad was the alpha male, and he wasn't moved at all by Mark's posturing.

"So we are going to be neighbors?" I asked Brad, trying to recover from the awkward interaction as we watched Mark's car pull out of my driveway onto the road.

"It appears we will," he said, seemingly lost in thought.

"Well, if there is anything you need, don't hesitate to ask and feel free to stop by anytime you want. That's just kind of how it works around here. As you know, it's a small town, so they won't let you in their clique at first, but if you or your wife or kids need help getting involved with anything, I will be glad to point them in the right direction," I said, rambling, all the while noting that he didn't have a wedding ring.

"No family, just me," he said, amused.

"Oh...good, I mean, okay...just let me know how I can help... you are both welcome to come to dinner tonight..."

A half smile crept across Brad's face.

Why did I do that? I have nothing to make for dinner.

"I don't think your boyfriend would like that, Laney," Brad teased as his eyes penetrated mine.

Breathe, Laney, breathe. I could feel my face going from a shade of blush to beet. It was amazing to me that ten years had passed, but he still felt so familiar to me.

"Who? Mark? He's just a friend. He's one of the locals that likes to check in on me since Sam died, and besides, our boys play football together...," my voice trailed off. I felt so drawn to Brad, I wanted to tell him everything about me—this was crazy! *Quit talking, Laney. He didn't ask for your life story.* I clamped my lips shut, thought for a moment, and then continued, "I don't want to keep you from your run, and these dandelions won't pull themselves." I smiled. My inner sex kitten coughed up a hairball, and my logical mind applauded. Brad flashed his perfect smile back at me.

"Of course, we won't keep you. We will see you around." He extended his hand out to me once again.

I shook his hand, looking into his eyes, and felt my breath hitch at the contact. This feeling was foreign but familiar. He was stirring something deep within me that I thought had been long ago extinguished. I released his hand and collected their empty water bottles from them. I watched them run back up the driveway to the street. Even the way he ran was in perfect form. I walked backward toward the porch, continuing to watch them, and almost tripped on the bottom step of my porch. It was hard to take my eyes off him. *Snap out of it, Laney. You deal with men all the time. Why are you acting like this?* My logical mind wrapped my knuckles with her ruler.

I kept going over the interaction in my mind. The memories of Brad poured out of my memory bank, flooding my mind.

I was an HR intern at Mendelson, just starting out after graduating college. Brad was a supervisor. I can still remember on my first day at Mendelson walking in and seeing him leaning up against the front desk, smiling at me as he greeted me. I had never seen someone so incredibly handsome in all of my life. Even though Sam and I were together at the time, nothing could touch the attraction I felt toward Brad. It wasn't purely physical attraction. There was something deeper, an energetic pull and flow between us. It scared me at first, knowing that there was someone out there that could affect me the way he could. We became close friends quickly, opening up to each other about the deepest part of ourselves. After about two weeks of long and intense conversations, late one night, our passions could not be held back any longer. For the next four weeks, it was the most amazing, intimate, and sensual experience of my life. I had never felt so close to someone. The only problem was, we were both married. After six weeks of knowing each other, almost to the day, he called me on the way out of town with his wife and said that he had to let me go. He had decided to work on his marriage with his wife, ending our affair.

That was the last time I had spoken with Brad. He and I had managed to avoid each other at work before he left the company only a short time later. To be honest, for the first time in my life, I had been completely living in the moment—no planning, no worries, no expectations. I hadn't considered where this path might take Brad and me, only that I loved being with him. Selfishly, I hadn't thought of Sam; I only thought of the fact that his long hours at the law office left me lonely and craving intimacy. Brad's phone call to break it off had happened on a Saturday. I cried the entire weekend and didn't really eat for the next month, subsisting on tea and cinnamon toast. I felt sick to my stomach for three months. Then it relaxed into a general queasiness until I reached a place of acceptance. I accepted the facts: He didn't feel the same way about me. I wasn't good enough for him, nor was I enough for him. Despite all of that, I have to admit that, all along, deep down, I knew there was something different about him and me, something otherworldly. Somehow I always knew he would return to me, which made the acceptance even more confusing. There had not been a day that I did not think of him. I shook my head, trying to bring myself back into the present moment.

The whole interaction with Mark had been weird, but what I told Brad was true: Mark was not my boyfriend. He would like more, but I didn't. But why didn't I? Mark was a very attractive guy. He was nice, he helped me all the time, had a kid the same age as mine. To tell the truth, I had shut down that part of me since Brad walked away from me that day. There was no one that could even compare to him, even Sam. I had dutifully fallen back into my role as Sam's wife until he died. After Sam's death, I tried dating a few men to appease my mother and well- meaning friends who were obsessed with ensuring that I was mentally stable enough to move on with my life. I had found that telling men that I was a widow or even, at times, a mother was similar to confessing that I had the bubonic plague. Or that my lack of apparent male attention left me a wanton slut. The few I did date felt similar but weren't Brad and would fizzle out after a few short months.

In reality, marriage had taught me that the commitment involved was so absolute one must make a wise choice and not settle for anything less than soul-ascending, toe-curling, "so happy you're giddy" type of love. Some would say that my standards were too high, but it made perfect sense to me. I had no time for one-night stands or "friends with benefits." I wouldn't settle because I was worth holding out for. With my plethora of lackluster dates and failed attempts at romantic encounters, I decided to give up on the whole scene. Each date made me miss who it was I really wanted to be with even more. I put my inner sex kitten in the pound and solely focused on Braeden and my job. I became numb. It was easier that way. Emotions were messy, and mine somehow could become all consuming.

A vision of Brad smiling at me as we walked through a local park all those years ago interrupted my thoughts. *Get him out of your head, Laney. I am sure he has a Barbie for a girlfriend. He was probably just looking at you because you look like a hot mess.* My logical mind had wrestled my inner sex kitten to the ground and put her in a cage. I smiled and shook my head, half-hoping to shake Brad out of my head. Now on to my next task of a shower before Jenna and Josh arrived for dinner.

Jenna Ford arrived it grand style, as usual, around six o'clock. She looked great in everything she wore, even worn-out jeans and a T-shirt. Her blonde hair was swept back into a perfect messy ponytail, her blue eyes beaming with a hint of mischief, as always. She was not only my best friend but my assistant at work as well. Her eight-year-old son, Josh, ran past me up the stairs looking for Braeden. I was pleased that the two boys had become fast friends as well.

"Laney, you are looking a little flushed. Something wrong with your air-conditioner?" she said with a sarcastic smile. This is when I hated that she knew me so well. Clearly, my guise wasn't working.

"Very funny, Jenna. I would never use your excuse of a broken air-conditioner anyway," I retorted.

"She's sassy tonight. I like it," Jenna said, giggling.

"I had a visit from my new neighbor today. He bought the property next door…," my voice trailed off as my mind brought up the memory of his face.

"Was he cute?" she said, scrunching up her nose at me optimistically and picking up a knife to assist me with chopping vegetables.

"More than…he is hot. There are no imperfections on him…or his friend," I added, winking at her.

"I like the sound of that. Does your hot new neighbor have a name?" she said, raising her eyebrows as she began to chop a head of cauliflower. I dropped my knife, and it went clanging loudly onto the counter.

Jenna gave me a quizzical look. "Careful, Laney! You're going cut a finger off, everything okay?" she asked, suspiciously eyeing me.

"Uh…yeah. He's Brad. I mean, his name is Brad Green, ironically, an ex-flame of mine. And the friend's name was Jesse something. I actually invited them to dinner," I said, completely straight-faced.

"You what! Are they coming?" Jenna gasped.

"No, they declined. I don't know what got into me," I said, chuckling.

"Laney Masterson, I am proud of you. I do believe you are coming out of your shell."

"I wouldn't go that far. Crap! I need to check the fondue!" I said as I put down my knife and went to the stove where the bubbling light-orange cheese mixture had luckily reached the perfect gooey consistency. I began stirring to make sure the concoction wasn't burnt. I removed the pot from the stove and set it on a hot pad on the counter. When I returned to my chopping station, I noticed that Jenna had poured us both a glass of wine. She raised her glass to me.

"To you, Laney. You took a wonderfully brave step today. And if I get you to drink enough wine, I want to hear all the dirty details about Mr. Flame," she said, looking at me with pride. It almost brought tears to my eyes.

"A baby step…and just a little more wine," I countered, smiling. Jenna rolled her eyes, and we clinked glasses.

The rest of the evening was wonderful, as it always was when Jenna and I were together. I had come to find there is nothing in the world like the company of a good friend, a best friend, soul family. After the third glass of wine after dinner, Jenna declared that she was going up to bed, and the boys followed her up the stairs. As I went into the kitchen to shut off the light over the sink, I stared out of the window into the darkness. I wondered what Brad was doing right now. My mind drifted to considering what life would have been like if we would have made the different choice of choosing each other instead of running away. I shook my head to clear my thoughts and flicked the light switch to off. There was no way to tell. Why even think of such things?

Chapter 19

I awoke Sunday morning to my cell phone vibrating on the night-stand, notifying me that I had received a text message. I swiped the screen on my phone to open the text message; it was from an unknown number.

"Care to join me for a run in the woods?"

I thought for a moment, squinting at the screen.

"Who is this?"
"Your new next-door neighbor"
"Hahaha…I don't really run anymore"
"How about a walk? Trillium Park in 30 minutes?"
"Deal"

I sprung out of bed, ran across the hall to the guestroom, and jumped on the bed where Jenna was sleeping. Jenna looked at me with one eye open and began to giggle.

"I didn't hear your bed squeaking last night. Why are you smil-ing so big?" she teased in her sleepy voice.

"Brad asked if I would go for a walk in the park with him this morning. Would you mind watching Braeden? I shouldn't be long."

"Sure thing. Take as much time as you need," she said,. winking at me. Then we both began to giggle.

After a moment, I darted across the hall and found my jogging shorts, sports bra, sneakers, and a tank top. I pulled my hair back into a ponytail and quietly sprinted down the steps to my car. On the drive over to the park, I took in the breathtaking sunrise before me and the beautiful pinkish-orange glow that illuminated every, tree, bush, and blade of grass. The weather was in the seventies with a light breeze. It was the perfect weather for a morning walk.

I pulled into the parking space next to Brad's Maserati and gave him a smile through the car windows. We both exited our cars. I walked to meet him standing in front of his car, which was parked conveniently at the opening of one of the tree-lined, pine-needle-covered paths that led to the main trail. He was dressed in athletic shorts, a T-shirt, and sneakers. It appeared he had rolled out of bed to meet here as well as his hair was a little mussed up. We just stood there smiling at each other. I felt the chaos, worries, and second-guessing in my mind become silent.

"It is good to see you again, Laney. You look beautiful, as always," he said as he tucked a piece of my bangs behind my ear. There was something about him. And standing in front of him now, I remembered how it felt to be completely out of control of my emotions.

"It's good to see you as well. And thank you, that is very kind of you to say. I haven't walked here in a long time. I'm excited to see the trail," I said, blushing.

"Shall we?" he said, motioning for me to start down the path first. He followed behind me.

After about twenty steps, the small path intersected a wider trail, where we could walk side by side instead of single file. We fell into step beside each other. I took in the beauty of nature all around us. I had always enjoyed being outside, but this morning, the leaves seemed more vibrant, the air smelled sweeter, all of my senses were singing. As we walked, I could see from the corner of my eye that Brad kept stealing glimpses at me.

"So what have you been up to the last ten years?" I asked, raising my eyebrows.

He chuckled. "Starting with the easy question, eh? Work, mostly," Brad offered. He wasn't going to make this easy.

"I see. By the car you drive, you have done well for yourself. What are you doing now?" I asked, hoping he would expand on his answer. I gazed at the side of his face, his strong jawline, his beautiful olive skin, his dark morning stubble that was barely peeking through.

"Management. What about you? Are you still at Mendelson?" he asked, clearly not wanting me to ask any more questions about his job.

"Actually...yes. I am surprised that Jack has tolerated me this long. I am the HR director now. Shocking, I know," I said with a chuckle.

"Ah, Madame HR Director. I'm not shocked. I knew you would do well. Everything you touch does well," he said as he turned his head to briefly look at me.

I was already enraptured with his presence, but his gaze was my undoing. Looking at him now, I remembered that I couldn't stop myself from falling in love with him all those years ago. I had tried to stop, tried to deny the feelings, but I couldn't. I shifted my attention to the trail in front of me, trying to be wary of any tree roots I may trip on.

"So you said no family, and I don't see a wedding ring on your finger. How is Kayla?" I asked, curious about his wife.

He smiled. "She is fine, to the best of my knowledge. She still lives in Charlotte." He paused for a moment. "I was sorry to hear about Sam. He was a good man. How have you been doing?" he asked.

I thought on his question for a moment. "At first it was hard, adjusting to life by myself. But Braeden is a great kid, and I was blessed with really great people that filled in to help me out. Some days I still don't know how, but it just works. I love my job and where I live. I feel content. How about you?"

He thought on my question for a moment, looking off to the side of the trail. "I will be there soon, but not yet," he said enigmatically as he paused. "But do tell me, how is someone as amazing as you still single?"

"Ha-ha, I am not *that* amazing," I said, smiling and looking at him.

He grabbed my hand, interlacing his fingers with mine. "Yes, you are, Laney Masterson...and I have dated all sorts of women," he said, squeezing my hand. "Tell me seriously. Why are you still single?" he asked intensely.

Whenever anyone else asked me this question, it made me uncomfortable because no answer I could supply would suffice, but with him, I knew he was not going to judge me.

"I guess it hasn't been my time yet," I said with a smile.

"No one serious?" Brad asked.

"No, I have been on a bit of a hiatus. Work and Braeden's sports schedule takes most of my time," I said, feeling my cheeks burning brightly with blush. I continued, "Any kids?" Brad seemed to be deep in thought after my answer to his question.

"No, no kids." He said still lost in thought.

"Well, what made you move to the area?" I asked, trying to get back to a safe line of questioning. Brad stopped, so I stopped. "Everything okay?" I asked.

He looked at me then looked in either direction of the tree and brush-lined path. I did the same, trying to find what he was looking for. There was no one else out this morning except us. He pulled my body to his. His lips delicately found mine. The contact of our lips was soul-quenching. I had forgotten how soft his lips were, how delicious his kiss tasted, how right this felt. His other hand slipped around my waist to my lower back, and he pressed me firmly against him. I let out a soft gasp. He smiled briefly; then his kiss became firmer, more passionate. I brought one of my hands to the side of his neck and the other to his waist, lightly gripping his T-shirt in my fingers. He entwined his fingers in my hair. I began to feel light-headed as our energies began to dance together. When we both came up for air, we were both awestruck.

"God, I have missed you," he said softly under his breath, resting his forehead on mine. "I could do a lot more of that," he said under his breath.

I was dizzy and trying to collect my thoughts when, as if on cue, his cell phone rang. He retrieved his phone from his pocket and swiped the screen to answer it, still holding me to him. "Green," he barked, "give me thirty." He ended the call and kissed me softly again. He parted from my lips and looked at me for a long moment. "Since

I have to cut our walk short, can I get a rain check?" he asked softly. I couldn't help but smile looking into his handsome face. I think he could have asked me to chew on a twig, and I would have done it.

"Of course," I said.

"Let's head back," he said softly, taking me by the hand. We walked in silence holding hands. Our pace was a little slower this time. I relished the physical contact.

When we arrived back to the cars, he walked me around to the driver's side of my car. I gave him a smile as I reached to open the door to my car. He turned me to him and leaned his body against mine, pressing my back against my car. His fingers tucked a few stray pieces of hair behind my ear, and then he studied my face.

"You are so amazing, Laney. I enjoyed this immensely."

"Me too." I smiled.

He leaned in and gave me another kiss. "We'll talk soon," he said as he winked. He stepped backward to release me and then reached around me to open my car door. I smiled and climbed into my car. He shut the car door behind me and gave a little wave. As I pulled out of the parking lot, I watched him make his way to the Maserati. All the way home, I couldn't stop thinking about him, yet I didn't want to call or tell anyone. I just wanted to enjoy the feelings in this moment all to myself. I didn't want to overthink this and give my insecurities a chance to take a stronghold. My phone buzzed; it was a text from Brad.

"Thank you for a wonderful morning walk"

I giggled in spite of myself. I felt like a schoolgirl with the amount of giddiness swirling around within me over one text.

"I did as well, I look forward to the rain check"

"Me too"

I pulled into my driveway and saw that Josh and Braeden were throwing the football in the front yard, and Jenna was sitting on the front-porch steps drinking a cup of coffee, thumbing through a magazine.

"Back so soon?" she said as she flashed me a wicked smile.

"Aren't you funny? You know I am too prude for that," I said, rolling my eyes.

"A girl can hope, can't she?" she said, laughing, as I sat down on the front-porch step next to her.

"Yes, yes, she can," I said.

"Well, how was it?"

"Wonderful."

"That's it? That's all you are going to give me? You come back glowing from head to toe, and that's all I get? Wonderful?"

"Yep."

"Mmmm, okay, Ms. Glowworm."

"Can I interest you in some breakfast?" I asked, wanting to change the subject.

"Yes, you may."

"Awesome. Bacon, eggs, and waffles sound good?" I said, getting up from the front-porch steps and heading toward the screen door.

"You had me at bacon," Jenna chirped.

I proceeded to get out the eggs, bacon, and waffle iron. While my pans were heating up, I sliced a fresh cantaloupe I forgot I had bought from the farmer's market. I went over to the cabinet and withdrew the waffle mix, stirring in the oil and water until the right consistency was reached. I heard Jenna cracking eggs into a pan and heard the sizzle from the bacon begin.

"What's so special about him?" Jenna asked softly, breaking the silence.

I thought on what she said for a moment, carefully considering my answer. "He's my person," I said, seeing Jenna's head whip around to look at me.

"Are you talking about soul mates or whatever?" she asked, almost in disbelief. I began to feel foolish talking about this.

"Something like that, except this is literally like he is my other half. I know it sounds ridiculous—"

"No, it actually doesn't, Laney."

"It's always been him. I just didn't realize it until this morning," I said softly, blushing, feeling foolish for talking this way.

"That's what everyone is looking for, and you've found yours," she said, winking at me.

Jenna left shortly after breakfast with Josh and Braeden. Braeden had begged me to go with Jenna so he could spend more time playing with Josh and promised to work on their science project that happened to be due tomorrow. I spent the rest of the morning cleaning the house. That afternoon, I was in the middle of my grocery shopping at the local supermarket when my phone buzzed. I answered it, assuming it was Jenna saying that Braeden was ready to be picked up from her house.

"Hello?"

"Hi, doll," I heard a man's voice say. It was Mark. I really should have checked the caller ID before I answered.

"Hi, uh…Mark, how are you?" I said, balancing the phone between my ear and shoulder as I grabbed a carton of milk from the case.

"I am doing well, just thinking about a beautiful woman that I can't wait to see again. And how are you?" he said, attempting to be charming.

"Not too bad. Just finishing up some grocery shopping, getting ready for my week, the usual," I said flatly.

"That's nice," he said, completely uninterested. "So I am going to be busy for the next couple of weeks and was calling to see if you wanted to go to dinner with me this evening?" he asked.

To be honest, I didn't want to, and everything in my body screamed at me, not to include the nausea in my stomach. All I wanted to do was pick up Braeden, put on my PJs, and watch movies at home on my couch. My head, however, was telling me that I needed to give Mark a chance. Maybe everyone was right? Maybe he would surprise me? Maybe I had put Brad on too high of a pedestal all this time, and I needed to give other men a chance? Brad wasn't a sure thing. We shared a kiss this morning, but I had no idea what his intentions with me were. So much time had passed. He was one of the "most eligible bachelors," per all of the celebrity magazines. Why would he want someone like me? I inhaled deeply.

"Sure, that would be lovely. I will call Jenna to let her know. What time should I expect you?" I said, kicking myself as soon as the words were out of my mouth.

"Great! I'll pick you up around six. I wouldn't want to keep you out too late on a school night," Mark teased with a chuckle.

"See you then!" I said, trying to be excited. As I hung up, I felt sick to my stomach. What had I done?

Mark arrived a few minutes past six. I had decided to wear dark jeans, a pair of peep-toe red pumps, and an off-the-shoulder blouse. I attempted to put on makeup and do my hair, but the effort was forced. I heard the doorbell ring. I answered it, and he gave me a bouquet of white calla lilies.

"For you. Beautiful flowers for a beautiful woman," he said, winking at me. I think he expected a kiss, but I gave him a smile instead.

"Thank you, how thoughtful. Won't you come in while I put these in water?"

"Sure," he said, scanning my house as he stepped into the foyer. I didn't like him being in my home, but I wasn't sure why. He was a police officer, after all; wasn't I safer with him than with anyone else?

He followed me into the kitchen where, he watched as I pulled a vase out of the cabinet and filled it with water. I could feel his eyes on my back, and sure enough, he was staring when I turned around. I placed the vase on the counter.

"Shall we go?" I asked, wanting to get him out of my house.

"Yep. After, you m'lady," he said, winking again. My stomach turned; this was such a bad idea. "Make sure you lock up. Wouldn't want anyone waiting inside to snatch you when you get home."

"Oh, right," I said, pulling out my key and turning the lock on the door. He opened the door to his truck for me, and I slid onto the leather seat. He closed the door behind me. I looked around and could tell it was usually a mess, and he had cleaned it for this occasion.

"I thought we would go out for Mexican? The place in town has phenomenal Pollo Loco."

"Sounds great." I gave a weak smile. The only benefit was that it was only five minutes away.

"So tell me, what were you talking about with Braxton Green and that other guy when I pulled up yesterday?"

"Not that it is really any of your business, Mark, but we were talking about the property and catching up."

"Catching up?"

"Yes, Brad and I are old friends."

"Well, look at you. I didn't realize you had such high and mighty friends," he mocked.

I rolled my eyes. "Mark, can we please change the subject?" I asked as we pulled into the parking lot. I opened my own car door before he had the opportunity to bring his muscle-bound self around the car. He tried holding my hand into the restaurant, but I kept moving away from him.

Once inside, my skin began to tingle. As we were being led to our table, we passed by a table with four people; one of whom was Brad. My heart stopped. We made eye contact, and he gave me a puzzled look. It appeared he was meeting with some architects with house plans.

"Laney! Over here!" Mark shouted. I gave a weak smile and continued walking. I was now fully distracted. "Of course, he had to be here, huh? Did you call an tell him we were coming?" Mark pouted.

"Get over yourself. He's probably here for the Pollo Loco."

"Is this how it's always going to be?"

"How what is always going to be?"

"Him interrupting our dates?"

"Mark, this is barely a date. You are my friend. Can we please just order and try to have a nice time?"

"Laney, I think we are more than friends...we should be at least."

"Well, I'm just not sure," I said. Thankfully, the waiter came to take our food order. I sipped on my water as Mark was droning on about how unfair life was, and I noticed Brad get up and go to the restroom. I thought about bumping into him on purpose, but it would be too obvious with Inspector Gadget watching my every move. Then I saw him return to his seat, glancing briefly in my direction. I hated this; I was miserable. As we got up to leave, we passed my Brad's table. Brad stood up and lightly grabbed my wrist.

"Laney, I didn't expect to be as fortunate to see such beauty come across my path tonight," he said, standing to his full height.

I smiled and blushed. "Thank you. It is good to see you too," I said.

Mark cleared his throat.

"You remember Mark?"

"Ah yes. Hello, Mark," Brad said with emphasis on the *k*, his eyes never leaving me.

"Hello, Mr. Green. It is good to see you again," Mark said, strained. Brad nodded, flicking his eyes in Mark's direction. "It appears you are serious about building next to Laney," Mark said, looking at the blueprints on the table.

Brad let go of my wrist. "Quite serious," Brad said, and I felt my stomach do a flip. I smiled at him again.

"Well, we must be going. I am going to take Laney home."

"I see," Brad said with curiosity in his eyes.

"Have a good evening," I said softly.

Brad nodded. I could feel his gaze upon me as I walked away.

As soon as we climbed into Mark's truck, the rant began. "The nerve of that guy…"

I didn't hear anything as I was thinking about Brad's eyes. I smiled in spite of myself, gazing out the car window.

"Laney?" I heard a few minutes later.

"Yes?"

"Did you hear me?"

"No, I'm sorry. What did you say?"

"I asked if you enjoyed the special?"

"Yes, it was delicious."

"To be honest, you're a cheap date, no alcohol. I got out of there under $20."

I nodded in response, not sure what to say to his crass and stupid comment.

Mark dropped me back off at my house at 7:15 p.m. "I can come in and check your place out?" he said, winking at me. I'm sure this worked with other women, but not me.

"No. Thank you for a wonderful evening," I said as I exited his vehicle. I could feel him looking at me like he wanted a kiss, but that sure wasn't going to happen. I slammed the car door and walked up to my door, unlocking it and tucking myself away inside until his taillights were out of view. As soon as I knew he was gone, I exited out of the side door to the breezeway connecting the garage to the house. I entered through another door and pushed the button to open the garage door. I climbed inside my car and rested my head on the steering wheel. I closed my eyes and took a deep breath. As I exhaled, I turned on my car and made my way to Jenna's to pick up Braeden.

Chapter 20

As it always did, Monday came around way too quickly, and the weekend was way too short for my liking. I was driving Braeden to school, and my cell phone rang through the speakers of my car. I answered in my standard professional HR director voice, "Laney Masterson?"

"Good morning, sweet pea! So we have an employee that refuses to submit a sample specimen for his drug screen. What do you want us to do?" It was Jenna. Right now she was playing her other role—that of my assistant.

"Well, what is his reason for not participating in the drug screen?" This ought to be good.

"He says that he can only pee, uh…er, I mean urinate once a day." Her response made me smile. Jenna was trying to be politically correct for such an odd topic.

"If he has a legitimate doctor's note, we can consider not terminating his employment. If he doesn't, we must proceed with termination." That's me—the judge, jury, and executioner.

"Okay, that sounds good. I will get the documentation from him and get back to you."

"Thanks, Jenna. See you shortly."

"See ya, Laney!"

Jenna had truly been a blessing to me. She intuitively knew what I needed or what I was going to ask for before I say a word. She was twenty-nine, only three years younger than me. My predecessor, who hired her, told me that Jenna was hard to get along with. I found it to be quite the opposite. Proof that under the right circumstances, a person can flourish.

"Mommy, why do you need to make sure people pee at work?" asked my inquisitive eight-year-old son from the backseat. I couldn't help but laugh out loud; then I looked at him in the rear-view mirror. I thought on how much I had come to enjoy dropping off Braeden at school in the morning. We always had very interesting discussions from boogers, to superhero battles between Superman and the Incredible Hulk, to pee. How was I going to tap-dance around this one?

"Well, honey, Mommy makes sure people have a special pee test at work to make sure they are safe and not taking any bad medicine that will make them act silly…in a bad way," I offered. He nodded, my answer seeming to satisfy him for the moment. As we pulled into the drop-off lane at his school, I gave him a kiss on the cheek, and he opened the car door. I watched him walk quickly into the school, his backpack bobbing up and down with his steps. Now off to work.

I loved my job. Every day was something different, and during my darkest days after Sam's death, it had been a much-needed distraction. The consistency of having a daily schedule amidst emotional chaos helped me tremendously. As HR director at Mendelson Industries, a manufacturer of electronic components, I had responsibility for ten locations and a staff of fifteen. I had worked at Mendelson since I graduated from college eleven years ago. Everyone at Mendelson was like family to me, even the ornery ones. I climbed the ladder fast; some would say too fast. I excelled in employee relations and had decertified a couple of the unions in Mendelson's manufacturing sites, which brought me much praise and professional recognition. What I had told Brad was true: I was content. I knew what was expected of me, the key players, and how to get things done. To tell the truth, I really didn't wish to climb the ladder any further. My plate was more than full trying to balance raising Braeden as a single mother and also maintaining my current position's duties.

I arrived at work and made my way up to the eighth floor. As I stepped out of the elevator, I briefly looked to the left, looking through the glass doors and confirming that the CEO, Jack Mendelson, was already in. When he was there, it was always a busy day. My office was down the hall from the C-Suite, in the opposite direction across the elevator lobby. Directly across from the elevators, there was a huge conference room that got a lot of use. It had been lovingly nicknamed "the war room." I veered to the right and scanned my badge, pushing through one of the double glass doors that led to a cluster of executive offices. HR shared the space with finance and legal teams. Needless to say, we didn't get a lot of visitors on this floor unless they were required to be there. My immediate neighbors consisted of various HR functional directors and my boss, the Human Resources vice president. Jenna's low-walled gray cubicle was situated outside of my office. I glanced at her cubicle and noticed she wasn't at her desk, but her computer was on. I unlocked the tall heavy wooden door to my office and made my way over to my cherry-colored contemporary desk. I pulled my laptop out of my bag and plugged it into the docking station, then sat in my leather executive chair and slid up to my desk, pressing the power button on my laptop.

I heard a tapping on my door and looked up to see Slade Brinkman, my boss, the HRVP. He walked in with his hands in his pockets, like he didn't have a care in the world.

"Hello, beautiful. I need a favor," Slade said like he was in a bar, completely inappropriate.

I looked up to see he was dressed in his dark-gray suit. He ran his fingers through his auburn hair. Slade's good looks were only rivaled by his other two strong attributes: he was a gifted bullshitter and arrogant womanizer. He still looked like a frat boy even though he was my age. It could be frustrating working for him some days because he really had no knowledge of human resources, but he was the chairman of the board's grandson. He relied on me for everything, which kept me busy, in "the know," and most importantly—employed. We worked well together because he gave me space to do my job and did *not* chase my skirt.

"Good morning, Slade. What can I help you with?" I asked in a calm yet chipper voice.

"I need you to prepare a brief for the executive board about our talent strategy. Halifax Corporation has been courting our talent, as you know. Jack is nervous that we won't be able to maintain our innovative edge if they keep fleecing us of our good people," he said as he ran his hand through his unruly auburn hair. This was a good step in the right direction. He sounded like he was beginning to understand his job.

"Sure thing, Slade. When do you need it by?" I asked, hearing *Jeopardy* music in my head as I waited for his answer.

"That's the thing. I need it tomorrow, and if you don't mind presenting it too—I don't like to get bogged down by all the details that are in the pretty little head of yours," he said, winking his baby-blue eye at me.

I sighed. "Tomorrow? I guess I will move some meetings today."

At least Slade was nice to look at even when he gave me last-minute deadlines. I had the privilege of meeting some of his latest conquests, all blondes with big boobs and after his money—or his family's money, rather. Slade reveled in the attention. He had probably slept with every woman in the office except Jenna and me, I mused to myself.

"Let me know if you need anything. Otherwise, I will see you at our meeting this afternoon," he said, making his exit toward the door and winking at Jenna as she entered my office. Jenna rolled her eyes as she came to lay some papers on the desk in front of me.

"Okay, so our pee-test abstainer could only provide a prescription for ibuprofen and no other doctor's note," she said with a twisted-up face. Ugh.

"Well, you know what to do, Jenna...he's gone," I said, disappointed.

Jenna smiled. "I'm on it, just as soon as you tell me how your date went with Mr. Police Officer last night?"

I twisted up my face slightly and chuckled. I had almost forgotten about my last-minute date with Mark. "He had pouted the whole evening and interrogated me about the presence of Brad and Jesse at my house on Saturday morning. Usually, I wouldn't go out on Sunday night, and I have decided to stick to that rule, at least with regard to Mark," I offered. I wasn't going to mention the small detail of Brad being at the restaurant.

Jenna raised her eyebrows. "Okay...so any sparks? You came to pick up Braeden awfully early, and you were awfully quiet. I thought you would at least go back to his place and get laid first?" she teased.

I chuckled. "I just don't feel that way about Mark."

"What is there to feel? It's just sex, Laney," Jenna said.

"I just can't—" I started to tell her that I just couldn't do it. She was looking at me quizzically, waiting for me to finish my sentence. "I still can't believe that Brad is going to be my neighbor. It is such a weird coincidence."

"Nice subject change, Masterson. Coincidence? You're kidding me, Laney Masterson. He just happened to buy the parcel of land next to yours that wasn't even listed for sale in one of the smallest towns in Virginia?" She gave me a doubting look. "Oh, and by the way, come jogging up your driveway to get a drink of water this weekend?"

"I know, right? It was terrible. When he and the other guy—uh, Jesse—came up my driveway, I looked like some bush woman with dirt on my face and leaves in my hair. And as they were introducing themselves, Mark was dropping off Braeden, so Mark had a caveman moment with Brad. I felt totally embarrassed for him."

Jenna tilted her head and raised her eyebrows. "Did Mark beat on his chest and try to drag you off by your hair?" she asked.

I pursed my lips. "A few more minutes, and he probably would have," I said, raising my eyebrows at her. Jenna narrowed her eyes and looked at me suspiciously.

"Okay...so no sparks with Mark, but with Mr. Flaming Hot and Handsome, there is something. You were more than excited for your Sunday-morning walk and glowing upon your return." She nudged me.

I blushed. "I never read those situations right," I offered, remembering the rejection of him walking away from me years ago.

Jenna's face softened, and she walked around my desk to give me a sideways hug. "I know it's hard, Laney. Sam was a great guy. When it's the right time, honey, you'll know." Jenna knew what she was talking about. She had her fair share of heartache too. Her "baby daddy," as she liked to call him, was killed in a motorcycle accident a few months after Josh was born.

"So you never told me...how was your date Friday night with the latest bad boy?" I asked, knowing this should be a colorful discussion. Jenna liked bad boys.

She let an evil grin slip. "As usual, it was hot, wild, sexy, and totally something I would not ever be able to sustain."

Both of us laughed.

"I will probably see him for the sex, but he's not the marrying type. How about you? When are you and Mark—uh, er, I mean Brad going to do the horizontal dance? Laney, you really need to get laid. It would help with all the stress in your life. By the way, Mark looks really hot at the football field in his police uniform. Just once might not hurt anything, while you're figuring out Mr. Flamethrower."

How does Jenna always turn the conversation back to me? I shot her a smirk. "How are you always so horny? Besides, I think it adds stress, not takes it away. I will admit, however, he does look good, but I am just going to let things progress, or not, at a good pace. I am not going to rush into anything, Jenna Ford."

Jenna winked at me with a huge grin. "So I will move some of your appointments today so that you can work on Slade's report—oh yeah! I want you to go with me today at lunch to go lingerie shopping. I need to keep my ten-night stand interested," she said, winking at me.

All I could do was shake my head. "Yes, please move my meetings. And what else would I rather do on my lunch hour than go shopping for five threads sewn together to arouse your soon-to-be eleven-night-stand man?" My logical mind was now poking my inner sex kitten with a stick.

Jenna laughed. "That's why you love me, Laney. I keep life interesting. You need to get some of your own for Mr. Flame or Mr. Police Officer. Ooooh, maybe he will use his handcuffs—that would be hot."

I could see Blake Hinkler, our CFO, approaching my doorway for our meeting. I had to interrupt her so he wouldn't hear our extremely inappropriate and unprofessional conversation.

"Let me know if you have any trouble moving the meetings," I interrupted.

Jenna immediately understood. She nodded and shot me a grateful look as she exited my office.

Listening to Blake's soft-spoken voice go on and on about sales, profit margin, labor costs, and other financial information almost lulled me to sleep. I detested budgeting season. Do more with less seemed to be the mantra in every meeting nowadays. I started to zone back in as I heard him wrapping up his thoughts.

"—so I will e-mail this spreadsheet, if you can input your budgetary needs for the upcoming year?" he asked.

I gave him my best smile. "Sure thing, Blake. When do you need this by?"

Blake was all business. Deep down, I know he has a sense of humor, but it did not show itself very often.

"By end of business on Friday would be superb," he said flatly as I typed this information into my calendar.

"I'll make sure that I run this by Slade before turning it into you," I said as I looked up at Blake from behind my monitor.

Blake exhaled loudly and nodded, clearly frustrated with Slade. "Thanks, Laney," Blake said, nodding appreciatively. No one liked working with Slade, especially Blake. Slade was always good for talking about sports scores and stats in the middle of a talent-calibration meeting, but facts and figures were not to his liking. When Blake opened my door to leave to exit, Jenna was waiting to come in again.

"Are you ready to go?" she asked as she breezed past Blake.

I nodded. "Let me just send this e-mail." My fingers furiously sped over my keyboard. "Okay, I am ready. I will drive?" I asked, grabbing my purse.

Jenna and I drove to the mall. It felt so good to just be a girl sometimes. We made our way into the mall and found the high-end lingerie store.

"Jenna, I feel so stupid going in here. I don't need anything. My cotton ones suit me just fine," I protested.

Jenna hooked her arm into mine. "Let's go, lame-o. We need to find something to match handcuffs or running shoes."

We both giggled like schoolgirls. I spent the first fifteen minutes walking around feeling the silky fabrics and tracing my fingers over the lace. A part deep inside me stirred and remembered wearing such beautiful undergarments. They had every color and pattern combination a person could ever want. I ended up buying some beautiful thongs, lace camisoles, bras, and sexy everyday panties. The stuff Jenna bought looked more like torture devices. I kept trying to rationalize in my mind that it was good to do this for myself. Score one for sex kitten.

Looking back, I used to buy all sorts of lingerie for Sam; he loved lingerie. I really didn't have a reason to since he died. We completed our purchases and headed back to the office. While driving back, my phone rang through the speakers of my car. I gave Jenna a glance. Jenna nodded, knowing she needed to be a quiet observer.

"Laney Masterson," I answered.

"Hi, Laney. This is Paul." Paul Henderson was one of Mendelson's corporate attorneys. These conversations were always interesting.

"Hi, Paul, how is Mendelson's legal world today?"

"Well, I received notification of a lawsuit by a firm that represents a gentleman that claims we unlawfully terminated him due to his workplace injury. He also stated that you and his site leader are out to get him," his loud, deep voice blasted.

I sighed. "I will send you all of our documentation when I get back to the office."

"Sounds good, Laney. We'll talk later." Paul hung up.

After our triumphant return from the lunch excursion, the day went fast as I feverishly compiled the requested report, and a grateful Slade stopped in at the end of the day. He owed me—as usual. He perused the report like a monkey trying to read a book.

"Phenomenal work again. Laney, you're a lifesaver."

I looked up at him from my computer screen. "Thanks, Slade. Are you okay to present the information, or would you still prefer that I present?"

Slade gave me a sheepish grin with a shrug of his shoulders. I knew what was coming.

"Well, tonight is poker night with the guys, so I will probably be in late tomorrow morning. If anything comes up, call me. I should at least be awake," he offered.

Before I would get frustrated at his immaturity, I had unfortunately grown used to it.

"Okay, sounds good. I am about to head out. Anything else you need?" I asked, shutting down my computer.

Slade thought for a moment. "I think we are good. Have a good night, Laney. See you tomorrow!" he said as he stood up and exited my office. I collected my laptop bag and purse; then I closed my office door and said goodbye to Jenna. I made my way to the parking garage, climbed in my car, and headed for home.

I actually left the office at 4:30 p.m., which meant today I would actually get to pick up Braeden from the babysitter's and take him to football practice. I truly enjoyed watching Braeden play football. It allowed me to reflect on my day and count my blessings, the biggest one practicing on the field in front of me. I picked up Braeden from the sitter's and headed over to the practice field. We stood behind my car, and I helped Braeden get his shoulder pads on. Then we walked over to the practice field, and I set my folding chair on the sideline with some of the other parents. I sank into my chair and allowed myself to get lost in watching Braeden practicing kicking the ball.

"Thanks for coming out with me last night."

The voice startled me out of my trance. I realized Mark was approaching from behind me. His newfound obsession with filling in all of my free time with his presence was beginning to feel suffocating, and this was only day two. I actually found it was odd that Mark was even at practice. I thought he was working the next two weeks straight. When I looked at him, he was in his uniform. I had to admit, Jenna was right: he did look good. Mark was walking testosterone. He was handsome with his light-brown hair, light-blue eyes, and tan skin. He was average height, slightly taller than me, and completely muscled up. I knew he spent hours in the gym and talked incessantly about the new supplements that he was taking. Even though he never said as such, it would not have surprised me if he was taking steroids. Most women would swoon at the sight of his handsome face and tall muscular body, but there was something about him that gave me an uneasy feeling. It was a mystery to me. He had been nothing but sweet and kind to me, but I had seen glimpses of his temper and possessive side these last few days, which was extremely off-putting. Thinking back, Mark and I started to talk because he knew the pain of losing a spouse as well; only, his wife had left him for another man. Sometimes football practices would get very interesting when his beautiful blonde ex would show up with her man of the week.

"You're welcome," I said, not wanting to say more.

He drew in close, leaning over me. This was too close for me; it was intimidating.

"Maybe next time you'll invite me in, see where this might go, you know?" He gave me a devilish grin while tracing my chin with his index finger. Then to my surprise, he kissed my lips. As soon as Mark's lips made contact, Brad's face flashed in my mind. My stomach squeezed, and my flesh screamed. I didn't like this at all; this felt wrong. I pulled away, half-hoping he hadn't noticed that I tensed up. I began to feel light-headed and confused.

"I'm sorry, I need to go slow. Give me time to process. All of this confuses me," I said and immediately felt vulnerable, wishing I hadn't shared that with him.

He shrugged and pursed his lips. "It's okay, Laney. I will accept a rain check, no problem," he said, trying to conceal his wounded ego.

Rain check. Brad owed me one of those, which I was looking forward to collecting on. *This* rain check, not so much. The contrast between the two men was amazing.

Much to my relief, the coach blew the whistle, signifying the end of football practice. Braeden ran toward me with a huge smile, hanging on to his helmet by the face mask. I stood and collected my folding chair. I began the trek toward the car, Braeden at my side. Mark and Lucas fell into step with Braeden and me.

I jumped slightly as Mark's large fingers interlaced with mine. I hated the contact. He leaned in slightly.

"How about I keep you company tonight? Lucas is going to be staying at his grandmother's house, and I know a certain two people that could use some fun," he said in a low, seductive tone.

I had a feeling this was coming. There wasn't a time when we were together when he wouldn't try to push my physical-affection boundaries.

"I have an early-morning briefing with the board of directors that I need to be well rested for. Besides, I have Braeden...I wouldn't feel right about it,." I said, unlacing my fingers from his, hoping this would end the conversation.

"Okay…but, Laney, you are always going to have Braeden. It wouldn't make you a bad mother," Mark offered defensively as he gave me a dejected look. In reality, this was our typical exchange. He would ask or try, I would reject, and he would get his feelings hurt. We reached my car, thank goodness.

"Maybe some other time," I offered.

"Sure." He managed half a smile.

Jenna's words were playing in my head, and she was right: I need to get back out there and quit acting like a hermit and lock myself away all the time. I had a perfectly great guy in front of me that was actually interested in me, and I kept pushing him away. What was I waiting for? What was my hesitation? Why was I taking sex so seriously?

"Have a good night, Mark," I said, smiling.

His expression softened as he offered me a smile and a wink. I climbed into the car, made sure Braeden was buckled, and pulled out of the parking lot.

It was only a five-minute drive home from the football field. I loved every minute of driving through my small coastal town. There were docks, marshes, and views of the river or bay everywhere you looked. Sam and I had fallen in love with our old house on the river, or "rivah," as most locals would say. Where our house was, the freshwater from the river meets the saltwater from the bay. The smell of the salt in the air seemed to go straight to my soul and cleanse me on even my most stressful days.

When Sam and I purchased the property, the house had fallen into disrepair. Bit by bit, he and I worked to remodel the entire place, trying to maintain most of the original character and charm as possible. I think Sam was just glad I had a project to keep me busy while he was at the office for long hours. Luckily, we had finished the renovation project before Braeden came along. I felt at ease as I pulled into the top of my gravel driveway, looking at my two-story 1900s white farmhouse with black shutters and huge wraparound porch

YOU ARE THE REASON

that was screened in on the back. It looked the same as I had left it this morning.

At Braeden's request, I bought hammock swings for my front and back porches earlier this year; it had definitely become my favorite late-night hangout either before bed or whenever I couldn't sleep. Looking at the house from the street, a view of the water peeked out beyond the house and the detached garage with a breezeway connecting it to the house. The water made the perfect backdrop to come home to. There was a small sandy beach at the water's edge that Braeden and I liked to play in when we couldn't go down to our Outer Banks beach house.

When we arrived home, I got out of the car to check the mail. After I collected the mail, I traveled down the long gravel driveway and put my car into park. Braeden was immediately out of the car and running up the steps of the porch. It was twilight, one of my favorite times of day. I stepped out of the car and let the feeling of being home wash over me—the summer chorus of frogs and crickets mixed with the distant sound of the waves lapping on the shore and the smell of the salt in the air.

I called after Braeden, "Buddy, can you please put your dirty clothes in the laundry room and then go ahead and hop in the shower?"

"Yes, Mommy," he said in an unenthused tone.

I walked inside the house and deposited my purse and laptop bag on a dining-room chair, removing my cell phone from my purse before setting it down. I checked my phone: six missed calls, zero text messages. I scanned my call log: two missed calls from Mark, one was from my mother, one from Jack Mendelson, the CEO, one from Slade, and one from Jenna. I was slightly disappointed there was nothing from Brad. Who was I kidding? I am sure he was busy with his job and didn't have time to think about me. I proceeded to return my calls; Jack first, of course.

"Jack Mendelson."

"Hi, Jack, it's Laney. I am sorry it is so late—" I started.

Jack's voice was always calm even when he was angry. "Nonsense. I just wanted to make sure you were ready for the briefing tomorrow?"

This made me smile. No matter how long I had worked for Jack, he always wanted to make sure I was ready. "I am. I submitted my report to your assistant. Thanks for checking on me, Jack. See you tomorrow."

"Have a good night, Laney," his exhausted voice came back. Next call, Slade.

"Hi, Slade."

"Laney! What a nice surprise," he slurred. This made me smile in spite of myself. I could tell by the amount of slurring in his speech he was drunk and didn't remember calling me. Either poker night was going really well or really bad.

"Just a reminder, I am not going to be there tomorrow morning," he sloshed out. I could hear him try to cover the microphone on his cell phone. He was talking to someone else in the room with him. I could only barely make out his muffled words.

"What type of sssshhhhit is that?" he said enthusiastically to this unknown person.

I had to choke down my giggle. "Slade, I spoke with Jack. It will be okay," I offered.

"You're right, Laney. You're always right, it will be okay…it will be reeeeaaally okay, like always," he said.

Thank goodness he couldn't see my eye roll.

"I know, Slade. Have a good evening. I will talk to you tomorrow."

"Good night, Laney," he slurred as we ended the call. I was not going to even try to call my mom. Anything after 7:00 p.m. carried a risk of waking her. I saved the best for last; Jenna answered and immediately began speaking.

"Hey, girlie, do you think if I wear a miniskirt, heels, and a low-cut shirt for the board of directors, I can land one of them? You know, finally have the sugar daddy I have always wanted," she teased.

I laughed. "Probably, Jenna. These are a bunch of old stodgy men that would probably appreciate your efforts but might not be able to keep up with you. That's the only reason why you aren't going to be in the meeting," I teased, and she laughed.

"So you ready for the briefing tomorrow right? Is there anything you need from me?" Per usual, Jenna was always looking out for me.

"Yes, I am ready. You have already done your part, thank you. I'll see you in the morning," I said as I laughed.

"See ya!" she chirped.

I was definitely not going to call Mark back. I just saw the man for goodness sake. Besides, if he asked why I didn't call him back, I would him the truth—I was just too tired.

With my calls complete, I shut off all the lights downstairs with only the warm glow of a small decorative lamp in the corner of the counter underneath the kitchen cabinets. I made my way up the stairs. When I reached the top of the stairs, I took in the familiar tan-painted walls with black-framed family photos on the walls. It had become almost a nightly ritual for me to look at the family pictures on the wall as I walked down the hall to Braeden's room from the stairwell. I looked to my left and see an open door into a room next to the stairs that acted as my office and guestroom. Continuing down the hall, I peeked into the hall bathroom on the left, scanning the room briefly, making out some of Braeden's dirty clothes on the floor by the glow of the nightlight. I quietly collected his dirty clothes and put them in the hamper. I walked across the hall and shut off the light in the guestroom, where Braeden sometimes liked to play, and continued to Braeden's bedroom, the last door on the left. I helped Braeden into bed. We said our prayers; then I kissed him good night and turned off the light.

As I walk into my room at the end of the hall, I went through a list of my tasks for tomorrow in my head. Specifically, I reminded myself that Lizzie Bushner, Braeden's babysitter, would be over extra early in the morning so I could go to work early for the meeting. As I changed out of my khakis, blouse, bra, and flats, I stopped briefly to look at my naked self in the mirror. My skin was tan with very strange tan lines from sunbathing out back and at the beach in different styles of swimwear and also my tank tops from yard work. My body shape was a true figure 8. I tilted my head to the side as I placed my palms on my chest above my breasts and slid my skin up just a bit. It made my breasts perkier. Then I released, and they fell back to their original lower position. My stomach was softer after having Braeden, yet still flat, my hips curved back out from my narrowed waist. My thighs were thick both with muscle and a little extra fat.

My eyes moved to my arms, still toned but a little softer than in my younger days. I played volleyball in high school and college, but I hadn't made much time for working out lately. My eyes caught the few small stretch marks on my hips and belly from growing my son. I exhaled. I felt overwhelmed by the thought of anyone seeing me naked. I had enough mirror time.

I walked over to one of Sam's dresser drawers and pulled out one of Sam's old T-shirts, slipped it on, then tucked myself into bed. I fell into a fitful sleep; I hadn't slept well since after Sam died. My pattern was to usually wake up after a couple hours and then toss and turn the rest of the night. I couldn't even remember the last time I actually slept through the entire night.

That night, I tossed and turned in my bed as I dreamed vividly. I could see myself in clothes from a different era—medieval times, it appeared. I was looking up a hill at the perfect silhouette of a knight on a horse. I could feel the breeze blowing my long blonde hair and tousling my dress. I instinctively knew I was going to see this knight off before he went into battle. I knew I shouldn't be there, but I couldn't help it; I had to say goodbye.

As I reached the top of this hill, facing this knight, the face was unrecognizable, but the energy was familiar. This was my love. He pulled me up onto his horse, and I kissed him.

"You shouldn't have come here," he said to me in a low tone.

"But I needed to see you before you left," I said to him.

"You know I'll always come back to you. Will you wait for me?" he asked.

"Of course, I will. You are my heart," I said.

He gently lowered me to the ground. He began to make his way down a dirt path. When he turned around to give me a wave, it was Brad. It didn't physically look like him, but it was him; I was sure of it. My heart began to flutter.

My eyes flew open, and I sat straight up in my bed. I was looking around my room, taking everything in. The dream had seemed so real. I glanced at my cell phone and then lay back down, taking deep breaths to calm the speed of my heart rate.

I had this dream at least once a week, and this was the third time this week. This dream and my lack of sleep was now beginning to affect my ability to concentrate at work. I glanced at my phone before picking it up. I pulled up my e-mail app and typed out an e-mail to my friend Carrie, a hypnotherapist. I really didn't believe in things like that, but I was desperate.

Chapter 21

I AWOKE TO THE SOUND of the radio from my alarm at four o'clock the next morning, trying to find the off switch to stop the radio, which was screaming "Teenage Wasteland" from the speakers. I found the switch. I sleepily swung my legs over the side of the bed and stood up. Then I shuffled to my master bathroom, one of the first renovation projects. We installed a huge soaker tub, double vanity, and two-person shower with showerheads everywhere. I walked into my huge two-person tile, stone, and glass shower and began to wash myself. Ugh. This was going to be the worst part. I always dreaded stepping out into the cold air after a nice hot shower. I braved the cold air—my towel did little to offer much warmth—and walked into my closet. I picked out my dark-gray suit and found a white camisole to go under it. I applied light makeup, eyeliner, mascara, eyeshadow, etc. and held my black spike heels in my hand as I crept down the stairs, trying not to make a sound as to wake Braeden. It was 4:45 a.m. Lizzie would be here at 5:00 a.m. I made myself the usual breakfast of a cup of tea and microwaved a few pieces of bacon. I heard a soft knock on the door. It was Lizzie. She was one of the bubbliest people that I had ever met, even at 5:00 a.m. Lizzie was a godsend after Sam died, she helped to keep both my and Braeden's spirits up in addition to our sanity. Lizzie's flexibility was also much appreciated, including these early-morning hours, and I made sure to pay her well for it. Without her, I really had little support for helping with Braeden during my work hours.

When I opened the door, Lizzie gave me a huge smile and a hug. "Hi, honey!" Lizzie whispered. When she leaned back from me, she held out a note motioning for me to take it. I noticed that Lizzie's smile was mixed with some concern around the corners of her eyes, a very unusual look for Lizzie. "As I was walking up to the door, I found this tucked in the screen door," she said in a tone much too serious for Lizzie.

I proceeded to unfold the piece of regular copy paper that had been folded in half. She rolled her eyes when I read the words inside under my breath:

> Laney,
> I can't wait to see you again.
> Love, Mark

I rolled my eyes and shook my head. "If I don't call him back, he does something like this," I said to myself as much as to Lizzie's benefit.

Lizzie looked at me sideways and squinted her eyes. "Do you really like him, Laney? He gives me the creeps. He is always watching you whenever we are at the football field and could probably be a certified stalker with how often I seem him drive by your house," Lizzie offered.

I slightly chuckled at her comments, wanting to believe that Mark wasn't as bad as she was saying. "He isn't a stalker, just a little insecure, emotionally confused, and a police officer. His wife left him, remember? I am sure he is just still a little mixed up. He'll come out of it," I lightly admonished, half-trying to convince myself.

Now Lizzie shook her head and rolled her eyes, still disapproving. "Whatever you say, Laney...do I need to take Brae to football this afternoon?" she asked with a huge smile.

"Hopefully not. This week doesn't look too bad for me, but I will call you when I leave." I sighed as I put my laptop bag and purse over my shoulder. Then I opened the front door and took in a deep breath of the salt air as I made my way to my car.

"Have a great day, Laney. See you this afternoon!" Lizzie called out in a loud whisper to me from the front porch. As I climbed into my car, I gave her a little wave. I then proceeded to check my phone, hopeful that Carrie had responded at this early hour. I was excited to see Carrie's response.

Laney—

It's great to hear from you! I would love to see if I can help. Today at 11?

I took a deep breath and responded.

Sounds great, see you then.

When I arrived to the office at 5:30 a.m., it was quiet on the first floor as I walked through the spacious lobby of large marble tiles and glass. The receptionist greeted me, "Good morning, Ms. Masterson."

I really needed to remember her name. "Good morning," I said as my heels clicked on the floor and echoed against the walls as I headed toward the stairwell. When I arrived to the eighth floor, everything was in chaos. People were hurriedly scurrying between offices, and I could hear voices from a very heated meeting taking place in the war room, completely opposite of the serenity I experienced only moments before. As I made my way through the glass doors, I looked over to Jenna's desk outside my office to find her crying; I gave her a confused look. I could hear Blake almost shouting on a phone call. For a moment, I thought maybe I was still dreaming and needed to wake up.

"What is wrong? What is going on? Why are you crying?" I leaned down and whispered.

Jenna opened her mouth to speak, but then she flicked her eyes in Slade's direction, who was, at the moment, pacing back and forth and running his fingers through his auburn hair. He looked like he hadn't slept much and didn't look like he had sobered up enough. His face came alive when he saw me. "Laney, there you are!"

"I didn't think the meeting started until seven, and you aren't supposed to be here...what is going on?" I asked.

No one was giving me an answer as to what was going on. I pulled my office keys from my purse, unlocked the door to my office, stepped inside, and deposited my belongings on my desk. Slade followed me in and shut the door behind him. I could smell the liquor coming from his pores even being across the room from him.

"Laney, we are being bought out by Halifax Corporation," he started anxiously and then stopped when he heard a controlled tapping on the door.

As my door opened, I could see it was Jack Mendelson, CEO of Mendelson. He was approaching seventy, but he still had an imposing figure, and his calm yet serious demeanor demanded compliance.

"Slade, if you will excuse us?" Jack said calmly. Slade nodded and then rushed out the door, closing it behind him.

"How are you, Laney? You look like you haven't been sleeping well," he said to me with genuine concern.

I chuckled, just what every woman wanted to hear. "Thanks, Jack. I am doing well, I think. These early-morning meetings don't help, and you don't look so good yourself," I said through my laughter.

Jack's face gave up a tired smile. His blue eyes seemed distant. "I have always loved to hear you laugh. We are going to need that these upcoming weeks," he said, his voice still steady.

I clamped my lips together and then flicked my eyes back to him. "You aren't here to lecture me about my sleeping habits, Jack. What's up?" I asked.

He looked at me, sadness tugging at the corners of his already deeply wrinkled eyes. "Laney, we are being bought out by Halifax Corporation. I know your situation, so I wanted to tell you first before someone else did. Obviously, I will be retiring, but you should know that they already have an executive team. In situations like this, they will most likely favor their own, end result being job cuts or demotions for our team. With your skill and reputation, I know you will easily get another job, but you may want to start looking," he said, monitoring my reaction.

Everything inside me froze. I hadn't ever considered leaving Mendelson, and now I was going to be out of a job.

Jack continued, "Everything happens for a reason. This may be the perfect time for a change, but you need to take care of yourself and your son. If you want time off to interview elsewhere, take as much as you need. I will also see to it that you receive a generous severance package if it comes down to that," he said, patting my arm.

I felt the floor falling away from me; my knees felt weak. *How will I support my son? How will I pay for insurance, my mortgage, my car payment, my bills?* I was starting to get a headache.

Then he continued, "I know you have a lot to deal with, but I need your help now more than ever. I have a concern for our employees. I want you to put together a business case and work with legal for an agreement with Halifax to keep them for some period of time postpurchase. Halifax's CEO is extremely sharp and also ruthless. He is a details guy, so make sure your data is flawless. We will need to be prepared to fight him for this. Our employees have been good to us. It is the least I can do for them," he said softly.

"Of course, Jack. I will get started right away. Thank you for telling me. I am glad this news came from you," I said, hooking my arm into his, and we walked over to the wall of windows behind my desk.

Staring out the window at the traffic and bustling people on the city street below, he said, "Laney, I want you to attend the meeting when we negotiate with Halifax. When the chips are down, you are my go-to person." At that, both of us let out a chuckle, silently understanding Slade's shortcomings without breathing a word of them.

"Of course I will." I paused. "Are you going to be okay, Jack?" I asked.

He turned to face me. "I will be fine when this is all over. It is hard to see the company that I built from the bottom up being dissected, sold, and transformed," he said with agitation. I knew Jack had never had children; this business had been the child that he loved and cared for. Jack hugged me. "Laney, I am glad you have been along for the ride. I don't know what we would have done without you," he said, both of us still staring out the window.

My heart felt like bursting. I smiled, tears welling up in my eyes. This was too real. How could this be happening?

"I know exactly what would have happened. You would probably have all females with blonde hair and big boobs working for you if it was left up to Slade," I said dryly.

Jack gave a hearty laugh and patted my arm before he released it. "Halifax's executive team will be flying in by corporate jet tomorrow. Why don't you talk to legal and then go home and rest. I am not sure what the future will look like, Laney." He hadn't even had to say it; I knew that was true.

With this new piece of news, the meeting with the board of directors was cancelled. I sat down at my computer and brought up Google. I typed in "Halifax Corporation" in the search bar. I briefly scrolled down to look at the news articles. They were a very active company, buying, dismembering and selling off unprofitable pieces of the business for a profit. They had already demolished a lot of smaller companies and competitors. From what I could gather, their stock prices had risen steadily since the new CEO took the helm. It was actually quite impressive. I was searching their webpage and was about to click on the photos of the executive team when my office neighbor Julia, the benefits director, came in.

I smiled, looking at the latest fashion creation she had managed to put together for herself. Today it was knee-high riding boots with a plaid dress from the 1980's, gold buttons down the front with complimentary shoulder pads. She wore thick dark-rimmed glasses with a short bob that didn't compliment the angles of her face. She had the potential to be quite attractive if she would just make a few changes. Jenna and I had mused that we thought about nominating her for one of those makeover shows.

"Hi, Julia," I said as I quickly closed the webpage.

"Hey, Laney…so you heard?" she said flatly. I don't think in the six years I had worked with Julia that I had ever heard any inflection of emotion in her monotone voice. She never seemed to be happy or excited about anything.

"I did. What do you think?"

"Just another moneymaking scheme for the bigwigs. They always make out like gangbusters. I am sure Jack is making a killing on this deal," she said, unable to hide her resentment. She was a bitter woman anyway as she was married to Blake at one point in time. Her bitterness was accelerated when he divorced her and married a much younger woman. From what I understand, she didn't do well in the divorce settlement. She also put in for my job when it came open, but Jack picked me instead. She was awesome with data but terrible with people.

"Well, we knew we had too much cash on hand. We were ripe for this," I offered.

"I guess. I heard the CEO is a real jerk, and the rest of his executive team follows suit. I also heard that he can't keep an HR team. He runs them off if they don't agree with him. He's got that bimbo Veronica, whatever her name is now. I guess she helps to manage his...temper, if ya know what I mean?" she said, rolling her eyes. It was true; Veronica Whitley was infamous for her salacious appetite for successful men.

"This should be interesting," I said with raised eyebrows. It was all I could offer at the moment as I was not interested in continuing this conversation with her. She offered the best smile she could manage and turned to leave. She was always such a ray of sunshine. I undocked my computer to meet with Paul and the legal team in the war room.

The meeting with Paul and the rest of the legal team hadn't taken long at all. Paul asked me to stay after. I could tell he wanted to say something, but he was being his typical stoic self. I spent a long awkward moment looking at him with my most friendly look, pretending this wasn't odd at all.

"Hey, Laney...," he finally said.

"Yes, Paul?"

"It's been really great to work with you over the years. I would be more than happy to be a professional reference for you, should you need it," he said genuinely.

I was surprised that he was so sure that I was leaving. But I knew his comments were thoughtful, and my brain did a quick flashback to our time together. Paul was my battle buddy. We had faced a lot of adversity together, lost, and won a lot of battles. Paul was mild mannered and soft-spoken, unless he was on the phone. He wasn't a typical attorney. He detested wearing suits, and when he had to wear one to the office, he wore a Hawaiian shirt instead of a dress shirt. He had even been known to throw a pair of sandals into the mix. His voice reminded me of late-night radio station DJs that played smooth jazz or took requests for love songs all evening.

"Thanks, Paul. If there is anything I can do for you as well, don't hesitate to ask," I said with a smile. I gave him a hug and then returned to my office. I found Jenna sitting in the chair across from my desk. I walked over and leaned on my desk, facing Jenna. She had a thousand-yard stare and tears welling up in her eyes.

"Laney, what am I going to do? I have a mortgage, I need insurance—what am I going to do? I will be on the street. I can't do that to Josh...what kind of mother would I be?"

I reached for her hand and squeezed it. "We'll figure it out, Jenna. Don't panic on me now. We still have a lot of work to do, and no decisions have been made yet," I offered.

She squeezed my hand and looked full up into my face then started nodding. "You're right Laney. We can do this," she said, sniffing.

After I finished my meeting with Jenna, it was 10:30 a.m. I made the short fifteen-minute drive downtown to Carrie's office in an old Brownstone. I rang the buzzer and saw Carrie make her way down the stairs to open the old wooden door. She smiled warmly at me.

"Laney, it's so wonderful to see you," Carrie said, pulling me into a hug.

"You too," I managed to say.

"Please, come in," she offered, holding the door open to me. We made our way up the stairs to small cozy office. Complete with salt lamps, crystal bowls, and candles. She motioned for me to sit in a reclining chair in the corner. I sat down.

"Okay, so tell me, what I can help you with today?"

"I am having this recurring dream, and I want to know more about it. I can't ever go back to sleep."

"Hmmmm, it sounds like a past-life issue."

"Excuse me, a past life?" I asked skeptically.

"Yes, we reincarnate here many times to learn lessons or for specific missions. Earth is like a school, if you will."

"How does my dream fit into that?"

"Sometimes, when we have lived a particularly traumatic past life, something needs to be remembered so it can heal and we can move forward. This can manifest as dreams, physical ailments, mental issues, etc."

"I see. So how do we address this?"

"So I will help put you in a deep meditative state. You are in control the entire time," she said.

I took a deep breath. "Okay, let's do this," I said.

"Okay, lie back and close your eyes. I want you to picture yourself in a beautiful garden. As we go find our seat on a bench in this garden, I will count backward from ten. Are you ready?"

"Yes," I said, beginning to relax.

"Ten…nine…eight…seven…"

The last thing I heard Carrie ask me was, "Where are you?"

"I am at my family's home. I have a mother with long brown hair, a father, three sisters, and a younger brother." I drifted into the dream I often would remember pieces of, but this time, I could fast-forward to different parts.

"Laney, Laney?" I heard a woman's voice say.

I came to from my hypnotic state.

"That was amazing!" Carrie squealed.

"Was it? What was?" I asked, still a bit disoriented.

"That past-life recall!"

"What?"

"That was quite a life you lived in France. I'm blown away, Laney, or should I say Annalise?" Carrie said, winking at me.

"It was so real," I said, lost in thought. "Liam…," I said softly under my breath.

"It's over now, Laney," Carrie said softly as I blinked, my eyes adjusting to the light.

"Is it?" I asked.

"Of course, it is."

"It doesn't seem over."

"It may take a while for things to dissipate, but let me know you're okay after a bit."

"Thanks, Carrie, How much do I owe you?"

"A hundred twenty dollars this time."

"Here you go. Thank you for the hypnosis session. That was surreal," I said, still in disbelief.

"Are you going to be okay?" Carrie asked with concern as she slid my debit card through the machine.

"Yea, I think so," I said, checking my watch; two hours had gone by.

"Okay…well, call if you don't feel better. Hopefully, that helps with your sleep," she said, eyeing me thoughtfully.

"Thank you," I said, taking my card from her and exiting Carrie's office.

I wandered in somewhat of a daze to my car. As soon as I made it to my car, I started to cry. All the loss, all the tragedy, all the love. That wasn't just a dream. It was as though I was remembering a memory that really happened hundreds of years ago. I cried until all the emotion drained out of me. I mourned my life, the family I lost, my love. I drove home in a daze. I didn't want to check my cell phone; I just wanted to be alone with my thoughts. I knew my son's bus would be arriving soon. I had to get myself together, but how could I forget their faces? The sensations were so real. I wished I could go back and save them, correct the past to let the love and light spread, defeat the darkness and set their souls free.

I decided to spend this beautiful sunny afternoon working outside in the yard, one of my favorite things to do to clear my mind. I texted Jenna and Slade, letting them know I wouldn't be back to the office. Then I called Lizzie on the way home to let her know that she could have the afternoon off, and I would be getting Braeden off the bus. I just needed get my mind off today's news at work and my session with Carrie. I arrived home. I looked at my house, wondering how long I could last without a job. I would definitely need to watch my spending closely from here on out. I checked the clock on my phone; I had two hours until Braeden would be getting off the school bus. I had already changed into my yard clothes. As I was standing in front of my porch daydreaming about pulling the regenerated weeds that had sprouted up between my azaleas, my phone buzzed and stirred me from my daze. I looked at the number on the display and hit the green button.

"Hi, Mom."

"Hello, baby girl, how are you doing honey?"

Since retiring from her nursing job, she had become so perky, and she also adopted the hobby of listening to self-help tapes constantly, which meant that I always got a lecture when she liked a particular lesson.

"I am fine, Mom, just taking the afternoon off to do some gardening." I couldn't tell her about my job yet; she would worry and drive me crazy.

"Oh, how lovely. You need some sunshine, and you may want to rest too. You are working yourself to death."

I must look downright awful. Everyone is telling me to rest. I opened my mouth to respond, but then I thought I saw something move out of the corner of my eye.

"Ummm, Mom, hold on a second." My heart started to race as I scanned the front yard, looking for any sign of movement.

I could hear my mother's squawking on the phone. "Laney! Laney! What is going on!"

"I am fine, Mom. Just thought I saw something out of the corner of my eye."

"Laney, what is going on?" she snapped.

"Nothing, Mom. Everything is fine. Just seeing ghosts out of the corner of my eye."

My mom continued her lecture, "Ya know, Laney, I burned my bra with the best of them, but I think you need a man to take care of you, honey, and to be an example for Braeden."

I hated this conversation. My mom started pressuring me to date men almost immediately after Sam died so "Braeden wouldn't forget how to be a man." It infuriated me. Even though my mom had been a single mom too, she said it was different because she was raising a girl. Agitated, I cut her off.

"The truth is, Mom, I don't have to have a man in my life to be happy. I like having time to myself and my own personal space. I am fine," I said firmly, but somehow I immediately felt like an adolescent girl.

"Laney, of course, honey, be happy. You deserve happiness. Don't settle for anything less. You have had more than your share of heartache. You deserve better," she said.

I smiled, recognizing the content of her message from an *Oprah* show. "Thanks, Mom. I need to get to these weeds, or I won't finish before Brae gets home."

"Okay, honey, talk to you later."

"I love you, Mom."

"I love you too, sweetheart."

We both hung up. I walked into the house to the kitchen; grabbed a bottle of water, my gardening gloves, and sunglasses; then proceed back out to sit down on the top step of the porch stairs, contemplating what I wanted to tackle first. I closed my eyes and tilted my face to the sun, letting its warmth wash over me.

After a moment, I stood up and walked down the steps; then I turned around and leaned to pick up my gardening gloves, mumbling to myself, "I'll need these to dig in the dirt." A chill ran up my spine, and all of a sudden I felt like I was being watched. I stood straight up, but before I could turn around, a muscular arm grabbed and held me by the waist. I shrieked; the other hand went to cover my mouth.

"I am ready to get dirty with you," a husky male voice said in my ear.

I instantly recognized it as Mark. I elbowed him in his bullet-proof vest. I was pretty sure it hurt me more than it did him. He released me and gave a hearty chuckle. Crap. With the day I am having, I really didn't want to see him today. After he released me, I turned to face him.

"What are you doing here, Mark? Were you lurking around my house a few minutes ago?" I said, trying to steady the tone of my voice.

"Laney, you need to be more careful, especially with how you are dressed," Mark said as he reached to touch the top of my breasts that were peeking out above my tank top. I swatted his hand away. He continued, "You should play nice, Laney. It isn't nice to hit—and I may have been checking out your house to make sure it was safe."

I knew a lecture was coming. Being a police officer made him over the top with all things security and safety related. I always felt uncomfortable being alone with him. His movements were domineering. He had an egotistical air about him, like he wanted me to fall at his feet and worship him.

"Mark, it's safe here, and it's broad daylight, and there is nothing wrong with my yard clothes…and you didn't exactly answer my question. What are you doing here?"

He had a smirk on his face. "Yes, there is. You are showing too much…skin…," he said as he reached to touch my cleavage with his pointed finger again. I swatted his hand away again. He flashed me a sinister smile. "And to answer your question, I was patrolling the neighborhood, and I saw your car. What are you doing here? You didn't get fired, did you?" he said, snickering.

I chuckled, realizing there may be some truth in what he said. "Mark, please stop trying to touch me like that. And to answer *your* question, I am going to be busy at work the next few weeks and wanted to take some time off to myself."

He eyed me warily. "Where is he?" Mark snapped.

"Who?" I asked, totally confused.

"Mr. Rich Breeches—where is he?" Mark's anger was escalating.

"Brad? I don't know?" I offered, confused.

"Is he here?" Mark said, walking toward my front door like he was going in.

"No—and please stay out of my house. Why are you acting like this?"

"You took off the afternoon to spend it with him, didn't you? Where is that asshole hiding?" he asked. "He knows I can kick his ass, doesn't he?" he snarled.

"Whoa, you just need to stop. Brad is an old friend, and he is welcome here anytime. You need to calm down. He is not hiding anywhere," I said calmly, wishing that Brad was actually here—or at least that I had heard from him.

"Did he give it to you the way you wanted it?" he said as a flash of jealousy bolted across his face.

"Don't you ever talk to me that way. I think it's time for you to leave!" I snapped, my jaw tightening.

"Or what? You're going to call the police?" he said, snickering. "I will give you some time and space, but I am not giving up on us. I am a stubborn man, Laney," he said, walking up the steps toward me. He grabbed my hand, pulled me to him hard, then he kissed me. Brad's face flashed in my mind's eye again. I pulled away; this felt wrong.

"Please don't...Mark. I think it is time I get started on my flower beds, and you should get back to your patrol," I said sternly.

His brightly burning eyes looked into mine. "One day, Laney...," he said and then eyed me for another moment longer. It made me feel uneasy. Then he strode down the steps and to his car.

As I watched his police cruiser pull out of my driveway, my irritation began to bubble over. I felt so mad. I was mad at Halifax for buying Mendelson. I was mad at Sam for dying, at Mark for being a jerk, and at Brad for dumping me all those years ago. I screamed and threw my gardening gloves like a child having a tantrum. Something burst within me, and I sat down on the stairs as the tears began to flow. It had been ages since I had cried so much in one afternoon. After a few minutes, I considered how ridiculous I looked. I collected myself and put on my gardening gloves to tackle the task at hand.

A couple of hours later, I finished my weeding. Braeden climbed off the big yellow bus and started running down the driveway with a huge grin. He was so excited to see me. "Mommy!" he yelled. Just looking at him made my heart melt.

"Hi, buddy, did you have a good day at school?"

"Yes, we got to touch a snake today in class, but it wasn't slimy," he rattled off excitedly. We walked into the house together. I gazed at his face while we sat at the counter together while he ate his snack before I had to take him to football practice.

"Braeden, I need to ask you a question," I said.

He looked at me, still chewing his apple slice. "Okay, Mommy."

"It's been just us...you and me, for a while. Would it bother you if mommy started to date a man?" I asked, watching his reaction.

He thought about it for a moment, then looked at me with his big hazel eyes. "Like Mr. Mark?"

"Well, I don't know...maybe someone like him."

"I like when you smile and laugh like you do when we are at the beach house or when Ms. Jenna comes over. Mr. Mark doesn't make you smile or laugh...and he is mean to Lucas."

I hugged him and kissed him on the forehead. He reminded me of Sam more and more every day. "What does he do that is mean to Lucas?"

Braeden sighed. "He yells a lot. I don't like going to his house."

My stomach squeezed. Now I wished I had taken him to football weigh-ins instead of Mark.

"I am glad you told me, honey. You won't have to go with him anymore." I paused and then went on, "You know there is no one who could ever replace you, right?"

He smiled at me. "I know, Mommy. I'm priceless. You tell me all the time."

We both giggled.

During practice, my mind drifted off contemplating my next career move. I would be attending a job fair on behalf of Mendelson soon anyway; maybe I could start networking there? I would need to check the list of attendees to see if I knew anyone. It made my heart hurt. I loved Mendelson. I essentially grew up there. It would be hard to leave, but I would just need to accept it. Maybe a change would be good for me, for us. Maybe life had been too stable the last few years? I noticed that during practice, Mark kept his distance, choosing to flirt with Tracy, another one of the football moms. Everyone knew Tracy's army husband was deployed to Iraq. It made the interaction seem a little sleazier, but Tracy seemed to be enjoying it, throwing her head back and laughing often. I never thought Mark was that funny, but good for Tracy.

That night, my dream was different. Liam met me by the stream where we had performed the red ribbon ceremony and made love for the first time. He said to me, "You didn't wait for me."

I tried to respond, "I did wait for you, but I was taken."

He shook his head. "I came back for you, and you were gone."

I woke up from the dream with a start. I shot up to sitting. I glanced at my clock; it was 1:44 a.m. I lay back down and fell back into a fitful sleep.

Chapter 22

I AWOKE IN THE MORNING to a malaise of emotion. I texted Carrie.

"Have any appointments today?"
"I just had my twelve o'clock cancel, if you are free?"
"Sounds great"
"See you then"

I was in a daze at work, thinking about the dream and how real it felt. I had hardly heard Braeden talking as I dropped him off at school.

To try to help get my focus for my day ahead, I had worn my navy-blue suit and pale-pink camisole. I felt powerful in this suit, like I could take on anything. Halifax's executive team walked in. I instantly recognized Veronica, the CHRO. I had many interactions with her at HR executive group meetings. Veronica was well known in the HR community for sleeping her way to the top. Jack gave me a smile and a wink. He was clearly aware of her reputation, or I wasn't hiding my disdain well.

"Mr. Green is just signing a few things. He will be here in just a moment," their CFO Frank Kaiser announced as everyone took their seats.

The blood froze in my veins. *Mr. Green*? It couldn't be. He said management; he didn't mention he ran a multibillion-dollar global company. I leaned forward casually to see that Brad's back was to the conference room, talking to his assistant. I couldn't believe Brad was the jerk everyone was referring to. He looked delicious dressed in his gray suit. It fit his tall, muscular frame like a glove. I could see that his short dark hair had recently been cut. I felt a familiar jolt of electricity, and the hair on the back of my neck stood up. As he turned around, I recognized him instantly. It was him…my new neighbor…my ex-flame. Now that I saw him from the front, I noted that he looked just as good in his well-tailored suit as he did in athletic shorts. Before I began salivating, I tried to collect my thoughts. I was beginning to feel that it wasn't normal to feel this enraptured in someone's presence.

He seemed to be in his element. He exuded confidence and power. His eyes seemed to glow electric hazel; they were rimmed with dark lashes, seeming to make them stand out all the more. His presence was commanding and intense. Self-control emanated from his being. He seemed so much more serious now, never smiling while he spoke. His eyes scanned the room; he seemed to make mental notes about each person at the table. And then his eyes rested on me. His face was serious and unreadable, not the flirty, affectionate man from the walking trail. But what did I expect? For him to walk in and spank me on the butt? I could barely breathe. I didn't notice that I was holding my breath, my thoughts still racing.

Slade must have noticed my breathing troubles. He leaned in and whispered, "Steady, Laney. You've been to these lame-ass meetings before, no worries."

Brad released his gaze from me and made introductions of Halifax's team. I noted that during Veronica's intro, she winked at Slade. At that moment, I was pretty sure Veronica would chew him up and spit him out for breakfast. Jack then made introductions of Mendelson's team. When he got to me, Brad gave me a penetrating look and nodded after Jack's brief biography. I thought he must find it odd that I was in here with all the executives.

"I know Ms. Masterson…and her top-notch work. She is well known in the industry. You are lucky you were able to hang on to her this long, Jack," Brad said as he maintained my gaze, not breaking a smile.

"Indeed," said Jack, sensing the tension. I felt the blush flood my cheeks, feeling the butterflies that had escaped my stomach now

YOU ARE THE REASON

multiplying in my throat. So I did what I do best in awkward situations: I put on my HR director face and smiled.

"Thank you for the kind words, Mr. Green," I said confidently.

Veronica's jealousy was palpable as she glared at me. I had come to the conclusion that Veronica most likely had achieved her position by sleeping with Brad, judging by her reaction. After completing all the introductions, Brad's eyes fell on me again, and mine on him—he was like a magnet; I needed to look away! I felt the same pull that I felt that day at my house and from all those years ago. I mustered all the self-control I had and broke our gaze once again, looking down to the table. I had to admit that he was even more handsome than I remembered him to be back when I first worked with him. Hs jawline and cheekbones seemed stronger. His face gave up any of its remaining boyish qualities to evolve into the angled face of a man. His larger muscles filled out his well-tailored expensive suit well. He looked rugged yet refined. Jack shot me a bigger smile and winked at me again, seeming to understand what I was thinking.

Frank, sensing the need to move on, said, "Okay, now that introductions are out of the way, let's get down to business."

Two hours later, the meeting had almost come to an end, with the exception of what Jack had asked me to complete before departing yesterday. I had felt Brad's gaze on me throughout the entire meeting. I intentionally focused on my e-mail, not wanting to look at him. I didn't want to seem too interested, like he could text me early on a Sunday morning, and I would spring out of bed to meet him for a make-out session in the park or something?

Frank was about to close the meeting and asked, "Is there any other business we need to discuss?"

I looked at Jack; he nodded at me.

"We need to discuss the matter of Mendelson's manufacturing location employees," I said, looking at Brad. He studied my face and tilted his head slightly, surprised to hear from me.

"What about them, Laney?" Veronica hissed from across the table.

My steely gaze shifted to her. "Well, Veronica, let's not beat around the bush. We all know the reputation that Halifax has for butchering purchased companies and selling their pieces. We are hoping for a different experience and want to ensure our employees are not caught in the crosshairs," I said. My tone was serious; my jaw was tight. I briefly glanced at Brad, who seemed to be amused.

"What are you proposing, Ms. Masterson?" Frank snapped. I had clearly pissed Frank off, typical finance guy.

Brad still said nothing; he was closely monitoring the exchange. I could see that he was contemplating what I had just said.

"We have approximately five thousand employees between all of our manufacturing locations. As we understand it, you will be taking them into Halifax, but we would like to work out an agreement to keep our same locations operational for at least three years postpurchase. I would assume that you don't want to discuss this today. Let's set a time for another day." My voice came out a little louder than I was trying for. Jack gave me a grateful look, nodding his approval. I could feel Brad's eyes staring at me. I believe he was surprised by my forwardness.

Frank spoke up again, "Do you realize the cost that we would have to incur to continue operating your locations as is? That would wreak havoc on our operational efficiencies—" Frank hissed but stopped as Brad raised his hand to silence him.

Brad's eyes were locked on mine, with no expression on his face. He had always been able to control the room regardless of his position. A slight smile was tugging at the corners of my mouth.

"Yes, we will consider it, Ms. Masterson. Let's set a meeting for tomorrow while I am still in town," Brad said, nodding at me.

I heard Veronica exhale loudly. Frank's face turned red, and he clamped his lips together, obviously extremely irritated but not about to argue with Brad. The meeting was dismissed. Brad walked over to me immediately and extended his broad hand to me. His expression was serious but mischievous; a smile tugged at the corners of his mouth. I extended my hand and shook his, my smile matching his, like we were sharing an inside joke. The touch of his hand made my breath hitch. His grip was soft but firm; his skin felt thick yet smooth. He was full of contradictions.

"What a pleasure to have the opportunity to work with you, Mrs. Masterson," he said, studying my face.

Clearly, we were going to play the "I have never met you before" game. I couldn't blame him. I was a peon back when we first worked together, and then he saw me after all these years like some mountain woman with dirt on my face and twigs in my hair. *I bet he was really impressed. Nice one, Masterson.* His proximity to me was intoxicating. The smell of his masculinity and his cologne was a heady mix.

I responded just as serious, "I look forward to working with you as well. And please, call me Laney. Mrs. Masterson was my mother-in-law," I said as I smiled.

He slowly nodded, his eyes lingering on my lips. I all of a sudden felt awkward and exposed. We were surrounded by twenty people, and I had briefly forgotten that all of them were there. Veronica was soon at his side, flipping her short blonde locks behind her shoulder, her shrill, irritating voice piercing my ears.

"Laney, it is good to see you again. How long has it been?" she said, extending her hand out to me. Her tone truly didn't match her beautiful purchased smile and the darts she was shooting with her eyes.

Brad's eyes were still studying me. I could feel my face begin to heat up, blush flooding my cheeks again as I thought to our walk in the woods. I shook her hand.

"Hard to say, Veronica. It's great to see you again as well. I look forward to working with you. If you will please excuse me, I have some work to get back to," I said.

Brad's eyes were focused on mine, and he gave me a nod. I gave him a slight grin and quick nod in return. Still feeling disoriented from our interaction, trying to clear my thoughts, I almost ran smack into Jenna in the hallway.

"Whoa, Laney, are you okay? You look flushed. Was it too hot in there? I told those damn HVAC guys to fix that room's—" She stopped as I started to shake my head. Jenna peeked around me into the boardroom where I had just came from.

"Holy shit, I see why you were flushed," she whispered.

I laughed. "For your information, Ms. Ford, that is my ex-flame that showed up to my house, a.k.a. the CEO of Halifax that is also going to be my new neighbor," I whispered back to her. "I really think I just need some water, and it was a little stuffy in there. Ready to go review our project list?" I asked innocently, returning to my normal business tone.

Jenna shot me a suspicious look. "Holy shit, Laney Masterson, he's hot…and you're in trouble. I was not born yesterday, and yes, as a matter of fact, I am ready to cover my project list. I will go get my info and meet you in your office."

I was shaking my head, smiling. I was about to head in the direction of my office two doors down the hall when I saw out of the corner of my eye that Brad broke away from a group of people from our meeting and came up beside me. His face was intense.

"Laney, if you will be ready tomorrow to discuss Mendelson's employee plan, I will have my assistant set up a meeting." He was all business.

I studied his face as he spoke. "Of course, please have your assistant work with Jenna to fit something into our schedules," I said, trying to sound confident. I gave him a quick smile and then walked away. He was too close; I desperately needed to come up for air. I could also still feel the glare from Veronica on my back, or maybe it was some more of those darts.

Chapter 23

AFTER MY MEETING WITH JENNA was done, I made my way to the parking garage to my car. I maneuvered in a haze to Carrie's office for the second time in two days. I climbed the stairs of the two-story brownstone that had long ago been converted to offices. I pushed open Carrie's office door. She was sitting at her desk in the corner. She rose and crossed the room, arms open wide to sweep me into a hug.

"How are you doing?" she said as she released me and took a long look at my face.

"I'm okay. I want to heal whatever this memory is. I want to set them free to live their life or detach from that life or whatever."

"Okay, let's do it," she said with a smile.

I relaxed into her comfortable reclining chair as she began her hypnosis speech. The last thing I heard her ask was, "If you could rewrite the story of that lifetime, what would it look like?"

I saw Petyr's wagon. I was unsure if he was looking for me. I hid in the woods as I was taught to do as a girl. I knew not to trust Petyr. Once he passed, I waited until I saw Henri's wagon also pass by. When both were well out of sight, I sprinted toward my parents' cottage. When I reached the dusty path, I walked briskly toward the cottage with my basket of flowers in hand. Jacque was playing in the garden as Ma worked, and he was the one who saw me first. He squealed with excitement and came running toward me. Ma looked up with her beautiful smile, grinning ear to ear. She was so excited to see me. It felt like it had been ages since I had seen her. I had missed her. Pa appeared in the doorway of the barn, his grin matching Ma's. It felt good to be home.

"Sissy! You're baaaaack!" Jacque squealed as I set down my flowers, and he ran into my arms. I squeezed him as I lifted him, then planted kisses all over his little plump cheeks. He giggled with joy. I carried him and lifted my basket of flowers. I walked over to Ma and set Jacque down. She had tears in her eyes as she smiled broadly and pulled me into a hug.

"My baby, I have missed you so," she whispered.

"Me too, Ma," I said, my voice breaking with the emotion. We held each other, not wanting to let go.

"What's all this crying business?" Pa's booming voice came from the barn. I spied that he had tears as well. Ma released me only to have Pa sweep me up into his strong arms. He squeezed me and swung me around like he always did. I giggled through my tears.

"That's one of my most favorite sounds in the world, my baby," he said, squeezing me tighter.

"I've missed you, Papi," I squeaked out.

"Oh, you have no idea how much I've missed you, baby girl." He set me down and wiped his eyes.

I felt Ma smoothing my hair. "How long do we have you for?" Ma asked.

"Well, I need to go and feed the livestock and check on things tomorrow," I said.

"We'll go with ye," Pa said, draping his arm over my shoulders and pulling me to him.

"We've been worried, my lovely. How have you been?" Ma asked, searching my eyes.

"I miss him. It breaks my heart every day he's gone. I'm not meant to live this life without him," I said.

My parents nodded their understanding. Jacque held my hand as we made our way inside. To my surprise, Pa took the rest of the day off working in the barn to sit at the table and be with us. I spied my apron still hanging on the peg next to Ma's. I retrieved it and promptly put it on. I began to peel and slice some apples as Ma made the pastry crust. Pa looked on at us, completely content.

"How long is Liam expected to be gone?" Pa asked.

"I'm not sure. I'm sure he'll be home soon. He was sent due to some tax money that his mother owed."

"That doesn't sound right," Pa said.

"No, it didn't sound right to me either. I believe he didn't want to displease his mother any more than he already has."

"Well, I would think that having to be apart from you all this time would have taught him a lesson about pleasing others at one's own expense," Pa said, winking at me.

"I think so too," I said, smiling.

"How long has he been gone now?" Pa asked.

"Two weeks," I said softly.

As I was cutting apples, I glanced at my wrist, remembering the day in the woods with Liam. I smiled. I knew he would be back soon; I could feel it.

"How is Bronwynn?" I asked.

"Sick and tired," Ma said, chuckling. "She's due in a few weeks. I'd imagine she'd like you to be there."

"I'd like that very much," I said, placing the apple mixture into the pastry crust shells Ma had shaped.

"Goodness me, Gwen, our babies having babies, where did the time go?" Pa said, scratching his chin.

"Aye, it does my heart good to see our family growing in all sorts of ways," Ma said, giving me a sideways glance. She and I both began to giggle.

"What's this giggling? Mercy me, I will never understand you women," Pa said.

That night, we ate apple tartlets for dinner until we felt like we were going to pop.

Jacque had fallen asleep on Pa's shoulder. I laid my head on Ma's shoulder, who was sitting next to me on the bench. She kissed my temple. None of us wanted to go to bed. I yawned.

"I think you need to rest my, sweet baby," I heard Ma say softly.

"Yes, ma'am."

"Aye, we'll all ride out to your place tomorrow together," Pa said.

I nodded. I kissed Ma on the cheek, and she smiled, raising her hand to her cheek as if to hold my kiss there. Then I walked over to Pa and kissed him on the cheek. He chuckled softly.

"I love you, lass."

"I love you too, Papi," I said softly as I made my way into my old room, which was now Jacque's room. To my surprise, Pa had squeezed in a fifth bed for Jacque; all of his girls still had a place in his home. I smiled as I saw that Ma had set a neatly folded nightgown on the bed for me. I changed and slid under the covers, feeling completely wrapped in love and totally safe.

I woke in the morning to hear Jacque's soft breaths. Pa had put him to bed, and I hadn't noticed as I had slept so soundly. I lay there quietly in my bed, taking in the room and the sounds. I could hear Ma quietly stirring in the kitchen. It sounded like Pa was still sleeping. I quietly slipped into my clothes and made my way into the kitchen.

"Sleep well?" Ma asked as I kissed her on the cheek.

"Yes, ma'am. I slept so well I didn't hear Pa come in with Jacque."

"It took everything I had to make that man go to bed. He kept wanting to go in and check on you."

"Why?"

"A father's love doesn't end when you leave the house, my lovely," Ma said, smiling. "Nor a mother's love either, for that matter," she added.

I smiled.

"You know, he's always been that way with you girls. He slept less than I did worrying about you all."

"I didn't realize..."

"You know, in all the years I have been married to that man, he has never slept through the night. He always has checked on you all at least once a night. He was beside himself when you moved out. I think he paced these old floors the first three nights you were gone, not sleeping a wink," she said, chuckling to herself.

After breakfast, Pa made his way out to the barn to hitch up the wagon. He and Ma climbed on the front bench as Jacque sat on my lap in the back.

We waved as we passed neighbors and bumped along. I gazed at the apple orchard as we made our way up the dusty path to Liam's and my cottage.

"You've done well with the upkeep. I'm proud of ye," Pa said.

"Thanks, Pa," I said.

He slowed the horses to a stop in front of the cottage, letting Ma and me out. He and Jacque continued to the barn. Ma and I made our way into the house.

"This is lovely, Annalise," Ma said, gazing at all of Liam's weapons.

"Thank you, Ma."

"Will this be his last assignment?" she asked.

"Yes, it's supposed to be. Then he can lay down his weapons and start a new chapter of his life," I said. "Our life, I mean."

She smiled. "Yes, that feels right," she said, pulling me into a hug. "Shall we get to washing and scrubbing so this place is ready for his homecoming?" she said.

I grinned in spite of myself. "Yes."

Ma and I scrubbed, scored, and washed most of the day. She had brought some of her dried herbs over and hung them over the fireplace. Pa would periodically pop in and blow us kisses. I heard him outside banging and fixing the waterwheel, adding thatch to the roof, tending to the things in the yard I had found difficult. He, of course, did these with ease.

Ma and I were cutting vegetables we had gathered from my garden in preparation for dinner when he heard a knock on the open door. I looked up to see Petyr standing in the doorway.

"Annalise, Guinivere, lovely to see you today," Petyr said.

I noticed Ma didn't put down her butcher knife either. "Can we help you?" Ma asked sweetly.

"I rode to your place. You weren't there, so I thought I would try here. Faith is feeling poorly."

My heart stopped.

"So I brought her with me to find you."

"Bring her in," Ma said.

Petyr nodded and returned with Faith, crumpled in his arms.

Pa appeared in the doorway. "What's this?" Pa asked.

"Faith isn't feeling well," I said quietly.

Faith's face lit up at the sound of my voice, and she raised her head to look at me. Ma nodded at Pa.

Pa clasped Petyr's shoulder. "Why don't you go help me with a waterwheel?" Pa said. Petyr nodded and exited.

"Well?" Ma said to Faith.

"Well what?" Faith asked innocently.

"Faith McShaman! How far along are ye?"

"A couple months."

"All this nonsense because you're feeling poorly from being with child?" Ma laughed.

"Yes, and I was worried about Annalise," Faith said, leaning her head on my shoulder.

"How's married life?" I asked.

"He's changed," she said.

"Oh, how so?" Ma asked.

"He's better, Ma. The dark is leaving him."

"Oh yeah?"

"Yes, ma'am. I'm going to start teaching at the little school down the way," she said, smiling. "I heard a rumor you might be interested in," Faith added.

"Oh?" I asked, raising my eyebrows.

"Liam's mother found a new suitor."

"Really?" I gasped.

"Yes, and a wealthy one at that," Faith said, grinning.

"And who might that be?" I asked, slicing one of the zucchinis into chunks.

"Marquis DeLaurent," Faith said.

"That's wonderful!" I said.

"It is. Now she can love and be loved the way she's supposed to. She can now let Liam go," she said and watched me as I set my knife down.

I looked at her and smiled. "That makes me so happy my heart wants to burst."

We all sat around the table that night talking late into the night. I was so happy, so content. Ma and Pa stayed in the extra room with Jacque. Faith and Petyr stayed in the loft. I placed my hand on Liam's pillow as I fell asleep with a smile, knowing within me that he would be home soon. I woke up to a knock on the door of the cottage. I sat up to answer, but Pa beat me to it. I heard the steps from the loft creak as Petyr made his way down the steps from the loft. The knocking got louder. Pa swung open the door.

"Liam, my boy!" I heard Pa say.

My heart burst as I sprinted from our bed to see Liam's grinning face standing in the doorway of our cottage.

"Arc, as much as I love seeing you, it's my beautiful wife—" He stopped as he saw me in the doorway of our bedroom. He released Pa's handshake and took a couple strides toward me. I sprinted toward him, and he swooped me up into a hug, kissing my hair, the side of my face, my neck. I giggled as tears flowed from my eyes. I squeezed my arms around his neck tighter as he carried me to our bedroom and closed the door behind us with his foot, making no apologies for our abrupt exit. We stood in our room locked in an embrace, not wanting to let each other go. I finally released him to smooth his hair and study his now-grinning face.

"I have missed you so," he said softly.

"And I you," I whispered back.

"I'm done with that old life, Annalise. I was released from my commission."

"I'm so glad," I said, kissing him softly.

"Do you think you can love me as I am now?"

"I love you for whatever you are," I said.

He kissed me, lifting me up and setting me on the bed, disrobing and lying down with me. We quietly lay together, not sleeping, drinking in the sight and feel of each other.

Chapter 24

WHEN THE SUN BEGAN TO peek over the horizon, we got dressed and exited our bedroom. To my surprise, all of our guests were still asleep. Liam lifted the bar on the door, and we quietly slipped out. We held hands as we walked toward the river.

"I heard your mother has a new suitor," I said.

He squeezed my hand. "I heard that as well," he said, lost in thought.

"Are you okay?" I asked, pulling him to a stop.

"I am more than okay. She released me, Annalise. She found her happiness and let me go. She wrote me a letter stating that she hopes you and I have an abundant life and that our children will come visit," he said, smiling at me.

I pulled him to my lips for a kiss. "We can make this life whatever we want it to be, my love," I said, resting my forehead on his.

"This is what I want," he said with his eyes closed.

"Me too," I said.

We continued to walk toward the river, the sounds of the rushing water luring us to it. We stood on the bank of the river. Liam stood behind me and wrapped his arms around my waist. I leaned my head back on his shoulder. Liam and I both jumped as Pa came to stand beside us.

"I wondered where you two ran off to," Pa said, smiling.

"I've been without her for far too long, sir," Liam said to Pa.

Pa smiled. "The day Gwen got her premonition that we needed to leave Scotland, I never hesitated. Sure, I had resistance from my family. They all wanted me to let Gwen go with Maribelle and my two babies while I stayed behind. My mother was the worst of them, using guilt and shame to try to get me to stay." Pa paused, thinking for a moment before he continued, "But the thought of living a life without Gwen, missing out on her smile, her laugh, her voice, her love, ripped me to shreds. For me, there is no life without her. I can be blind, deaf, dumb, or destitute, but as long as my Gwen is there, I'll be the happiest man in the world," he said, his eyes misting.

"*Pa!*" I chided, wiping my eyes. Liam kissed my temple. Pa chuckled. The three of us walked toward the cottage.

"Gwen and I would like to hold a celebration in honor of your return and Faith's good news. We have much to celebrate. We will give you two some time alone but want to have a family get-together in three days' time. How does that strike ye?"

"We will be there," Liam said, squeezing my hand.

After everyone ate breakfast, they all headed home. Liam and I decided to make our way into town. We opted for riding on his horse as opposed to our wagon. We arrived at Tomas's shop. Liam helped me down and then scanned the area for Tomas.

"Tomas!" Liam hollered out.

"I heard you were back!" Tomas said, exiting one of the sheds.

"Annalise," Tomas said, nodding his head.

"Tomas," I said, greeting him back.

"Your sister misses you, Annalise., I'm beginning to think she would rather live with you than with me."

"She's always welcome to stop by," I offered.

"Well, we were going to give you two a couple days before swinging by," Tomas said, winking at Liam.

"Did I hear—" I heard Raquelle say from behind his shop. "Annalise!" she shrieked as she pulled me into a hug. "I thought I was hearing things," she said, wiping her eyes and then pulling Liam into a hug. "I heard you were back. I'm so excited to see you both."

I heard a male voice clear his throat from behind us. We both spun around to see Henri. Liam nodded. "Henri."

"Captain, it's good to see you," Henri said and then moved his eyes to me.

"You look like you are well," Liam said.

"I am indeed. I just came from getting married at the courthouse."

"Who is the fortunate woman?" I asked.

"Well, Annalise, since the captain here took one of the most exquisite creatures, I had to find another. I married Madame Deveroux. It seems I have an instant family," Henri said, smiling.

"Congratulations, Henri," I said.

"Thank you, and to you both as well."

"Thank you," Liam said, shaking Henri's hand.

"Well, I must be going." Henri nodded and climbed into his carriage.

Liam pulled me closer to his side and kissed me. I giggled.

"Hopefully he'll be in a better mood now that he's getting laid." Raquelle said as she came up beside us. We all started laughing.

"Liam! Annalise!" we heard a woman calling to us from down the street. It was my aunt Maribelle. She was walking as quickly as she could with a huge grin. She pulled me into a huge hug and then Liam and then Raquelle and then Tomas. "I haven't seen you all since your union ceremony!" she said.

"Will you be able to make it to the family gathering?" I asked her.

"Of course! I wouldn't miss it! We're going to bring some of the kids," she said. Since Maribelle was married to the man that ran the orphanage, she tried to bring the kids out as much as possible. "We just got a new baby, so I need to be getting back to the kids, but I will see you soon," she said as she pulled Raquelle and me into a hug. "I love you so much," she said, then turned and rushed back to the orphanage down the street.

We said our goodbyes to Tomas and Raquelle; then Liam helped me up onto the horse. He climbed up behind me and held the reins. A couple of men on horses came trotting toward us.

"Captain!" one of the men said

"Hello, Ric, how are you?" Liam asked.

"Pretty fair. Hello, madame," Ric said, nodding at me. I smiled and nodded back.

"Glad to hear it," Liam said.

"I heard you're out of the Lord's guard now," Ric said.

"I am. It's a new life for Annalise and I."

"Well, drills aren't going to be the same. I might actually get a moment's rest every now and then," Ric said, chuckling.

"We need to get going. Good luck with everything," Liam said.

"You too, sir," Ric said.

Liam and I made our way back to our cottage. With the exception of our daily chores, we locked ourselves away for the next two days to enjoy each other.

Chapter 25

WE ARRIVED TO MY FAMILY'S cottage. I could smell the pig roasting on the spit. By the grin on his face, I could tell that Liam was as excited to see everyone as I was. Pa spotted us and called out from the doorway of the barn.

"Annalise! Liam! There you are!" As we drew closer, Pa helped me down off the horse and pulled me into a huge hug. "Your ma has missed you these last couple days she'll want to see you straight away," he said softly.

I smiled at him. Liam tugged on my arm and pulled me in for a kiss. We smiled at each other, and then I turned and made my way into the cottage.

As my eyes adjusted to the dim light, I saw Ma walking toward me with her arms open. I hugged her. As I did, I looked to see Maribelle kneading dough on the table and a pregnant Bronwynn sitting next to her shelling peas. Raquelle was stirring the custard; a queasy-looking Faith was slicing potatoes. They all looked at me and smiled. I made my way to each of them and hugged them. Then I retrieved my apron from the peg on the wall and went about churning the butter. My soul was at peace with its family.

Per Ma's request, Pa placed a long table outside, similar to the one inside the cottage. It had a chair on each end for Ma and Pa and two long benches on either side that could seat all of us. We lit some candles and placed them in between the platters of food. Between the dance of the candlelight and the hues of the setting sun, it seemed magical. I looked at my family's beautiful faces, illuminated by the flickering candlelight. Then I looked to my right, looking at Liam's profile. He turned and gave me a kiss. My heart felt like it was going to burst; it was filled with so much love. This felt right. This felt like the life I was supposed to be living.

As I came to, I glanced at Carrie. She had tears in her eyes. "Laney, that was beautiful. How do you feel?"

"I feel so much more peaceful," I said as I sat up.

"Are you going to be okay?" she asked.

"Well, I'm going to need to be okay. I have some meetings and a new executive team I need to entertain this afternoon," I said as I paid Carrie.

"Thank you for allowing me to help you, Laney. Please call if you need anything else," she said as I hugged her and exited her office.

I drove back to Mendelson. I made it back thirty minutes before my meeting started with Paul.

I finished my last meeting of the day with Jack. It was around 5:00 p.m. Lizzie would be expecting me at Braeden's football practice soon for the hand-off. I heard the group that was going out to dinner outside of my door. I heard Brad ask Slade, "Is Laney not attending dinner this evening?"

I then heard Slade's response, "No, she has previous engagements."

Brad's voice, clearly flustered, was quick and sharp. "Please excuse me a moment." He walked into my office as I was typing out an e-mail. I paused my typing a moment as I looked up at him. I gave him a half smile and returned to typing.

"I understand you aren't going to dinner this evening." His voice was crisp. He was sexy when he was agitated. Down, kitty, down.

I looked up from my monitor. "No, I am not. I need to take my son to football practice," I said matter-of-factly.

Brad was having trouble controlling his temper; he was clearly used to getting whatever he wanted. "Next time I expect you to attend dinner with us, Laney."

His comment irritated me. Who was he to try and dictate what I had to do? My logical mind told me that he was the new CEO (i.e. my boss); then I told my logical mind to shut up. I smiled only with my mouth. Nothing else on my face moved.

J.M. TRASK

"Maybe next time," I said, enunciating each word. Then I continued typing.

He was standing in front of my desk, tapping his fingers on my desk. "Laney, I would suggest you learn to comply with my requests and expectations, or your life is going to become very hard over the upcoming weeks," he snapped.

Now I was furious, I threw my logical mind into the sex kitten's cage. I stood up and leaned forward over my desk in a very aggressive stance. He still dwarfed me and was seemingly amused.

"Obviously, you don't understand my role and its purpose here. I am sorry if your HR department is run under your thumb, or something else—and if so, clearly *you* are going to have some difficult days over the upcoming weeks," I hissed. You could cut the tension between us with a knife. Our eyes locked on each other, his eyes set on fire and his jaw tight, neither one of us backing down.

"Don't be so sure, Laney," he said through his clenched jaw.

I realized I couldn't feel my legs. Was it the bravery or the fact that I was really turned on? The blood was flowing somewhere other than my legs. Truly, I just wanted to run out of the office and get some fresh air, be anywhere but here. He held my gaze for another moment. My mouth was going dry; I swallowed hard. He nodded slowly as though he was agreeing with something unspoken, his mouth spread into a devious smirk, and then he left my office. I heard the *ding* of the elevators and the doors close. They were gone. I immediately plopped myself into my chair and rested my head back, closed my eyes, inhaling and exhaling once deeply.

Jenna peeked in the door. "Holy shit, what was that, Laney? Either you have the biggest balls here, or you just made the worst career-ending decision possible?" she said in disbelief.

I laughed, my eyes still closed and head back. "Probably the latter." I sat up and started packing up my things for the day. "I am heading home and then to football practice. I have done enough damage today. I will see you tomorrow," I said, winking.

"Have a good night, Laney! Don't put any of the other football parents in a headlock!" Jenna called as I walked down the hall. I

226

began laughing and heard Jenna snickering as the glass door closed behind me.

Football practice went smoothly as usual. I was pulling into my driveway and saw a figure sitting on my steps, a monstrous black tinted-out Chevy Suburban in my driveway. Braeden squeaked from the back, "Mommy, is that your friend...Mr. Green?"

My stomach did a somersault, and I swallowed hard. *Shit.*

"Yes, I believe it is. Mommy works with him...for now. I think you can call him Mr. Brad," I said, swallowing hard again.

As I pulled in closer, I could see that he was still in today's work clothes, but he had removed his tie and suit jacket. I noticed that his shirt sleeves were rolled up to his elbows; I could see the veins in his well-defined forearms. Was there anything he didn't look stunning in? I figured I was really in trouble. Jack had only ever made a house call after I gave birth to Braeden. I pulled into the garage and put my car in park. Braeden jumped out and ran toward Brad.

"Mom said I can call you Mr. Brad. Is that okay?" Braeden excitedly yelled as he ran up to Brad.

"Yes, it is." Brad gave a half smile.

"If you are here for dinner, all we have is leftover pot roast." Braeden leaned in closer and whispered, "It's a little dry."

Brad seemed amused. "Thank you for the offer, but I brought you dinner instead," he said, and Braeden's eyes lit up. I smiled in spite of myself, my heart melting just a little.

"What did you bring me?" Braeden shrieked, jumping up and down.

Brad reached his arm around behind him and held out a white plastic bag containing two takeout containers. "Well, I hope you like spaghetti," Brad said.

"I love spaghetti!" Braeden said as he grinned from ear to ear, taking the bag.

"What do you say, buddy?" I said as I readjusted my laptop-bag strap over my shoulder.

"Thank you, Mr. Brad! Hey, if you are going to live next door, I will need to show you all the good fishing spots."

Brad flashed Braeden his radiant smile. "I would like that. Maybe I will take you up on your offer sometime," he said.

I walked up. As I made my approach, Brad's eyes scanned my body up and down slowly. I pretended not to notice, but my lady parts definitely did not ignore it.

"Brae, can you please take that inside and get started on your dinner? You will need to go take a shower and get changed for bed soon. I will be there in just a few minutes, okay?"

Brae's face twisted up. "Awww, bummer. Okay, Mom. See ya later, Mr. Brad!" He gave Brad a high five and ran into the house. I watched after Brae through the screen door to make sure he actually went into the kitchen.

"You're welcome," he said as he stood up. The look on his face was soft.

"You didn't even give me a chance to say thank you," I said, snickering.

"You're welcome," he said again.

"Thank you for dinner…you didn't have to do that," I said, feeling like a complete ass for how I behaved today.

"I didn't have to. I wanted to," he said softly.

I could feel my heart thumping inside my chest. "How long were you waiting for us?" I asked.

"Not long," he said as he took a step toward me.

I could feel the butterflies beginning to flutter their wings in my chest. His frequency was scrambling my brain; I needed to focus.

"What brought you all the way out here, Mr. Green? I can't imagine it was just to bring us dinner. If this is about today and not going to dinner…," I started, sounding more seductive than I meant to.

He took another step toward me. He was now only inches away from me. My breath caught. *Keep it together, Laney.* My logical mind was hissing at me. His look was so intense as he lifted my laptop bag off my shoulder and took my purse from my hands. I watched as he placed them on the porch.

"You said you were going to football practice, and I didn't think you would have time to eat. Besides, I wanted to check out the view from my property this evening," he said, studying my face. Somehow I knew he wasn't talking about the water views. I began feeling weak all over and slightly light-headed.

"A-and what did you think?" was all I could squeak out, my mouth going bone-dry. His eyes lingered on my lips.

"It's breathtaking," he said in a low tone.

I began to feel disoriented—his look, his smell, his…everything. We stood there in the dark with lightning bugs all around us, the frogs croaking their chorus, the yellow porch light casting shadows.

"A-are you going to start building soon?" I asked, swallowing hard.

"I have some unfinished business to attend to, then I plan on breaking ground." The words somehow dripped from his lips like melted chocolate. "I can see that there is something else you want to ask me, Laney. Why don't you ask me what you really want to know?" he said, his eyes looking deeply into mine. I really wanted to ask him if he would stay and take me one hundred ways and then do it again, but I didn't think it was entirely appropriate to ask the new CEO that question.

"How was dinner this evening?" I said, immediately feeling stupid.

"Boring. Is that really what you wanted to ask me, Laney?" he said, moving his gaze to my lips again. I could see my chest moving more than usual from the intensity of our interaction.

"I want to know if the views are the only reason for your visit?" I somehow mustered up enough courage to ask. He reached up and slowly tucked a stray wisp of hair behind my ear and studied my face. My breath hitched yet again at his touch.

"No. I wanted to bring you dinner as well." He shot me a sexy half smile. "I want you to call or text if you ever need anything," he said as he handed me his business card.

I was confused. I already had his phone number. After I took it, I read it. The cell-phone number on his business card was different. He had two phones. I flipped it over to the back; it was his apartment address. I recognized the part of the bordering city he lived in from the street address.

"Have a good night, Laney. I will see you tomorrow." He brushed my arm as he walked past me to his car.

"Wait," I said softly, not sure that he had heard me. I heard the crunching of the gravel stop. I turned around to see that he was standing with the driver side door of the Suburban wide open.

"Laney?" he said.

"I never stopped thinking about you," I said. I wasn't sure where it came from, but it needed to be said. He closed his eyes and tilted his head back, looking up at the stars in the night sky, exhaling. I wasn't sure if that was good or bad.

After a moment, he looked at me again with a soft smile. "Me either," he said.

I smiled. "Have a good night, Brad," I said softly.

He nodded. "You too, beautiful," he said, seemingly lost in thought as he climbed into his SUV and closed the door.

I was now careening down the side of a slippery slope of memories in my mind. The night before Brad broke it off with me, he showed up at my house, telling me that he was going to leave Kayla. He said that he wanted me to leave Sam so we could be together. He wanted me to be the mother of his children and spend our days laughing and growing old together, just being together. He even said he wanted to show everyone what true love looks like. It was the last time we made love; it was passionate and powerful. The last thing he said to me before leaving my apartment that night was, "I love you, beautiful"; then he broke it off with me the next day. I was so lost in the memory of that night involuntary tears had begun to roll down my face, unbeknownst to me. I quickly wiped them away.

I tried to collect myself, and by the time my brain fog cleared, his SUV was turning onto the street. I watched as his taillights disappeared, evoking a strangely familiar sadness that hung over me. I walked inside and into the kitchen. I opened the remaining Styrofoam container in the bottom of the white bag sitting on the counter and pulled the plastic bag off the plasticware it contained. I opened the lid and twirled a few of the noodles around my fork. I took a bite; it was delicious. After a few more bites, I closed the lid and put the rest in the refrigerator.

I made my way upstairs to tuck Braeden in. Then I went to my bedroom and closed the door. I robotically changed out of my work clothes, completely lost in thought. I didn't put on one of Sam's T-shirts tonight. I put on a pair of yoga pants and a tank top. I climbed into bed, closing my eyes and feeling as though Brad was there with me. I drifted off into a deep sleep.

Chapter 26

I WAS TIRED OF SUITS. I arrived to the office in my camel-colored pants with cream-colored cashmere sweater and brown ballet flats. I was going to need to be comfortable if I was going to win this battle with Brad and Frank. I had gotten up early to review the data that Blake had sent me on operations costs so that I could at least appear somewhat intelligent about the subject. Jenna was on her desk phone when I got to the office. She just winked at me and handed me a pink piece of paper as I passed by her desk to unlock my office door. I was relieved to see that the voice-mail indicator light on my phone was not glowing. I hated voice mails. I turned my attention to the note that Jenna handed to me: "Meeting with Mr. Dreamy Green @ 9." Her note made me smile.

I sat in my chair, shaking my head, and proceeded to turn on my laptop and begin the task of answering e-mails. I was so engrossed with my e-mails that when I looked up at the clock, it was 9:04 a.m. "Oh crap!" I whispered to myself. Luckily, the conference room was just down the hall, and I only ended up being a total of six minutes late to the meeting. I entered the room confidently; all eyes were on me.

Veronica spoke first, "Nice of you to join us, Laney," she said with her best fake smile.

"My apologies, gentlemen…Veronica," I said in the most steady voice I could manage. As I hooked up my laptop to the projector cord, I was anxious to get their eyes off me, especially Brad's.

"Please direct your attention to the screen. I have put together a presentation exploring the cost-benefit analysis of our request and also some basic figures that I worked out with Blake." Blake gave me a nod of approval.

The conversation was long, frustrating, and tedious. Veronica spent most of the time alternating between glaring at me and picking her nails. She would also adjust her blouse every so often to ensure her she was showing adequate cleavage. Slade was playing with his Blackberry; I was not sure he even knew how to send an e-mail from the device. The rest of the attendees zoned in and out. Frank was completely engaged. After several circular and detailed discussions, there wasn't much more to talk about.

"With this information, we may be able to consider this, but before we would give approval, I would need to verify your financial data," said Frank.

Brad spent the meeting not saying a word, just running his fingers over his knuckles as he stared at me, his mind clearly somewhere else, or checking e-mails on his phone. I felt good; this felt like a victory.

"I will send you what I have, and Blake can meet with you to discuss any questions. Thank you, gentlemen…Veronica," I said as I stood up and began to collect my things.

Brad spoke, "If you will please excuse us."

I assumed he wanted his team to stay behind to discuss. I looked up at him to verify. "Laney…stay. The rest of you may go," he barked.

I looked at him with raised eyebrows. Veronica looked like she had been slapped in the face; I gave her my most insincere smile. Jack squeezed my shoulder and winked at me on the way out. Slade was the last to leave the room and shut the door behind him. I was irritated at the tone Brad had spoken to me with in front of everyone. Brad had taken a seat at the end of the conference-room table; I had taken the seat caddy corner to him. When I was crossing my legs, I accidentally brushed his calf. I felt a tingle run up my leg.

"Before you say what you are going to say, let's get one thing straight, I am not a servant to be ordered about by you," I said in my stern HR director voice, pretty sure steam may be coming out of my ears. We were sitting two feet away from each other.

Brad tilted his head to the side with an amused look on his face. "You are angry with me?"

"If we are going to work together for these next few weeks, I would ask that you don't bark commands at me like a dog."

"Ha, you *are* angry with me! I am going to sign this expensive one-sided deal you proposed, and you are angry with me!" he said, amused.

I was flabbergasted. "You are? I thought…"

"Well, you thought wrong, Laney Masterson. I suggest you don't make any more assumptions about me." His tone was stern and smug, his eyes matching his voice.

"Why did you dismiss everyone? You could have just signed it at the end of the meeting," I asked, confused.

He was quick with his matter-of-fact response. "I don't complete business transactions in group settings, only in one-on-one meetings."

I felt my face flush. "Why are you signing the agreement if you feel it is unfavorable to you?" I asked.

Brad pulled the thick legal document from his leather portfolio and handed it to me, his eyes never leaving mine. "Because it's you." His tone had changed to husky and seductive; it made a hot charge zap through my lady parts. I was starting to realize that Brad could possibly always have an underlying meaning behind what he actually says. I scanned the document, flipping through the pages, checking for all the required signatures and date stamps. Brad smirked, still amused.

"But wait…you accidentally put yesterday's date. I can have legal reprint it, and we can correct the date—"

"It is correct, Laney. I signed it yesterday after you gave it to me," he said, his eyes still watching me.

My mind was racing. "What? Why did we have this meeting if you already signed it?" I said, getting irritated.

He leaned in across the corner of the conference-room table close to my ear, speaking in a hushed growl. "So next time, you will think twice before turning me down for dinner. This isn't the only form of punishment I like to use, as you know." His lips barely brushed my ear. I could smell his masculinity and cologne; he smelled good. I swallowed hard, trying to manage my breathing and the Sahara desert that developed in my mouth.

"Excellent work, Laney," he whispered.

Then in the moment, he was rising from his seat and exiting the conference room without another word. *What the hell was that? Was this meeting a form of punishment?* I guess in a way it was, like torture listening to the finance people drone on. I gathered up my belongings and opened the conference-room door where I almost ran head-on into Jenna.

"Okay. So the conference-room door makes it a lot harder to eavesdrop than your office door. Spill it, chica, why were you the bad kid who was kept after class?" she hissed.

I laughed, the irony of Jenna's words not lost on me. "Yes, Mother, I am fine. Are you still good for tomorrow night? Lizzie is still coming over to watch the boys."

Jenna and I had a girls night planned for tomorrow night; this was the only time I let my inner sex kitten scratch and claw at my logical mind.

Jenna gave me a wink. "Umm, hell yeah, we are going to have the hottest dates in the place!" She and I both set about giggling.

I spent the rest of the day behind closed office doors; I was booked solid with meetings. I was thankful for the time that I could hide out from Brad. I was wrapping up my final meeting of the day with Paul when Brad walked into my office unannounced.

"I need to speak with Laney. Please excuse us, Paul," Brad barked.

Paul looked up at me with surprise. "We were just finishing up…Laney, we can get the rest of the affidavits organized tomorrow."

I managed a smile for Paul's sake, but I had a great deal of trouble hiding my anger.

"Sounds good. Have a good evening," I said to Paul. He gave me a nod and then exchanged nods with Brad as he exited the office.

Brad locked his eyes on mine and walked toward me. "You should manage your time better, Laney. Your calendar was packed today."

Was he checking my calendar, or did Jenna tell him? If it were possible, steam would have been coming out of my ears yet again, and I would be spitting fire.

"Thank you for your feedback. The last time I checked, I did not need your permission to have meetings. I would prefer you do not barge in on my meetings. If there are topics in which you have an interest, I can add you to the invite," I hissed. I was having trouble unclenching my jaw while speaking.

Brad continued to control my eyes. "We are going to dinner tonight, I expect you to attend—" he changed the subject.

I stared just as intensely back. "I am sorry. I have previous plans. I will take a rain check." I broke the eye contact, my heart still racing, and started packing up my things.

Brad was still staring at me, mostly in disbelief. His eyes narrowed as he spoke, "Laney, I thought we covered this after the meeting this morning," he hissed back.

"I don't listen to threats or commands," I said as I zipped up my laptop back and gathered my purse.

"I have never worked with someone as defiant as you," he snarled.

I looked up at him as I hoisted my laptop-bag strap over my shoulder. "That explains a lot," I said as I walked past him, saying to Jenna on my way out, "Can you lock up for me?"

She slowly nodded, her eyes wide. From her expression, I knew she had heard the whole thing.

Braeden was excited after practice. He had made some tackles, ran the ball, and fared well on their other drills. After practice, I raced Braeden to the car.

"Come on, Brae, are you going to let your old mom beat you to the car?" I asked as we ran side by side. He replied with a giggle and surge of energy. We tied. I was helping Braeden take off his shoulder pads when Mark came from around the car. It startled me, and I jumped.

"Laney, how are you?" he asked. Lizzie was right, he could be stalkerish sometimes.

"Mark! Hey! I didn't see you there. I am doing well, swamped at work as usual. How are you?" I asked as Braeden climbed in the car.

"I can't complain. I had a question for you. I wanted to see if you would be interested in going to the mountains with me this weekend, just me and you?"

I tilted my head to the side, glad I already had plans this weekend with Jenna and knowing I was about to reject him. "That's really sweet of you to ask me, Mark, but Jenna and I are going away this weekend."

"Oh, okay, I see. Maybe next weekend?" His face was not hiding his disappointment well.

"I'm not sure. Have a good night, Mark," I said as I climbed in my car and headed toward home. I watched Mark still standing there in the parking lot as I drove away in my rear-view mirror.

When I arrived home, I did not have a visitor on my front porch. Oddly enough, I was kind of disappointed.

Chapter 27

TGIF. I WAS GLAD IT was Friday. It was hard to focus because Jenna and I were having a girl's night out. Thankfully, Lizzie had agreed to stay the night with Josh and Braeden at my house since we never knew where the night would take us. This was one night out of the month that Jenna and I let our hair down and just enjoyed ourselves. Jenna was outside of my office door, tapping her foot when I finally got off my last conference call of the day.

I laughed. "Well, you could have already changed while you were waiting on me," I said.

Jenna's face erupted in a smile. "You know just as well as I do that half of the fun is getting ready together. Besides, I want to see what my hot date is wearing tonight," she teased.

This made me chuckle. We both grabbed our duffle bags and went into the ladies' restroom to change and freshen up our makeup. I usually only wore light makeup to work, but tonight I put on black eyeliner and smudged it so it had a smoky effect. I put on a low-cut spaghetti-strap flowy print tank top and my designer jeans that fit like a glove. Then I slipped on my wedge sandals with a nude-colored strap. Since my hair was long and fine, a few scrunches of hair gel would give me a sexy curly look, so that was what I proceeded to do. To my delight, the effect was a heap of sexy, messy curls. I felt sexy. My inner sex kitten nodded her approval.

I smiled at Jenna, who was curling the last chunk of her blonde hair with a curling wand. Jenna was only a couple inches shorter than me. She had the same figure 8 body shape. She had blonde hair that went to her shoulder blades and blue eyes that seemed to change colors. What I loved about Jenna was that we were never in competition with each other; it was all love between us. I was applying my lipstick. Jenna had just finished her own and smacked me on the butt.

"Ready to go, sexy?" she asked.

I smiled and winked at her. "Only if you promise me a good time tonight," I retorted.

At that, both of us started laughing, pulled our duffle bags over our shoulders, and exited the bathroom. I noticed that Brad's office light was on, but his door was still closed. His secretary had already gone home, but Jesse, who I learned was his personal security guard, was still stationed outside. We gave him a little wave as we headed for the elevator. His expression went from surprise to amused.

Jenna and I arrived to the bar; happy hour was in full swing. We were lucky that when we arrived, a group of business men was leaving a table in the bar area. We quickly maneuvered through the crowd to claim it. Both of us set our clutch purses on the tall table and hopped up into the barstool chairs.

The waitress came over immediately. "Good evening, ladies. What can I get you this evening?" she said as she placed the small square drink napkins on the table.

"We will both start with cosmopolitans," Jenna said, winking at me.

I smiled. I loved this game: we would take turns ordering drinks for each other. "You are being nice to me tonight," I said.

Jenna laughed. "Well, I have learned that payback is heck."

In moments, our drinks arrived. We clinked our martini glasses and took a sip of the delicious pink liquid. I was contemplating telling her about the meeting. But as usual, she read my mind.

"So tell me what happened after the meeting." Her eyebrows were raised.

I let a half smile slip. "It's the strangest thing, Jenna. He held me back to give me the signed agreement. Only thing was, he signed it the day before," I said, taking another sip.

Jenna's face twisted up in confusion. "Wasn't that the point of the meeting, to convince him to sign it?" she asked, perplexed.

I started to chew the inside of my cheek. "Yes...that is what I thought. Then he told me the meeting was punishment for not going out to dinner the other night," I said, hesitating to make eye contact with her at first.

Jenna's eyes got big. We both picked up our glasses, clinked them again, and took a huge sip.

"Wow, Laney. That's kind of hot. Was he so…like this before?" Jenna said, raising her eyebrows up and down several times.

I giggled, more from nerves than anything. I didn't want to share about my time in the bedroom with Brad. It was too private, too personal, too intimate. I decided to only share a little.

"Jenna, only you would turn a work meeting into something sexual, and yes, he liked to be in control. It was fun," I said as I winked.

"So would you do it again?" she asked eagerly.

"Do what, Jenna? Sleep with my maybe-soon-to-be boss again? Is that what you are suggesting?" I said with mock offense.

"Well?" she said, clearly not buying it.

I smiled and looked at my drink. "In a heartbeat. Who wouldn't? You should have seen him the day he ran up to my house. I have never seen a body to rival his," I added.

Jenna smiled. "Nothing wrong with that," she offered.

I winked at her.

We were three quarters of the way through our drinks. I was beginning to feel relaxed, and my buzz was sinking in quite nicely. Two gentlemen came up to our table; they were average-looking. I assumed they were some sort of professional type; they both wore khaki pants and dress shirts. The tall blond one with glasses seemed to take a shine to me, or he had just too much to drink. Either way, he stood way too close. His friend, who was the same height but had black hair and blue eyes, stood close to Jenna. Jenna and I smiled at each other. We knew this scenario very well. It happened to us almost every time we went out for ladies' night.

The blond one spoke first, "Hello, ladies, how are you this evening?" I noted the smell of alcohol, obviously, but he wasn't slurring.

"We are doing well this evening. How are you?" Jenna answered.

I proceeded to finish my cosmopolitan and made eye contact, signaling for the waitress to come over. It was my turn to order. Jenna followed my lead and slurped down the rest of her cosmopolitan. The waitress came up. "What can I get ya hon?" she asked, heartily chewing on a piece of gum.

I grinned. "We would both like a Long Island iced tea," I said, making a face at Jenna.

Jenna smirked, shaking her head and silently mouthing the word *nice*. The black-haired gentleman spoke this time. By the way he was staring at Jenna's chest, he was clearly wanting to engage in a conversation—or more likely something else.

"Well, we saw two beautiful women over here and thought you could use some company," the dark-haired one offered.

Jenna turned to look at him. "Do they teach you that line at 'guy school' or something?" She turned to look at me. "How many times have we heard that line?"

I shook my head. "Too many to count. You are going to have to do better than that," I said, looking at the black-haired stranger. The waitress returned with our drinks, and we both immediately took a sip.

The blond stranger now chimed in, "Let's try this. Your legs must be tired because you have been running through my dreams all night." At this terrible try, all four of us laughed.

"Okay, since you made us laugh, my name is Jenna, and this is Laney," Jenna responded.

The blond smiled and introduced himself, "My name is Riley, and—"

The black-haired man interrupted him, "And my name is Trent."

We all shook hands. We came to find out that they both worked at an IT firm that Mendelson contracts with. Both men eventually gave up that they were twenty-seven. I was feeling the effect of my Long Island pretty well now. I knew I was being giggly and flirty and pretty sure that this was going to be my last drink for the evening. Jenna gave me a look from across the table. I knew what she meant: we needed a sidebar discussion. So Jenna and I hopped off our chairs, looked at Riley and Trent, and said, "We need a bio break. We will be right back."

"We will be here," Riley said, winking at me.

Jenna and I departed to go to the restroom. As we were washing our hands, Jenna spoke, "Laney, did you want to sleep with either one of them?" she asked me like she was writing her grocery-store list.

"No, did you?" I responded just as casually.

Jenna smiled. "Nope. We both know that nerd is not my type."

We both let out a drunken giggle. We held hands on the way back to the table so as not to lose each other in the huge crowd of professionals that had formed around the bar. As I was leading Jenna through the crowd, I had turned around to look at her and ran smack into a column; then Jenna ran into the back of me. As I turned around, I realized it wasn't a column; it was the backside of Brad's hard body.

"Oh crap," I whispered.

Brad spun around and looked at me. "Hello, Laney." Brad eyed me, and a half smile slowly spread across his face. I tried to clear my thoughts to speak. Of all of the people to run into, literally, it had to be him.

"Oh…excuse me, Brad. I'm sorry, I was talking to Jenna and wasn't watching…," I stammered.

He seemed amused. "I almost didn't recognize you, Laney…I like this," he said softly as his hand reached up and lightly touched my hair. My breath hitched. I needed to get away from him so I could breathe again. I also did not need my new boss to see me drunk.

"Thank you, it's good seeing you. I hope you enjoy your evening," I muttered as I tugged Jenna, who was waving at Jesse as we departed to our table.

"Did you see all the women around him?" Jenna said as she pulled back on my arm and whispered in my ear.

"I didn't notice," I lied. Of course, I noticed all the women around him; they would have to be crazy not to try.

As we approached, we noticed that Trent and Riley were still at our table; they hadn't given up. Luckily, with where we were sitting, it was difficult to see Brad. We hopped up into our seats and sipped on our Long Islands some more. After about fifteen minutes, I started to feel hot; my skin felt like it was on fire. I actually wanted to be touched, I wanted to dance, I wanted to talk, I wanted to have sex—I felt like touching everything and everyone within reach. I felt like I was on sensory overload. I had never felt this way before, and now the lighting in the bar didn't seem right. Jenna gave me a funny look; I could tell Jenna was feeling it too.

A new drink that was in a highball glass was being set down in front of each of us by the waitress. Both men were leaning in closer; their hands were beginning to wander. The weird thing is, I didn't want to stop Riley, even though I knew I didn't like him. I never went home with a man from the bar, especially one that I just met. This was a new sensation for me. I knew I didn't want to, but I felt like I just need to relieve the buildup of sexual tension in my body.

"It's hot in here. I need to step outside for some air. Jenna?" I said, fanning myself with my hand. I could see a fine film of sweat that had formed across Jenna's face too. As we got up from our barstools, I almost rolled my ankle, but Riley caught my arm. "Easy there, sexy," he whispered. I usually could walk in high heels with ease, but apparently not after a Long Island iced tea. Note to self: effects of Long Island iced tea should only be enjoyed in privacy of my own home.

I looked in Brad's direction and saw Jesse whispering in Brad's ear. Brad's eyes flicked up to me and intently watched as I walked by. I hadn't noticed, but Riley had his hand in my back jean pocket, guiding me out. Trent had his arm draped around Jenna's waist, and his hand shoved down the side of her jeans by her hip. It was a weird sensation. I knew all of this was going on, but I didn't want to stop it. We made it through the crowd of people and pushed through the outside doors. The cool night air felt amazing on my sweat-covered skin. I could feel my hardening nipples push against the fabric of my bra.

Riley spoke into my ear, "Why don't we go back to my place, and I will make you feel even better? I know what you want, Laney. I know what will satisfy everything you are feeling," he said.

I looked over to where Jenna was. Trent was running his hands over Jenna's butt. She was in the same boat; she was having trouble maintaining control. I watched as Trent shot Riley a hopeful smile.

This didn't feel right. *Why am I acting this way? Why am I not stopping this?*

"Jenna, is it hot out here still?" I said, fanning myself with my hand again. The pleasurable coolness of the air had worn off.

"Yes, I can't seem to cool down. I think we probably need some water," she said, looking over her shoulder at me.

"Everything's okay. We thought you would want something to keep your buzz going. We thought you two ladies would want go home with us this evening," Riley was explaining to me. The hair on the back of my neck stood up, and I felt the familiar tingling all over my skin. Before either Jenna or I could respond, Brad's voice came from behind me. Jenna raised her eyebrows.

"That won't be necessary," Brad said sternly.

At the sight of him, I felt my insides turning to goo. My inner sex kitten had transformed into a rabid tiger. I spun around to see him. He looked hot. He was in his dress shirt and jeans. My body leapt at the sight of him. In my current state, I wanted to have sex with him right where he stood. Riley's hands were on my waist; he pulled me to him. Brad's face was grim. Jesse approached with Brad. Both looked tense but confident as ever.

"What are you doing here?" I blurted out.

"I came here to have a drink…and thought you might need an escort home," he explained as his eyes dropped from mine to Riley's hands, which were still planted firmly on my hips. He was being a smartass, I thought.

Trent spoke next, "Do you ladies know them?" Trent asked in disbelief.

I spoke. Even with my world spinning, I could answer this. My eyes were locked on Brad. "Yes, we do. He's my b—" I started, and Brad interrupted me.

"Boyfriend, and I am taking her home," he said through his clenched jaw. I was in shock, but Riley and Trent turned from confident and horny to angry. Riley postured up—big mistake.

"Look, dude, I don't know who you think you are. They didn't mention anything about having boyfriends, and we were just leaving," Riley said, pulling me even closer to him. "She seemed to be enjoying herself plenty without you. Some boyfriend you must be." Riley snickered.

Brad ignored him and spoke to me and Jenna. Alphas clearly aren't required to respond to conversations if they don't want to. Soon I thought one of them would club us and drag us away by the hair like a caveman.

"Let's go, Laney...Jenna," Brad commanded, clearly irritated.

Jenna turned toward Brad and Jesse. Trent released her. She stood next to Jesse; she immediately began rubbing and kissing his clean-shaven head. Jesse didn't seem to take notice of being molested by Jenna; his eyes were intensely focused on the two men. I took one step toward Brad and couldn't go any farther. Something was holding me back: it was Riley. He had a hold of my back jean pocket. He pulled me back to him by my pocket.

I turned to look at him. "The boss says I have to go," I said matter-of-factly. Riley wasn't going to give up. Even in my altered state, I knew this wasn't a good idea...for him. "Riley, don't do this...I need to go." I tried backing away again, but he clung to me and pulled me back to him. I looked over my shoulder at Brad, now slightly alarmed.

"No, Laney, look at me. You are coming home with me. We are going to have some fun tonight," Riley snarled, holding my face and turning it to face his with one hand. I could see he was angry and losing control.

I had no chance to respond. Brad was swift as he stepped between us, breaking Riley's grip on me, and picked him up into the air by his shirt. I stepped back, and Jesse grabbed me. He pushed me behind him so I was standing next to Jenna. Jenna and I exchanged looks. Then we interlaced our arms into each other's. Trent took one step toward Brad, and Jesse stepped forward, putting his arm out, motioning for him to stop all forward motion.

"You slipped ecstasy in their drinks, you stupid shit. That's the only way they would ever go home with you two stupid fucks. You're pathetic," Brad growled through clenched teeth.

Riley narrowed his eyes at Brad. He shouldn't have challenged the alpha. Brad threw him to the ground and was on him. Brad pinned Riley down with his knees and began punching him, alternating punches with his right and left fist. Riley couldn't even land a punch. Jesse came over and pulled Brad off him. Riley was bleeding from his nose. His eye was starting to swell, and he had a busted lip. As Brad was getting off him, Riley spat a wad of his blood on Brad's shirt. Brad stepped forward and made a quick motion with his hand, connecting it somewhere on Riley's neck, I assumed. I was totally focused on watching Riley gasp for air as Brad came over to stand in front of me, looking at me. Brad's eye color had changed to brown. I had known a few people with "mood-changing eyes," but I didn't know Brad was one. I had never noticed this about him before, most likely because I had never seen Brad angry before now. Anger was dripping off him.

I saw one of his knuckles was bleeding. I reached down and grasped his hand to look at it, his gaze was on me as I looked at his knuckles. I could hear his breath from adrenaline, and I felt his eyes continuing to watch me. But then I let go of his hand as soon as I heard the bar doors open.

"Brad! Baby, where did you run off to!" a shrill woman's voice called from behind us.

The three of us spun around to see a scantily dressed, highly inebriated woman calling from the doorway. She stood there with her arms crossed, rubbing her upper arms. She looked like someone that Brad would date. She was beautiful with bleach-blonde hair, green eyes, large fake boobs, and pouty lips. Brad flicked his eyes at her, and then I felt his hand grasp mine. He didn't say a word to her. I turned to look at him as he turned and pulled me away. Jesse and Jenna fell in behind us. This had really turned into a circus.

"Aren't you going to answer your date?" I asked, offended at his rudeness. He didn't speak. I realized I may have just ruined his date. "If you were on a date, we can just call a cab—" I tried offering.

"No, we're not," he snapped. I wasn't sure which question he was responding to.

As Brad was leading me away by the hand, I turned around to see that Riley was still lying on the sidewalk grasping his throat, trying to catch his breath, Trent leaning over him. Another man, who I assumed was on Brad's security team, was leaning over Riley.

Brad's touch made my skin tingle. My skin was on fire. I began to rub his forearm, lightly caressing his fine hair, all of my senses were on overdrive. It felt like I could feel every fiber of his muscular forearms. He was tolerating my silly state very well.

"So...ecstasy. Is that why I want to have sex with everything, including that lamppost?" called Jenna from behind us. Jenna and I laughed so hard tears came to my eyes.

"Yes," Brad hissed, still irritated. He clearly did not enjoy Jenna's comment as much as I did.

I pulled against his grip. "Slow down! My legs can't walk that fast," I squealed as he tugged on my hand. I turned back to see Jenna talking and rubbing all over Jesse. Jesse was trying to mask his smile. They really looked cute together; they looked like they were truly enjoying each other's company. As for me, Brad slowed his pace slightly, then snapped at me.

"If you wouldn't have drunk so much tonight, you could walk faster," he said through a clenched jaw. My head was spinning. I was horny, really horny. For some reason, every word out of his mouth sounded like, *I want to have sex with you, Laney.* He continued his lecture, "You really need to exercise more control, Laney. And you never leave your drinks unattended—ever. Do you know what could have happened to you tonight?" he hissed.

"I am not a child, Brad, and I did not mean for any of this to happen!" I said, feeling bold and foolish simultaneously.

"What if you would have left with them? What if they—" He paused, clearly flustered. "What if they hurt you?"

"Why do you care?" I shot back.

He stopped immediately, and I bumped into him. Brad nodded at Jesse as he continued past us with Jenna in tow. Jenna winked at me as she walked by. Brad's gaze returned to me. We stood there looking at each other until they were out of earshot.

"Did you really just ask me why I care?"

"Yes, I did."

"How can you ask me that?"

"Because you walked away from me, from us!" I blurted out, not realizing that was going to come flying out.

"I know I did, Laney! Do you think I haven't regretted that decision every day since?"

"I wouldn't know! I've been here, missing you every day, and you were nowhere to be found!"

"And you think because we weren't talking I wasn't missing you too?"

"How would I know? And what type of fucked-up logic is that? If you care about someone, you don't walk out of their life!"

He turned, and we started walking again. I was still agitated. I yanked my hand out of his grip. We stopped again. He glared at me.

"What are you doing?"

"Answer me."

"Answer what?"

"Why did you leave me here?"

"I didn't know what else to do. I thought I was the problem," he said, exasperated.

"I see, and in your mind, leaving me was the best idea?"

"It was never the best idea." He grasped my hand, and we started walking again.

"Where are we going?" I asked as I began to smooth the fine hair on his forearm again. Brad kept looking forward as he tugged me forward.

"My place," he growled.

I was surprised. "Wait...what?" I was shocked.

He looked angry. He was hot when he was angry. Who was I kidding? He was hot all the time.

"You're drunk, Laney, and now you have ecstasy in your system. You can't go home, and God only knows what you would do if you were left to your own devices," he snarled.

My mouth seemed to have no filter from my brain. "I'm not a child! We were doing just fine. I didn't need you to—" I began, but he cut me off.

"Yes, you did. What were you going to do, Laney? I didn't see you fighting him off," he hissed.

I thought for a moment, looking at the blood on his shirt. "No, we didn't. We were just about to...," I started.

Brad chuckled sarcastically. "What? Get rid of them? Go back to their place and—" He paused and looked at me intensely. He could have stopped a train with his look. Then he continued, "I don't think so, Laney."

"Well, what if I don't want to go back to your place?" I blurted out.

"You don't have a choice. You are," he snarled.

"We aren't at work. You can't order me around, Brad," I hissed. He exhaled loudly. Before he could say anything, I looked at him and asked, "Why can I go home with you but not him?"

"He's not me," he hissed.

Wait. What? That statement had so many meanings. I felt like I was in an imaginary world where bosses kept too close of an eye on their unruly adult employees. It was only moments later when we walked into a beautiful lobby of white marble, glass, and water. Of course, he had an apartment at the Waterside Towers. It was one of the most elite and expensive places to live in the area. There was a huge write-up in the paper when they were first built. I had never had the opportunity to go into them. I saw that Jenna and Jesse were waiting for us. Jenna was leaning her head on Jesse's shoulder. We walked over to a private elevator that went only to the penthouse and required a thumbprint, which Jesse supplied. We were all silent in the elevator. Brad had let go of my hand when we stepped in the elevator. Jenna and I stood next to each other, leaning against the back wall. Then we both leaned our heads onto each other.

Jenna sighed. "You ruined my date with Laney, gentlemen. I was trying to get her liquored up so I could get laid tonight. It was her turn to be on top."

At this, Jenna and I broke out with a case of the giggles. I thought I actually spied a smile tugging at the corners of Brad's mouth. The elevator came to a stop, and the doors opened. Jenna and I were holding hands, still giggling, when we stepped out into the hallway.

Chapter 28

JESSE OPENED THE DOOR TO Brad's apartment, and we filed in. Jenna and I were in awe. We took in the expensive furnishings. It was immaculate; however, it looked somehow sterile: no paintings, photographs, or warm colors of any kind. Brad disappeared down the hallway and returned wearing a new T-shirt. He walked over to his wet bar at the side of the room and poured himself and Jesse a drink over ice. Then he leaned against the wet bar and watched me as I wandered around his living room, touching his expensive furnishings lightly with my fingertips—the feel of his wooden side table, the smooth wall, the lampshade. Everything felt erotic. The sensation of the different textures on my fingers were euphoric.

Jesse was sitting on the arm of the chair, and he spoke for the first time all evening. "Care for a drink, ladies?"

Jenna and I both shook our heads and simultaneously said, "No thanks." We erupted into giggles.

"How about some water?" Brad dryly said as he appeared next to me and handed me a bottle of water. I was thirsty. I drank as he watched me. Jenna was engrossed in the stereo system. I knew what was going to happen next. Jenna turned on some rock music. Jenna stood up and pointed at me.

"Hey, beautiful, come hither. I want to dance with you," Jenna said seductively.

I giggled. "Then pick a better song to dance to," I retorted as I slipped off my high heels.

Jenna twisted up her lips. "Fine," she said, crouching back down to fiddle with the stereo system.

Brad had sat down on the couch, seeming to have relaxed, and he started quietly talking to Jesse. I was holding my bottle of water walking around Brad's expansive den, studying the pictures and furniture, and continuing to touch whatever I could get my hands on. In a moment, I heard, "Ladies Night" by Kool and the Gang blasting through the built-in speakers.

I shook my head. "You are killing me, Jenna. You can do better than this."

"Aha, I'll get you dancing, Laney Masterson," Jenna screeched. I heard "Stayin' Alive" by the Bee Gees blast out of the speakers.

I began to laugh as Jenna danced her way over to me. I put down my bottle of water, and she grasped my hands in hers; then we began to dance. After some time of acting silly, Jenna and I needed to catch our breath. I picked up my bottle of water and took a sip. Jenna was kneeling in front of the stereo, back to playing DJ. I turned to see that Brad was looking at me, even though he was sitting on the couch talking to Jesse and mindlessly rubbing his knuckles with his fingers. In this moment with my drug-induced sensory overload, I was enjoying the attention.

Then in true Jenna fashion, Jenna announced she need a bio break. As she departed, the song changed to "Bed of Roses" by Bon Jovi. I turned to ask Jesse a question, but he was gone. It was only Brad and me. My artificial boldness still raging through my body, I smiled at him and slowly walked toward him. He didn't smile back. His eyes slowly scanned my body up and down, lingering at my curves.

"Are you still mad at me, Mr. Green?" I teased.

"I'm not mad. You need to be more careful about your personal safety, Laney," he said sternly.

"How did you know we were at the bar tonight?" I asked.

"I know a lot of things about you," he said as he finished his drink.

"Like what?"

"Like you are the HR director at Mendelson, and you can't hold your liquor." He was being a smartass again.

I laughed and nodded. "Guilty on both accounts," I said through my laughter. As I looked at his face, I was lost in memories. "Do you remember the night we went out for happy hour, and

George couldn't get the lime out from between Rita's boobs?" I asked, laughing.

He gave a half smile. "Yes, I remember. And that was the first night you came back to my place," he said, maintaining my gaze.

My smile disappeared as my mind played the intense and passionate first night that Brad and I were together. Brad's anger was gone; his eyes had gone back to their rich hazel color. I was closing in on him, making sure to sway my hips just enough. His eyes fell to my overflowing cleavage. I swallowed hard.

"It was…," I said, getting lost in my flashback. I cleared my throat. "You've been looking at my outfit all night, Mr. Green. I can tell you where I got it from if you want one," I teased.

He pursed his lips. His eyes had fire dancing within them; he looked devious. Brad had been sitting back on the couch, relaxed, his legs separated. Once I was within range, he leaned up, hooked his fingers through the side belt loops on my jeans, and pulled me onto his lap. My breath hitched. I was straddling him on the couch. My knees were on either side of his hips.

He looked at me. "You know that I prefer you in no clothes at all," he huskily said.

I was surprised and elated at the same time. I am pretty sure my face gave me away. "I work with you, Brad…you are kind of my boss now," I said, tracing my fingers on the collar of his shirt. My brain was trying to process this but couldn't.

"That never stopped us before. And if I am your boss, then why don't you ever do what I tell you to do?" he whispered and then nipped my ear.

"Because I don't trust that your interests are in alignment with mine," I whispered, trying to get up.

He held me onto his lap. "I can assure you, Laney, that my interest is in perfect alignment with yours." His jaw was tight. I could tell he was trying to maintain control.

I was trying to will myself to climb off him again. The close proximity of our bodies made it hard to pull away from him. I felt the familiar pull toward him, like a magnetic force. I felt like I was in a trance due to all these new sensations.

"Do you feel that?" I breathlessly said.

"Yes." He exhaled heavily.

"I want you to touch me, Brad," I whispered, sounding like a seductress.

"It's the ecstasy talking, Laney," he growled.

"No, it's not. I want to feel your hands on my skin." I had to admit, I was sounding very needy and whiny and forward at this point in the night.

I leaned in to kiss him on the lips. He turned away, saying, "Laney, no…"

My insecurities flooded my brain. He didn't want me. He was just pacifying me until I sobered up. *Why would he want me? A widowed single mother with an eight-year-old son and stretch marks? This is Brad Green. He is hot and very rich. He could have anybody.* It was like a bucket of cold water was thrown on me. My inner sex kitten was thrown into a swimming pool of ice cubes.

"I don't do relationships…I am not ready for a commitment yet," he snapped.

"Then what is all of this? Why did you bring me back here? Were you going to use me?" I hissed. I grabbed his hands off my hips and attempted to climb off him. I could tell I was still very inebriated because as I tried to stand, I lost my balance.

Brad immediately stood up and caught me; he was gazing at my face. "No, spending time with you is special enough. Anything else would have just been a bonus," he said as he gazed into my eyes.

His words took my breath away. I don't think someone had ever said something so nice to me. We gazed at each other a long moment, not saying a word. The silence was broken by Jenna walking down the hallway, talking in a too-loud tone, "Holy cow, Brad, I took a wrong turn out of the bathroom, and I got lost in this place."

As Jenna walked in the room, I was still in Brad's arms. Jenna stopped talking and tiptoed backward. Brad leaned his head back and closed his eyes, then looked back down at me.

"Laney, I think you need to go to bed now."

"You're right. If you would please call me a cab, I would like to go home," I said.

"I insist you stay here," he snapped back.

"Fine. I will call my own cab," I said as I reached into my back pocket and pulled out my cell phone.

"Quit arguing with me, Laney," he snarled as he plucked my cell phone from my hand. Then he picked me up and put me over his shoulder. My butt was right by his ear and upper body and arms dangling down his back. In moments, he had laid me down into his huge king-sized bed. He turned and went to his dresser.

"I can stay in another room. I don't have to take your bed," I said.

"You're staying here," he barked.

I sat for a moment, contemplating; then I began to unbutton my jeans and slipped out of them. I paused, forgetting what I was doing. He handed me one of his T-shirts, his eyes lingering on my legs. He turned and walked to his bathroom. I slipped off my blouse and was about to put on his T-shirt. When he stepped back out of his bathroom, I was down to by bra and panties. He took a moment and gazed at my body.

"You may want to take some ibuprofen," he said, handing me the pale-red pills. I could tell my high was coming down because I didn't feel as confident as when I had climbed on his lap only moments ago. I quickly slipped on his T-shirt and then popped the pills into my mouth and took a sip from the bottle of water he handed to me.

In my still fresh feeling of rejection, I couldn't even look him in the eye. I did, however, look around his master bedroom. It was very masculine, black wood and grays throughout.

"Good night, Laney," he said as he exited his bedroom and flicked the switch to turn off the overhead light.

I tossed and turned. At one point, after lying there for what seemed like hours, I sat up and took a drink of water. I looked around the room. It was pitch-black except for the city skyline lights coming in through the huge floor-to-ceiling windows. I swung my legs off the bed and walked over to the windows, wrapping my arms around myself. I leaned my forehead against the cool glass, watching all the people below on the sidewalks that were on their way to somewhere.

"Laney...," I heard Brad's voice, and I jumped. I put my hand over my heart.

"You scared me...how long have you been there?" I said softly, catching my breath as he stood up from the chair in the corner and walked over to stand beside me. I could see out of the corner of my eye in the darkness he had a T-shirt and sweatpants on.

"Long enough. Are you okay?" he asked, his body still facing the window but turning his head to look at me, the city lights illuminating the side of his face.

"I'm fine, just couldn't sleep," I said, offering a slight smile.

"Why don't you ever sleep, Laney?" he asked in a tone that quietly demanded an answer.

I inhaled, allowing a few moments to pass. He didn't flinch.

"I just never sleep," I said, unable to look at him.

"Why?"

"Before you, it was because I never felt safe," I said, pausing for a moment, thankful the dark was hiding my blush in the darkness. "After you, it was because something has been missing," I said quietly staring out the window, my mind flashing back to memories of giggling under the covers and falling asleep in his arms. "I guess you could say I have some emotional baggage that would be a good topic to discuss over drinks one day." I paused and then wanted to move away from this topic. "Besides, if I wasn't awake right now, I wouldn't be able to watch all the people down there. I wonder where they are all going and what the evening holds for them...," I said, trailing off, realizing I probably sounded like an idiot.

"Like those guys," he said, pointing to a group of men walking below us. "Maybe they are going to spike some beautiful woman's drink with ecstasy and try to take her home," he said dryly.

I pressed my lips together. "Maybe...or maybe they are going to make sure those guys"—I pointed at another group of men walking below us—"don't take advantage of a woman having a drink with her best friend on girls' night?" I offered. We continued to watch the people walking around below us. "You didn't have to get involved this evening. Why did you?" I asked, still staring out the window.

"I didn't want anything to happen to you," he said, looking out the window. "You are very...valuable to me, Laney," he offered, and I let out a breathy chuckle.

"Well, thank you, I think. Look, if you want your bed back, I can sleep somewhere else...that chair can't be comfortable," I said as I tucked my hair behind my ear.

Brad turned to face me and grasped my wrist. It didn't hurt, but his grip was firm. He pulled me to him. Our faces were close. If I moved slightly forward, our lips would touch. I froze as I was enraptured by the glow coming through the window reflecting off his beautiful face. Up close, I could see his eyes had yellow flecks in them, almost making them glow.

"You must know what I mean when I say that, Laney," he said quietly. I could see that he was staring at my lips.

"What do you mean?" I said, slightly out of breath from our proximity.

He was silent, his chest moving up and down.

"Why won't you kiss me tonight?" I asked breathlessly, wanting to taste his lips so badly. They were right in front of me. I wanted him so badly it hurt.

"I can't...," he said, releasing me.

I closed my eyes and inhaled deeply. "Can't or won't?" I asked.

"Both," he said with his jaw clenched.

"I feel like this is some sort of game you are playing with me. Why are you doing this?" I asked and then looked down at my hands.

"It's not a game, Laney," he said sternly.

I was starting to get a headache. I turned to walk back to the bed. He didn't let go of my wrist and pulled me to him again. My breath hitched, and I swallowed hard. I thought he was going to kiss me this time, but he didn't. "I don't play games," he whispered with urgency. His lips lightly brushed mine as he spoke.

I studied his face for a moment before responding, "You will kiss me in the woods but not in your bedroom," I barely squeaked out as I turned to walk away.

"Don't walk away from me," he said under his breath.

"That feeling sucks, doesn't it?" I asked, not realizing just how much of the hurt from long ago was still inside of me. He remained silent. "Why didn't you pick me?" I said, my eyes misting.

"Don't do this...," Brad whispered, searching my face.

"Why was I the one you walked away from?" I asked. This was the million-dollar question I wanted to know all these years.

"There were a lot of reasons...none of them were good ones... none of them were the right ones," Brad said under his breath.

"Why? Why was a life with me not worth anything to you? Why was I not good enough?" I said and then swallowed hard. The charge between us was making it hard for both of us to breathe. I think you could have plugged a car battery up to us, and we would have made it run. This was insane; I had never felt anything like this.

"Dear God, no...you are so amazing," I heard him say under his breath.

He pressed his hand against my lower back, the front of our bodies making complete contact. His lips found mine. His kiss was soft yet urgent. What started as a gentle kiss soon grew more passionate, more demanding. It was better than any fantasy or memory I had about him over the past ten years. I didn't want to stop. I felt like my world was spinning around me. I was so engrossed in our kiss that I didn't realize he had lifted me up and carried me to the bed. He slowly laid me down. He lay on top of me, his waist positioned between my legs, our lips never parting. I could feel his hard member pressing against the fabric of my panties. I ran my fingers through his hair as his tongue parted my lips and overtook my mouth, my tongue swirling with his.

All of a sudden, he leaned up, separating his lips from mine. I opened one eye at a time. I lay there, my chest heaving as I caught my breath. He rested his forehead on my sternum.

"Not like this...," he said.

"What!" I said.

"I can't do this...not to you, Laney," he said softly, catching his breath and standing up.

Holy cow, I had been rejected twice in one night. I lay there paralyzed and on the verge of tears. Not sure if it was the rejection, the pent-up emotions from the last few days, or all the events from the evening. He rose up off me and walked out of the room. I continued to lie there a moment, in shock, rejection tearing through my psyche. A tear escaped my eye. I slowly crawled under the covers and closed my eyes. How stupid was I? I must have really changed after all these years. Maybe I wasn't a good kisser anymore, or maybe it was the cellulite on my thighs, or the stretch marks on my stomach. I knew I should have bought that high-end wrinkle cream for my face. I know for a fact he was aroused, but maybe I was just a fling all those years ago. Maybe he just wanted to be friends? Maybe he just wanted sex? My mind was spinning.

The only problem with all those explanations is that he had acted contrary to all of them at some point. I wiped my face, sniffed, and soon I drifted off to sleep.

In the morning, I woke up in Brad's bed, at first unclear as to where I was. I was wrapped in covers and cloaked in severe embarrassment. *What had I done?* My head was a little foggy, but I wasn't sick, and no headache. I checked my phone: it was 7:17 a.m. I slowly turned my head to look around the room. He wasn't there. Memories of last night all came back to me at once, my level of embarrassment continuing to rise. I rubbed my face. *Holy crap, I just spent the night in the CEO's bed.* I reached over to his nightstand and drained the remaining water from my water bottle into my mouth. My aching bladder was telling me that I needed a restroom break. I snaked out of Brad's bed, collected my clothes from the oversized chair in the corner, and walked into his bathroom. I was in awe of what looked to be a five-person shower and a huge soaker tub. I looked in the mirror and attempted to clean up the makeup that was smudged down my face. I gazed for a moment at my unruly hair in the mirror and pulled it back into a ponytail. Relief flooded my body as I relieved my bladder; then I slipped on my jeans and shirt from last night, depositing his shirt into the hamper. I needed a plan on how to get out here with minimal interactions. First, I had to find Jenna and then make a run for it. I was halfway across Brad's room and was bending over to pick up my shoes off of the floor when I heard his voice.

"How did you sleep?" he asked, seemingly amused.

I gazed at him. My brain was foggy, but the hurt from the rejection last night struck me like a bolt of lightning. He was sitting in the chair my clothes occupied only moments ago. He must have supersonic hearing. My eyes caught sight of his swollen and scraped knuckles resting on the armrest. This man had saved me from a monumental mistake and possibly my life last night, and I was sneaking out of his house like a thief. My logical mind was wagging her finger at me.

"I slept well...I'm sorry if I ruined your plans for the evening. I noticed you had a very pretty girl waiting for your return at the bar," I said softly, looking down at the shoes in my hand. He was scanning my body up and down. *Why does he do that? He doesn't want me, yet he checks me out like I am a prime slab of beef.*

"You didn't ruin anything," he said with a smirk.

"I need to go find Jenna. We should really get going," I said nervously, fidgeting with my shoes that I held in my hands. He nodded, not saying a word. I looked down at my hands again. "I never properly thanked you last night. If you hadn't of been there, I don't know what—"

"Those guys were pricks. You need to be more careful, Laney. You are too beautiful to waste your time on guys like that," he said, cutting me off and standing up. His large muscular frame dwarfed me, especially when I was barefoot.

I scanned his body, noticing how his muscular arms nicely stretched his T-shirt, and his jeans accentuated his muscular thighs. I didn't know what to do. This whole situation was surreal to me. I was looking at the future CEO of my company, in his bedroom, after just spending the night in his bed, albeit by myself. I gave him a little smile and nod then walked out past him, out of his room into the hall, looking for Jenna. She was awake in the guestroom. Her night had clearly been more active than mine. The bed looked completely destroyed. I lay on the bed facing her.

Jenna was the first one to whisper, "I know you are wondering, so here is my summary—Jesse is as good in bed as he is hot."

I gave a quiet laugh and then sighed. "Are you ready to go? We can talk more at breakfast." I was completely sober and realizing the need to put some distance between myself and Brad's penthouse.

Jenna eyed me. "What is better than morning-after breakfast with my best friend? Nothing! Did you get some from Mr. Grumpy CEO?" she whispered.

I shook my head. "No, he didn't want me. I feel so stupid, Jenna. I am going to have to work with him, ya know?" I whispered back.

Jenna quietly laughed. "Well, work just got more interesting," she said as we both got up to make our escape.

We were almost to the door. I thought we were going to escape Brad's penthouse apartment without any more interactions, but Brad called out from the kitchen, where he was sitting at the counter on his laptop with no shirt on, just his athletic shorts and sneakers. "Leaving?" he said without looking up.

Jenna spoke, "Yes, thank you for your hospitality. We will see you on Monday."

Jesse appeared from the corner to give Jenna a wave and wink. Brad was smirking, still looking at his screen.

"Have a good day, ladies," he said wryly.

I felt so ashamed I wanted to slip into a crack on the floor and hide for a few days. We walked out of his building and down the sidewalk to our favorite diner, just past Mendelson's office building.

Jenna and I sat in a booth. We were famished. I realized we hadn't eaten any dinner last night. Jenna had just swallowed a huge bite of waffle. "Do you have Jesse's number?" she said with wide eyes.

I laughed. "No, I don't. Why would I?" I said, sipping my tea.

Jenna groaned. "Shit. He asked if I wanted his number last night, and I was playing it cool, so I said no because you have it."

I squinted my eyes at Jenna. "Jenna Ford, why would I have that man's number?" I asked.

Jenna looked at me innocently. "You're the HR director. You have everyone's number," she said as she batted her eyes at me.

I pursed my lips. "Jenna, darling…sweetie pie, honey bunch, my lovey…he is not a Mendelson employee," I offered.

Jenna laid her head on the table and groaned. I let out a hearty chuckle.

Chapter 29

AFTER BREAKFAST, WE FOUND OUR cars in the parking garage across the street. Jenna followed me to the football field to watch Braeden's game. We found Lizzie in the bleachers with Josh. After the game, Jenna left with Josh, and then I paid Lizzie, and she departed soon after that. I was walking with Braeden to the car when I looked up to see Mark leaning against my car. *Not today.* I thought to myself.

"Mark?" I acknowledged.

"Laney, I haven't seen you around. You must be working too hard," he said, almost sounding like a game-show host.

"The job pays the bills. When were you looking for me? I just saw you the other day?" I said with my fake smile.

"So it does…you know, I am always around town. I like to drive past your place to make sure everything is quiet on the homestead."

"I see," I said, unamused.

"So I just got a new hot tub at my place," he started and then paused, looking to make sure Braeden was out of earshot. "How about you and me get naked and break it in tonight? My mother can watch the boys," he said with his eyes dancing dangerously.

I let out a nervous laugh. Truthfully, that was the last thing I wanted to do. "Sounds interesting, but no thank you. I had a late night last night and want to spend some time with Braeden tonight." I paused then restarted again. "I really just want to be friends, Mark," I said, opening my car door, which made him move out of the way. I checked the rear-view mirror to see Braeden already engrossed with a game on his tablet.

"Friends? Come on, Laney…," he said.

"Have a good night," I said as I shut the door and waved to him. I drove home, lost in thought.

Braeden was occupied with a movie in the living room, so I took the opportunity to take a shower. When I got out of the shower, I checked my phone: no text messages. I went downstairs and cuddled up with Braeden on the couch. After the movie was over, we went outside and lit the yard debris in our fire ring by the water. It was beautiful, the flames dancing in the dusk sky. Braeden and I each sat in an Adirondack chair with our designated blankets. I had wine; he had grape juice in a wineglass. We giggled and told "knock, knock" jokes until darkness settled in. When I looked over to see that he could barely keep his eyes open, I walked with him back to the house and tucked him in. Then I grabbed the opened bottle of wine and returned to the fire ring, setting the bottle of wine on the ground to the side of my chair. I added a few more logs to the fire and sat in my seat, pulling my legs up to my chest and covering myself with the blanket. I took a sip of my wine and then leaned my head back against the back of the chair, setting my glass down on the armrest. I watched the flames dance. As I gazed into the fire, I thought about Sam, but then my thoughts quickly shifted to Brad. I tried to console myself that I may have struck out with Brad, but there would be others. *Wasn't that something that people just say to console the brokenhearted?*

In truth, there would never be anyone else like him, no one that made me feel the way he did. There was something special about him, something so much deeper about our connection. I needed to stop thinking that way, I told myself. I needed to get over him. People change. Maybe we had just changed too much for each other and what we had needed to be left in the past. I just need to let him go this time. It would be difficult, I decided, since I had thought about him every day for the last ten years, but I would figure out a way to go on. I knew the sadness would eventually tame itself some.

"Should you be out here by yourself?" Brad's voice said from behind me.

I jumped and knocked my glass off the armrest. With one swift and fluid move of his arm, he caught it. I looked up at him. He had jeans and a navy-blue fleece pullover on. The fleece clung to his strong arms. I could see the flames reflecting in his eyes. He looked relaxed.

"Oh shit, Brad! You scared me...," I said, holding my hand over my heart, feeling the poor organ thumping loudly against my ribs. I leaned my head back, closing my eyes. He set my wineglass back on the armrest. "Thank you," I murmured. I swallowed hard. "Please, take a seat. I just put Braeden to bed," I said softly. He sat down, moving the blanket to the side. "I didn't bring an extra wineglass. I can go in and get one for you."

"This will be fine," he said, taking my wineglass and draining the remainder of my wine down his throat. Then he smiled at me and set the glass back down. I smiled back and reached down to grab the wine bottle, pulling the cork out with my teeth. Then I filled my glass again. He started to laugh, and then so did I.

"What brings you out here so late, Mr. Green? I would think one of the most eligible bachelors in America would be on a hot date. It is Saturday night, you know?" I said, smiling, still staring into the fire, partially afraid to look at him from embarrassment and partly jealousy.

"I had to see you, Laney," he said as he took my glass of wine and took another sip. Then he set it back on my armrest. I figured since we swapped saliva last night, I already had whatever cooties he had.

"Is it work? Did something happen?" I said, turning to look at him.

He started laughing. "Work is fine. Relax, Laney," he said, looking back at me.

I turned my head and looked back at the fire. "Then why did you need to see me?" I said, hugging my legs into my chest. I wanted to make myself as small as possible—suck in all my flaws and hide them under the blanket.

"I couldn't stop thinking about you," he said in a hushed tone.

I exhaled. "What? Really?" I said under my breath as I turned to look at him.

"Yes. Is that really that hard to believe?" he said, looking back at me.

"You are so confusing to me, and I can't read you at all. I am really rusty at these games, so I need a freaking neon sign if you are trying to tell me something," I said, feeling myself getting upset; I needed to calm down. "Look, I know from last night that I'm not your type anymore—completely get it. I remember how much fun we had when we worked together before, and I would love to be friends again, but...," my voice trailed off. I was frustrated, and my emotions were clogging my communication neurons. I stood up to get another couple pieces of firewood. I caught Brad drinking in my body out of the corner of my eye. I was wearing my black yoga pants and tank top; I wasn't really expecting company. After I tossed the wood in the fire, I was walking in front of Brad to return to my seat when he grabbed my hand and completely derailed my emotional outburst.

"Come here," he said, pulling on my hand. My heart squeezed as I looked at his face, which was illuminated by the dancing flames. How was I supposed to unlove this man? I sat down on his lap and leaned my back on his chest. His body was firm. His cologne was mixed with the natural male scent of his skin. It smelled so good; he was so warm. I laid my head back on his shoulder, and he covered me up with the blanket. His long arm reached to bring the wineglass over. He took a sip, and then I took the wineglass from him and took a sip. I set it down on the armrest.

"Is this okay? I mean, am I hurting you?" I asked, starting to sit up.

He softly chuckled. "It's perfect, Laney. Quit worrying so much," he said, pulling me back onto his chest. He leaned into my hair and inhaled. "Laney, I need to explain something," he said softly into my neck.

"Please don't. I can't take any more this weekend. I am cool with being friends and a cuddle by the fire every now and then," I offered.

"But I'm not okay with that," he said softly, his lips brushing my neck. This man was about to make my head explode. I picked up my wineglass and finished it. Then I felt over the side of the chair with my hand for the wine bottle. I found it and emptied the remaining dark-red liquid contents into my glass.

"Okay...then maybe I am going to need you to explain," I said, sitting up and twisting my upper body to face him. He patted his chest. I smiled; he wanted me to lie back down. I did, and he wrapped his arms around me.

"When I said I needed to see you, I meant it. I have been distracted by thoughts of you all day, Laney," he said into my neck, his lips brushing the sensitive skin on my neck as he spoke. As his words registered, my heart squeezed, and butterflies commenced fluttering around my stomach. I wasn't crazy.

"Then why didn't you want me last night?" I asked, afraid of the answer.

"You deserve better...Laney, there are things about me—" He paused. "I don't want to hurt you," he said in a low tone.

"Like what? I am tougher than I look," I said, staring into the fire and watching the log pop, sending sparks cascading into the grass. I felt his chest move as he gave a soft chuckle.

"Ha, I am well aware of that. But—" he started, but I cut him off.

"But—let me guess—you just want to be friends?" I asked.

He didn't respond for what seemed like the longest time. "I would say yes, but I am finding that I can't stay away from you, Laney," he said as he proceeded to kiss my neck and then softly sucked on my ear lobe. I turned my head to face him and to look into his eyes, my ear lobe slipping from his mouth. "And the thought of another man touching you enrages me," he said as he leaned in to kiss me.

I closed my eyes, heightening all the sensations. I reached up and held his face, and we continued to taste each other. His hand slowly slid down my abdomen and slipped under the top of my pants, and then he made his way under the top of my panties. *Oh my.* My heart began to beat like thunder in my chest as I anticipated the feel of his fingers against my ever-moistening and sensitive lady bits. His fingers found their target and went to work dividing and massaging my wet folds. I gasped as his other hand reached under my tank top and squeezed my swollen nipple. My hips twitched as he found my most sensitive area. It had been so long since I had been sensually touched by a man. I felt the building of tension throughout my body begin. I was on sensory overload—the taste of his kiss, the feel of his lips, the urgency of his tongue, his scent, his rock-hard body, his obvious desire pressing against me, his skilled hands—it was all too much for my novice body to handle. I gripped his hand, causing his motion to stop. I felt his lips form into a smile, and he withdrew his hand from my pants. I parted from his lips.

"You are still just as responsive," he said as he kissed my neck. "Why aren't you this compliant for me at work?" he whispered in my ear as he slipped his hands from underneath my clothing.

I started giggling under my breath. Then I took a sip of wine and handed him the glass. He took a sip. He kissed the side of my head. I turned to look at him, and he softly kissed my lips again, his tongue softly teasing my lips. I smiled at him as I parted from his lips then laid my head back and lifted his hand so that I could see his bruised knuckles in the soft glow of the dying fire. I felt his cheek move against my temple from his smile. Then he began to slowly and softly kiss my neck, ears, shoulder, and chin. The feel of his lips on my skin felt so incredible.

"Did it hurt?" I asked softly as I gently ran my fingers over them, feeling the roughness of the scabs alternating with the smoothness of his skin. I tried to maintain my focus as his lips distracted me.

"Did what hurt?" he asked in between kisses.

"When you punched him?"

"I don't know," he said flatly. He stopped kissing me.

I quietly chuckled. "How do you not know?" I asked.

He didn't answer for a couple of minutes. "I blacked out, Laney," he said, shifting underneath me, and withdrew his hand from my grasp.

"What do you mean by 'blacked out'?"

"It's late. I should really get going," he said, shifting again underneath me.

I struck a nerve. I sat up and twisted to the side so my legs draped over the armrest. "Tell me," I said.

He exhaled out of frustration. "Laney, like I said, it's getting late," he said more firmly.

I reached up and held his face in my hands, gazing into his eyes. "This is me...tell me," I whispered.

"I have a bad temper," he said, trying to shake me from the subject.

"Okay, and I have PMS," I said matter-of-factly. This made him smile and seemed to lighten the mood, if only temporarily. "Tell me what you meant by black out?" I asked, removing my hands from his face, my eyes holding his gaze. I saw his chest decompress as he slowly exhaled.

"Certain triggers cause me to experience intense anger. When I don't control it, I slip into rage. When my rage reaches a certain level, I black out and have no recall of my actions." His eyes searched mine, waiting for my response. I had so many questions.

"How do you control it?"

"Lifestyle modifications help, exercise, diet, sleep, sex, and—" He paused. I could tell he was contemplating if he wanted to tell me more. "Therapy. Most of the time, I feel it coming on and can stop it from going too far," he said, still studying my face for my reaction.

"What triggers it?" I asked, still not flinching.

"Laney...," he chided.

"If it's too personal, that's fine, but tell me what triggered it last night," I urged softly.

He closed his eyes and leaned his head back. I didn't think he was going to say anything, but then he began speaking.

"You," he said, barely audible.

"Me? I made you that angry?" I asked in disbelief. I was acting silly last night, but I didn't think it was that bad. He leaned his head up and looked at me; his gaze was intense.

"One member of my security team was at the bar the whole time you and Jenna were there. He told Jesse that they slipped ecstasy in yours and Jenna's drinks. Then a few minutes later, we saw them taking you and Jenna outside. He was touching you, his hand was on your waist..." He swallowed hard, as though feeling some remnants of the intense emotions he felt the night before. "When I walked outside, he was still touching you." He stopped, and his eyes looked away for a moment. Then he looked back to me. "I got tunnel vision.

All I could see was you…his hands on you…I knew I was slipping into a rage…and when he kept you from me, I didn't care anymore," he paused and swallowed hard. "I blacked out," he said, his jaw tightening, instinctively preparing himself for my reaction.

"When did you come out of it?" I asked.

"When Jesse was pulling me up, and I turned around and looked at you," he said, watching my face, fearing my rejection.

"Is that how it usually happens?" I asked.

"No. I haven't blacked out in a while, and it usually takes me longer to come out of it. But you…," he started and stopped.

I was so touched by his openness and vulnerability. I did what felt natural: I wrapped my arms around his neck and hugged him. He tensed up at first, surprised at my response. Then I felt him relax and his arms wrap around my back, squeezing me. "Laney, I was out of control of my actions. Aren't you afraid…of me…now?" he asked into my shoulder. His question broke my heart.

I released him from my hug and looked at him. "No," I said with a smile. "You're going to have to do better than that," I said playfully. He reached his hands up to either side of my face and held me for a moment, looking into my eyes, searching for something, then pulled my lips to his. When we parted, he studied my face a moment before removing his hands. I could tell by how dark it was that only ashes remained where our fire once was. I knew he would be leaving; I didn't want him to. Beyond the physical attraction, I genuinely enjoyed his company.

"I need to be going, Laney," he said softly as he kissed the top of my hand.

"I wish you didn't," I said softly, leaning in to kiss him once more.

"Me too," he said softly. I smiled then stood up and collected the blankets, wine bottle, and wineglass. I found my phone on the ground next to my chair. I checked the time: it was 1:11 a.m. As we walked around the front of the house, I saw his huge SUV parked behind my car. I stood in front of the porch in almost the exact spot where I had seen him that day he jogged up my driveway. He stood in front of me and tucked a stray piece of hair behind my ear.

"Thank you for coming over. This was a wonderful surprise," I said softly.

He nodded, not saying anything, gazing at my hair. I knew the longer we stood here, the more the sexual tension was going to build between us. He leaned in for a soft kiss. "I will see you Monday," he said. I nodded with a smile, and he turned to leave.

Then I turned to walk into the house. Once he saw that I was inside, he turned and got into his car and left. I had a huge grin on my face. What was that? It was so unexpected, so amazing. Proof that some surprises are a very good thing.

I woke up only a few hours later to Braeden bouncing on my bed. "Mom! Get up! You promised we could play in the water!" he was saying as he was bouncing.

"Okay...okay...let's get some breakfast first," I said, swinging my legs out of bed. I picked up my phone: no messages. Braeden shrieked with excitement as he ran down the hall. After breakfast, we changed into our swimsuits and played in the river until late afternoon.

As we made our way into the back door, I noticed a white unmarked van turning out of our driveway. I quickly changed and went back downstairs. I opened the front door to see a beautiful bouquet of white with red-tipped roses sitting on my welcome mat.

"Those are pretty, Mommy. Who sent them?" Braeden asked.

"Well, let's find out." I smiled as I picked them up. I took in their scent as I walked into the dining room and set them in the middle of the table. I plucked the card from the clear plastic fork it was sitting in. I smiled as I read it:

I thought these were aptly named. Thank you for last night.

-B

"They are from Mr. Brad," I said, lost in thought as I took a picture of the flowers and searched them on Google. I chuckled to myself when the search results came back: "fire and ice roses." I pulled up my text messages and selected Brad's name.

"Thank you for the flowers, they are beautiful."

"Did you look up the name?"

"Yes…fire and ice…perfect. Now my new favorite flower."

"I'll remember that."

"He must really like you to send you pretty flowers," Braeden said.

"I think you're right, honey," I said and smiled as I put down my phone and went to make dinner in the kitchen with a huge grin on my face.

Chapter 30

MONDAY MORNING ROLLED AROUND. I was a little nervous about interacting with Brad in the workplace after our weekend. The whole thing still left my head spinning, and I would prefer to question him to death, but I decided that I needed to just focus on my work and let whatever might happen naturally unfold. I also decided that I would pretend like nothing happened between us; I decided that it would probably be easier. I scrolled through the appointments in my calendar. I noticed I had a meeting with Brad at 3:00 p.m.; that would be the true test of my resolve. Slade came in a few minutes before three.

"So did you complete the labor analysis for each of the sites?" he said, out of breath.

I laughed. "Slade, our meeting is in five minutes. Don't you think you should have asked me this earlier? And yes, I sent it to Brad's and Jack's assistants this morning," I said, chuckling.

Slade nodded. "Perfect. I was planning on presenting the data. Jack thought it would be good for me to get face time in front of Brad," he said confidently.

I smiled. "By all means," I said.

We walked into the conference room together. Brad was watching me even though he had Frank in his ear talking to him. It seemed he was trying to figure out the nature of the relationship that Slade and I had. Frank finished talking, and we began the meeting. Slade ran through the first fifteen slides. My eyes fell to Brad's scratched knuckles. A pang of guilt seized my stomach as I remembered this weekend's events.

Brad spoke up and broke my concentration, "Mr. Brinkman, can you please tell me how you calculated your 2013 number?"

Slade stumbled through his answer. Brad narrowed his eyes and nodded, then let him continue. I could tell he wasn't believing a word Slade was saying. After a few more slides, Brad questioned Slade again.

"These numbers are different than what I had been given by Veronica. What do you classify as attrition?" Brad asked.

Slade thought for a moment and looked to me with desperation in his eyes. So I did what I always do: I answered for him.

"We classified attrition as retirements, voluntary resignations, and involuntary terminations. This is what we have always classified attrition as. If there is another subcategory, I would be glad to work with Veronica on harmonizing this information," I said without a trace of a smile.

Brad seemed satisfied as he gave me a subtle smirk. Slade continued, but Brad's eyes stayed on me, studying me. When the meeting was over, I jumped up. Jack was at my side. He walked me to my office, chatting about his weekend. As I was watching Jack go back to his office beside Brad's, I noticed that Jesse was stationed outside Brad's office. I smiled as I walked over to him and spoke in a whisper.

"Jesse, I wanted to let you know that Jenna had a great time Friday night. Thank you for everything."

He raised his eyebrows at me in surprise. "Ma'am?" he said innocently.

I smiled and nodded. "Here is Jenna's number," I slipped him a piece of paper. I turned and walked back to my office. It was quitting time, and I had made it through my first day this week without any one-on-one meetings with Brad. My confidence grew slightly each day that I could actually handle this.

Tuesday and Wednesday, my days flew by with no sighting of Brad at all nor a text or phone call. I had developed a sore throat. I was convinced that I was getting a cold. I hadn't been sleeping that much due to all the reports that were being requested for the acquisition team. Unfortunately, that was the price of doing my job and Slade's job. In a normal world, Slade would be able to take some of the workload. With all the changes and stress, it was no wonder I was sick; but in typical strong-willed Laney fashion, I refused to acknowledge anything was wrong. I felt like all I did was bathe in antibacterial gel and eat ibuprofen like candy. Thursday had been going well until 1:00 p.m. I received a call from Brad's secretary, Gladys.

"Ms. Masterson, could you please meet Mr. Green in his office?" her chipper voice squeaked through my phone.

I sighed. I felt terrible. This was really the last thing I wanted to do right now.

"Yes, be right there," I replied, my voice expressing more exhaustion than I had wanted. As I approached Gladys's desk, she smiled sweetly at me.

"Ms. Masterson, I beg your pardon, you are a beautiful woman, but, honey, you look terrible. I think you should tell Mr. Green he can wait, and you should take yourself right home and rest in bed," she said with genuine concern.

I felt slightly embarrassed. I didn't know Gladys that well, and for a semistranger to tell me I looked like shit was a new low for me.

"You are really sweet, Gladys. I truly appreciate your concern. I plan on meeting with Mr. Green and then taking the rest of the afternoon easy. I will hopefully be done soon," I said as I gave her a weary smile.

She nodded. "Please let me know if you need anything, sweetie," she said.

I nodded, and she motioned for me to enter Brad's office.

I walked into Brad's office. He was leaning on the side of the desk closest to me with his arms crossed. He looked up at me and said, "Close the door, Laney." I inhaled and shut the door, then turned back around to face him. I stopped about three feet from him. I felt dizzy.

"What can I help you with, Mr. Green?" I said flatly.

He tilted his head, his gaze cold. "I would appreciate if you didn't meddle in the affairs of my security team," he snapped.

My eyes narrowed. "What are you talking about?" I said with as much energy as I could muster.

"My security team doesn't need to be distracted by the opposite sex."

It hit me like a ton of bricks. He was talking about Jenna; I tampered with his territory. I laughed. "Well, Mr. Green, let's speak in specifics, not generalities. I gave Jenna's number to Jesse because she likes him. He is a human being that deserves to get his rocks off the same as, I am sure, he has to watch you do all the time!" I hissed.

"Laney, I am warning you...," he hissed back.

I glared right back at him. "Warn me all you want, Brad. It's not going to change a damn thing that I do," I hissed.

The jugular vein in his neck was pounding rapidly. "Damn it, Laney! Why are you so defiant?" he snarled as he slammed his hand on his desk.

"Because you are so controlling!" I blurted out, not quite understanding where my comment came from. It stunned Brad too. I turned on my heel, opened the door, and walked back to my office. That exchange took every last bit of energy that I had. I walked over to Jenna's desk.

"You don't look so good. Why don't you head home for the day?" she said with concern.

"I will explain it to you later. I am fine. I just haven't been sleeping a lot lately. Different subject. How about you, me, Josh, Braeden, and a few bottles of our favorite wines go to the beach house this weekend?" I said in a hushed voice even before she could begin to inquire.

"You had me at bottles of wine. For real, Laney, are you okay? You look awful."

I smiled. She was always so concerned about me.

"I'm fine, Jenna. Are you still okay for Braeden to spend the night?" I asked. The room felt like it was spinning, and I felt weak. I needed to sit down.

"Yeah, Josh can't wait to work on their history project!" she said, giddily clapping.

I smiled weakly and nodded as I went back to my office. I plopped myself in my chair. I began to feel hot and then get chills. I found a sweater in one of my desk drawers to put on over my blouse. On his way out, Jack had brought some legal briefs in for me to review.

"Laney, go home. You look like a ghost," Jack commanded.

"I will. I am almost done," I said as I gave him a weak smile.

"I mean it. You are running yourself into the ground. This place isn't worth that. I will carry you out of here myself if I have to," he barked.

"All right, all right, just another few minutes, and I will head out, I promise." This seemed to appease him.

"Okay then, have a good night. See you tomorrow," he said as he eyed me suspiciously.

"Jack, go home," I said. He winked at me and turned to leave.

Contrary to what I told Jack, I was on a short timeline with a lot of these reports, so this was going to be a late night. My throat was killing me. I tried to drink water, but it was like swallowing razor blades. Around 9:30 p.m., I decided that it would be okay if I laid my head on my desk for a little rest before resuming my work. I crossed my arms on top of the desk and laid my head down. I was roused from my sleep by a cool hand brushing my hair from my forehead. My eyes were heavy and didn't want to open.

"You're burning up, Laney. Why are you still here?" Brad said softly.

I opened my eyes to look at him sitting on my desk, next to me. I wondered how long he had been there. My head was pounding. I squinted at him; the light hurt my eyes.

"I had some things I needed to get finished for Jack...what time is it?" I asked softly.

"Ten forty-four p.m. The legal briefs can wait," he said firmly.

"Really, I'm fine," I said as I tried standing up. My knees felt weak. I steadied myself against my desk, closing my eyes to make the room stop spinning. I began to tremble. I tried to control my jaw so that my teeth wouldn't chatter. Brad stood up next to me. I could feel his body heat. He took off his suit jacket and wrapped it around me. I leaned closer to him. "Thank you," I murmured, feeling slightly embarrassed.

"Laney, you are sick. You need to rest and take care of yourself. You shouldn't be here," he admonished me. I closed my eyes and nodded. I was starting to believe what everyone had told me

275

all day. The room was spinning again, and my leg muscles gave out on me. As my knees began to give way, he pulled me to his warm body and wrapped his arm around my waist as he picked up my purse and laptop bag then helped me to the elevator. Once in the elevator, I leaned against the cold brushed nickel back wall. I heard the elevator *ping* as it opened. He swung my legs up, cradling my body like a child.

"No…Brad, you are going to hurt yourself…I am too heavy…I can walk…if you will just bring me to my car, I can drive home," I softly protested.

"You can't drive, Laney. You aren't walking, I am carrying you," he sternly said.

I leaned my head into his chest. As we exited into the parking garage, the cool night air hit me, and I began to furiously tremble. This time, I couldn't stop my teeth from chattering. The familiar black Suburban pulled up. Jesse was waiting for us as we approached. He opened the door to the backseat. Brad gently set me on the seat and hopped in beside me, closing the door. Jesse was in the driver's seat. I briefly opened my eyes to see him looking at me with concern. I brought my knees up toward my chest and turned my body toward Brad, laying my head on his shoulder. He wrapped his arm around me and pulled me in closer. I felt him lay his head on top of mine. I had to admit, my body felt like I had been hit by a Mack truck, but I liked being close to him, however odd this situation was. I felt the car come to a stop and heard the door open.

"I want to walk…," I softly protested, hardly able to open my eyes. I felt Brad begin to move away from me to exit the car, and I slowly sat up, immediately missing the warmth of his body. I had a death grip on his jacket as I pulled it tighter around me.

He stepped out of the car and turned to face me. I scooted to the edge of the seat, and he pulled me into his arms. He held my waist from behind me as we walked together to the elevator. Once in the elevator, he leaned against the back wall and pulled me to him. I turned to face him, craving his warmth. I closed my eyes and laid my head on his shoulder. He smelled delicious. He tightened his jacket around me and then wrapped his arms around me. My knees felt weak again and gave way. He gripped me tighter and swung my legs up yet again to carry me.

"I-I-I'mmmm s-s-sorrryyy," I said quietly through chattering teeth.

"You never need to apologize to me," he said softly.

"Y-y-y-ou c-c-cannn d-d-droppp m-m-me offfff attttt th-th-the ER ssso I d-d-don't r-r-ruin yourrrrr p-p-p-lansssss for thisssss evening," I said through my chattering teeth.

"You aren't going anywhere," he said softly.

The elevator doors opened. He carried me to his bedroom, which now looked familiar, as it dawned on me that I had been here less than a week ago.

"The doctor should be here in a few minutes," he said as he laid me down on the bed. The sheets were cool against my hot skin. He removed my shoes, and he covered me up. I turned to my side, facing him, and hugged my legs to my chest in the fetal position. I pulled his jacket tighter around me.

"D-d-doctor? B-b-brad, it'sssss eleven o'c-c-c-clock-k-k at n-n-night-t-t?" I weakly countered.

"My personal physician, Dr. Balldrum," he said, sitting next to me on the edge of the bed, brushing wisps of hair from my forehead.

"I-I-I c-c-couldn't impose onnnnn h-h-himmm. I-I-I jjjjusssttt n-n-need r-r-r-rest," I offered.

"You're sick, Laney. You need a doctor. I already asked him to come. You are going to get checked out, and that's final. Now quit arguing with me and just rest," he barked.

I closed my eyes and swallowed hard, feeling the ever-present razor blades in my throat. In moments, I heard a soft tapping at the door. I felt the bed shift as Brad stood up and walked to the door. I opened my eyes to see a very in-shape gray-haired man who looked to be about sixty with a kindly smile and small oval glasses.

"Laney, I presume?" he said, walking over to the bed.

I sat up slowly. "Y-y-yessss," I said, feeling stupid I couldn't control my shaking.

He came to sit next to me, setting his black medical bag between us. "I understand you aren't feeling well?" he asked as he felt my forehead with his hand. I nodded instead of talking this time. He fished his thermometer out of his medical bag and stuck it under my tongue. I looked at Brad. He looked concerned from his position in the doorway, leaning against the doorframe with his arms crossed. I caught a glimpse of Jesse standing slightly behind him. Every so often, I would see Brad rake one of his hands through his hair. I heard the thermometer beep, and Dr. Balldrum clicked his tongue.

"Your temperature is 104.6 degrees. Let me see your throat. Open up and say *aaahhhh*," he said as he brought out a tongue depressor.

I did as I was told, feeling like a small child.

"You have strep throat, Laney. Are you allergic to any medications?"

"No," I said softly

"I am going to give you a shot of penicillin. It is long release so you won't need to take any further antibiotics. I will give you the injection in the thigh. We will need to get your fever down as well. Take some ibuprofen and a lukewarm bath to bring your temperature down. Please keep personal contact down to a minimum as you will be contagious for the next twelve hours."

I nodded as he pulled out a fresh needle and vial of clear liquid. "Now before I do this, is there any chance you could be pregnant?" he asked, eyeing Brad's jacket. I couldn't look at Brad.

"N-n-no," I responded.

"Okay," he said, clearly not believing me. He obviously thought Brad and I were together. I could understand why. Brad made his way across the room to his bathroom, and I heard him turn on the faucet to his huge bathtub. Dr. Balldrum popped the cap off the needle and stuck the sharp tip into the end of the vial then turned both upside down, slowly draining a precise amount of the clear liquid out of the vial. Brad returned to the room and stood next to the doctor.

"Mr. Green, could you please help her to standing. Laney, I will need your bare thigh please," the doctor said as he stood up from the edge of the bed.

I swung my legs around to the edge of the bed. Brad helped me to standing and then began to unfasten my dress pants. My eyes watched his hands move with ease. My mind brought forward memories of nights long ago where that led to different activities than a penicillin shot to the thigh. As my pants slid down my legs to the floor, a new wave of trembling came over me as a layer of warmth had been removed. My legs had goosebumps everywhere; I looked like I had alien skin. How embarrassing. Brad eased me back onto the bed and swung my legs up. The doctor cleaned the area with a small alcohol pad and, in an instant, shoved the needle into my thigh. I winced; then he removed it after all the liquid had been forced out of it.

"Your thigh is going to be sore for a few days, but go ahead and get in that bath and take these." He handed me four ibuprofen tablets along with a glass of water.

I sat up, trying to cover my panties with my blouse. I looked at my legs; they were still covered in goosebumps.

"It was nice to meet you, Laney. No work tomorrow. Do you need a note for your employer?" he asked.

"No, she doesn't. I'll make sure everything is taken care of," Brad said firmly.

Dr. Balldrum turned to Brad. "Very good. If she isn't better in the morning, call me right away," he said.

Brad nodded and left the room with Dr. Balldrum to see him out. I sat on the edge of the bed, willing myself to move in the direction of the warm bath. Brad soon returned. His face looked so soft, completely different from the expression he wore at work. Brad's eyes lingered on me for a moment as he walked into the room, and then he quickly walked to the bathroom, and I heard the rushing water from the faucet stop. He returned to the side of the bed.

"Come on, baby," he said softly.

I was now hearing things. I know he must have said *Laney*, not *baby*, as he scooped me up in his arms and carried me to the bathroom. He slowly set me down. The tile floor was cold on my feet. My body stiffened, and I immediately began to tremble. I could feel my nipples swelling against the fabric of my bra; it was almost painful. Brad stood there a moment, both of us unsure if he should stay or go. I began to try to unbutton the three buttons on the top of my blouse. My hands were shaking so badly I couldn't keep a grip on the small delicate buttons. I felt so helpless and frustrated I began to cry.

"Hey, hey, what's this? Why are you crying?" he crooned.

"I hate this. I feel so helpless. You shouldn't have to do this... and now I'm crying," I said, sniffling, my shaking hands unsteadily wiping my cheeks.

"It's okay to need people sometimes, Laney, and to let yourself be vulnerable," he said, looking intensely into my eyes. I knew he was speaking more deeply than my illness. In a moment, his large steady fingers were next to mine, unbuttoning my blouse, gently moving my hands out of the way. He was so close to me I could feel his breath blow the small wisps of hair on my forehead. He slid my blouse off my shoulders and down my arms; then he tossed it into the sink. I realized that I was too weak to get into the bathtub by myself and would need his help.

His arm reached around me and unfastened my bra with one hand. I smiled. "Nnnnothing yyyyou hhhhaaaven't seeeen beeeeforrre," I said as my body shook violently.

He looked at me for a long moment. "And you are even more stunning now," he said softly, tucking a stray piece of hair behind my ear.

How could he look at me and say that? My bra released its hold on my breasts, and it slid down the front of my arms. My erect nipples grazed the fabric of his shirt. He then gently reached down and hooked his thumbs into my panties, giving them a firm tug, allowing them to slide down my legs. He gripped my upper arm as I stepped out of them and into the huge tub. I lowered myself down into the warm water. His eyes took in my body and would rise back up to mine. I lay back, sloshing water, my breasts bobbing, the water harassing my swollen nipples. I closed my eyes and sank deeper into the water. I began to feel better as my trembling ceased. I opened my eyes to see Brad sitting on the edge of the tub with his back facing me, still in his suit pants and collared shirt, his sleeves rolled up to his elbows. He was mindlessly rubbing his knuckles, staring across the bathroom at the wall. I slowly sat up, hugging my knees to my chest, feeling my wet hair cling to my back.

"Thank you," I said softly. He turned his head back to look at me. It made me smile in spite of how terrible I felt.

"Laney, you really need to take care of yourself. You are working yourself into the ground," he snapped. He gazed for a moment at my wet skin, then looked away.

"This lecture coming from you?" I countered.

"I don't have a son that needs me to take care of him," he said as he turned back around.

"I've told you before that I don't sleep...well," I softly mentioned. "That's why I get sick sometimes."

"If you are worried about work, Laney, you shouldn't," he said.

"Life just feels really out of control right now, and working has always been a way for me to cope," I said quietly. I closed my eyes tightly and then reopened them. "Boy, I bet you think Mendelson has a real winner for an HR director. I promise I am not always like this," I said, feeling embarrassed that this was the second time in less than a week that Brad had helped me out of a bad situation. I could feel my cheeks blushing.

"That is not what I was thinking at all. Mendelson's HR director is pretty magnificent. Even if she doesn't know what is good for her and never backs down from an argument with her boss," he said, smiling.

A smile crept across my face. He stood up and held out a towel. I stood up, the water running down my body, the air feeling cool on my skin. I began to shiver again. My nipples could have cut glass; they were so hard. Brad's eyes immediately moved down to take them in. I was usually more bashful about my body, but in my sickly state, I didn't have energy to care. I took the towel and wrapped it around me. We didn't move. He studied my face and hair for a moment; then he handed me one of his T-shirts and then walked into his bedroom, closing the bathroom door behind him. I towel-dried my hair, hung up the towel, and slipped on his shirt. I opened the bathroom door and scanned his bedroom. I didn't see him. I walked over, and I slipped into his bed, burying myself beneath the billowy covers. Waves of trembles would wash over my body and then cease.

"How are you feeling?" he asked as he walked back into his bedroom a few minutes later, setting a bottle of water on the nightstand next to me.

"I f-f-feel f-f-f-ine, th-th-thank you," I said through my chattering teeth.

"Damnit, Laney, you're shivering," he hissed as he hurriedly unbuttoned his dress shirt and pulled his white undershirt over his head by the back collar. He unfastened his pants, and they fell to the floor. He gathered up his clothes and laid them on top of mine on the chair. He looked good in only his boxer briefs. He climbed under the covers and wrapped his muscular arms around me, pulling my backside to his front. He inhaled my hair.

"God, you smell good, Laney," he said under his breath. "You should have told me you were cold," he whispered, or at least that was what I thought he said. His words sounded so tender. It amazed me that he could switch from being demanding to soft so quickly.

"Brad, I'm contagious. You can't be getting sick…I'll be fine, you don't have to do this," I said softly as I tried to wiggle out of his grip.

He tightened his grip to keep me from wiggling. Another wave of trembling came over me.

"I'm not going anywhere. You are safe, Laney. Sleep," he quietly commanded.

I relaxed into his warm body. I had to admit to myself that this felt good. I soon fell into a deep sleep.

Chapter 31

I WOKE UP IN THE same position I fell asleep in. I did a mental scan of my body before I opened my eyes. The aches were gone, my throat felt better, I knew my fever was gone. I could feel that Brad's body was still against my back, and his arm draped over my waist. My eyes fluttered open to see the sun pouring in through the massive windows. Panic coursed through my body. I reached for my phone from the bedside table.

"Good morning," Brad said softly into my hair. "How are you feeling?" he whispered.

I looked at my phone. *Crap!* It was 11:30 a.m. I leaned forward and rested my head on the mattress. "Shit, it is eleven thirty. I slept too long Jenna will be worried sick...and you should be at work. Holy shit," I said as I leaned back against him and began flipping through my phone.

He grabbed my phone from my hand and set it on his nightstand so I couldn't reach it. He gently pushed my shoulder so I was lying on my back. He was on his side, facing me, propping his upper body up with his elbow.

"Stop worrying about everyone else. I called her this morning. I told her that you wouldn't be coming in," he said sternly.

"Fuck," I said under my breath, rubbing my face with my hands.

"What are you so worried about?" he said.

"Brad, I'm in HR. My reputation is all I have. If people knew that I stayed here last night...plus, I am going to the beach this weekend...I need to pack."

"Only Jenna and Jesse know that you are here. Who are you going to the beach with?" he asked.

"Jenna, Josh, and Braeden," I said, lost in thought, counting how many meetings I missed in my head.

"How long will you be there?" he asked without humor.

"Until Sunday," I said, now feeling like I was being interrogated.

He studied my face. "Laney, you need to be careful…and rest," He barked.

I smiled. "Thank you for everything you did for me last night. I knew I wasn't feeling well earlier in the week, and I pushed myself too hard. I didn't mean for you to pay the price for it," I said, blushing, remembering that I had no underwear on.

"Pay the price? It's okay for you to need to lean on someone, Laney," he said, looking into my eyes. He hit the nail right on the head. It was like he read my mind. I hated to need anybody. It was easier to be independent because people always let me down. I had always been that way.

"But, Brad, look at what I have caused…think of all the meetings you missed this morning. You stayed up way too late last night because of me. I messed up Dr. Balldrum's night. If you would have left me there, I would have made it home—"

"Enough!" he snapped. He took a deep breath and then continued, "Everything you just said were choices that I made. You don't own those, I do. And you need to remember, I am the boss, so I make the rules," he said in a very serious tone.

I wasn't sure if he was talking about work or something else. Brad sat up and swung his legs off the bed. His back muscles rippled as they contracted to move him off the bed. When he stood up, my eyes kept drifting below his defined lower back, and then down to his perfectly sculpted round butt. I closed my eyes, remembering when I would dig my fingers into his glutes as I screamed his name in the throes of passion. Brad made his way to the bathroom, I took one last look at him as he walked to the doorway, noting the perfect definition in his calves. Why did he have to be so flipping hot? I retrieved my cell phone from the nightstand and began answering e-mails. I knew I couldn't move until he was out of the room. When he opened the door from the bathroom, I looked up from my phone to see that he was fully dressed.

He was wearing a collared Oxford shirt, jeans, and dock shoes. He looked scrumptious and was looking right at me.

"Let's go get some lunch," he said with a smirk.

"I would love to," I said, glancing over to the chair where my dirty clothes once were, which now were gone. "Where are my clothes?" I asked.

Brad smirked. "They are being dry-cleaned. You should have some new ones in the drawers over there. My personal assistant picked up some for you." He motioned to his dresser. I had clothes in Brad Green's dresser?

"Why did you buy me clothes?" I asked, searching his face, completely blown away.

"I had a feeling you would be spending more time here and might need them," Brad said confidently, a satisfied smile resting across his face. "I will give you a moment to get ready." He crossed the room and closed his bedroom door behind him.

After he left, I sprinted over to the drawers. I found lacy panties, bras, shirts, jeans, shorts, athletic shorts. I pulled on a pair of the lacy panties and matching bra. They fit perfectly, of course. I pulled on a tight-fitting T-shirt and pair of designer jeans. Everything fit like a glove, of course. I couldn't even find myself clothes that fit like this. I went into the bathroom and relieved my bladder, then found a spare toothbrush and sample-size toothpaste. I looked in the mirror. I wasn't used to seeing myself well rested. It looked good on me. My skin actually glowed a little. I pulled on a pair of women's dock shoes that I assumed were for me and made my way down the hall. I looked in the various rooms, but I couldn't find Brad. I heard talking coming from the dining room.

After collecting my purse from the counter, I walked into the dining room, not realizing he was actually meeting with someone.

"Oh, I-I am sorry. I will come back," I said as I turned to leave, but Brad called out to me.

"Laney, I believe you know Veronica," he said dryly.

I gave my best fake smile, taking in Veronica's appearance. I noticed how low cut Veronica's blouse was and how close she stood to Brad, making sure she rubbed her left breast against his arm. She looked at me as well, confusion registering across her sinister face, eying my outfit and just as curious as to why I was there as I was as to why she was making a house call. I was screwed; she would tell everyone at work.

"Fancy seeing you here. I just stopped by to see if Brad had signed off on some…budget changes for me. I think you and I have a meeting set up to go over policies on Monday, don't we?" I asked, trying to pretend this wasn't one of the most awkward interactions ever.

Veronica looked at me with an equally fake smile. I am not sure she bought my story. "I didn't know you knew where Brad lived, much less made house calls. I heard you were sick today. It seems you are feeling better. As a matter of fact, Brad and I were just going over some policy changes to the severance policy you might be interested in," she said with a seductive smile, looking at Brad.

I imagined in that moment walking over to her, gripping her by her overdyed blonde hair, and slamming her face into the table. My daydream was interrupted by Brad's voice. Brad turned to Veronica, visibly flirting with her.

"As always, thank you for all of your help, Veronica. We can continue this discussion later." If I didn't know better, I would have thought that Brad was *trying* to make me jealous.

Veronica leaned in close to his face and batted her eyes. "No problem, Brad. Call me when you get finished with her," she said seductively.

I wasn't sure she was really talking about work at this point. As Veronica was walking out, she looked me up and down and then gave me a little nod with her sinister grin. I stood there for a couple minutes silently. It was obvious Brad was toying with me.

"Are we going to lunch?" I asked, pretending not to be bothered.

He looked at me. "Yes, I almost forgot," he said, feigning innocence.

I narrowed my eyes. "You almost forgot! But you only asked me twenty minutes ago, and I was standing right here for that purpose. Maybe we should just forget it!" I hissed, unable to hide my irrational irritation.

"Why are you so upset?" he said, tilting his head to the side. He was clearly getting a lot of amusement out of this.

"It isn't polite to flirt with demons. Did you know she was coming over?" I snapped.

He looked at me with a smirk and then shrugged his shoulders. He seemed to be amused. "I did, but I don't care that she knows you're here," he said, standing up from his leaning position.

"What! How can you say that? You know how much trouble she can cause for me, for us? I just gave you the speech about my reputation!" I said in disbelief.

He slowly started walking toward me. I felt myself beginning to turn to goo as he approached. He leaned into my ear. Our cheeks were all but touching, his lips brushing my skin ever so softly as he spoke. His intoxicating scent was swirling around me. The chaos in my mind was calming as it always did near him.

"I would never allow her to harm you. Do you believe me?" he said softly.

"Yes," I answered truthfully. I felt his energy pulling me in again.

"Then ask me what you really want to know," he continued so softly it was almost a whisper.

"Have you slept with her?" I blurted out, fully realizing it was none of my business.

"No," he said, holding my gaze. "Need I remind you that there is only one woman who has been able to keep up with my tastes? And from what I can recall, you tasted delicious," he spoke softly and methodically. I tried to contain my smile that was trying to blossom. "Speaking of delicious, are you ready to go to lunch?" he said as he stood up straight to face me.

A huge smile spread across my face. "I'm famished. Let's go," I said, shaking my head and smiling. He winked at me. Then he reached to collect his cell phone off the table, lightly grasped my elbow, and ushered me out the door.

The ride over was interesting. I had never been in such a beautiful, expensive car, and Brad commanded it. He was flawless in the way he drove the manual sports car, just like everything else about him. Was there anything he didn't do well?

"I honestly didn't realize that Veronica made house calls. She seemed very familiar with your apartment," I said, my cattiness getting the best of me.

He looked over at me in his Ray-Bans. "I have had after-work get-togethers for my executive team at all of my homes. Veronica has attended a few," he said, disinterested.

"How nice," I said in my most polite tone.

"Sure," he said, eyeing me.

Since I couldn't think of anything nice to say at the moment, I gave up and watched the scenery of the city go by. His iPod was connected to his car stereo. I turned on stereo and selected the auxiliary button. "Style" by Taylor Swift came blasting through the speakers. I was amused and started to giggle. This got his attention, and he looked at me.

"I wouldn't have guessed that you were a Taylor fan?" I said playfully.

He grinned. "Kayla liked it...and sometimes you just need to 'Shake It Off,'" he said with a cheesy grin.

Hmmm...his ex. I chuckled in spite of myself. "Were you able to stay friends after the split?" I asked.

"I guess you could call it that," he said cryptically.

As we arrived to the restaurant in his beautiful, sleek sports car, everyone stared when we pulled into a parking space. I mused that he must be used to this reaction everywhere he went. He came around to my door and opened the door for me. I stepped out, and he smiled at me. He closed the car door, and we began walking toward the restaurant. He put his hand on my lower back.

"What happened with you and Kayla?" I asked, somehow feeling jealous, which I had no right to be.

"We grew apart," he said.

"How long ago did you break up?"

"I moved out seven years ago," he said.

"Right after you left Mendelson...," I said softly, mostly to myself.

"Yes," he said, studying my face. He opened the restaurant's door for me.

The hostess was all smiles and giggles when Brad asked for a table. This made me smile as he didn't seem to notice that the young girl was openly gawking at him and suspiciously eyeing me. Maybe he did know or, more likely, didn't care. We were seated outside on a patio next to the river that ran through the city. I could hear the water flowing next us. The sunshine felt warm on my face. Looking at Brad, he looked glorious in the sunlight. Clearly, there was no lighting that he looked anything but good in. The friendly college-aged waiter came up. He was tall and lean, black hair and brown eyes. He looked like he was recovering from the previous evening's fraternity party.

"Hello, my name is Todd, and I will be your waiter. Can I start you off with something to drink?" I grinned as he was mostly speaking to me with an arrogant smile. I decided that two could play Brad's little game. He wanted to flirt with Veronica; I would flirt with the young waiter.

I shot Todd my most flirty smile. "Yes, Todd, I will have a water," I said, winking at him, and his smile broadened. I couldn't help it.

"And you, sir?" his surfer voice asked Brad.

Brad was unamused. "I will have the same," Brad said flatly.

Todd left, so I thought I would try conversation again.

"I have always wanted to try the Waterside Grill. I don't know why I haven't before now. Have you eaten here before?" I asked.

Brad looked up at me, his face unreadable. "I remembered you loved the water. That much hasn't changed from when I knew you before, Laney," he said keeping his eyes on the menu. Then he looked up at me. "You shouldn't flirt with underaged waiters, Laney. It isn't polite." At that moment, Todd returned with the water and took our food orders. I ordered a salad in my flirty voice.

"Delicious choice!" Todd winked at me; then he turned his attention to Brad. Brad ordered a sandwich while staring Todd down, looking like Brad was going to saw him in half with his butter knife. Todd departed yet again.

"So tell me, Laney, what are your future job plans?" he said, attempting to get our conversation back on the rails. I thought on his question for a moment.

"Am I being fired?" I asked.

He gave me a half smile. "As much as I would love to fire you for your defiant behavior and outburst yesterday, Jack is the only one who can do that right now. When the merger is over, I will have the authority."

I raised my glass of water and did an air toast before I took a sip. "Thank goodness. Now that we got that out of the way, I am not sure what I am going to do. I am rewriting my résumé and plan on reaching out to some colleagues to do some networking. Jack has been good to me, like a father. I want to make sure I do everything I can for him before I go." I gave him my most genuine smile.

Brad was lost in thought, studying my face. I needed to break the tension.

"So this must be quite a life that you lead, Mr. CEO—sports cars, supermodels, magazine covers?"

Brad's face gave way to a sad smile. "It is quite a life." He clearly wasn't going to say anything further on that subject. Then he reached across the table and squeezed my hand. I froze and swallowed hard.

"Laney—" Brad began; then Todd interrupted our discussion and delivered our food. Brad stared him down, not removing his hand from mine. It seemed that he was keeping the physical contact with me for Todd's benefit. Brad was not good at hiding his irritation with Todd. After Todd departed, Brad's phone began to vibrate. He swiped the screen to answer.

"Green...I understand...I will be there shortly." He snapped and then looked at me. "I have to go in to the office. Let's get Todd to pack this up, and Jesse will give you a ride home." He hailed Todd over to the table. He dropped some cash on the table, and we made our way to the front of the restaurant. We stood outside in front of the doors on the sidewalk, the sun warming my face. It felt amazing. I closed my eyes and tilted my head back. I turned to look at Brad.

"Thank you again for everything. Please let me know how much I owe you for the doctor," I said, smiling at him.

"You don't owe me anything, Laney," he said, looking into my eyes. I felt the intensity level growing between us. I cleared my throat.

"So we need to cover some staffing plans next week. My days are pretty full, so if you didn't mind coming in early…," I offered.

"I don't mind." Brad stopped as Jesse pulled the car in front of us. Brad opened the door, and I climbed in. I looked back at him, our gaze lingering.

"See you Monday," he said. His words made me a little sad. Brad closed the door and gave a little wave. No kiss this time, I mentally noted, but I had been sick.

I immediately called Jenna. "I am going to go home and pack for the beach. Meet you down there?" I said quickly.

"Ummm…I hope you have more to say to me than that?" Jenna said.

"Tonight," was all I said, acutely aware of Jesse's keen sense of hearing.

"Fine. I am just going to finish up a few things, and then I will see you in a few hours."

"See you then!" I said, hanging up the phone.

Twenty minutes later, Jesse pulled up to my house. He exited the Suburban and walked around the back door and opened it for me. I smiled at him.

"Thank you, Jesse."

"Have a good time at the beach," Jesse said as I climbed out of the car. He closed the car door behind me and walked around to the driver's side. I gave him a little wave before he turned the massive SUV around, and I watched it pull onto the street and out of view.

Chapter 32

BRAEDEN AND I ARRIVED TO my beach house in Duck, North Carolina. The town is part of the Outer Banks, a string of land that hangs off North Carolina's mainland. It was created by a hurricane hundreds of years ago. My beach house was a cottage, older and smaller than the monstrous beach mansions that surrounded it. It had a total of four bedrooms, two master bedrooms on one side of the living room and kitchen area and two bedrooms on the other side, one with bunk beds and one with a queen bed that shared a bathroom. It was a one-story house on pilings with salt-air-aged shake shingle siding, with a deck that surrounded the entire house. Attached to the deck there was a private access to the beach via a small wooden walkway that extended over the sand dune to stairs that led down to the beach. Over the years, my neighbors had upgraded with pools, miniature putting greens, and sod, but I hadn't.

This house was perfect the way it was. A few cans of paint, and it shone. This was my dream. I had wanted to own a home here since I was a small girl vacationing here with my mother on the weekends. Two hundred and fifty-two more payments, and she would be mine. This was my place that I could think, that I could be at peace, that I could escape. The days and weeks after Sam's death, I took refuge down here, mourning by myself and then later with Braeden. This place had helped to heal me. I had saved and scrimped until I had enough money for a down payment on this house when Sam and I were first married. Sam was not a fan of the idea. He told me that it was a waste of money; all we would be doing is flushing money down the drain with home repairs. I finally prevailed and bought this little slice of heaven when it was being auctioned off. Even though its purchase did not make sense to Sam, it made sense to me. This was something I knew I needed to do for me, and I didn't question it.

Jenna arrived thirty minutes after I did, and the party began. We made the boys meatballs for dinner; then Jenna and I proceeded to sip a Riesling we had never tried and nibbled on cheese cubes. Once the boys were content watching a movie and we were sure they weren't listening, the questions began.

"So spill it, girlfriend. What's going on with Dreamy Green? How was lunch? I love this outfit. Is it new?" Jenna said with raised eyebrows.

I exhaled loudly. "Lunch was good, especially after the night I had with him." I looked at her. She was completely engrossed in my response. I loved Jenna.

"Laney! What happened? What did he say, or better yet, what did he do?" she asked excitedly.

I continued, "I was working late last night. I didn't feel well, and as you may recall, I didn't look well either. I began to feel tired and ended up falling asleep at my desk. Brad woke me up around eleven. I was running a fever and was really weak. It was hard for me to stand actually. He literally carried me to the car and took me back to his apartment. Then he called his personal physician. His physician said I had strep throat and gave me a penicillin shot. Brad drew a bath for me. Nothing happened as I know you are wondering, but he did hold me all night. It was totally sweet. I haven't slept through an entire night since I can remember. I woke up at eleven thirty this morning." My smile fell. "And…it was completely inappropriate. He is going to be our boss soon at least until…"

Jenna nodded and finished my thought, "We lose our jobs."

I nodded and gave a half smile.

A smile spread across Jenna's face. "He's so into you, Laney, and you should know that everyone in the office is talking about it. They notice him looking at you in every meeting. He requested access to your calendar, the IT guy told me when he was fixing my computer, 'restart my computer, my ass.' Funny how he always knows where you are and shows up at the same place you are…," she trailed off, taking a sip of her wine.

I felt myself blush, or maybe it was the wine. I thought about telling her about the night in front of the fire, but now it seemed like a distant dream.

"Let me start by saying, as far as access to my calendar, I am sure he is just tracking my time to make sure I am still a value-added resource. They say he is ruthless," I said in a mock serious tone, wagging my finger.

Jenna rolled her eyes. "Right. So when are you going to tell me the history of Brad and Laney?" she said nonchalantly.

"Our story is short. I was starting out at Mendelson. He was a supervisor. We were both married and let our passions get the best of us. It was amazing, it was intense, and it was beautiful. He ended it after six weeks and left the company soon after," I said, taking a huge sip of wine.

"Tell me honestly, Laney, do you really still love him, or is this just something that the memory is better than it actually was?" she asked.

I looked at my wineglass. I was running my finger around the rim slowly. "If it were just a memory, I would be able to forget. A love like that is unforgettable," I said quietly, finishing the contents of my wineglass and then looking at Jenna.

She was looking at me with understanding. "You just fit the missing puzzle piece in for me. Is this why you don't date?" she asked softly.

I nodded. "Yes. Once you have a taste of something like that, being intensely connected to someone mentally, physically, emotionally, spiritually...it was something that was so perfect, but the timing was just wrong. Every other person just doesn't compare, and when you think you are in a place to start seeing someone, all they do is remind you of the one you really want to be with," I said with feeling.

"Holy shit, Laney, what are you going to do?"

"I don't know. We are getting used to each other again. I get so mixed up when I am around him. I don't know what to think, I forget to breathe...," I said, looking into my wineglass.

Jenna gave me an understanding smile; then she came around the counter and hugged me. "Laney, maybe it's finally your time.

Maybe you need to be mixed up. Maybe you need someone that challenges you and takes your breath away. You deserve this, you deserve him, you deserve happiness, Laney," she crooned.

I smiled in spite of the tears that were pooling in my eyes. "Thank you, Jenna. I am so lucky to have you as my friend. I don't know what I would do without you," I managed to squeak out, trying to keep my emotions from descending into a sob. At that, a tear escaped my eye and rolled down my cheek.

Jenna smoothed my hair. Her voice cracked as she had tears in her eyes now too. "Laney, I feel I need to say this...I know that no one could replace Sam, but you have the best part of him sitting in there watching *The Avengers* with Josh. I hope you have forgiven yourself for what happened between you and Brad in the past so that you can move on and have a future. Life is messy. We can't choose who we love. Our heart does that for us. You were allowed to care about someone *in addition* to Sam."

I nodded, overcome with emotion. We both chuckled through our tears. We both quickly wiped our eyes. Jenna returned to her stool on the other side of the counter. I cleared my throat.

"So any word from Jesse?" I asked, wanting to change subjects.

She finished her glass of wine and began refilling the glasses. "Ummm, he texted and told me to have a safe trip. Thank you for giving him my number, Laney," she said, smiling at me.

I winked at her, then straightened in my seat and recrossed my legs. "So tell me about your sixteen-night-stand man. Is he gone?" I inquired.

Jenna rolled her eyes. "Ugh, I am afraid to get rid of him. He's pretty good in the sack. Jesse and I have been talking at work, but his time is very limited due to a certain CEO. Maybe you can invite Brad to dinner so we can actually spend some time together?" she teased.

I laughed, thinking of the explosive conversation I had with Brad about Jesse's social life and fully understanding the truth in Jenna's statement: Brad dominated everyone's time. Then Jenna continued, "I don't know how you do it, Laney, I just get so horny," she confided.

I rolled my eyes. "I do too, but rejection is a wonderful deterrent. And besides, I have never been as good at picking up men as you are, Ms. Ford."

We both laughed. Approximately an hour later, I was really feeling the bottle and a half of wine Jenna and I had shared. I knew in Jenna's mind there was only one thing to do: turn off the TV, turn up the music, and dance around the house. The four us were so caught up and laughing so hard that I had to do a double-take out the window. There was a man standing in the driveway staring at us through the blindless windows. When I tried to refocus my eyes, the man was gone. It had a sobering effect on me.

"Jenna, did you see him?" I said in disbelief.

"Who?" she said, peering out the window.

"The man in the driveway?" I said, still in disbelief.

Jenna laughed and then yawned. "Laney, there is no one out there, and I don't like the spooky stories you tell. Besides, if there was someone there, it was probably some neighbor seeing two grown women acting like fools."

She had a point. I raised my eyebrows and nodded. "Touché, Jenna."

"I guess since the hallucinations have begun, we should be off to bed." Jenna yawned again.

I just nodded, still getting over being startled. Both of us ushered our very sleepy boys into their bunk beds, hugged them, and went off to our bedrooms. As I lay there awaiting sleep to find me, I thought about Brad, wondering what he was doing. Did he have fun on Friday nights, or did he work all the time? Was he watching a football game with friends? Was he still at the office? Was he on a date? What type of women did he date? Was he seeing anyone now? I realized how little I knew about him and felt silly for having feelings for him still, after all this time. I couldn't even be sure that his feelings were reflections of mine.

The next day was filled with walks on the beach, seashell collecting, boogie boarding, paddleboarding, sandcastles, paddleball, boccie ball, and a picnic on the beach. When we returned that evening, Jenna and I were already through our first bottle of wine when my phone buzzed. It was Brad. I almost spilled my wine setting down my wineglass. I contemplated letting it go to voice mail as I didn't have a great track record of talking to him after having alcohol. In my defense, the ecstasy those two pervs slipped us probably played a part…probably. My logical mind was pleading with me, *but he may need something important.* Shit!

"Laney Masterson," I answered in the most professional tone I could muster.

"Laney, it's Brad. I wanted to—"

I could barely hear him. It sounded like he was at a bar. "Brad, it's hard to hear you," I said, cutting him off. There was a pause.

"Hold on a sec. I'll walk outside," he said. I could hear him cover up the microphone as he was walking "I was calling to see— have you been drinking?" he asked accusingly.

I pursed my lips and closed one eye. "Ummm, maybe just a little," I had to admit, I slurred a little bit that time.

"Laney, you are recovering from an illness! Where are you?" he snapped.

"I am fine. I am at my beach house, and we aren't going any- where," I said, making a face at Jenna.

"Laney, you really need to be more careful. Your health is important, and as you know all too well, things can happen when you drink." He sounded mad. I hated being lectured by him, and I felt myself getting irritated.

"I am a grown woman, Brad. I don't know what difference it makes to you—actually, I have a friend that you should meet. You two have a lot in common."

"Is that so, Laney? Who, Mark? Remember, we have already met. Have you slept in his bed too after having too much to drink?" he came back quickly and angrily.

Shell-shocked from his reaction, I couldn't find my words. My wine-soaked neurotransmitters were slow to fire. When my brain finally came up with a response, I began with a stutter. "H-h-how dare you…of course not…and I don't know how who I sleep with is any of your business," I hissed, so as not to get the attention of the boys. I had made the alpha mad. I knew he expected me to back down, but I wasn't going to. I stood up and walked outside. I wasn't sure where this conversation was going.

"Laney, what is the nature of your relationship with Mark?" Brad demanded.

My mind was racing; I was still trying to gather my composure. "I told you...he...he is a friend," I said, not meaning to stutter.

Brad came back with a low growl, "Are you fucking him?"

"No! But like I said, I don't know what business that is of yours—"

"Are you fucking anyone else?" he growled.

"Brad..."

"Answer me, Laney!" he snapped.

"No! What has gotten into—"

"Good," he cut me off before I could finish my tirade. I was trying to process this interaction, but my poor wine-saturated neurons were very sluggish. It was Brad who spoke next.

"Get some rest, Laney. I will talk to you later," he snapped.

I opened my mouth to speak, but the line went dead. *What was that?! Why did he actually call?* I looked to Jenna as I walked back into the house, who was now openly gawking at me. Even Jenna seemed very confused and was actually speechless for a few minutes. I went to sit next to Jenna on the couch. We sat there silently for a moment; then Jenna broke the silence.

"What the heck, Laney? He's got it bad for you, or working for him requires a lot of personal information. How does that fit into your value proposition determining whether you can stay or not?"

Both of us laughed until we had tears in our eyes.

It was two in the morning, and I couldn't sleep. The effects of the wine had worn off, and my conversation with Brad kept running through my mind. So I decided to do something I was pretty sure was against all the advice written in every relationship book: I picked up my phone and sent a text to Brad. I had to make peace with him for my sanity.

"U awake?"
"Yes. Why aren't you resting like I told you
     to?" (He responded immediately.)

"I am, but I can't sleep"

"Why can't you sleep?"

"I am thinking about you"

"What about?"

"I am so confused. Why did you ask me about Mark earlier?"

"You shouldn't be sleeping with him or anyone else."

"I still don't understand how that is any of your concern"

"I don't want to share you with anyone else"

His response was perplexing and hot. All of my internal organs proceeded to do backflips, not to mention my inner sex kitten was loudly purring. I began to tremble. Before I could respond, I received another text from him.

"Like I said before, get some rest, Laney. I will talk to you later. Sleep well, beautiful."

I put my phone down on the nightstand in disbelief of what just happened. Who was he to control my life? *What did this mean?* Eventually, I fell into a fitful sleep, dreaming of two little girls with hazel eyes.

Sunday we arrived back home around noon, just in time for lunch. I was unpacking the car when one of the football dads, Greg Allsberg, pulled up the driveway. I was surprised by his visit. Greg was divorced. He owned a local construction company and seemed to do very well for himself. He was a nice-looking man with brown hair and brown eyes, slightly taller than me. He had always been very pleasant to talk to at practice.

"Laney! I was in the neighborhood and thought I should stop by and say hello," he said, closing the door to his pickup truck and resting his Costa sunglasses on top of his head.

"That was very nice of you, Greg. Can I offer you a drink or anything?" I said, feeling slightly off balance.

"No, thank you. I won't be staying long," he said.

"Oh, okay. What can I help you with?" I said.

"Well…how about we take the boys to a movie tonight?" he asked, blushing slightly.

I was charmed; his offer was sweet. I was still slightly miffed and confused about Brad trying to control my love life—what right did he have? What harm could it do? So in an act of rebellion, I accepted Greg's invitation.

"Yes, Greg, that would be lovely," I said.

A huge smile spread across Greg's face. "H-how about I pick you guys up around six?"

"Sounds great. See you then!" I said, smiling.

"Great, Laney, sounds great." He gave me a peck on the cheek and climbed back into his truck.

With all the unpacking, washing, and other chores, 6:00 p.m. came fairly quickly. We were going to go see *How to Train Your Dragon 2*, and the boys were ecstatic. It had been forever since I had gone to a movie theater. Greg looked handsome: he had a golf shirt on with nice-fitting jeans and sneakers. When the movie was over, we made it back to my house about 9:00 p.m. Braeden had been quiet all evening. Barely before Greg put the car in park, Braeden jumped out and gave a little wave. I noticed he never turned around; he just kept marching toward the house. I quickly pulled the handle on my door to open it.

"Thank you, Greg. I had a lovely time. And thank you, Logan. We had fun with you!" I said with a smile. Greg smiled and leaned in to kiss me. I couldn't do it. I turned, giving him my cheek only.

"Have a good night, Greg," I said.

He exhaled. "You too, Laney. Thanks for such a great night," he said with a smile.

I gave him one last smile and wave then turned to go into the house. I watched as Greg drove away. Then I climbed the stairs, thinking on my evening, I did have a nice time with Greg tonight. We both had kids. He understood what it's like to be a single parent. Maybe I had been excluding potential dates prematurely. I put Braeden to bed and lay there with him a moment.

"Were you okay tonight, buddy?" I asked.

"Yeah, I guess," he said quietly.

"You were very quiet. Did you not like the movie?"

"I liked the movie."

"You know, you can tell me anything," I said as I kissed him on the side of his forehead.

He thought for a moment, staring straight up at his ceiling. "I don't like Mr. Greg. I don't want to go to any more movies with him," Braeden said.

"I see," I said softly.

"Does that make you sad, Mom?"

"Honey, I love you. That does not make me sad. It means that we won't do this again, okay?"

"Okay," he said, snuggling in closer to me.

"Can I ask you one more question?" I said.

He giggled. "Yes!"

"Why don't you like Mr. Greg? I'm just curious."

"He doesn't make you laugh, and he doesn't open doors for you, and he could have bought you flowers."

His explanation was simple. In that moment, I realized that I was doing okay. My son was getting an idea of what good looked like and how a man was supposed to act.

"You're right," I said, kissing his forehead again. "I love you," I said, and he gave me a sleepy smile.

"Good night, Mommy."

"Good night, sweetheart," I said as I walked out of his bedroom and headed for mine.

I climbed into my own bed. I fell into a fitful sleep. I dreamed that I was standing in front of a mirror in a beautiful wedding dress, but it wasn't the one from Sam's and my wedding. I just kept staring into the mirror, looking at myself. Then the mirror cracked and shattered all over the floor. I woke up at 1:11 a.m. out of breath and sweating. I lay there awake until my alarm went off at five.

Chapter 33

I WAS AT THE OFFICE bright and early, dreading to see Brad after our odd text discussion over the weekend. Luckily, I was booked all day. I had seen him briefly in the hallway and thought he was going to speak to me, but his attention was pulled away by Frank. As luck would have it, I was on my way out that evening.

Brad called to me from his office. "Laney, a word please?"

I felt like a kid being called into the principal's office. Usually, that is the feeling I gave to other people. I stepped into his office. "How can I help you, Brad?" I said in my HR director voice. He was walking toward me, his eyes intensely locked on mine.

"Shut the door please," he barked. I could see his jaw was tense.

"Okay," was all I could say. He was clearly the apex predator, and I was the prey. I closed the door. He kept coming toward me like a lion approaching a gazelle. I set my laptop bag and purse on the ground next to my feet. As he walked toward me, I slowly backed up so my back was against the door. As he drew near me, he stretched out both his arms, his hands resting on the door on either side of my head. I swallowed hard. My breath quickened or stopped, I can't be sure…

"I thought I told you I didn't want you seeing any else," he said in a low growl.

How did he know I went out with Greg? His face was so close to mine. I could smell his cologne and the masculine scent of his skin. I tried not to look at his lips, but I had to admit that I wanted to kiss him so badly. It made it hard for me to focus on the task at hand. I swallowed hard again and gave a smirk.

"Wait, how did you know? I still don't see—"

He cut me off, "I told you I know a lot of things about you, Laney. No one else, Laney, including Greg. Don't argue with me about this," he snarled.

"A-are we seeing each other exclusively?" I asked softly, a bit confused.

"I don't want anyone else touching you," he growled.

"Brad...I...," I said. My breath was becoming labored from the tension between us.

His face softened. "You need to remember to breathe, Laney," he huskily whispered, softly tucking a piece of hair behind my ear.

I swallowed hard yet again, my eyes still locked into his, feeling as though I was in a trance. His intensity, his smell, my attraction to him—he had completely dominated my thoughts and was silently willing me to allow him access to my inner self with just his presence. He was truly a remarkable creature. I couldn't come up with any other answer but the truth.

"You take my breath away," I whispered.

Brad let out a soft growl, leaned in slowly, and brushed his lips against mine. Then he softly kissed me. The contact of our soft lips made me quiver and want more. I could feel the electricity running through my body. My skin felt like it was standing at attention, waiting in anticipation for his touch. He was careful to make sure that only our lips touched. What started as a soft kiss turned into a desperate lip-lock from two people that were clearly in need. The kiss was so passionate that when our lips parted, I had to try to remember where I was. I felt like I had stood up too fast. When I opened my eyes, he was still intensely looking at me.

"How many men have you slept with since me?" he asked, studying my face.

"Three," I said quietly.

"Who were they?" he said without humor.

I felt my cheeks blushing. "Sam and two other men I dated—not Mark," I said quietly.

"How were they for you?" he asked.

"What do you mean?"

"Did you like being with them?" he asked. His eyes were as intense as his tone.

I swallowed hard. "No," I said quietly, then swallowed the lump in my throat and continued, "The two, I slept with a couple of times. And Sam—" I paused and clamped my lips together.

"Why didn't they satisfy you, Laney?" he asked.

I closed my eyes for a moment and swallowed hard. When I opened them, I was prepared to speak my truth. "They weren't you. I would try to close my eyes, but I would see you. I just wanted you," I said softly, looking down at my hands, feeling foolish for showing him how much my feelings for him controlled my life.

He held my face with his hands and tilted my face up to his. Then he kissed me. I could feel the energy pouring out of him into me. My hands held on to his waist. He parted from my lips and rested his forehead against mine.

"You are mine, Laney, do you understand?" he growled. "I don't want you *seeing or sleeping* with anyone else, Laney. Promise me now," he said in his husky voice, now staring intensely into my eyes.

I exhaled. "When I am with you, I can't think straight...I don't know what to say..." I didn't move; I just kept my eyes on his.

"No one else, Laney...promise me," he said, and then he kissed me again. This time, his hands gently cradled my chin.

I became so wrapped up in his being, his touch, his taste. I reached up and ran my fingers through his hair, clutching him to me, pulling his mouth tighter onto mine—I wanted this. I wanted him. I hadn't realized there was such a deep well of need within me. I hadn't felt like this in such a long time that when my desire began rising, I almost didn't know what to do. I felt ravenous.

There was a tapping at the door. It startled me out of our moment. Brad was calm and in control as usual. We parted lips, and he started searching my eyes.

"Promise me, Laney," he whispered.

I looked in his eyes and nodded. "I promise," I softly said.

Then he backed away from the door, seeming to be pleased with my answer. I gathered up my laptop bag and purse. I started to feel embarrassed for my behavior and that I had gotten so carried away—in the office, no less. I blushed and murmured, "I really have to go get Brae. I will see you Wednesday. I have the career fair tomorrow, so I won't be here. Have a good night, Brad." I was rambling, still feeling disoriented.

Brad grabbed my hand and reached his other hand up to my lips and began tracing them with his finger. "You never have a reason to be embarrassed when you are with me, Laney," he paused for a moment, studying my face. "Have dinner with me Wednesday night," he spoke softly, and obviously my face gave me away. I thought of Jenna's words from our beach-house weekend. Maybe she was right; maybe it was my time to be happy.

"I would love that," I said softly and smiled.

Brad gave a slight nod and had a look of satisfaction on his face. He studied my face for one more minute, released my hand, and quit caressing my lips. "Remember what I said, Laney," he warned, looking deep into my eyes.

I nodded then turned to open the door. It was Frank. He slowly eyed me then Brad.

"He's all yours. Have a good night, Frank," I said in a slightly too perky of a voice as I rushed by him.

The next day was the job fair at the workforce development center. I had to focus and figure out which companies I wanted to pursue. I also had to keep yesterday's meeting with Brad out of my mind so I could focus. I had been applying for jobs online, but I thought this would be a great place to network.

"Well, well, well, if it isn't the great Laney Masterson."

I spun around to see the blonde she-devil Veronica coming toward me, looking like she just devoured a baby kitten for breakfast.

"Hello, Veronica, how are you? I love your blouse," I lied.

Veronica was wearing a sheer black blouse with a gray miniskirt and stiletto black high heels. If I didn't know better, I would think Veronica belonged on a street corner. She didn't wear a tank top underneath her see-through blouse like she should have for a professional function. She wore her laciest black bra that only seemed to barely cover her nipples.

"I might as well wear these while I still look this good," she said.

I just smiled as I wasn't in any position to give her a piece of my mind. "So are you conducting interviews today for Halifax?" I asked.

Veronica flashed her vicious smile at me, like she had just zoned in on her prey. "My team does most of it, but I will do some. Since you won't have a job shortly, are you interested in a position on my team? I have an HR assistant spot open," she said, pleased with the insult.

I wasn't hung up on titles, but she was clearly trying to put me down.

"Thank you for the information, Veronica. I will keep my options open for now and continue looking," I said with a fake smile, knowing full well that if I couldn't find something, I may actually have to beg this horrid woman for a job.

Veronica wasn't going to leave. She obviously wasn't finished toying with her prey before she ripped it apart. "Oh, Laney, come on. Brad and I were talking the other night that it might be nice for you to join my team. What do you think?" she asked as she batted her eyes.

Here it goes. I was startled at the sound of Brad's name but managed to choke out a response. "You and Brad? Really?" I managed to say.

Veronica laughed. "Yes, Laney. You know, the CEO of Halifax? I wasn't sure if you knew, but he and I are *very* close, if you know what I mean." And she gave me a wink.

I was already starting to feel sick to my stomach, and unfortunately, she wasn't finished with me yet. Had Brad's lips touched Veronica's too? Was this just something he did with all the women he worked with? Did he have a thing for HR people?

"Brad and I were talking about you and your career prospects. We just felt so bad for you and your situation," she said in a tone that did not hide her hate for me.

I felt gutted, vulnerable, exposed, and was becoming agitated. I tried to keep my emotions level. "My situation, really? And what situation is that?" I asked through my plastic smile.

I could see by the gleam in her eye that Veronica knew she had won.

YOU ARE THE REASON

"Yes, Laney, a widow, raising a child on her own, about to lose her job. Such a sad story. It just didn't seem right to let you beg for food on the streets, and Brad agreed," she said, offering me a sympathetic smile.

I stared off in the distance, trying to collect my words, a dagger tearing through my heart. I knew it didn't make sense as to why he would be interested in me, and now I knew why—I was a pity project.

"Thank you, Veronica. I am going to keep looking," was all I could manage to say. I couldn't show this evil woman how she had hurt me. It hit me like a Mack truck. Brad must think I was really pathetic. I truly did feel embarrassed that I was thought of as a charity case and people discussing it behind my back, especially him. I had worked so hard to not come off that way, but it made sense I could not manage myself out at the bar and even my own health without his intervention. I must truly look like an incapable fool to him. I could feel tears were going to start threatening my eyes.

I looked up at Veronica. Her delicate face would be very attractive if hate wasn't emanating from her pores. "I am going to head out. I will see you in the office tomorrow," I said with a weak smile.

"Sure thing, Laney. Glad I could help!" Veronica called after me.

Veronica knew she had been triumphant at what she was trying to accomplish. I was determined to make it out of the convention center before I started to cry. I made it to my car, and the tears began to flow.

I needed to drive, create some space between her and me. Here I had thought he was still in love with me like I was with him when all he was feeling was sorry for me. I felt so stupid. Why would he want to be with me after all these years? Jenna's phone call broke my concentration.

"Hi, Jenna," I said, trying to hold my voice steady.

"Hey, Laney, where did you go? I went to go get a free bagel from the snack table, and you were gone," she said.

In my haste, I forgot she had gone to get a quick bite to eat, so she wouldn't know that I had left. I really needed to pull myself together.

307

"I'm sorry. I was feeling light-headed and just needed some air. Can you handle the booth by yourself today?"

"Sure I can. Is everything okay?" she asked with concern.

I couldn't go into it with Jenna right now. She may actually punch Veronica in the middle of the career fair if she knew what she said to me.

"Everything is fine. I just need some air and time to think. The stress of this whole situation is getting to me today."

"Okay, Laney. If you need anything, I am here. I am still taking Braeden to football practice tomorrow night, right?"

In being wrapped up in the emotions of the day, I had forgotten about dinner with Brad the following evening. I knew that what I had to say to say to him, I wanted to say to his face.

"Yes, thank you so much, Jenna."

"No problem! Have a great night. See you later—and don't do anything I wouldn't do!" she said as we hung up.

I turned up my driveway, got out of my car, and sat on the front porch. I had twenty minutes until Braeden's bus would arrive. I felt so insecure, so vulnerable, so judged. I wanted one of Braeden's hugs. I was lost in thought when the bus arrived.

Braeden ran up to me. "Mommy!" he squealed as he ran into my arms.

I closed my arms and squeezed him, reminding myself that despite what anyone else said, I was a good mom, and I was raising a good kid. I released him. "Hey, buddy!" I gave him an ear-to-ear grin.

We ate a snack then went to football practice. After football practice, we ate pizza and played UNO until 10:00 p.m. I was going to bed and heard my phone buzz. It was a text from Brad:

> "How was your day?"
> "Great…I was at the career fair with Veronica, you are lucky to have her."
> "Are you ok?"
> "Looking forward to dinner tomorrow night. Nighty night!"
> "Good night, Laney."

I put my phone on the nightstand and fell into yet another night of fitful sleep. I dreamed that I was sitting on the deck at my beach house at night listening to the ocean, covered in a blanket. The waves kept coming farther up the beach until a huge wave engulfed my house. I began to drown in the violent undertow of the huge wave. I woke up out of breath and sweating profusely.

Chapter 34

WEDNESDAY MORNING, I ARRIVED AT work at my usual time. I had been in a daydream all day at work. Brad had appointments all day and an off-site meeting right before dinner, so I was going to meet him at the restaurant. I was out to lunch and had just finished discussing the interaction with Veronica at the career fair with Jenna when my phone buzzed.

"Laney Masterson."

"Laney, where are you?" It was Slade. I was getting irritated that my whereabouts mattered so much to everyone. I felt like lately I couldn't pee without checking in with someone.

"I am out to lunch, I—"

Slade cut me off, "The Department of Labor is here for an unexpected visit. Can you get back here? He's been in with Veronica for thirty minutes, and he's already talking about penalties and fines. It would be detrimental to the merger," he said, panicked.

I sighed. "I'm on my way," I said, giving Jenna a look.

When we returned to the office, I deposited my things on my desk. I could hear the auditor's booming voice from my office. I recognized the voice as Curtis Jackson's; he was friendly enough. I could hear the party had moved from Veronica's office to Brad's; this couldn't be good. I took a deep breath, put on my warmest, most engaging smile, and walked into Brad's office. The auditor, whom I now verified was Curtis Jackson, was severely agitated. Brad's eyes were cold. He looked like he was ready to decapitate Curtis with his pen, if it were possible. I walked in just as Curtis was midway through his lecture, which sounded more like a rant.

"—sloppy mess. Since you can't answer any of my questions—"

Brad's posture was tense. He looked like he was about to come across the desk at him. I cut Curtis off.

"Curtis, long time, no see. I wish you would have called before you came," I said as I walked in.

He turned around to look at me. I walked over to him and shook his hand. He was trying to conceal his smile. I had worked over the years to have a good relationship with Curtis.

"You know I don't do that, Laney. Tell me what is going on here. I spent an hour with Ms..." he said, motioning to Veronica.

Veronica looked shell-shocked and squeaked out, "Whitley."

He gave his head a shake of disgust then continued, "And she can't tell me where any of your records are or answer *any* of my questions," he snapped.

I smiled at him and tilted my head to the side. "Curtis, you have my number. You should have called me. Why don't you sit down in my office, and we can go over what you want to see. Would you like to start with seeing our business scorecard?" I asked.

He exhaled. "Yes, let's start there." But he didn't move. I then went on trying to get his feet moving in the direction of my office. "Would you like a cup of coffee?" I offered.

He nodded. "I would love one," he said, still not moving.

"Well, why don't you get your things, and I will show you the new fancy coffee machine," I said, faking my excitement.

He was staring down Brad. *Oh no.* Curtis motioned toward Veronica. "You need to fix that. If this is representative of the haphazard way in which you run your company..."

Brad's jaw clenched. Brad was about to respond. I spoke; my pitch was a little too high and breathy I almost didn't recognize my own voice. "Now, Curtis, Mr. Green is not part of the audit. If you don't get yourself in my office, you are going to get on my bad side. Let's go," I teased.

He let out a little chuckle. "Okay, okay, Laney" he said. He waddled into my office.

I spent the next four hours going over time-card entries, personnel records, applicant-tracking data, and anything else he asked for. The rest of my meetings and reports would be postponed until tomorrow.

If I hadn't have been so hurt by what Veronica told me at the job fair, I would have been happier to see Brad and would have been looking forward to our dinner. Even though our interaction was always intense, I always looked forward to seeing him. I arrived at the restaurant. Today I had intentionally wore a black pencil skirt, teal low-cut blouse, and black heels. I felt sexy and confident. Brad was sitting at the table when I arrived. He looked relaxed, casually scanning his phone. The maître d' walked me to the table and pulled out my chair. Brad stood up and was going to lean in and kiss me, but I pretended not to notice by looking back at the maître d' as he pushed my chair in and placed the napkin on my lap. Brad sat back down. I flicked my eyes over to Brad. He looked good in his navy-blue suit. He had removed his tie and unfastened the top button on the collar of his white dress shirt.

"Laney," Brad started. He was eyeing me suspiciously. Thankfully, before he could continue, the waiter arrived for my drink order. I noticed that Brad had a golden-brown liquid in a highball glass with no ice that he was slowly spinning with his thumb and middle finger. I ordered a Crown and Sprite—I meant business tonight. I needed to quiet my nerves with some liquid courage. Brad was looking at me curiously, trying to figure out why I was drinking hard liquor tonight.

"I heard the audit went well," he offered.

I took a deep breath. "Yes, it did. We can keep operating the business and do not have to pay any fines. That is always a good thing in my book," I said, trying to maintain my emotional control and offering a plastic smile. Luckily, the waiter returned with my drink, which I proceeded to gulp down.

Brad looked partly amused and partly confused, tilting his head to the side. "Everything all right? You might want to slow down, Laney," he said with a crooked smile.

I looked straight at him, not able to control my emotions anymore. "I am sorry. Does this embarrass you? Wait, I guess this adds to my charity-case quality. Now you can feel even more pity for me thinking that I am an alcoholic," I hissed in a whisper.

Brad looked perplexed. "What are you talking about, Laney?" His eyes were searching mine.

My eyes narrowed. This was my moment. "I had a nice little talk with Veronica at the job fair yesterday. She seemed to be very intimate with you. She said that you two talked about how sad my situation was, and *that* was the reason you considered hiring me into Halifax! As an HR assistant, no less! You are an ass! And another thing, I don't want Veronica's sloppy seconds," I hissed at him.

Brad hit the table with his hand. It was loud and rattled the silverware and glasses. I jumped. "Enough! Calm down, Laney!" he said with a clenched jaw. Then he continued calmly, "If you have a question about my conversation with Veronica, then ask me." His calmness was pissing me off. I felt my emotions continuing to rise. Tears were going to start threatening my eyes if I didn't get it under control.

"Which part is true?" I hissed. The waiter returned. Before he opened his mouth, I looked at the waiter and snapped, "No, we aren't ready to order. Please come back in a few minutes."

Brad raised his eyebrows at my assertiveness. "Laney, I did talk to Veronica about you. I want you on my team. You're the best player in the people-strategy business. Why would I not try to keep you?" he said, still confused as to why I was so upset.

"Yeah, she mentioned she had an HR assistant position open on her team that I could take! You would want me to work for that awful of a person? At least Slade knows he's a dufus. She's got no clue and has the soul of Satan to boot. How many times has she slept with you to make you so delusional as to think it would be a good idea for me to work with her? Is that how pathetic I come off that you think that I should sink that low!" I hissed.

"Contrary to what you believe, and as I told you before, I have not slept with Veronica," Brad calmly replied. His eyes were steady on mine.

Brad was about to speak, and I cut him off, "I am sorry that I have come off as a charity case to you, but I want to be clear—I don't need your handouts or your pity. I-I need to get out of here." I took my napkin from my lap and placed it on the table.

Brad looked intense as he grabbed my hand. "No, Laney, don't go, I—" he snapped through his clenched jaw. I didn't let him finish. I yanked my hand out of his and walked toward the front of the restaurant. Brad followed, grabbing my arm, stopping me in the foyer in front of the hostess stand.

"Laney, don't do this," he said through his clenched jaw.

Rage was pumping through *my* veins this time. "Screw you, Brad. I don't want anyone in my life that is there because they are taking pity on me—especially you!" I hissed. My eyes started to well up with tears. I jerked my arm out of his grasp and walked out the door. I cried the whole drive home, disappointed in myself for thinking that after all of this time, he might still care for me like I cared for him. My phone buzzed as soon as I was walking in the door to my house. It was from Brad; his timing was impeccable.

"Did you make it home safely?"

"Shouldn't you be checking on Veronica instead of me?"

"Stop it, Laney! Don't do this! Did you make it home ok?"

"Well, I had to go to my single widowed mothers' club on my way home...but I made it."

My phone began to vibrate; it was Brad. I hit the red button to dismiss the call then sent him a text:

"I'm not talking to you. Have a good night."

He never replied. It hurt, more than I cared to admit. It felt like I had just tied my stomach in a knot and then put it in a vise. I found Jenna in the laundry room. She was depositing Brae's dirty football clothes into the washing machine.

"Hey, girl! You're home early. How did it go...oh." She realized when she looked at my face and saw that I had been crying. I was thankful that the boys were in Brae's room playing.

I leaned up against the doorframe, inhaled, and looked down at my hands. "He is only being nice to me because he feels sorry for me and 'my situation.' I guess he and Veronica talked about how pathetic I am, and that's why he wants to keep me with Halifax," I said as a tear rolled down my cheek. I wiped it immediately.

Jenna's face showed her disappointment. "What? Laney, there must be some mistake…a misunderstanding. He is crazy about you," she countered.

"He's not, and there isn't. Veronica told me, and he confirmed it. How big of a loser do I feel like right now?" I said, wiping my tears again.

"I am sorry, Laney. I really thought he was different. He seemed to really care for you. At least you looked hot when you went off on him," she said, winking at me. We both giggled.

"I remember now why I don't date." I sighed.

Jenna laughed. "Are you okay if we camp out here tonight? I don't feel like driving home," she said, giving me a tired look.

I smiled; it was music to my ears. "I would love if you would stay," I said, needing my best friend tonight, especially as I licked my wounds.

Jenna and I sat up in my bed. We stayed up talking. I recounted everything to her, my discussion with Veronica and my argument with Brad. We clasped hands, and soon we were both asleep.

Chapter 35

My phone woke me up three hours later at 11:17 p.m. I was trying to get my bearings. "This is Laney."

"Laney, it's Jesse. Sorry to wake you, ma'am," he said with urgency.

"It's okay, Jesse, what—" He didn't give me a chance to finish. At the sound of his name, Jenna's head popped up off her pillow. She was squinting at me, trying to figure out why Jesse was calling me, same as I was.

"Laney, there has been an accident…Brad's car hit a tree. He is being airlifted to St. John's Hospital."

My mouth went dry; my heart was pounding in my ears. *Not this nightmare again. I remember how it ended last time.*

"Oh my God, how is he?" my voice sounded panicked.

"He's still unconscious…they will know more when he gets to the hospital, which should be any minute now."

"I will meet you there," I said. The line went dead.

Jenna had heard everything. "Get going, Laney. I'll take care of Braeden. Everything is going to be fine this time," she said, reading my mind and tucking a stray wisp of hair that escaped my bun behind my ear. "Keep me posted."

I arrived at the hospital wearing my T-shirt, jeans, topsiders, and my hair in a messy bun. I maneuvered my way through the hallways until I found the ICU registration desk. I asked for Braxton Green.

"Only family members can go back, sweetie. Are you of some relation to the patient?" the portly nurse at registration said.

Before I could respond, Jesse came up beside me. "She's his wife," he said with authority.

The nurse eyed us suspiciously. "And you're the brother, right?" her eyes narrowed.

"Yes, ma'am." Jesse nodded.

After thinking on it a moment, she responded, "Okay, you can take her back. You know where to go," she said flatly. He guided me down the sterile hallway.

When we were out of earshot, Jesse spoke first, "I am glad you came, Laney. I wasn't sure you would after…," his voice trailed off.

Jesse knew about our argument. I finished the sentence for him, "The blowup at the restaurant. He told you?" I asked, looking straight ahead as we walked.

"Yes, ma'am." Jesse nodded.

I felt terrible about the way I acted, and now I might not even be able to apologize. "Is he conscious yet?" I asked, trying to conceal my nerves.

Jesse shook his head, sadness in his eyes. "No, they say there is swelling in his brain, and he might not wake up." Jesse swallowed hard. He was one of Brad's closest friends; this had to be hard on him.

"Does, he have family that is coming?" I inquired, realizing that Brad and I had never talked about his family.

"No, ma'am, no family," Jesse said quietly. My heart sank.

As we entered the room, I took in everything. This time, my breathing stopped. I scanned Brad's motionless body, taking in the damage. His muscular chest and chiseled abs were bare except for the four round monitor stickers placed around his chest. He was covered in dried blood. It appeared an attempt had been made to clean it off, judging by the circular faded red residue pattern all over his upper body. The deep gash on his lower right side was oozing a dark substance onto the white dressings that covered it. He had tons of more shallow superficial scratches with a couple pieces of glass still lodged into his left arm. He had a large bruise on the left side of his forehead that matched his blackened, swollen-shut left eye. I spied some dried some dried blood under his nose; at some point, his nose had been bleeding. He had a split upper lip that had swollen. I swallowed hard. It was difficult to see this beautiful man who seemed so strong and in control only a few hours before lying here so broken and helpless. I quickly wiped the tears that inadvertently cascaded down my cheeks.

The doctor came in briefly. "Hello, Mrs. Green. I am Dr. Brimley. I will oversee Braxton's care."

I had forgotten about the lie I told to get back here. "Hello, Dr. Brimley, I'm Laney...Green. Can you update me on his status?" I caught a weak smile from Jesse out of the corner of my eye.

The doctor eyed me for a moment. "He has swelling on his brain, and a piece of metal from his car was lodged into his side abdomen. He is at a high risk for infection. We aren't sure how much internal damage he has. As I told your brother-in-law, I am not sure when or if he will wake up. If he can make it through the next twelve hours, it will be a good sign. You should know that there may be extensive brain damage, but we will be able to learn more when we can do a CAT scan."

I could hear the heart monitor's sad ballad as the background music to our conversation. The doctor left, and Jesse stepped up beside me. I was the first one to speak, talking to myself almost as much as Jesse.

"My late husband died down the hall in almost this same scenario. We had an argument about something that morning before work, and then a few hours later, I got the phone call that he was here. He died minutes after I arrived. Funny thing is, I can't remember what the argument was about." I paused and then looked at Jesse. "Why was Brad out driving so late anyway? Where was he going?"

Jesse inhaled and looked at the floor, avoiding eye contact with me. "When Brad is angry, he likes to drive his car. Sometimes he drives it too fast," Jesse said.

I nodded, fully understanding: this was one way of controlling his rage.

"It was our argument...," I offered quietly.

Jesse didn't respond; he just kept his gaze on the floor and clamped his lips together. I inhaled. I was trying to process everything. Jesse put his arm around my shoulder. "Laney, all I am going to tell you is this: there is no other place that Brad would rather be as long as you are there. Even if it is here, like this."

In that moment, I realized that in spite of what Veronica and Brad had said about me, I knew I loved him, and that was all that mattered.

"So he doesn't think I am a charity case?" I asked.

"Are you kidding?" Jesse said, searching my eyes. "You would have to be blind and deaf to not know that what I said was true."

"Thanks, Jesse. I really don't deserve someone like him. He deserves a lot better than me...," I said, shaking my head.

Jesse gave me half a smile. "In my humble opinion, I think you deserve each other—on all accounts. Now I am going to get coffee and make a few phone calls. Do you need anything?" he asked.

I gave a weak smile. "No, I am going to stay here," I said.

Jesse nodded and exited the room. I pulled up a chair next to Brad's hospital bed. I interlaced my fingers with his, leaned forward, and laid my head on the mattress by our interwoven hands. I stared at his large, thick hands, seeing the scars from his scuffle with the guy outside of the bar. Yet these same hands delicately tucked pieces of hair behind my ear.

I was awakened an hour later by the shriek from the heart monitor's alarm that something was wrong. I looked up to Brad's face. His eyes were closed, his skin was covered in perspiration, his breathing was rapid. As his eyes flew open, they looked wild and panicked, I squeezed his hand. "It's okay, Brad, the doctor is coming," I said softly, trying to calm him down. His throat was dry. He was trying to say something, but it came out as a silent whisper. I stood up, still holding his hand, and leaned my ear over his mouth. I was still barely able to hear.

"Wait for me, Laney, please don't leave me...," he softly whispered through his ragged breath. His eyes closed again, my heart squeezed. The doctor and two nurses rushed in.

"Mrs. Green, you will need to step out of the room. Your husband's temperature is elevating. We are afraid an infection has set in," the doctor barked at me.

Jesse came running in from the hallway. "Come on, Laney, let's go for a walk," Jesse suggested.

I blinked for a moment. My mind was clear now. This beautiful alpha male was strong and in control for everyone else, and in this moment, he was vulnerable and needed to be protected. I shook my head.

"No, I am not going to leave him," I said.

The doctor looked up at me. "Mrs. Green, I must ask you to—"

I cut her off, "I am not leaving. He asked me to stay, and I'll not leave him," I said sternly.

The doctor narrowed her eyes at me. "He spoke to you?" she asked me in disbelief.

I looked into her eyes. "Yes, he did," I said more calmly.

Jesse raised his eyebrows. The doctor retorted, "That's impossible," the doctor hissed.

I just shook my head. "He can verify it when he wakes up. Please just help him…," I said, my tone softening.

At this, the doctor nodded and proceeded to hook up a strong antibiotic and a various cocktail of bags to his IV. The nurses began to clean his oozing abdominal wound. When they were finished, I resumed my position next to Brad. I could feel the heat from his body due to a running fever radiating off him.

I was awakened by the sound of the doctor coming in and speaking to someone. She was speaking to Brad—he was awake! I quickly sat up and had to let my eyes adjust to the early-morning light. When my eyes came into focus, I saw Brad was looking at me with a crooked smile on his face. He motioned for me to lean in closer.

"You waited for me…," he whispered.

I looked at him, with his black swollen eye and split lip, tears pooling in my eyes. I chuckled in spite of myself. "Yes, I did," I whispered back. Then I smoothed his hair with my free hand. He maintained his crooked smirk and closed his eyes at the contact of my hand.

"So this is what it took for you to spend the night with me again. That wasn't so hard," he whispered as he opened his eyes. I let out a soft chuckle and shook my head, my eyes unable to leave his. I can't describe how much I missed seeing his hazel eyes.

The doctor cleared her throat; it made me jump.

"Mrs. Green, you seem to be a good-luck charm. Your husband came very close to leaving this world for the next last night. It seems that after the incident with the infection last night, his vital signs started to improve. Maybe you should think about volunteering here?" she said dryly.

"Yeah, I'll probably stick to my day job." I blushed, forgetting about the far-fetched lie we had told to get in the room last night. The doctor left, and I immediately looked at him, searching his eyes.

"I…I'm sorry. We had to lie to get me back here to see you."

He put a finger to my lips to stop me from talking and shook his head. He looked exhausted. "You can use my last name anytime you want. You know, I haven't forgotten that I told you all those years ago that I wanted you to be my wife," he said softly. I couldn't describe the feeling of hearing him validate our conversation all those years ago. So many nights I thought I had dreamt it.

I smiled. "I wasn't sure you remembered," I said softly.

"Of course, I do," he said.

I was lost in the memory of the night he uttered those words to me. I was so immersed with him I would have run away with him that instant. I shook my head, trying to clear it. "Thank you," I said softly. "Why don't you rest? I need to make some phone calls, and I will come back," I offered. He all of a sudden tensed and squeezed my hand. I brought his hand to my cheek. "It's okay. I promise I will come back," I crooned.

"Promise?" he whispered.

"Promise," I said.

He settled back down, seeming to relax, and eventually dozed off to sleep. I released his hand and tiptoed out to use the restroom.

On the way out, I saw Jesse in the waiting room. He looked more worried than usual.

"Are you okay, Jesse?"

He frowned at me. "Actually, no." He paused, considering his words. "I am looking into a few things that concern me about the diagnostics that came back from Brad's car after the accident…

it looks like someone may have tampered with it," he said, lost in thought.

My heart dropped. *Someone would do this to him?* My head was reeling. I felt like I was in the middle of a James Bond movie.

"Who would want to do this to him?" I asked, still in shock.

"That's the problem. The list is long. The price of being wealthy, famous, and successful, unfortunately." Jesse sighed.

I nodded, understanding that this was one of the things Brad was trying to shield me from. "Well, let me know if there is anything I can do to help," I said as I picked up my phone and dialed Jenna.

"Hey, Laney, how is he?" Jenna answered. It was good to hear her voice.

"He's awake today. I am still at the hospital with him. The accident was pretty bad, and then he developed a really bad infection last night. He's on the mend now, I think. How is my little man doing?"

"Braeden is doing great. I am going to take the three of us to breakfast. Then he can stay with me until you are done with Mr. McDreamy Green, okay?" she teased.

"Thank you, Jenna. I owe you," I said.

Jenna chuckled. "No, you don't. Just promise me you won't mess this up with all those thoughts in your head."

"Do you know how hard that is for me?" I sighed.

"Laney! I will see you in a few." Jenna giggled.

I returned to Brad's room to see that he was sleeping. I sat in the chair next to the hospital bed. I sat there quietly scanning e-mails on my phone with my left hand and resting my right hand on my lap. I felt his large warm hand pick up mine and interlace our fingers. I looked up to see that his eyes were still closed. I smiled and went back to checking my e-mails and holding his hand. I hadn't realized it, but I dozed for a while and woke up to hear a booming voice talking to one of the nurses right outside the doorway.

"I am Mr. Green's attorney. I will handle all of his decisions while he is incapacitated," he said as he barged into Brad's hospital room, breaking the peaceful silence. "Who are you?" he demanded, eyeing our hands and then me like I was a bug to be squashed. He continued, "Actually, it doesn't matter. I would appreciate if you would use discretion when leaving the hospital, and I think we would both agree that it is better for everyone if you don't make a scene," he said as he scrunched up his face.

I was perplexed. "What are you talking about, he—" I started, racking my brain for what he was talking about.

Brad's lawyer cut me off, "I know, I know, honey…he is the love of your life, and this could only be true love, blah, blah, blah, blah. It doesn't appear you were hurt in the accident, so how much is it going to take to make you go away and forget about him and this whole incident?" he snapped.

I was still in shock. I was trying to get my mouth to move. "I think you are mistaken. I am—" I started, but he cut me off yet again.

"I know, you are the one, he loves only you, blah, blah, blah. Look, what is your price to go away, 100 grand, 150 grand? If you videotaped last night, I will throw in an extra 50 grand for all video-graphic material," he said in a condescending tone.

I was still racking my brain, but I kept coming up empty-handed. I was now thoroughly confused and pretty sure I should be offended. "I don't want his money—"

He cut me off for the third time. Now I was starting to get really irritated.

"Oh, one of those with a high moral code. Look, darlin', he doesn't want you. Why don't you just let go of his hand and get out before I call the police? How about that?" he snapped.

I didn't release Brad's hand, but I did stand up. "Look, Brad is a good friend of mine. I am here to provide support—" I started to explain.

He cut me off for a fourth time, "Just leave. This sad display of pretending to be Brad's friend, wife, whatever is pathetic. Name your price. Cash or check?" he snarled.

I couldn't control it anymore. "Don't interrupt me again! I appreciate that you are trying to protect his interests, but I am not some whore that you need to pay off! Maybe he needs to be protected from bloodsucking parasites like you charging him a retainer fee just to listen to yourself talk! And one more thing, you can take your checkbook and shove it. I don't want a dime from him!" I snarled.

Jesse had heard the commotion and came in. A grin broke across his face as he looked at Brad. Our exchange had woken him up.

"She's a feisty one, Brad, that's for sure," Jesse said to Brad.

Brad just grinned and spoke in a loud whisper, "Dale, this is Laney Masterson."

It looked like Dale had just been slapped in the face. He stared at me for a long time, the color draining out of his face, apparently he knew who I was. "A thousand apologies, ma'am. I beg your pardon, Ms. Masterson," Dale said, continuing to stare at me like I was a ghost.

"Think nothing of it," I said as I offered my hand for a handshake, which he gladly obliged.

"I appreciate you coming, but your services aren't needed here. We have this under control," Brad said to Dale.

"As you wish, sir. I will continue to work with Sue for a statement to the media," Dale said.

Brad just nodded his approval. Dale then left with his briefcase in hand. Jesse followed behind him. It was just Brad and me. Even in his broken state, the sexual tension between us was palpable. His eyes were smoldering.

"I was surprised to see you here, after last night…," he whispered.

A twinge of pain ran through my gut. Memories of our argument, the hurt, the anger, everything came back. I sat back in my chair next to his bed. I removed my hand from his and looked at my hands, which I began to anxiously rub together. He grabbed my hand again, raising it to his lips and kissing it. My breath hitched, and my insides clenched.

I looked at him. "I'm sorry I overreacted. I was hurt that you would talk about me to Veronica and that you viewed me as incapable. Anything else I could say right now would just sound like a cheap excuse," I said quietly.

"Laney…you have to know, it's never been about that with you, and I have never slept with Veronica. My taste is much more…you," he whispered.

I gave him a smile. "Jesse told me that you were out driving last night because you were angry," I said softly.

He thought for a moment. "I was," he said, looking at me soberly. "You were so angry and hurt...I couldn't stop you from leaving...and then you were crying...everything felt so out of control. The emotions were all consuming. I just had to get the energy out. I tried working out, but it kept eating away at me..." His face was twisted slightly from the memory.

"Where were you going?" I asked. I looked full into his eyes.

"To you," he whispered. "I just didn't care, Laney, I had to see you," he said.

I pulled his hand, still intertwined with mine, to my cheek. "We need to get better at working things out, but if you aren't around for me to work things out with...," I said with a smile, my voice catching. He shut his eyes and swallowed hard. Then he nodded his agreement. I noticed he was starting to look sleepy again. "One more thing...," I said. He slowly turned his head to look at me. "Was what Dale said true? Do you really pay women to leave after...you have... have been with them?" I asked.

His eyes were searching mine as he slowly nodded his head. "Yes, and they sign an agreement," he whispered, still searching my eyes for a response. "Do you find that disgusting?" he asked.

To tell the truth, it made me sad. He had isolated himself from the emotional part of life. I could understand it, but my heart broke for him all the same.

"Not at all. Just seems like a waste of money." I stood up and leaned next to his ear. "Especially when I would do it for free," I whispered.

He groaned. I was about to walk away when I felt Brad firmly cup my apex. He motioned for me to lean back down with his other hand. "Mark my words, babe, I will claim this as mine once again... soon," he growled.

I smiled. "I'm counting on it," I whispered. He groaned softly again, closing his eyes. He released me from between my legs. I turned around and was about to take a walk down the hall when I almost ran into Jesse.

"They are going to discharge him tomorrow if he keeps improving, but I will need a place to keep you until you are well and until I figure out what happened to your car. Or *who* happened to your car. I would prefer you don't stay in your apartment until I make sure it isn't bugged. And I don't want to take you back to Charlotte yet. I have checked into other rentals, but they won't be ready until Tuesday, earliest."

I thought for a moment; then the lightbulb went off. "My beach house," I said.

Jesse considered it and then cocked one eyebrow. "As long as you don't have any more dancing parties," Jesse teased.

My face turned beet red. I knew I wasn't crazy; I did see someone. "That was one of your guys! I knew I saw someone in my driveway!" I said.

Jesse's face turned serious. "Laney, I am going to be in and out, so I won't be able to provide care all the time, especially while I am investigating his accident the next few days. I have already called some nurses, but they can't start until Monday—and to tell the truth, I am not a good nursemaid. He won't like my bedside manner," Jesse said, winking at me.

I nodded. "I can stay until Sunday. I will need to talk to Jenna. She is watching Braeden. I will have to see if she can watch him or bring him down Friday afternoon after school," I offered.

Jesse nodded. "Very good. I am going to step out for a while to make some additional arrangements. I'll be back in a few hours," Jesse said.

I nodded. Brad had already gone back to sleep. I did a mental scan of my body. I felt gross. I needed a hot shower. When Jesse returned, I decided I would go home for a little while to work, clean up my house a little, and pack for the beach.

"I'll only be gone for a little over an hour," I said to Jesse.

"I don't think that's a good idea," Jesse said hesitantly.

"Everything will be fine. I'll be right back."

"Laney, I will get you whatever you need. Please stay," Jesse said, on the verge of pleading.

"I just need an hour."

"Laney—" Jesse started.

I shook my head and picked up my purse. "See you in a few!" I said as I exited the hospital room.

Chapter 36

As SOON AS I GOT home, I took a deliciously hot shower and changed my clothes. I was getting Braeden off the school bus when I felt a strong urge to call Jesse. I swiped the screen of my phone and selected his contact information. But an incoming call disrupted my dialing. It was Jesse.

"Hi, Jes—" I started, but he interrupted me, his voice was more urgent.

"You need to get back here, Laney." Jesse sounded panicked; he never sounded panicked.

I closed my eyes. "Crap," I whispered. "I'll be right there." Then the line went dead. I looked at Braeden. "We need to go to the hospital and make sure Mr. Brad is okay," I said, looking at my handsome little boy's face.

Braeden nodded. "Okay, Mom, let's go," Braeden said like a superhero.

I arrived at the hospital with Braeden in tow. We quickly made our way up to the floor where Brad's room was. I could hear Brad's strangled growls from the hallway. I asked Braeden to stay in the hall. I quickly walked into Brad's room. A combination of doctors and muscular nurses were trying to force Brad to lie down. Brad's face and body were red. Veins all over his face, neck, and shoulders were bulging. The whole scene made me sick to my stomach. A nurse rushed past me with straps. My heart sank they were going to try to strap him to the bed.

Jesse was standing back, rubbing his head. "Don't you dare tie him down!" Jesse commanded, ripping the straps from one of the nurse's hands. "Get the fuck off him, or you're going to have another problem!" Jesse threatened, about to start fighting one of the male nurses.

"Do you see him right now? He is a risk to himself and to our staff! Nurse! Call security and have this man escorted out of here!" the doctor hissed.

"Fuck you—don't strap him down! Don't fucking touch him!" Jesse growled. He looked up at me and gasped. "Thank God."

Brad was fighting them to sit up. He looked like a caged animal.

"Let him go!" I demanded in a voice that was more powerful than I had ever heard come out of my mouth.

Brad had heard my voice and stopped fighting. They immediately slammed him onto the bed and held him down. I heard him loudly groan from pain. His eyes were wild. He was looking at me, gasping, trying to catch his breath from his physical exertion. The orderlies began to prepare the straps. The doctor looked at me. The security officer showed up in the doorway.

"Excuse me? We will NOT! We are going to give him a sedative and strap him to the bed," she hissed.

"No, you are not! You heard me, take your hands off him. Do you know who my husband is? I am sure your CEO wouldn't appreciate you treating one of your largest donors in this manner. Go ask him for me," I barked at one of the nurses. "And while you are doing that, consider if you do not comply with my wishes, I will sue this hospital and you personally! Or would you prefer that I get your CEO on the phone right now and see what he prefers to do?" I commanded in my most snobby voice, pulling out my cell phone from my back pocket.

The doctor's eyes narrowed. "Look at him. He's opening up all of his wounds. How do you know he won't just get up and leave before we can treat him? Or worse, attack me or my staff!" she hissed.

My eyes were on his now brown eyes. I softened my tone a little. "Because he is looking for me," I said. I knew with every fiber in me that is what the issue was. "Tell them to get away from him. I've got this," I said more quietly.

She eyed me for a long moment, then motioned for them to move away from him and pointed to the door for them to leave. They all stood back, most of them walking backward toward the door, watching nervously, anticipating a fight. Jesse was watching with satisfaction, a subtle smile stretched across his face. I smiled at Brad and walked to his bedside. He immediately grabbed my hand and held it to his heart.

"Laney…where…," he said in between gasps for air. He laid his head back on his pillow and eyed the crowd for a moment. Then he returned his eyes to me.

I turned to the crowd of nurses and doctors. "The show is over. Can you all please give us a moment. He could use some space," I said, looking at the medical staff staring at him. They all filed out of the room. I pulled up my chair and sat down next to him. I interlaced his fingers with mine and smoothed his hair, now wet with perspiration with my other hand. I looked at him tenderly. "I'm sorry I wasn't here," I said softly.

"I didn't know where you were…I woke up, and you were gone. I needed to find you…I blacked out again. I don't know why this keeps happening," he said, distraught. Jesse looked down at the floor.

"How often has this been happening?" I asked.

"Daily," Jesse said, avoiding eye contact.

"Why now?' I asked.

"We aren't sure. We think…," Jesse responded.

Brad was looking to the ceiling until now. "No," Brad said.

"What?" I asked, looking from Brad to Jesse.

"It's you," Jesse said.

I felt like I had been punched in the stomach. "Oh…," I said, my gut clenching.

"It's not you," Brad snapped, glaring at Jesse.

"What can I do?" I asked, confused, searching Brad's eyes for an answer.

"It doesn't happen at all, or he comes out of it immediately when you are around," Jesse responded.

"Can you excuse us for a second?" I asked, looking at Jesse.

"Yes, ma'am," Jesse said, slightly surprised, and then walked out of the room, closing the door behind him.

"Is that true?" I asked Brad, still searching his eyes.

"Yes. When I am with you, the chatter in my mind stops, my stress disappears, and I'm…happy, fulfilled…content. And when you're not...," he said quietly. "This can't be happening to me," he said, rubbing his face.

"We'll figure it out," I offered.

"No, Laney, you don't understand...," Brad said, exasperated.

"Then explain it to me! You know, someone once told me that it is okay to be vulnerable and need people sometimes," I said, raising my eyebrows at him.

"God, you are so beautiful," he said, holding his hand to the side of my face.

"Thank you," I said, blushing. "Will you please explain it to me?"

"Not right now. I don't want to talk about this," Brad said. I opened my mouth to argue, but he cut me off, "Please, Laney."

I gave him a little nod, realizing I was pushing too hard. "I brought a special guest to see you," I said, shifting subjects. Brad's eyes moved to the hallway where Braeden was waiting patiently with Jesse. He nodded and drew in a slow breath. I went to the door to get Braeden for him to come in. Braeden walked into the room and immediately went to where I had been previously standing.

"Hey, buddy," he said, his voice still gravelly. I came around the side of the bed to stand next to him. Brad gave Braeden a high five and then grabbed my hand again.

"How bad are you hurt, Mr. Brad?" Braeden asked, looking at his stomach, where his bandage was ever reddening.

"Just a few scratches," Brad offered.

"Why were you so upset when we got here?" Braeden asked.

"Because I woke up, and your mommy wasn't here," Brad said, looking at me.

Braeden smiled and nodded his head. "I understand. The same thing happens to me when I wake up at night, and I'm scared. She's brave. She will even check the closet for the boogeyman if you want her to," Braeden offered.

Brad chuckled. "I might need her to do that," Brad responded.

Jesse came in with the nurse who was going to clean Brad's now oozing stomach wound.

"Braeden, do you want to go get something to eat in the cafeteria with me?" Jesse queried.

Braeden's eyes lit up. "Can I, Mom?" Braeden shrieked.

I chuckled. "Sure, you can." I had barely responded when he ran out the door. Jesse gave a little wave. Brad's face winced as the nurse was cleaning his abdominal wound. I smoothed his hair again with my free hand.

"You can't do this anymore, Mr. Green," I softly scolded as I looked at his beautifully broken face.

He closed his eyes at the feel of my hand on his head. "Then don't leave me, Laney," he gravelly retorted.

"Brad…," I chided, not wanting to get into this conversation in front of the young nurse. Luckily, she was collecting the soiled bandages.

"No, Laney, listen to me," he said, visibly pained either from his wounds or the conversation. "When you walked out of the restaurant…," he said, his voice going from hoarse to a whisper.

"We can finish this tomorrow. You need to rest," I said softly. The nurse was finished collecting the dirty bandages and left the room.

"No, we can't. When you walked out of the restaurant, I had never felt as low as I did in that moment, except that day ten years ago when I let you go. I have already made that mistake with you and know the pain that comes with it…," his whisper trailed off as he sleepily looked at my face. This exchange had taken a lot out of him.

"Can you try to sleep please?" I said, softly caressing his temple with the back of my hand.

His eyes flicked open. "Are you going to leave?" he whispered, trying to fight his exhaustion.

I smiled. "No, I am not going to leave. I won't leave the hospital without you."

"Promise me, Mrs. Green."

"I promise," I said as I leaned in to kiss his broken lips softly.

He studied my face. "Then I will sleep," he whispered. Brad closed his eyes and was asleep within minutes. I was checking work e-mails on my phone when the doctor came back in.

"I hope you don't mind me saying, we treat a lot of executives in here, and we usually only see a few members of their entourage, not any next of kin. You and your husband must be very close, Mrs. Green. I have never seen a patient react the way he did earlier. How did you know that he was looking for you and not having a reaction to the medication or something else? I see here on his chart that he is a veteran. Could his outburst have been caused by PTSD?" she asked.

I smiled at her. "Possibly, but who knows? The simple fact is that everyone needs to be protected and cared for at some point. We can't be strong all the time. He and I have an understanding," I said as I gazed at him, listening to his breathing.

She tilted her head and looked at me. "I hope you will be staying," she said, raising her eyebrows.

I let out a soft chuckle. "Yes, I will be staying until he is discharged."

Jesse brought Braeden back to Brad's room in addition to some food for me. The doctor excused herself. Jesse, Braeden, and I played rummy on the sliding bed tray. I felt Brad's hand rub my back. I turned slightly so see him smiling. I smiled back at him. After a couple more games, Braeden started to get the yawns.

I pulled out the convertible bed for Braeden and covered him with a blanket. In moments, I could hear his soft breathing as sleep found him. Jesse was camped outside the room, alert as can be. I swear the man never slept. I walked around the room to flick off light switches. I walked back around to my seat.

"Here, Laney," Brad whispered as he patted the spot next to him on the hospital bed. I scooted up on the bed next to him. I lay on my side and faced him. I interlaced our fingers together. He kissed my hand with his broken lips. My heart squeezed. I laid my head down and fell asleep.

Chapter 37

It was Friday morning. I awoke in the morning to the sound of two men talking. I sat up with a start, looking over to the corner where Braeden was sleeping. He was still covered in the blanket I put on him last night. As the fog was clearing my mind, I realized it was Jesse and Brad who were talking. I also noticed that I was still holding Brad's hand; he hadn't let mine go either. Jesse grinned at me.

"The doctor is going to release him into your care today, Mrs. Green, after his CAT scan, of course. I think you made quite an impression when you walked in last night. She thinks that you can handle it," he teased.

I let out a laugh. "I think they are afraid to keep him here any longer. Even with six guys, they were struggling," I said, swinging my legs of the side of the bed. At that, both Jesse and Brad chuckled. I stood up and stretched, releasing Brad's hand. He looked at me and winked with his good eye. Then I went into the hall to use the restroom. On the way back to the room, I called Braeden's school to tell them he wouldn't be there today. When I returned, Braeden was awake. He walked over to me and gave me a sleepy hug. I kissed him on the top of the head. Jesse volunteered himself and Braeden to get breakfast from the cafeteria.

After they departed, the doctor returned to take Brad to his CAT scan. They had him sit up and slowly swing his legs off the bed. When he stood up, he made even the hospital gown look good. Then he sat in the wheelchair.

"How are you feeling this morning, Mr. Green?" Dr. Brimley asked.

"I have a slight headache and am a bit sore, but other than that, I feel fine."

"Very good. Well, let's go see what's going on with that brain of yours, and we'll get you ready to go home with your wife and son," she said, winking at me.

"Sounds good to me," Brad said.

My heart squeezed. It sounded perfect to me. I proceeded to call Jenna and let her know the plan. She said she would be down to help. Braeden and Jesse returned with breakfast. I picked at the breakfast sandwich they brought back for me; then Jesse took Braeden to the arcade.

About an hour later, Brad returned with the doctor.

"Mrs. Green, your husband is free to head home. You will need to help him clean his wounds twice a day, then once a day after the first ten days. Please keep an eye out for infection. Please help him move for brief periods to keep his blood flowing. He will need your assistance in rising and walking. He should lie flat on his back for approximately five to ten days depending on how he is feeling and how his stomach wound is healing. The stiches should dissolve, so he should not need to come back to have them removed. He should not participate in any strenuous activities. You can return to normal sexual activity in fourteen days. Any questions, Mrs. Green?"

I clamped my lips and then took a deep breath. "No, I don't think so. I think that covers everything," I said. I felt Brad's eyes on me. There was no way I could even look in Brad's direction.

"Great. Well, I see you have clothes for him to wear. I'll leave you to help him to get dressed."

"Thank you," I said. I eyed Brad as he sat on the edge of the bed. I heard the door close behind us. "Can I help you get dressed, Mr. Green?"

"Laney...," he said apprehensively. I grabbed his boxer briefs out of his duffle bag. I slid them over each of his feet and then pulled them up his legs. He stood up to allow me to slide them up the rest of the way. Then I stood up to face him while I reached around to untie his hospital gown. He let his slide off his arms. I tossed it on the bed and grabbed his T-shirt out of his duffle bag. I gently pulled it over his arms and head. Then I kissed him.

"What's that for?" he asked.

"Do I need a reason?" I asked.

"Never," he said, kissing me.

I pulled away and pulled his fleece pants out of the duffle bag. He stepped into them one leg at a time, and I pulled them up. I then found his fleece jacket and slid it on one arm at a time.

"Thank you, Mrs. Green," he whispered.

"You're welcome, Mr. Green," I said as I kissed him.

Chapter 38

BRAD WAS SLIGHTLY RECLINED, SLEEPING in the passenger seat of my car, Jesse following in a black SUV behind us. My phone rang through my car speakers.

"This is Laney."

"Hi, sweetheart! How are you?"

I smiled. I never knew what was going to come from my mom. "Hi, Mom. I am doing well. How are you?" Brad was looking at me with an amused expression on his face. The call had woken him up.

"I am fine, dear. I have a new casserole recipe that I wanted to take to the beach, but it has quinoa in it. Do you think Braeden will eat it?"

"Yes, I think he will try it. If he doesn't eat it, then more for you and me!" I looked in my rear-view mirror at Braeden watching his movie with headphones on.

"Changing subjects, dear, I saw on the news there was a terrible accident down your way, some rare expensive sports car belonging to the CEO of Helicopter something. I know it's a small town down there. Did you know the man?"

I felt my face reddening with Brad's gaze on me. "I do know him. I am going to see if I can do anything to help," I said, giving Brad a look.

"Well, that is sweet of you, dear. You know, being a CEO, he is probably very wealthy, Laney. Maybe you can convince him to take you on a date if he's single. I would assume he is with that type of car. Just make sure you put on something nice, dear, not your gardening clothes."

Now I was positive that my face was the color of a beet yet again. "We will see what I can do. Hey, Mom, I need to go. My cell reception is going to get bad," I lied.

"Okay, honey, have a good day! Love you!"

"Love you too, Mom!" I clicked the button to hang up the phone. I looked at Brad. His eyes were closed. Maybe he had dozed off and not heard my mom's last comment.

Then he spoke, eyes still closed. "Why didn't you tell your mom the wealthy single CEO did try to take you out for a date, and you walked out on him?"

I scrunched up my nose. "Funny...I forgot to tell her that part," I said sheepishly.

Brad just grinned and reached for my hand, grasping it in his. My phone started to ring through the speakers. On my navigation screen, it showed the caller ID. It was Mark. Before I could stop him, Brad hit the green answer button.

"Hello?" I said, giving Brad a look.

"Laney! How are you?"

"I am fine, thank you."

"Did you hear that neighbor friend of yours got into an accident?" he said.

"I did. What do you know about it?" I asked, giving Brad a look. I think Brad was surprised I would ask.

"I was first on the scene. I was pretty sure he was dead. It was bad, Laney. Who knows, he may have died. Have you heard anything? I thought he was taken to St. John's, but the hospital staff won't confirm anything."

"I haven't heard anything. I'll let you know if I do," I said as I squeezed Brad's hand.

"Thanks, babe. Hey, where are you? I drove by your house, and you haven't been there the last few of nights."

"I'm on a business trip."

"Really? I called your work, and they wouldn't tell me anything."

"I'm about to get into some traffic. I need to get off here," I lied.

"Okay, drive safe. Call me when you get back to town."

"Bye, Mark!" I hung up. I opened my mouth to speak, and my phone rang again through the speakers of my car. It was Slade.

"This is Laney," I answered.

"Masterson!" Slade said in a hushed whisper.

"Yes, Slade?"

"Where the hell are you?"

"What do you mean? I told you I would be out a few days."

"It wouldn't be a coincidence that you and a certain CEO happen to miss the same days, would it?"

"What are you suggesting, Slade?"

"I'm not suggesting anything. I'm telling you it's pretty fucking obvious," he said, laughing.

I started laughing too. "Slade, I need you to cover for me, okay?"

"Anything, Lanes, you sure you know what you're doing? That's a pretty dangerous game you're playing. He's a powerful enemy to have if it goes sour?"

"I know, Slade. I got this."

"Okay, girl, be careful, I'll see you Monday?"

"Thanks, I'll see you then." The line went dead.

"So they are catching on at work, huh?" Brad asked, attempting a boyish grin.

"Ummm—yes!" I said, slightly panicked.

"Why are you upset?"

"Brad! I can't be known as the CEO's whore!"

"And what if you are?"

"Wait, what?"

"What if people think we are sleeping together? What's the real problem, Laney?"

"They will think the only reason I am working there is because I am sleeping with you. Not because I have skill or talent."

"Who cares, Laney? You never have anything to worry about."

"How can you say that? I have a lot to worry about. I have a mortgage payment, insurance, bills. I'm not independently wealthy, Brad. I need my job."

"That's not what I meant."

"Well, what did you mean?" I asked, slightly miffed.

"I meant that you will always be taken care of," he said.

I thought for a moment. "I...," I started, but I saw we were about to pull into the beach-house driveway.

We arrived at the beach house around 12:00 p.m. Jesse and I helped Brad to one of the master bedrooms while Braeden ran straight to the beach, as usual. I could tell the trip down had exhausted Brad as he had quickly fallen asleep after I had covered him up. Braeden came running into the house. I promptly told Braeden to get his swimsuit on so we could enjoy this beautiful fall day on the beach. Braeden and I spent the whole afternoon on the beach. Jesse had the first shift with Brad. It was almost dinnertime. Jenna was bringing dinner for everyone. Braeden and I collected our beach towels, beach bag, and boogie boards, then headed into the house. I noticed that Jesse's car was gone. I rushed into the house and went to check on Brad. He was awake, answering e-mails and texting on his phone.

"How's the patient?" I asked playfully.

He gave me a half smile. "Fine. Where were you?" he asked nonchalantly, but his eyes were more intense.

I smiled. "I was right outside your sliding glass doors, on the beach, playing with Braeden. That reminds me, there is something I want to show you. Are you up for standing?" I asked. Brad nodded. I walked over to him and hooked my arms under his arms. We were face-to-face. The familiar pull was getting stronger the longer we were positioned like this.

"Now lean on me to get up," I ordered.

He eyed me. "Laney...just call Jesse. I don't think this is going to work."

"He's not here, and like I told you before, I am stronger than you think," I said, and he smiled. He looked like he was going to kiss me. He stood up, using me to pull himself up. Brad then wrapped his arm around my shoulders, and I kept my arm around his waist. He limped as we walked over to the sliding glass door at the side of his room. I opened the sliding glass door and led him out onto the deck. The breeze from the ocean immediately began whipping my hair around. I tried to tame it with my free hand. I looked at Brad's face, now being bathed in the beautiful oranges, reds, and pinks from the sunset. He looked like the truly magnificent creature that he was.

"This is the best spot in the entire house. If you look to the east in the morning, you can see the sunrise over the ocean. If you look to the west"—I let go of my unruly hair and gently turned his head—"you can see the sunset over the sound in the evening," I said.

Brad smiled; then he turned to look at me. "You really love it here," he said quietly.

I smiled, still looking at the sunset and feeling his eyes on me. "I do. It has always been my favorite place to escape. I bought this place shortly after Sam and I were married. Sam didn't want it so much. He was always working, so I would come down here on the weekends and fix it up."

"I bet that was lonely for you," Brad said.

I gave him a half smile and nodded. "When Braeden came along, he and I would come down here all the time instead of just sitting at home missing Sam. After Sam died, I came down here with Braeden for a few weeks to grieve. I needed a place that didn't have Sam's stuff everywhere to remind me."

Brad looked at me and squeezed my shoulder. "I'm sorry, Laney. I know that was hard for you," he said softly.

"It was. This place was therapeutic after I lost you too. I had never felt so alone," I quietly said.

"That was the hardest thing I have ever done," Brad said, tilting my head to look up at him.

I continued, "Me too." I was still able to feel the sting of his departure all those years ago.

"It's beautiful here, Laney." His comment truly touched me. This outrageously wealthy man who was used to the most decadent and finest of everything thought this simple beach town and my small haphazard cottage was beautiful. I was distracted from my thoughts as I heard Jenna calling for us. I gently nudged him to move, but he wouldn't. His gaze was still on me. He leaned in and kissed me. My world began to spin. Our kiss grew more passionate; then I heard Jenna calling for us again. I parted from his lips.

341

"We need to go back inside. It's time for dinner," I softly murmured, suddenly feeling shy. He nodded. His look was still smoldering. I helped Brad to the living room and helped him to lie down on the couch. He was asleep within moments. Then I went to help Jenna unload groceries in the kitchen.

Jenna whispered to me, "Laney, it is kind of weird to be hanging out with our CEO like this."

I laughed. "I know. Just think of him as Brad, the guy from the bar," I whispered and winked.

"Yeah, okay, that's not much better…some guy from the bar who has supercrazy fighting skills," she said, rolling her eyes.

Dinner was delicious as always when Jenna made it. Jesse was helping Brad off the couch and into his bedroom. Jenna and I went to put the boys to bed and then poured ourselves each a glass of wine. We sat outside whispering together about all the happenings at the hospital for about two hours. When we began yawning as much as talking, we knew it was time to retreat to bed.

I went into Brad's room to check on him. He was awake, his fingers flying across the keyboard of his laptop. I walked in with a smirk. "How are you feeling?" I asked.

He looked at me over his computer screen. "Fine. I was just waiting up for you," he said flatly.

I shook my head. "You need your rest. Do you want your pain pills?"

Brad reached for my hand, and he shook his head. "No, I want you to lie with me," he said softly. His tone was so alluring it melted my heart. It reminded me of the Brad I used to know.

"Brad…," I chided.

He cut me off, "Laney, the first time I slept through the night in nine years was when I brought you home from the office sick," he said sternly.

I was searching his eyes for a moment and didn't say a word. "Why?" I asked, lost in thought.

"I don't know…I…I just want to hold you," he started then stopped.

"Me too," I said in a small voice that I barely recognized as my own.

He tugged my hand, pulling me toward him. He kissed me. We parted and smiled at each other. Then I climbed up on the bed and lay on top of the comforter and covered myself with a throw blanket. My hand found his again. I interlaced my fingers with his, and he brought my hand to his lips for a kiss. I turned toward him, placing my hand on his chest, and fell asleep.

I dreamt I was running in a dark forest away from a masked man. I kept running, chasing after Brad, but he was always just out of my reach as the masked man came upon me. At that moment, I woke with a start due to a strangled growl. I opened my eyes, looking around the room, to see that Brad was standing, slightly crouched, approximately four feet from the end of the bed, pointing a gun with a red laser light toward the sliding glass door. He was approaching slowly. I was immediately alarmed. My heart started to thump loudly in my chest. I held my breath, listening for anything that would hint of a malicious guest. I could only hear the roaring sound of my heart rapidly pumping blood through my body, ready for fight or flight. I saw that Brad was bleeding from his stomach wound. He must have strained against his stitches when he got up. He didn't seem to be in any pain.

"Brad? Did you hear something? Is someone out there?" I whispered as I slowly pulled the blanket off me and scooted to the edge of the bed. I stood up slowly and took a step toward him. At that moment, Brad slowly turned his head to look at me; there was no recognition in his eyes. I froze. My immediate instinct was to put my hands out in front of me. "It's me, Laney...," I said softly as I walked toward him. At the sound of my voice, he slowly shook his head and then looked up at me. He looked at his hand, where the gun was, and then looked at me.

"Oh fuck! Holy shit! Are you okay?" he whispered. He clicked the safety on his gun, then limped over to his duffle bag. He released the clip from the handle and deposited it into his bag. I watched as he paced the room back and forth, running his fingers through his short hair. Then all of a sudden, he began to feel the pain of his inju-

343

ries. His adrenaline must have finally come down. He doubled over with pain, clutching his lower abdomen.

When I returned to him, standing at the edge of the bed, his face was pained as he bent over in pain and held his bloodstained dressings, grimacing.

"I am fine...can you come back to bed please? So I can clean that?" I asked softly, caressing his arm.

"Laney..." He looked like he was in agony.

"Everything's okay. Come back to bed, and I will change your dressings," I offered.

"You don't understand...I'm messed up...I could have killed you...I would never forgive myself...you can't stay here...I don't want to hurt you," he said, gasping.

"I'm not going anywhere," I said softly as I put my arm around his waist, pulling him over to the bed. He lay down, and I began changing his dressings.

He gazed at my face. "It was so real...it must be the stress from the accident," he said, mostly to himself.

"What must be the stress?"

"The stress is triggering my night terrors. I can't believe they are happening again," he said and winced as I poured saline solution on his wound.

"Braeden has those too," I said as I placed the bandage over the top of his would and tore off pieces of tape.

"Fuck...Laney, aren't you listening? I could have really hurt you...maybe even...," he said softly as he rubbed his face with his hands.

"I am not afraid, and I don't need to be protected from you," I said as I held his face and ran my fingers through his hair. After a moment, I walked around the bed, slipped off my jeans, and climbed under the covers. I turned to him and wrapped my legs around his and clung to his chest. He kissed the top of my forehead. I felt the tension slowly dissipate from his chest. I watched his chest rise and fall with his peaceful breathing. I settled back down and fell back asleep.

I woke in the morning to find Brad on his cell phone, typing an e-mail. When I stirred, he looked at me. I tried focusing my sleepy eyes on him.

"Are you okay? You should have woken me up. How long have you been awake?" I asked sleepily.

He gave me his playful smile. I hadn't seen it from him in a while, and it was hot. *Big surprise there.* "I was surprised to see you still here," he teased.

I let out a soft chuckle. "I need to go start coffee for everyone," I said, rubbing under my eyes. When I got up, I had forgotten that I had taken off my jeans and that my shirt was too short. This allowed Brad to see my black lacy panties, one of the purchases I made with Jenna on our lunch excursion. I am not sure why I was embarrassed; it wasn't anything he hadn't seen before.

"Laney," I heard him growl. I turned to see his eyes were on fire. As I drew near, I could see the pressure from his massive erection pushing against the sheets. Truth be told, I wanted to jump on him immediately. I craved to feel him inside of me. My body betrayed me and immediately felt moistening between my legs. I swallowed hard. His eyes stayed on mine as I walked slowly back to him. When I reached him, he reached down and grabbed my left butt cheek hard. I let out a gasp. It didn't hurt so much as it surprised me.

"Brad...," I said, sounding very breathy. I almost didn't recognize myself.

"Laney, I may not be able to do anything about what you're wearing right now, but I will take care of this issue eventually," he hissed. His eyes were serious.

I smiled and nodded. "Duly noted. Remember, doctor's orders," I said mockingly.

"You should know by now that I make the rules and give the orders, Laney." He gave me a smirk. He grabbed my hand, pulling me to him. Our lips found each other's. As we kissed, our lips continued to press more firmly as the desire grew between us. I parted from his lips and held his gaze for a moment. I smiled at him, and he let go of my butt cheek. I turned to walk to my duffle bag sitting on the floor in the corner and pulled out a sports bra, tank top, and mesh athletic shorts, then made my way to the bathroom to change. Once dressed, I gave Brad a wink before tiptoeing to the kitchen and pushed start on the coffeemaker.

I was the first one up, it seemed. I wondered how Jenna fared, most likely with Jesse, last night. I stepped into the hall bathroom and looked in the mirror at what a mess I was. My loose bun had all but fallen out of its band. I took down my hair completely and swept it up into a ponytail. Then I walked back down the hall to the kitchen. Jenna was up now and searching for her hair band in her purse.

"Good morning," I whispered. She gave me a huge smile and a wink. We must have been too noisy for Jesse. He popped up from the couch and came into the kitchen.

"If you drink coffee, it will be done in a minute," I offered, watching him rub the sleep out of his eyes.

"That would be great, Laney, thanks. Where are you two off to this morning?" he asked.

I grinned from ear to ear. "We are going to take a walk on the beach. Do you mind watching the patient and listening for the boys?"

"Not at all. Just make sure you have your cell phone with you," he warned.

I smiled at him. "Sure thing," I said.

Then Jenna and I were out of the back door and onto the beach. I loved the salty morning breeze, watching the sun come up over the water. The sand felt amazing between my toes. This was where I felt free; this was where I have felt that I belong. I've always done a lot of thinking on these walks. When Jenna was with me, we always did a lot of talking. Our walk took us over an hour. When we walked back into the house, we heard Jesse and Brad loudly whispering. I assumed they were trying not to wake the boys. "Damn it, Brad, I hate you as a patient." *Oh no.* I raced to the back master bedroom. Brad was standing near the side of the bed. The two men were staring at each other like they were about to throw punches.

"Jesse, I ordered some breakfast at the Salty Paw Café. Can you pick it up for us?" I asked like this situation was normal. My words broke their stare down; both turned to look at me. When Brad saw me, he sat down on the edge of the bed, like he had deflated.

"With pleasure," Jesse hissed and trudged out of the room. I walked over to Brad and kneeled in front of him to get a look at his stomach wound, which appeared to be bleeding through his shirt now. I heard the front door slam as Jesse left. I looked up into Brad's face, searching his eyes.

"What were you doing? I told you to behave, Mr. Green. You have to rest, and you need help getting up so this can heal," I lectured.

The anger he felt was displayed across his face. "Where were you? What took you so long?" he snapped.

I shook my head and returned my eyes to the bleeding wound on his stomach. "I need you to take off your shirt so I can get you a clean one. I need to change the dressings, and we may have to go back to the hospital if the bleeding doesn't stop."

"Not until you tell me where you went and why it took so long," he hissed.

I looked up at him. "I took a walk on the beach with Jenna. We got lost in enjoyable conversation so we lost track of time," I said.

He studied my face; then he grimaced as he lifted his shirt over his head. I drank in the sight of him. His body was immaculate with the way his clothes hung on him. I never got tired of seeing him without his shirt on either. Every muscle in his upper body was toned and strong. His abs were tight. I could count each one of his six-pack muscles. I noticed the various scars on his chest and arms; they made him that much sexier.

"Do you want me to lie down?" he asked and broke my gawking.

I blushed. I cleared my throat and swallowed hard. "Uh…yes. I am going to get the dressings and saline. I will be right back," I said. I caught my breath as I picked up the supplies from the dining-room table and returned. Brad grimaced as I peeled off the old dressing, now saturated with blood, and began to clean his wound.

"Where did you walk to this morning?" he asked, his face unreadable.

"Jenna and I went a couple miles down the beach. I needed to clear my head," I said, still focused on my task.

"What's clouding your head?" he asked.

"There is this guy in my life that is confusing me. I seem to have trouble getting him out of my head. I also wanted to think about the move for my career," I said as I focused on his wound.

He shook his head. "You aren't going anywhere. The staffing model for the HR department hasn't been finalized yet," he snapped.

"You already have a very highly qualified HR director. There is no reason you wouldn't keep her," I said, tearing strips of tape.

"She isn't you, Laney." He seemed agitated, like I had taken his favorite toy.

"As much as I love to hear that, it's not fair to her or Veronica. And after everything that has happened, there is no way I could work for her. She offered me an HR assistant job, remember?" I said, and as much as I hated that she-demon, it was true.

He was now agitated. "I am not going to lose you," he said, staring at my face. I didn't reply. "Who is this guy you speak of, and should I be jealous?" he hissed, trying to be playful through his irritation.

I smirked. "You should be very jealous. There is this really hot guy that I work with, kind of high-ranking, most-eligible-bachelor type. All the ladies in the office swoon over him. He is controlling, jealous, domineering, and mysterious, but there is something about him. I can't seem get him out of my head. Do you want me to tell you a secret?" I asked, playfully flicking my eyes at him.

His mood seemed to be lightening. "Sure, I love secrets," he said, seeming to be enjoying this.

I leaned over to his ear, making sure my lips brushed his ear as I spoke. "I even think about him when I am playing with myself." I leaned away from his ear and tore the last strip of tape.

He nodded and smirked with satisfaction. "Laney...," he whispered.

"The only thing is, he gives me mixed signals, and I am not sure how he feels about me." I looked right at him.

He began to open his mouth to speak; then we heard the front door open and close. "Breakfast is served," Jesse said with pride and had clearly returned in a much improved mood, for him at least. I quickly placed and taped the new dressing over his right abdomen. He let out a groan and stiffened his body.

"Are you okay? Are you ready for something to eat for breakfast?" I whispered. I could see his chest moving from catching his breath.

"Yes, but there is something else more delicious that I want to eat," he said as he ran his hand up my thigh and underneath the leg of my shorts. I closed my eyes when his hand found its target.

"Brad...," I whispered, lost in the all-consuming feeling of his fingers inside me.

"Yes, Laney?" he said softly.

"I...I...," I started and clamped my lips shut; my brain was failing me.

"What's that, babe? Is there something you wanted to tell me?" he teased softly. I couldn't get my mouth and brain to work with his fingers massaging my most sensitive spots. He tightened his grip; my breath hitched. "This is mine, do you understand?" he said softly. I leaned in and kissed him hard. He caught my lower lip between his teeth and gently tugged and released. "Did you hear me?" he said softly, keeping his lips out of reach of mine.

"Yes...," I said breathlessly.

He tightened his grip even more. I let out a quiet moan. "This is mine, do you understand?" he said in a more firm tone.

"Yes...," I said, panting.

Then he released his grip and pulled me in for a kiss. My lips broke into a smile, and he leaned back and looked at me. "You are so beautiful." He withdrew his hand from underneath my shorts and licked my juices off his fingers. "And just as delicious as I remember," he said as his eyes danced.

I blushed and cleared my throat. "Are you ready for breakfast?" I asked.

"Sure," he said with a grin.

I felt my face flush. "I will go get it." I got up and walked toward the door. I could feel Brad's eyes following me.

I almost ran smack into Jesse as I was exiting the room. He caught me by my arm and pulled me back into the room with Brad. Jesse seemed to be a bit out of breath.

"Some of the tests came back from your car. It was tampered with. The SOB loosened the bolts on your wheel shaft, put coke in your gas tank, and cut the brake lines three-fourths of the way through. Not a professional. He was clearly inexperienced," Jesse said, trying to control his temper.

"The police said they are investigating, but I don't trust them, especially since it may be one of their own." Jesse immediately looked like he wished he took his last comment back.

I stood there, a cold chill running down my back. I crossed my arms. "You think Mark...," I said, barely able to get it out.

Brad eyed me. "It's possible, Laney. How well do you know Mark?" he asked me.

"He is, or was, kind of a friend. I thought...," I said. Jesse nodded.

Brad was all business. "Who do you think did this?" Brad asked Jesse.

Jesse cocked his right eyebrow and gave a smirk. "It is hard to say since you have so many enemies, but obviously we are narrowing the list. In my professional opinion, it could be the usual, Kayla or her new lover...or a dozen other people that don't want you taking over Mendelson. I warned you what all this attention would do," Jesse said. Brad was lost in thought, rubbing his knuckles. Jesse continued, "I will find out for certain and get back to you. Also, Laney, you may start being linked to Brad. It doesn't take too long for the reporters to find him. We were lucky that they didn't catch us leaving the hospital. The person who did this may go after you too, so be careful," he said sternly.

Me? Linked to Brad? Go after me? How am I going to keep Braeden safe? Panic ran through my mind. Jesse looked from me to Brad and back to me. "Well, I am going to go for a run. I will be back in a couple of hours. I will keep you posted," Jesse said as though we had just been discussing our favorite wines. He departed, and I followed him to the kitchen, where I picked up a container with Brad's breakfast. I numbly carried it back to the room. I walked over and handed it to Brad then turned to leave, not saying a word.

Chapter 39

"LANEY?" BRAD SAID, TRYING TO get my attention.

I didn't respond.

"Laney!" Brad hissed.

I jumped from being startled and spun around to look in his direction. "Wha-what? Did you say something?" I asked, lost in thought.

"You look like you have seen a ghost. Are you okay?" he asked.

"Yes...no! Holy shit! What if they come after me too? How am I going to keep Braeden safe? What am I going to do?" I blurted out. I covered my mouth with my hand. I felt like I was going to have a panic attack.

"Hey, hey, hey...stop," he said.

I looked at him.

"Come here," he said as he motioned with his hand.

I was lost in my anxiety. I went over and sat on the edge of the bed next to him and put my face in my hands. I looked up from my hands. "Brad, I can't..."

"Laney! Don't!" he snapped. His expression softened. "It's going to be fine," he said firmly.

I wanted to believe him. I felt so much nervous energy that I had to keep moving. I realized that I hadn't brought Brad a clean shirt after I changed his dressings.

"I want you to answer something for me," I said as I walked over to his duffle bag to search for a clean shirt.

"Okay."

"What happened with you and Kayla? Why would she want to kill you?" I asked as I walked over to help him put on his shirt.

He exhaled slowly then spoke, "We separated shortly after I left Mendelson to go work as a finance director at Halifax. She didn't do anything to provoke it. I just couldn't be with her anymore. We fought constantly about everything. When I was with her, my mind was always somewhere else..." He sucked his breath in suddenly due to the discomfort of raising his arms to put the shirt on. "I guess she has never gotten over me. Since I haven't remarried, she thinks that I still have feelings for her."

After I helped to lay him back down on the pillows, I sat on the edge of the bed, looking down at my hands, then turned to look at him. "Do you still have feelings for her?" I asked before I could take it back.

His face was serious. "I guess in some ways I will always care about Kayla. We have been through a lot together. She was very loyal to me when I was deployed, but..." He reached his fingers to my lips and softly ran his finger over them. "Now I have other interests that I would like to pursue." His eyes were penetrating me. "Tell me more about this guy in your life that is confusing you?" he asked softly as he dropped his hand to my thigh.

I swallowed hard. "You know who it is," I chided.

"What is so confusing?" He was searching my eyes. I could tell he was getting sleepy again, and I was trying to collect myself.

"Everything. My head starts to spin when I am close to you." I paused then went on, "I can't breathe, I can't think, I can't speak...I just don't know where you see us going..." I looked down at my hands.

"Then why are you here?" he urged.

I shook my head. "I don't know," was all I could manage to say. My mind was racing. I wasn't ready to tell him that I was still in love with him. He laid his head back on the pillow.

"Well, feel free to tell me when you do know," he said, devoid of emotion. He looked at me, the hurt registering in his eyes. I got off the bed and walked out of the room.

I looked out the sliding glass doors to see Braeden playing on the beach with Jenna and Josh. I wanted to do a little work before I joined them. I pulled my laptop out of my bag, powered it on, and started to go through a few days' worth of e-mails. Jesse returned from his run. He showered and returned to the kitchen where I was.

"So, Jesse, I am going to have to go back to my house tomorrow morning, but please stay here as long as you need to."

He looked at me with a smirk. "I don't think my boss is going to like that very much," he said as he withdrew a bottle of water from the refrigerator.

I sighed and nodded. "I know, but I need to get back to my life, find a job, be a mom, clean my house, all sorts of things!" I said, laughing.

"I understand completely. I will talk it over with Brad. The nurse should come by Monday. Thank you for letting us stay here." His voice stopped, and he paused. His mind was chewing on a thought. "One more thing, Laney. Be careful around Mark. I think you will find he is not who he says he is."

"This is the second time you have brought this up. What do you mean?" I asked, somewhat flustered. "I mean, is he an ax murderer? Does he have a record? You and your boss seem to have access to everyone's information," I asked.

He thought for a moment. "Let's just say it is in your best interest and his if you two stay away from each other. I am going to hop in the shower," he said, departing down the hall to the hallway bathroom. His riddle-like comment stayed with me the rest of the day.

Braeden giggled as he ran in the house from the beach, startling me from the e-mail I was writing. "Mommy! Is Brad feeling better? Can he come out and play with us? Are you ready to surf? I found my extraspecial surfboard with the shark on it!"

I turned to face him and squeezed him. "Mr. Brad needs to rest, and yes, I am ready to surf. How about you, Josh?" I looked to Jenna's son.

"Me too!" he squealed.

"Why don't you two go get your surfboards, and we will meet you out there?"

"Yay!" they both screamed as they ran out the door and down the stairs.

Jenna was out of breath after climbing up the stairs from the beach. Jenna looked around to make sure everyone was out of earshot. "I can't find my birth control pills." She frowned.

"And why would you be concerned about that, Ms. Ford? Is there a certain clean-shaven gentleman that might have something to do with it?" I whispered with a conspiratorial smile.

She gave an ear-to-ear grin and continued, "I need to get that contraption you have," she said between breaths.

"Thank you for being here, Jenna. I don't know what I would do without you." I gave her a quick hug. Jenna blushed and gave a little wave to Jesse as he stepped out. I noticed they had been MIA several times during the trip and had a certain glow about them. I needed to ask Jenna about this in greater detail later. I went to the bathroom to go change into my bikini. I was determined to be part of the movement to "be proud of your postbaby mommy body." I was far from perfect, but I was learning to accept myself. I had even convinced Jenna to wear one.

Braeden came running back in the house. "Mommy, aren't you ready yet? Are you sure Brad can't come with us?"

I motioned for him to come over to me. I wanted to talk to him about Brad. Braeden tilted his head and looked up at me. "I'm coming, I'm coming. Mr. Brad won't be coming with us this time, honey."

"Is Brad going to be okay?"

"Yes, I think he will be."

"Well, okay, I still want to take him fishing…can I see him?" he asked me with wide eyes. We walked into the bedroom. Luckily, Brad was awake.

"Hello, Braeden, thank you for letting your mom take care of me," Brad said, giving Braeden a high five.

Braeden smiled. "It's no problem. If you say *please*, she will give you a popsicle when you are sick. Works every time," Braeden loudly whispered.

Brad gave a smile. "Thank you for the tip. I will try it out," Brad whispered back.

"Do you like to surf?" Braeden inquired.

"I used to when I was stationed in Hawaii, but I haven't in a very long time."

Braeden thought on this for a moment. "Well, that's okay. Mom's not very good either. She falls off the board all the time. I can teach you though."

"Thanks, buddy." Brad chuckled.

Braeden turned to look at me. "Can we go out and play now?"

I held his hand, and as we were walking out the door, Brad called out to me, "Laney, come here."

I looked down at Braeden. "I will be out in a minute." Then I walked over to Brad. "Did you need something before I go out to the beach?" I asked.

He was glaring at me. "What are you wearing?" he said in a low growl.

"It's called a bathing suit. People wear them on the beach," I answered.

"That is not a bathing suit. That is a bikini."

"So what? Does it look that bad on me?" I asked, my ego starting to wilt, remembering my "tiger stripes," as I liked to call them, on my hips. Maybe this was a bad idea.

"You look fucking hot, Laney, and people are going to see you…"

"And?" I asked, thoroughly confused.

"Laney, you could attract the wrong kind of attention," he said with a clenched jaw.

I shook my head. "You are a worrywart. And what, pray tell, is going to happen? They are going to kidnap me in the middle of the day and keep me on their pirate ship?" I teased.

"Laney—" Brad started, but I cut him off.

"I am going to go surf with my son and get some sunshine," I said as I slowly walked backward out of the room, turning quickly at the doorway and hastily exiting the room.

The sunshine felt glorious on my body. It was warm with just a hint of a breeze. The water was mostly warm, but we would wander into cool pockets every now and again. Since it was beginning to be the off season, the beach wasn't crowded, mostly locals that chose to live here year round. As I was lying on my towel reading my book, a pair of men caught my eye. Normally, I would have thought nothing of it, but now since everyone in my life belonged in a James Bond movie, I paid attention to everything. They entered the beach at a public beach access point and began to walk down the beach toward us. They looked out of place. They were extremely in shape, with military-style haircuts. Both had brown hair; one had a slightly lighter shade than the other. They were both approximately the same height. They were wearing board shorts and a surf shirt, but I could make out the outline of a gun tucked by their side close to their armpits. I looked to see that Braeden and Josh were sitting at the edge of the water on their boogie boards letting the wet sand bury their feet. Jenna was sitting on a beach chair next to me reading her book. She casually looked at me and then glanced at the men. The men seemed to be watching us and taking in the whole environment to see who and what was around.

"Do you find the scenery odd?" Jenna leaned her head to me and asked quietly. Even though my body was warm, I got chills.

"I was thinking the same thing," I said with a smile.

The men began to approach. I could see Jenna tense just as I did. She put down her book and casually pulled out her phone, pretending to play with it. I knew she was texting Jesse.

"Hello, ladies," the man with the darker shade of brown said.

"Hi, there!" I said, like this sort of thing happens every day. Jenna looked up from her phone. As they drew closer, I could see that the lighter-haired man had a scar across his eye in spite of his sunglasses and baseball hat.

"You didn't happen to see a black Lab run by here, did you?" the dark-haired one asked.

I noticed that even though they were both talking to me, they kept their eyes moving, constantly taking in the details of the environment, the same as Jesse did all the time.

I sat up, feeling vulnerable, looking up at them. "No, we haven't, I'm sorry," I said with pretend sympathy.

"How long ago did you lose him...her?" Jenna asked, playing along.

I could see past these two men that another two men were jogging down the beach, but I recognized the joggers as part of Brad's security team. One had a baseball cap; the other did not. Both had sunglasses, earbuds with an iPod strapped to their muscular arms. They looked like a pair of friends enjoying a morning run on the beach. They were jogging, but not sweating—no surprise there. I felt uneasy as I looked at the faces of these two strangers.

"Just this morning. We let her off the leash to run for a minute on the beach, and she took off," he said, trying to sound concerned.

I was no profiler, but this interaction felt tense, almost dangerous. "What's her name?" I asked.

"Molly."

"Sara! Sara, honey, my mom called and said the baby is sick. We need to get back."

The two strangers turned around when they heard one of the joggers call out, making their way up from the edge of the water. I realized the one with the baseball cap was talking to me.

I nodded. "Oh sure, sweetie. We have already been out here too long anyway. How was your run?" I said, smiling sweetly.

"It was great, a beautiful day for it. Let me carry these," he said, picking up my beach bag.

"Wait, these gentleman lost their black Lab, Molly. Did you see anything while you were on your run?" I asked, looking at him, standing up, and shaking the sand out of my towel. I waved to Braeden that we were leaving. He and Josh slowly got up to their feet. The second muscle-bound jogger from Brad's security team walked down to the water and started walking with them toward the public access point.

"No, not a trace. Sorry," he said curtly.

"We better go dry off the boys. My husband will be furious if they get his iPod wet!" Jenna said as she forced a giggle. Jenna made her way to the boys and walked down the beach with her pretend husband, Braeden, and Josh. My pretend husband took my beach bag as he started to walk down the beach, putting his arm around my waist.

"Good luck finding your dog," my pretend husband said and smiled as we walked away.

"Sara?" one of the two men called out.

My fake spouse and I both turned around.

"If you find him, please call me," one of the strangers said as he handed me a piece of paper with a phone number on it.

I didn't recognize the area code. I looked at him. "Did you say it was a female?" I asked.

My fake husband lightly squeezed my waist. "She is. Slip of the tongue, I guess. I am so emotional. They are part of the family, you know?" he said, sounding like a robot and clearly unemotional. I nodded and smiled. We walked together down to the public access point. When we were up the stairs and out of sight and earshot of the two men, my pretend husband spoke.

"My name is Kyle. Brad sent me, if you didn't guess already, Ms. Masterson," he said very businesslike, removing his hand from my waist.

"Please, call me Laney. I think I remember you from the bar. Who were they?" I asked.

"Some people that Mr. Green would prefer you not keep company with," he said cryptically.

"All of you talk in riddles. I am assuming Jenna and the boys are back at the beach house?" I asked, flustered.

He softly snickered. "Yes, ma'am," he said softly.

We made our way into the beach house. I looked around to see that Jenna was already changed into normal clothes in the kitchen making dinner. The boys were watching a movie, and Jesse and Brad were in the back bedroom behind closed doors. I opened the door anyway. Brad was sitting up in bed, and Jesse was sitting in a chair alongside the bed. Both of them looked up at me.

"Well?" I said. "Who was that?" I asked.

"If you will excuse me," Jesse said as he rose from his chair and rushed out of the door, closing it behind him.

"Come here, Laney. We need to talk," he said quietly.

I inhaled sharply and walked over to sit in the chair Jesse had vacated. I leaned forward, resting my forearms on my thighs. "Okay, I am all ears," I said.

"I should not have come here and involved you in this. I have a lot of enemies or people that wish to do me harm, both from my life as a SEAL and in business. Unfortunately, most of these people have the means to make life difficult. I can't have anything happen to you, and as much as it pains me to say this, we should probably not"—he stopped; I heard him swallow—"not continue to see each other in a personal capacity." His words were so formal it hurt. Even when he had broken up with me before, it was full of emotion.

I nodded, knowing he was right. "I agree," I said, not sure what else to say. I stood up and walked out of the room. I heard him call my name, but I didn't turn around. It hurt, even though I knew it was the right choice.

When I walked into the kitchen, Jenna was in the process of making her special spaghetti dinner. In truth, there really wasn't anything special about it. We had made a joke about it a long time ago, and it had stuck. She and I stood in the kitchen sipping wine, leaning against the counter. Jenna and I were enjoying gossiping about people at work while the boys watched a movie, and Brad and Jesse talked in the bedroom. The timer went off, and I removed the baked spaghetti from the oven. We let it cool for a few more minutes before dishing it out onto plates.

"Dinner's ready!" Jenna called out. Josh and Braeden came running and then ran back to the living room. Jesse came out of the bedroom after a few moments to sit alongside them. I brought Brad's plate to him. He was working on his laptop.

"Hungry?" I asked as I brought his plate over to him. It stung to look at him.

"Where's yours?" he asked.

I smiled as I gave him his plate. "Be right back." I went to get my plate. Even though I was hurt, I didn't think it was right to make him eat by himself. I came back into the room, balancing my plate and wineglass. Brad took my wineglass and took a sip. I climbed on the bed and sat cross-legged, setting my plate on my lap. Once I was situated, he handed my wine back to me, and I leaned back to put it on the bedside table.

"Did you see Slade's e-mail?" he asked. At that moment, he was back to being my CEO. He was referring to a termination request for some members of the Halifax finance team that were bullying a member of the Mendelson finance team. Kindergarten-playground stuff unfortunately.

"I did."

"What are your thoughts?" he asked, twirling spaghetti noodles around his fork.

"Contrary to Veronica's opinion, I am in support of termination. Our legal risk is relatively low as opposed to the risk we take if we keep them. Plus, there are higher stakes because of their level and positions within the company. These were managers. Do you know if Frank knew them well?" I asked, taking a bite of spaghetti.

"I don't know. He may have hired a couple of them," he said as he took a bite of garlic bread.

"This also sends a zero-tolerance message of bullying and of overall team cohesiveness, especially right now," I said, setting my plate to the side of me and reaching back to get my wineglass. I took a sip, and then he took the glass from me once again. As I took a sip and handed it back, my fingers brushed his, and he flicked his eyes up to me. When he had cleaned his plate, he picked up his phone and began typing. When he put his phone down, my phone buzzed. I gave him a look as I reached into my back pocket to get my phone. I checked my e-mails. I smiled as I read his e-mail. He supported what I had told him, countering Veronica's opinion.

"I'm going to pay for that," I offered, thinking about Veronica's evil face.

"Pay for what?" he said narrowing his eyes.

"Your decision, turning you against her—you name it," I said, taking another sip of wine.

He took my wineglass from me and drained the rest into his mouth, then set the glass down on his nightstand. "This was business, not personal," Brad said confidently.

"I don't think Veronica separates the two. Why did you hire her anyway?" I said, remembering my discussion with her at the career fair.

"She was my second choice. She came as a recommendation from a friend of mine."

"Is your friend a male?"

"Yes, he is."

"Makes perfect sense now. I don't know too many HR people in the Charlotte area, but who was your first choice?"

"Do you even have to ask, Laney?" he said, making me blush.

"Oh...I...I didn't even know you were interested," I mumbled, in shock.

"When the job came open, I contacted Jack about you, and he got pissed off. He is very protective of you, Laney, you know? Besides, I didn't want to ask you to move with Braeden," he said, his mind suddenly somewhere else.

"Ahh yes, the poor widowed single mom," I said,` scooting off the bed, standing up and collecting our plates.

"Laney, that is not what I said...," he said calmly.

"Yes, it is. Why couldn't I have moved for a new job? You didn't even ask me if I was interested."

"If I did, I would risk my relationship with Jack." His tone was steady. It made me mad how calm he was.

"Since you can't get up to drive your sports cars recklessly, let's have this conversation. What do you think of me, Brad? How do I come off to you? Do you support my ideas and opinions because you want to get in my pants? Or is it truly pity that makes you want to help me? Please enlight—"

Brad cut me off, "Enough, Laney!" he hissed. "You want to know what I think of you?" His eyes were angry and intense. I was a little scared of what he was going to say next.

"Professionally, I have never met another person like you. You know the business and the people. You are able to influence the most stubborn assholes we have. Our people love you because you are fair, consistent, and kind. Your team would walk on hot coals for you, and even that auditor was nicer the moment you walked in my office. You are tough when we need a kick in the ass, and you give us a hug when we need to cry. When you speak, people listen because you have their respect. That is why I want you on my team—no other reason," he hissed, sitting up further, wincing.

"I...I...don't know what to say...," I said quietly, feeling humbled and looking down to the dirty plates in my hand.

"I'm not finished," he said sternly.

Oh no, here it comes.

"Come here, Laney," he said, patting the spot next to him. I set the dirty plates on top of the dresser and sat next to him on the edge of the bed. I looked at him, holding my breath. "Breathe, Laney," he said softly. "Personally, I think you are smart, generous, funny, beautiful, strong, caring, courageous, confident, humble, and extremely sexy."

I averted my eyes and looked at my hands. I could feel the heat in my cheeks. I felt embarrassed. "Brad—" I started.

He interrupted me softly, "Kiss me, Laney."

I looked at him, smiling. "What? But you said—" I started but stopped talking as his hand slid underneath my hair to the side of my neck. He pulled my lips to his. I could feel his need pouring out from his lips into mine. My mind screamed at me, reminding me that he didn't want to see me in a personal capacity anymore, and the door was open, and anyone could walk in. I pulled away from him, looking into his eyes briefly, then stood up to collect the dirty dishes.

The dishes were clean. It had been a long day, and the delicious carbs from dinner had done us all in. Everyone was sleepy. I tucked Braeden in while Jenna was tucking Josh in. As we were walking into our shared bedroom, it dawned on me that I should check on Brad. I hadn't gone back in since our kiss.

"I am going to go check on Brad, and then I will be in, okay?" I said.

Jenna smiled and winked. "I won't wait up," she said as she smacked me on the butt.

I hadn't told her what he said earlier. I went into Brad's bedroom. He was typing out an e-mail on his laptop. It seemed to me that he was getting better by the hour. He still had some trouble sitting up, standing up straight, and walking unassisted, but his recovery was going well otherwise. His color was much improved.

"Do you need anything before I go to bed?" I offered.

He looked at me with a distant look.

"When are you leaving?"

"I will be leaving tomorrow morning, but I want to show you the sunrise before I go…if you are still interested," I said, trying to avoid any further arguments with him.

He nodded.

"See you in the morning," I offered with a smile.

"Good night, Laney," he said. I noticed he didn't ask me to stay. I figured he was trying to create distance between us. It stung.

Around 1:00 a.m., I was woken up by a thump. It wasn't very loud, and I thought I was hearing things. I noticed Jenna was absent from the bed. It made me smile. I couldn't lie in bed and ignore it, so I got up to checked it out. I quietly stepped out of my room. First, I checked the couch; Jesse wasn't there. *Crap.* My heart was pounding in my ears. I tiptoed back to Braeden and Josh's room; they were sleeping peacefully. I made my way to Brad's room. I started to make out his shape in the darkness. As I walked in and drew closer, I could see he was on his knees, his bottom resting on his heels. He was close to the bathroom door. I could hear his ragged breathing and quickly walked to him. I got on my knees in front of him. He wouldn't look at me. I put my hands on either side of his face and turned his head to face me.

"Don't, Laney…," he quietly growled, still catching his breath.

I didn't move my hands. "What are you doing?" I softly asked.

He took my hands off his face with his strong hands. "I had to take a piss, Laney…and no, I didn't want to ask for assistance like a feeble invalid," he snapped.

I continued to sit on my knees in front of him, silent for a moment, just looking at him. "Will you let me at least help you up? I quietly asked.

"Get out of here, Laney, go back to bed," he snapped.

"I am not leaving you here," I hissed.

"Tell me, why are you here, Laney?" he hissed back. I realized his words had a slightly deeper meaning than just why I was here to help him up to pee.

I inhaled deeply. "I am here because…because I was heartbroken the day you let me go, and there hasn't been a day since that I haven't thought about you. There were days when you first left that it felt like my heart was being carved out of my chest. I don't know what it was for you, but it was real for me. I don't know why or how it happened so fast, but it did, and I don't regret a moment of it. Now, you have walked back into my life, and I almost lost you again. All of this is scary, but I want to face it together, with you. Please don't push me away again," I whispered.

He reached his hands up, which had been resting on his thighs, and held my face, then gently pulled my face to his. Our lips touched, and we were lost in a slow intense kiss, fully tasting each other's lips. In moments, his hands released my face and reached around, finding their way under the back of my night shirt, grabbing a butt cheek in each hand, his strong arms pulling me onto his lap. His desire was pushing against the crotch of my panties. I wrapped my arms around his neck. He claimed my mouth, kissing me harder, and I pushed back just as hard. I ran my fingers through his hair.

"Was it real for you?" I whispered, still panting.

He rested his forehead against mine. "It was real for me too, Laney," he said softly.

Brad kissed me again, his tongue searching and filling my mouth.

"Let me help you up," I whispered into his ear, trying to maintain control of my desire.

He leaned in to kiss me again. I leaned away, tilting my hips up to climb off his lap, but he gripped my hips and pulled me down firm onto him.

I gasped. "Brad…," I chided.

"Tell me you don't want me," he whispered

"I can't," I said truthfully.

"Then let me feel you," he cajoled.

I kissed him, fully committed. Then a lamp fell on the floor in the living room. I felt him tense too. The day's earlier beach interaction put everyone on alert. We both rested our heads against each other and exhaled.

"Let me help you up," I whispered again.

He was irritated, for obvious reasons. He hesitantly released me. "Fuck!" he hissed. "What are we, in grade school? Jenna and Jesse fuck like rabbits—I don't give a shit if they see us!" he snapped.

I tilted my head. "Do you want help up, or do you want to crawl to the bathroom by yourself?" I whispered, and he begrudgingly fully released me. I stood beside him, and he pulled himself up on me. He kissed me softly, making a point of brushing his erection against my abdomen. He then draped his arm over my shoulder, and I walked him to the bathroom. I sat on the edge of the bed while he used the bathroom. He opened the door, and I stood to walk to him.

"Laney, stay with me tonight," he whispered.

"Okay," I said as I helped him back to bed, easing him back down. I climbed under the sheets beside him and rested my head on his shoulder. He snaked his arm around my waist. This felt good; this felt right. We both fell asleep quickly.

As promised, I woke Brad up in time to look at the sunrise. He looked hot when he first woke up. His eye wasn't swollen anymore and now only had a tinge of yellow around it. The bruise on his forehead had disappeared, and his lip only showed the slightest hint that there was ever a cut. He was a fast healer.

"Your bruise has all but disappeared," I said softly.

"Yeah, but I can tell something else is blue today," he teased softly.

I blushed, understanding full well what he meant. "Sorry," I said with a girlish grin.

"It is worth the few moments of heaven from last night," he said in a sleepy whisper.

I smiled. "Come on, sleepyhead, I want to show you the sunrise," I whispered. He winced as I helped him up and outside onto the deck. This time, I turned us to face to the east, overlooking the ocean and the sky filled with beautiful shades of oranges and violets.

Brad was looking at me.

"This is beautiful, Laney." He leaned in to kiss me. I could hear Jenna in the kitchen clanging pots around, making her delicious breakfast casserole. When our lips parted, I looked into his eyes.

"I should go help Jenna and start packing up," I said softly.

He exhaled. "I need to take care of something first before breakfast," he said, winking at me.

Chapter 40

JENNA'S AND MY CARS WERE packed. Braeden was in my back seat already watching a DVD. Brad was standing on the deck outside the front door; he looked forlorn. Even in that state, he looked powerful. It was emanating from his being. I walked up the stairs to kiss him goodbye.

"I wish you could stay," he quietly urged, tracing my chin. His face was searching mine.

I sighed. "I wish I could, but I can't. Don't give Jesse too much hell. You are a really grouchy patient. I'll let you know when we get home." In truth, if I didn't have other responsibilities, I would have loved to stay there with him.

Our kiss was slow and deep. I parted from his lips and gave him a smile, then turned to walk down the stairs. I waved when I got into the car. Jesse had just gotten back from his run and met me at my car window. I rolled it down to talk to him.

"Be careful, Laney. Try not to be alone with Mark. Call me if he comes around," he said while catching his breath.

"What is this all about, Jesse? I mean, Mark and I have been friends for a while. I have never seen anything that would suggest—" I started, but he cut me off.

"Brad was right. You are defiant. My number is in your phone. Use it." He walked up the stairs to stand next to Brad.

As I was driving down the street, I looked in my rear-view and saw both men entering back into the house. To tell the truth, we all had too much togetherness for a while.

It was Sunday night. I had put Braeden to bed and was enjoying listening to the frogs and crickets singing a musical chorus while enjoying a glass of wine on my bench swing on the front porch. As

I gently swayed back and forth, the gentle night breeze caressed my skin. I thought on how much I loved it here. My thoughts drifted to Brad and questioning his every word and touch. My dreamlike state was shattered when I felt an uneasiness come over me. I heard the creak of one of the porch boards behind me. My blood ran cold. I reached for my phone and swiped the screen as I started estimating how quickly I could make it inside the house.

Maybe it was all imagined, and Jesse's words had me spooked. Then I felt two large rough hands grab my shoulders. I tried standing up, but the person shoved me back down. My cell phone went sliding across the porch. My hands flew to my shoulders as I tried to try to pry the hands off. Once I got them off, I spun around to see the person's face. Shit, it was Mark. He smelled like a distillery. *Keep him out of the house and away from Braeden*, kept pumping through my mind.

"Mark, what are you doing?" I hissed. Jesse's words kept replaying like a broken record in my mind.

"I had told you to be careful, and you didn't listen to me...I wanted to show you what could happen," Mark slurred.

I was infuriated. I stood up a little too fast. I steadied myself against the siding of the house. "How dare you come over here and lay your hands on me!" I hissed at him. "How did you make it over here in this state?" I asked, looking for his car.

Mark dropped to his knees. "Please don't be mad, Laney. I need you. I need to feel you..." He walked to me on his knees and buried his face into my abdomen, kissing me on top of my clothes.

I cut him off and tried pushing him off me. "Get out of here, Mark. We are done talking. It is too late for you to be here anyway, and you are drunk," I said, still trying to push him off.

"Did you think that I wouldn't find out you were seeing someone else? I am a police officer, remember?" he slurred.

I was enraged; maybe it was the wine making me feel brave. "You and I are not together, Mark! How many times do I have to tell you this? If I am seeing someone else, it is none of your business! You need to leave!" I hissed. He stood up. We were face-to-face. He reached one hand around and shoved my lower back into him so that I could feel his erection pressing on my groin. It made me sick to my stomach.

"Mark! Let me go," I hissed as I pushed away from him. He shoved his tongue into my mouth; he tasted like stale beer. I tried turning my face, and he grabbed my face with his free hand, ensuring tight lip contact. The harder I pushed away, the harder he held me to him. Then he parted from my lips, still maintaining the pressure on my back. I was pushing to get away from him.

He leaned into my ear. "Did he give it to you how you like it, Laney? Did he pay you afterward like the whore you are? I heard he likes to do that with his women. You're after his money, aren't you? What, am I not rich enough for you? You greedy bitch!" he snarled.

"Fuck you, Mark! How dare you do this! Let go of me. I'm not yours, I never was!" I screamed at him, forgetting that I was trying not to wake Braeden.

"You think some rich fuck can come in here and take you away from me? You will be mine, Laney. The harder you fight, the more fun this is going to be for me," he growled in my ear.

"Let go of me," I screamed and slapped Mark on the face. It seemed to shock him out of his drunken demonstration. He threw me to the ground and began to take off his belt as he slowly walked toward me. I tried getting to my feet, but he shoved me down again.

Just then, I saw beyond Mark's silhouette a pair of headlights turn into my driveway. I began to tremble. I was afraid that Mark had invited friends because I sure wasn't expecting anyone at this hour. Mark let out an evil laugh. "Scared, Laney? Don't worry, this won't hurt a bit. I'll make it feel really nice," he said with a sinister smile. Mark's smile fell when he looked to see the car fast approaching. He reached for where his gun should have been, but it wasn't there.

The car picked up speed, sending gravel and dust flying into the air. As it rapidly approached, I saw that it was Travis's, my son's football coach and next-door neighbor, SUV. Relief flooded my body. His car skidded to a stop, and he jumped out barely before the car stopped.

"What is going on? Laney, are you okay?" Travis shouted to me as I saw his tall, lean frame quickly approaching.

"Yes, I'm fine," I said as I stood up. I dusted off myself.

Mark was perplexed. "What the fuck are you doing here?" Mark yelled at Travis.

"I feel like I should ask you the same thing," Travis said to Mark accusingly.

Mark's jaw tightened. Both Mark and Travis were locals. They had grown up here together. Travis was on the Marine police in the next city over. I would sometimes see him patrolling the waterways behind our house.

Travis shifted his attention to me. "Are you hurt? Do you need medical attention?" Travis asked me softly as he slowly walked up the stairs on the porch.

"No, I…I'm fine," I said.

"Good, let's get you inside. And, Mark, you need to go home and sleep this off," Travis said, staring him down. I nodded.

"Who the fuck do you think you are?" Mark said, making a move to shove Travis's shoulder.

In one swift move, Travis grabbed Mark by the wrist and twisted him like a pretzel, slamming the front of his body into the side of the house. It took me a moment to realize that Mark's feet were off the ground, and therefore all of his body weight was on his twisted-up joints—ouch.

"Listen, you are drunk, and you need to go home. If you don't, this won't end up well for you."

"Let me go, Travis! She's fucking you too, isn't she? The biggest whore in town!" Mark said as he spat.

"You should be ashamed to wear a badge," Travis snarled then set Mark on his feet and let him go. Mark loudly groaned as he massaged his arm and shoulder. Travis came to stand in front of me as Mark stared him down and trudged down the stairs and stomped back to his car, which I now saw was hiding in the woods at the top of my driveway. Then we watched as he sped out of my driveway, kicking up dust and gravel and fishtailing as he squealed his tires out of the driveway.

"Thank you," I said softly, feeling embarrassed, rubbing my arms.

"I'm glad I showed up when I did," he said with concern.

"Me too. Why did you show up?" I asked, now curious.

"I was out feeding my chickens, and I heard shouting, so I thought it couldn't hurt to drive over. You and Braeden are usually really quiet at night, so the yelling seemed very suspicious," he said, picking up my cell phone and handing it to me. "You have our number. Don't hesitate to call if you ever need anything, Laney. I know Melissa would love to take that stained glass class you two are always talking about at practice," he said, trying to make the situation less awkward.

I smiled, thinking about his beautiful wife. "Thank you again. I am sorry about all of this," I said sheepishly.

"No thanks needed. If you don't mind me asking, what happened?" he said.

"I was sitting on my porch, and Mark was lurking around, trying to scare me. He has a theory that something bad is going to happen to me because I live alone with my son. The feelings of affection are not mutual between us, and he doesn't like to be told no obviously," I said.

Travis nodded, eyeing me for a minute. "That sounds like Mark. Have you ever thought of getting a security system?" he asked.

"I am now," I said, and we both chuckled.

"Well, I will leave you to the rest of your evening. Are you going to be okay?" he asked.

I smiled. "I will be fine. Nothing some sleep and a hot shower won't cure," I said.

He nodded and headed back to his car. I waved as he left and quickly made my way inside, locking the door behind me, then systematically checking all the doors. Next, I ran upstairs to check on Braeden, praying he hadn't heard anything. He was sleeping peacefully. *Thank God.* I had begun to shake uncontrollably. I wanted Brad here so bad right now. I went into my room and picked up my phone from the nightstand. Tears spilled from my eyes. I wiped them and brought up Brad's number. Then I texted him:

"U awake?"
"Yes, what are you still doing up?"

"I miss you, how is the beach?"

"I miss you too. We will be leaving tomorrow for my 2 week trip to Europe, are you sure everything is ok?"

"Are you sure you are ok to travel?"

"Yes, why aren't you answering my question?"

"I wish you were here"

"Me too"

"I am off to dreamland, goodnight and safe travels!"

"Good night beautiful."

I had forgotten that Brad was going on a two-week trip to Europe. I was more than a little bummed out. I fell into a fitful sleep.

I woke up the next morning sore, and every time I would shift my body or recross my legs throughout the day, my body would remind me of my incident with Mark the previous night. Monday, Tuesday, and Wednesday went without incident. I didn't even see Mark at football practice. Mark's ex-wife brought Lucas. I noticed that Travis would always look for me and give me a wave. Thursday, I worked from home. The security company had arrived to install all sorts of cameras, motion sensors, window alarms, anything one could imagine.

Later that evening, practice was rained out, so Braeden and I sat on the back screened-in porch watching the thunderstorm roll in from over the water while we played Monopoly. I heard the doorbell ring and looked at Braeden.

"Are you expecting company?" I teased.

He giggled. "No, Mommy," he said with a smile.

I walked through the house and opened the door. No one was there, and there was no package on the doorstep. I looked around and didn't see anyone. *Freaked out* would have been an understatement. I quickly closed the door and locked it. I calmly walked back out to Braeden.

"Who was it?" he asked.

"I don't know. No one was there," I said, and the doorbell rang again. I knew Jesse was with Brad on his trip, so I texted Kyle, my pretend husband.

"Can you come over and check my doorbell?"
"Yes"

The response was immediate, and he didn't ask any questions. The doorbell rang again. Braeden was looking at me with curiosity.

"Mommy is going to have a friend come and look at the doorbell. I think they messed it up when they put in the security system today," I said quietly to him.

The doorbell rang again. It was odd that the intervals were not even. I heard the siren of a police car give off a short chirp. *Mark was here.* Then I heard the crunch of the gravel and grass as Mark walked around the house.

"There you are," he said. "I've been ringing the doorbell for a few minutes now. Didn't you hear it?" he asked, grinning, looking at Braeden and me through the screen. I made no move to open the screen door for him.

"We weren't expecting company. You should have called first. That is the polite thing to do," Braeden said, not pleased Mark was interrupting our time.

"You are correct, young man, but we received a call that the alarm went off at your house, and since we are friends, I said I would check it out. Otherwise, the city will charge you," Mark said.

I knew he was lying about my alarm going off. "Thank you for your concern. We are fine. I will call the security company to check it out tomorrow," I said with a tightened jaw.

Mark's baby-blue eyes locked into my brown ones. I felt angry that he was here, invading my peaceful home space.

"You can leave now," Braeden said

"Well, young man, you should learn some manners," Mark said, agitated.

I heard another car pull up. I prayed silently it was Kyle. "He has very good manners. He was telling the truth. There is nothing wrong with that," I hissed. The tension was thick.

"Laney?" I heard Kyle call from the house, not even sure how he got in but thankful he did.

"We're back here!" I called to him, keeping eye contact with Mark.

Kyle appeared in the back doorway and stepped out onto the porch. "Is everything okay, Officer?" Kyle asked.

"Who are you?" Mark snapped, perplexed as to how Kyle got in my house.

"I am a friend of Ms. Masterson's," Kyle replied calmly. "Is everything okay here, Officer?" Kyle asked with a bit more force.

"Yes. I was just telling Laney the alarm went off from her house and notified us at the police station. She should get it checked," he said, trying to be polite.

"Very well. Is there anything else?" Kyle asked.

"No, have a great day," he said, staring down Kyle and then me.

Kyle walked through the house and watched him leave, then came back to the screened-in porch. "You guys okay?" Kyle asked.

"We're fine. Is Mr. Brad with you?" Braeden asked. I was surprised.

"No, he's on a trip. He'll be back in a little over a week. Do you want me to tell him something?" Kyle asked.

"Can you tell him I really want him to come back so we can go fishing?" Braeden asked.

Kyle smiled. "I will tell him. How about I look at the doorbell? Do you want to help me?" he asked Braeden.

"I don't think there is anything wrong with the doorbell. I think it was Mark. I think he was trying to scare Mom into liking him," Braeden blurted out. I was floored. I thought I had done so well hiding it.

"Really?" Kyle asked.

"Yeah, but he's stupid. Sorry, Mom…I mean silly because girls don't like being scared. They like funny jokes, flowers, and necklaces and fancy food and stuff," Braeden added. I was proud of my son.

He was a better man already than a lot, especially the Marks of the world. He motioned for Kyle to lean down. "Tell Brad my mom loves chocolates," he whispered. I pretended to not hear anything.

Kyle nodded. "Will do," he whispered back and winked. Braeden attempted to wink back and scrunched up half his face instead. We all chuckled. "Let's go check out the doorbell anyway."

After taking it apart and putting it back together, checking the wiring, everything possible, my doorbell was given a clean bill of health. I was sitting on the front-porch steps, staring across my front lawn. Kyle came to sit next to me.

"Thank you," I said, "I am sorry to interrupt your evening."

"Ma'am?" Kyle asked, perplexed.

"I am sure there are other things you would prefer to do than take apart my doorbell," I said, laughing.

"It's my job, ma'am," he said.

My smile fell, thinking about Mark's certain impending return.

"Are you sure you're okay?" he asked me.

"I guess, I don't know. This whole thing has me spooked. I don't know how we got to this point. How did things get so crazy?" I asked, more to myself.

"It's not you. Mark has a record of domestic abuse. Supposedly, he is well connected enough to keep getting his job back," Kyle said.

"That makes sense now. I can never thank you enough. I don't know what would have happened if you hadn't showed up," I said, my eyes misting a little.

"I can...Mr. Green would have put me in a meat grinder instead," he said, smiling. I let out a soft chuckle. The mention of his name made me want him there with me. "Mr. Green would like me to stay here tonight, ma'am," he offered, trying to gauge my response.

Brad knew what happened. They had been in contact, yet I received no texts.

"I would honestly prefer that," I said, too tired to argue or fuss. "I am going to try to get some sleep. Please make yourself at home. There are extra beds upstairs or the couch. Please feel free to eat any food you see or drink and beverages you see. The bathroom is down the hall or there is another one upstairs. Mi casa, su casa," I said.

"Thank you, ma'am, that's very generous," Kyle said. "Ma'am?"

"Yes?"

"Don't forget this," he said, picking up my cell phone from where it had fallen out of my pocket onto the porch step.

"Thanks." I nodded and turned to head into the house. I walked into my bedroom and placed my phone on my nightstand. I sat up on the bed and pulled my legs to my chest and did something that I hadn't done in a while: I wept. How did my life get so crazy? Due to exhaustion, I slept through the night. I had to admit, it was nice having Kyle there.

Lightning Source UK Ltd.
Milton Keynes UK
UKHW012115120819
347845UK00003B/1236/P